One Drunk Night In Miami 2

A Billionaire Romance

Alecia J.

One Drunk Night In Miami 2

Copyright © 2024 by Alecia J.

All rights reserved.

Published in the United States of America.

All rights reserved. No part of this publication may be reproduced, distributed, or transmitted in any form or by any means, including photocopying, recording, or other electronic or mechanical methods, without the prior written permission of the publisher, except in the case of brief quotations embodied in critical reviews and certain other noncommercial uses permitted by copyright law. For permission requests, please contact: www.colehartsignature.com

This is a work of fiction. Names, characters, places, and incidents either are the products of the author's imagination or are used fictitiously. Any resemblance of actual persons, living or dead, businesses, companies, events, or locales is entirely coincidental. The publisher does not have any control and does not assume any responsibility for author or third-party websites or their content.

The unauthorized reproduction or distribution of this copyrighted work is a crime punishable by law. No part of the book may be scanned, uploaded to or downloaded from file sharing sites, or distributed in any other way via the Internet or any other means, electronic, or print, without the publisher's permission. Criminal copyright infringement, including infringement without monetary gain, is investigated by the FBI and is punishable by up to five years in federal prison and a fine of $250,000 (www.fbi.gov/ipr/).

This book is licensed for your personal enjoyment only. Thank you for respecting the author's work.

Published by Cole Hart Signature, LLC.

Mailing List

To stay up to date on new releases, plus get information on contests, sneak peeks, and more,

Go To The Website Below…

www.colehartsignature.com

1. Melani

"Wait. What? Come again?" Miracle asked, her forehead creased with confusion as she struggled to absorb the shocking news I had just disclosed.

Miracle and I were cool, so I had given her a little insight into my past relationship with Sincere. However, when it came to telling her about my current relationship with Sincere, I chose to shield her from the knowledge of me rekindling things with him while I was still involved with Kelan for a multitude of reasons.

"Miracle, what I'm about to tell you has to stay between us. Meaning, it *cannot* leave this car!" I stressed. "I haven't even spoken about this to Tiece, and she's my *best* friend. No offense."

"None taken," she replied.

"But yeah, it's crucial that what I'm about to tell you stays between us, not only for my protection but if this information gets into the wrong person's *ear*, people could be coming after you, too," I forewarned.

Alecia J.

"Melani, you have my word. I'm not going to say anything. But you're starting to scare me, so what's up?"

I took a deep breath, steeling myself for what I was about to reveal.

"So, I've told you about my ex, Sincere, who's... really *not* my ex."

"And that's what I'm confused about. Like, when did the two of you start back talking? Hell, *how*, or even *why*, when he's in jail?" Miracle rambled.

"I'm getting to that part. So, I already explained to you the reason he ended up in prison, didn't I?"

"Yep, you mentioned something about numerous drug charges, and most of them occurring from his ex snitching on him or something."

"Well, yeah, but that's not exactly how it went down. But we'll get back to that in a minute. I have a feeling that Sincere's ex is the same girl who is fucking Kelan."

"What?! No way! But what makes you think that?"

"He said that he's seeing someone else, and I've seen *her* around him twice lately."

"But that's no proof, Melani."

"My intuition is really all the proof I need. Whether it's her or not, though, he's with some bitch because he said so."

"Well, if she's the guilty party, then this is definitely a small world," Miracle said.

"Tell me about it. Now, let's get back into Sincere's case. His ex had no involvement in him going to prison or receiving additional time."

"Then, who was responsible?" Miracle quizzed.

I lowered my head and let out a sigh.

"Oh, God, Melani, please don't tell me that it was you!"

"No, but I know who it was. It was my dad," I softly confided.

"Your dad?" she gasped. "Did he not like him or something?"

"Not at all."

"Dang. But what kind of pull did he have on the inside to make that happen?"

"Miracle, I'm sure I've never told you this because I rarely talk about my dad, but he's a judge," I divulged. Those words left a bitter taste in my mouth.

"A... a judge?!" she shrilled incredulously.

"Yes. You still have a lot to learn about me," I said with a wistful smile, knowing there were secrets I hadn't yet unraveled.

"Clearly," she agreed.

"Does the name Dean Hampton ring a bell to you?" I asked.

"*Judge* Dean Hampton? *He's* your dad?" Her eyes widened in realization.

"Unfortunately, *yes*," I answered in an unenthusiastic tone.

"Girl, that's the man who gave my cousin ten years for a minor drug charge! I mean, I know they found enough dope on him to keep him locked up for at least five years, but ten years was a bit of a stretch!"

"Yeah, he takes his job *very* seriously, especially where drug cases are concerned."

"Why is that?"

"Ever since my mom passed away from an overdose, he's been handing out lengthy jail sentences to drug dealers left and right."

"But isn't that considered biased?"

"Pretty much."

"But aren't judges supposed to disqualify themselves from a case in those matters?"

"Keyword... *supposed to*. Often, a party needs to *prove* the bias and then file statements of fact and all the accompanying documentation. However, my dad is widely recognized, highly regarded, and deeply respected throughout this state. Adding to that, he has connections with damn near everyone, so I seriously doubt that anyone would go against him and take such action, even if they know that to be true. If you're wondering how I know so much about the law, well, let's just say I followed in my father's footsteps, and he taught me a lot."

"So, you have a degree?" she inquired in astonishment.

"I do," I responded with a sense of accomplishment. "I have an associate degree in criminal law. I had completed almost all the credits needed for my bachelor's degree before I made the tough choice to drop out of school."

"And why did you do that?"

"Let's circle back to my father's involvement in Sincere's imprisonment to get to that understanding. So, during the time I dated Sincere, he was with the Jenesis chick."

"So, *she* was the main chick, and *you* were the sidepiece?" Miracle's coy smile hinted at her amusement.

"Yes, I was," I shamelessly confirmed and hated to do so. I could already foresee her using that information against me in the future, especially since I had always emphasized the importance of staying away from another woman's man.

"Nah, now! Not Ms. 'Always on *My* Ass About Playing The Other Woman' when you've played the role as well."

"Whatever, Miracle, and it was only for a short period of time," I said, attempting to diminish the significance of my role as a side chick.

"Short or not, you still did it, and I'm guessing it would've been longer had he not gone to prison."

"Okay, Miracle, you made your point! You're right! You win! I was once a side-chick! Whoop-de-do! Now, can I finish telling the story?!"

One Drunk Night In Miami 2

I wasn't trying to come off so aggressive, but I was already agitated by Kelan's and my situation, and her actions only added to my frustration. Despite Miracle's honesty, I couldn't stand being in a position where I was the center of attention and being perceived in a negative light.

"You may proceed," Miracle replied with a self-satisfied smirk, her eyes gleaming with triumph.

"As I was *saying*, I started dating Sincere about six months before he went to prison. Yes, I knew he had a girl, and he made it *very* clear that he wasn't leaving her for me or anyone else. Still, we did things as couples would do... in different cities, though. He even met my dad, but all it took was that one time for him to know, as he said, that Sincere wasn't the one for me. I really couldn't understand what led him to that assumption because Sincere was a complete gentleman when they met. Moving forward, a little over a month after Sincere was sent to prison, my dad revealed to me that *he* was the one who had the additional charges added to his case."

"Really?! Surely not just because he didn't like him."

"I thought the same thing. Like I said, Sincere and I didn't date that long, and he only met my dad once, so I figured it couldn't be for that reason alone. Besides, I've talked to plenty of men that my dad disapproved of, and some, hell, most of them were thugs, too. Still, he never went to that extreme to have one of them removed from my life, so there has to be another reason."

"What other reason do you think he would've done that?"

"Miracle, until this day, I have *no* idea. I've been trying to figure that out for all these years, and I always come up empty-minded. At the time, when I questioned him about it, the only answer I'd get in return was 'You wouldn't understand,'" I mimicked him.

"You said he's has been in jail what... five years now, right?"

Alecia J.

"Yes."

"So, you and your dad haven't talked about this topic since? If not, surely, he can provide you with a better answer than *you wouldn't understand* by now."

"He probably can, but it's been *five* years since we've last spoken. We got into a big argument over that same simple question. I was tired of hearing the same answer, so I left, and when I did, I changed my number and never looked back."

I told Kelan a story about how my father's actions had led to my mother's struggle with drug addiction, causing our relationship to suffer. However, the narrative I shared with her was not an accurate reflection of the situation at all.

"Wait. So, are you telling me that you haven't spoken to your dad in *five* years because of a *man*?"

"Precisely," I replied in a measured tone, though the emotion in my voice revealed the truth that I missed him deeply. Aside from one of my cousins, he was really the only family I had, well, could rely on.

"Wow! But you're saying that like you don't care if he's even alive. Do you really hate your dad that bad, Melani?"

"Miracle, I don't hate my dad, well, at least not anymore. Right after all that shit happened, yes, I can say I left because I was livid at what he did to Sincere, but as the years passed, I was more stuck on the principle of the matter, as I still am to this day. Like, why couldn't he just tell me the real reason behind him wanting to put Sincere away for all those years? Because there's definitely another reason behind that other than him dating me.

"As for me caring about his wellbeing, I have a cousin who I trust not to tell him my whereabouts, and every so often, she goes to visit him and lets him know that I'm alive and well and vice versa. He has even sent me money by her."

One Drunk Night In Miami 2

"Do you miss him? Hell, does he even cross your mind these days?"

"Miracle, despite what he did, he's my dad, and at one point, he was all I had. So, of course, I miss him, and I think about him all the time; actually, a lot here lately. Still, I don't know if I could ever face him again. Again, it's not so much what he did. It's how he went about doing it! I probably would've still been against it had he told me his plans beforehand, but it's the fact that I found out *after* the fact. I hated my dad for *so* long for doing that, and probably more so now."

"Why?"

"Because Sincere is getting ready to get out... *soon.*"

"He's getting out? But how is that possible? I thought you said he was done for?"

"Or so I thought. So, to answer your question, I don't know, but if he's getting out early, then he knows something that I don't know and has yet to tell me."

"Or probably *won't* tell you," Miracle countered. "Maybe he snitched on someone, like gave up the plug's name. You know they do shit like that to get an early release."

"Snitched? Nah. That's one thing Sincere doesn't believe in."

"Doesn't *or* didn't?"

"Miracle, if there's one thing I know or can remember about Sincere, it's that he's *big* on loyalty, so I find it hard that he'd do something like that. Trust me, if he did, which again, I don't think he has done, why wait this long?"

"Five years in prison gives a person a lot of time to reflect on things," Miracle pointed out.

"True. Still, I don't think that's it," I said, refusing to believe that he would engage in such behavior.

"Well, how *soon* will he be getting out?" Miracle inquired.

"I don't know the answer to that either. He won't tell me."

Alecia J.

"So, what I really want to know is if the two of you have been talking this *entire* time? Like, has this been an ongoing, never-ending thing while you've been with Kelan?"

"Girl, no! I went to see Sincere before they sent him off, and he *told* me to move on because, at the time, he felt like he'd never get out of prison. With the charges he had, I kind of believed the same. Moving on wasn't as hard as I thought it would be, though. Shortly after I left home, I met Kelan."

"So, when exactly did you start back talking to him then?"

"Early last year. Sincere hit me up out of the blue on Facebook, told me to send him my number, and the rest is history."

"So, y'all just been communicating over the phone, or... you've been going to see him too?"

"Both. And they haven't just been regular visits either," I hinted.

"Hold up. Hold up. So y'all have been fucking too?! How?! I thought conjugal visits were for married couples only."

"Well, when you know people and have a *lil'* money, rules can be bent a little, even broken in some cases," I winked.

"Hmph. So, I hate to ask this, but I gotta know. Was that even Kelan's baby you were carrying?"

I sighed. "No, it wasn't. Kelan and I *always* use, well, *used* condoms."

"Melani, why am I just now finding out about all of this?! I mean, I know you haven't given me the 'best friend' title yet, but goodness! You've been walking around holding all of this in! You do know that stress can kill you, right?!"

"Yes, Miracle, I'm well aware!" My voice rose. "I just wasn't ready to tell anyone. Hence, why Tiece doesn't know!"

"Melani, I'm not trying to make this situation more difficult for you than I'm sure it already is. I'm just trying to make sense of all this. I mean, if he's getting out, then why aren't you happy, especially since you're no longer with Kelan?"

"Because what if Sincere knows that it was my dad who pinned all those charges on him? And if he doesn't know but later finds out, he might just kill me. Hell, both of us! Or he might just be done with me completely and try to get back with Jenesis! I honestly think that would hurt worse!"

"Him getting back with his ex will hurt you more than him killing you?! Melani, do you hear yourself?!"

"Miracle, you don't understand how much I *envied* that girl when she was with Sincere, and other than the fact that I knew she was Sincere's girlfriend, I knew absolutely nothing else about her ass! So, imagine how I feel knowing that there's a possibility that she's had *both* of my men!"

"Well, technically, Sincere was *never* yours, at least not while he was with her."

I found Miracle's bluntness to be both refreshing and challenging, especially when she spoke the truth. Miracle's honesty was what set her apart from Tiece. Tiece was always agreeable and down for whatever, while Miracle was the complete opposite. She wasn't afraid to hold me accountable for my mistakes, and she always motivated and encouraged me to be better. Despite her distasteful reputation for sleeping around with men who already have women, Miracle had her life in order, with a stable job at a bank and her own home. Nonetheless, Miracle and Tiece played complementary roles in balancing out my life.

"What I do find funny is, if you *envied* her so bad, how did you not know that was the same girl when you saw her with Kelan?" Miracle continued. "If it was me, I'd know a bitch's phone number, where she worked, her favorite color, hell, zodiac sign, and I damn sure wouldn't forget how a bitch looks that I don't like!"

"Like I said, I didn't know much, hell, anything about the girl at the time, except that she and Sincere were together. I

Alecia J.

never knew her name because Sincere chose to never share that *valuable* information with me. It wasn't to keep her a secret; he just felt it wasn't my business to know. I only saw one picture of her while I was with him, and that was the one of her on his phone's screensaver. So, it was always brief when it would pop up, but her face remained a *familiar* one."

"Okay, so what about Facebook? Instagram? You couldn't go lurking on there to find her?"

"Trust me, I tried *multiple* times, but I soon learned that with Sincere being in the drug industry, he didn't believe in having his face all over social media. So, since he didn't have any accounts, there was no way for me to find any pictures of them together, at least not anything that she would've tagged him in or vice versa."

"Gotcha. Well, until he gets out, what do you plan to do in the meantime, girl?"

I blew out a breath of exasperation.

"Honestly, I don't know. I'm not really worried about Sincere right now, though. I'll cross that bridge with him when the time comes. Right now, all I'm focused on is this shit with me and Kelan and seeing what his plans will be with Emmy. Fuck everything and everybody else."

"I know that's right. Well, I already told you that you're welcome to stay at my house, but knowing what I know now, you're welcome to stay *as long* as you need to. I'm even willing to let you stay three months free of any bills, but after that—"

"Look, Miracle, I get it. Nothing in life is free."

As much as I appreciated Miracle's generosity in allowing me to stay at her place, I knew if I didn't come up with some money soon, it would possibly lead to daily conversations filled with her frustration and complaints, something I definitely wanted to avoid. Since I happened to have some cash, I made the conscious choice to offer her a modest sum.

One Drunk Night In Miami 2

I carefully retrieved five thousand dollars from the envelope that Jewelynn had given me and handed it to Miracle.

She looked quizzically at the money, then back at me and asked, "What is this for?"

"My half on rent and other bills for the next three months. You can also look at it as a small token of my appreciation for being the friend that I *really* need right now. I have more where that came from, so if that's not enough, just let me know. I promise to start looking for a job soon. I just need to get everything squared away with Kelan first."

"Alright, but Melani, I really think you should consider going back to school to finish getting your bachelor's and go even further to get your master's. Do you know what type of money you could be making?"

"Believe it or not, I have considered it."

"Good for you! I also think you should go see your dad."

I scoffed. "Okay, you're pushing it now."

"Melani, I understand what he did was wrong, and I get why you're so angry with him, but life is unpredictable. I'm sure you wouldn't want something to happen to him before you get the chance to understand his reasons or make amends." Miracle placed her hand atop mine. "Melani, besides you, my other friend, and a few cousins here and there, my dad is *all* I have, and I can't imagine life without him. That's why it baffles me to know that you've gone this long without communicating with yours. Would you just *try* to put your personal feelings aside and have a conversation with him, even if forgiveness isn't on the table right now?" she urged.

I rolled my eyes and kissed my teeth. "I'll give it some thought; no promises, though," I finally responded, my mind filled with uncertainty about the prospect of facing my father. "Let's go because I'm sure Kelan will be pulling up soon."

Alecia J.

Wordlessly, Miracle deftly maneuvered the car into reverse, ready to make a quick exit.

As we were departing, a rush of bittersweet emotions overcame me, and tears filled my eyes. It was at that moment that I fully grasped the depth of the wonderful life I once had. I was fortunate to have a caring, handsome, wealthy—not to mention great-dick having—man, a beautiful and brilliant daughter, and the luxury of not having to work. I had been living a charmed life, and I lost it all for a man who likely wouldn't even be mine once he was released from jail, nor could he compare to Kelan in any aspect. I made that statement because if Sincere hadn't reentered my life, Kelan and I would likely still be together, perhaps even engaged or married. Nonetheless, I had no one to blame but myself.

I should've gone with my first mind and never responded to Sincere's message when he wrote me on Facebook. Unfortunately, that's when things started going downhill for Kelan and me. I found myself devoting more attention to Sincere than anyone else, and my *heavy* drinking began when I learned about his impending release from prison. Although I assumed that Sincere would've brought it to my attention if he had knowledge of my father's role in his charges, I still wasn't certain, and the unknown is what feared me the most. For all I knew, Sincere not telling me could've been part of a plan he was orchestrating to kill me and my father after his release.

Regardless of my conflicted emotions toward my father, I felt compelled to visit him and issue a warning. Following Miracle's advice, I grappled with the idea that I might have never forgiven myself if he 'miraculously' passed away or was killed without attempting to mend our relationship. So, yeah, I had to go see him, and *soon*.

2. Dior

"Mmm," I groaned, squinting my eyes as I slowly regained consciousness. When I finally managed to open my eyes, I was taken aback to find myself not in a room but on a plane.

"What the fuck?" I muttered.

As I sat up, a surge of panic swept over me when I realized that one of my wrists was restrained by a handcuff connected to the bed.

"What the hell is going on?" As I uttered those words in confusion, flashbacks of someone breaking into my house and forcefully injecting something into my neck flooded my mind.

"Oh, no! I've been kidnapped!" I whispered frantically, trying to keep my voice low. "Somebody really managed to kidnap a bitch!" I added in disbelief.

Fear and curiosity warred within me as I sat there, unable to leave the bed. With no other option, I raised my voice and called out, desperate for answers amid the overwhelming sense of dread toward finding out who the kidnapper was.

"Help!" I repeatedly shouted until *Kane* and his goons

Alecia J.

entered the space. "Kane!" I bellowed in astonishment and anger.

"In the flesh, baby." He grinned mischievously.

"Kane, what the hell is going on?! And why do you have me chained to this bed?!" I yelled, yanking at the handcuff attached to my wrist.

Kane stood with his arms crossed and a calm expression on his face.

"Calm down, Pretty Eyes. I was just taking precautions."

"I will *not* calm down! And take precautions for what, exactly?! Nigga, did you *really* kidnap me?!" I asked incredulously.

"Blocking me and thinking I wouldn't *kidnap* you is crazy. Since you blocked me on everything, I took it as you wanted to see me in person. So, here we are, baby."

"I'm dreaming! That's what this is! That's what this has to be!" I tried convincing myself.

"Oh, nah, baby. All of this is real. Do you need me to pinch you so you can believe it?"

"No! What I need you to do is uncuff me, tell me why the hell I'm here, and then have the pilot turn this plane around and take me back home!"

"I can't do that, Pretty Eyes. Well, I *can* have the pilot take us all back to LA, but then, all of my hard work would've been a waste of time, and what lesson would you have learned if I did that?" He chuckled. "I will uncuff you, though, and we'll talk in a minute."

"Kane, you've really gone too far this time! And why the hell are y'all just standing there, doing nothing like this nigga didn't just confess to kidnapping me?! Y'all do know there's such a thing as being an accessory to a crime, which all of you are guilty of at this moment!" I shouted to the men who came in with Kane. "What the hell am I thinking? Y'all probably was in on the shit! Well, Kane, I'll have you know that I have a man now, and he's going to be looking for me!" I fibbed. "So, you won't get away with this!" I included.

"Pretty Eyes, I hate to be the bearer of bad news and tell you this, but... I've already gotten away with this, baby." Kane smirked conceitedly, and then his demeanor quickly changed as if it dawned on him what I said about me having a man. "And you said you got a nigga? Since when did you get a nigga?"

"Since a few days ago! That's why I blocked you!" I continued with my lie.

"Well, if you call yourself done went and got a nigga, you can dead whatever shit y'all got going on because from here on out, you're mine! Now, to answer your question, yeah, I *ordered* the kidnapping, but I wasn't the one who came to your crib," he admitted.

"Well, I'd like to know the muthafucka you sent! The nigga broke my vase, which was new and expensive, by the way, *and* he called me a bitch!"

Kane's brows furrowed in confusion and anger. He turned around and looked at all the men, then focused his attention back on me.

"Somebody called you a bitch, baby?"

"Yeah, one of your henchmen did! Probably one of those muthafuckas." I pointed at the other men.

What happened next took me by surprise. Kane pulled out his gun and pointed it at all the men.

"All I want to know is which one of you niggas called my girl a bitch?" Kane demanded.

"It wasn't me, boss! I was just the driver!" one of them quickly confirmed, hoping to exonerate himself.

Another man, visibly nervous, raised his hands in surrender and commented, "And I was outside as the lookout person."

Alecia J.

"Look, Boss, I went inside with Jay, but I swear I didn't touch shit or say anything to her. Well, I was the one who broke her vase... by mistake," the third guy explained and confessed.

"Maybe I should just kill you *by mistake*." Kane's words seemed to send a chill down ol' boy's spine as fear etched itself onto his face. "On any other day, I would've broken something of yours to be even, but since you owned up to breaking the vase, I'll let you live to see another day. Apologize to my girl, though. Her name is Dior, by the way." Kane glanced back and shot me a kiss.

"My apologies, Dior."

I nodded in acceptance.

"Just know, whatever was the cost of her vase, I'ma take that shit out of your pay... *triple*."

"Aight, Boss."

"So, since the three of y'all stories add up, that only leaves you," Kane aimed his gun at the last remaining guy's chest, who I assumed was Jay, "as the one who called my girl a bitch. Now, Jay, what was one of the orders I gave y'all before going to her crib?"

"To... to go in and get her," he struggled to speak, stuttering over his words.

"Mm-hmm." Kane nodded. "And anywhere in my orders, do you recall me telling you to say *anything* to her?"

"Na–nah, boss."

The tension in the room was palpable as sweat seemed to dot the guy's forehead, betraying his nerves.

"I didn't think so. I just had to make sure *I* wasn't trippin'. Now, before I kill you, which I'm about to do in a few seconds, I'ma need you to apologize to my girl as well."

"Kane—" the guy Jay started to plead, but Kane shushed him by pressing a finger to his own lips to silence the guy.

One Drunk Night In Miami 2

"Just answer the question, man. The sooner you apologize, the sooner you can meet your maker," Kane callously said.

This nigga is insane, I thought.

Although I had a few words of my own for the nigga Jay, him calling me a bitch wasn't worth his life being taken, so I knew I had to intervene because Kane was serious about killing him.

"Kane," I calmly called out to him.

"Yes, baby?"

"Are you really about to kill that man, all because he called me a bitch?"

"Hell yeah! I would never disrespect you like that, so I'm damn sure not about to let another nigga do it!"

"Kane..." With my free hand, I paused and rubbed my forehead in frustration. "Look, if you want to beat his ass, I'm all for that, but do *not* kill him!" I ordered.

With his gun pointed in Jay's face, Kane's eyes darted back and forth between me and him. His expression was tense as he contemplated his next move. After a few seconds, he made the decision to lower his gun.

"Nigga, this must be yo' lucky fuckin' day. Then again, it's not. I'm not going to kill you, but I'ma let these niggas beat yo' ass, and when we get to our destination, we gon' leave yo' ass stranded there. As a matter of fact, we might just drop you off somewhere along the way because I'll probably still be liable to kill yo' ass if I see you around. Get this nigga the fuck out of my face and tie his ass up for the rest of the flight," Kane commanded to the other three men.

Once they were out of view, Kane came over to me and removed the handcuff from my hand.

"I'm sorry about that, baby."

"Which part exactly? The handcuffs or the fact that you

Alecia J.

almost just killed a man in front of me?!" I countered, rubbing the sore spot on my wrist.

"And his ass would be laid out right now if you hadn't been Ms. *Captain-Save-A-Nigga*."

"Anyway, are you ready to tell me why you *had* me kidnapped?"

Kane took a seat on the bed next to me.

"Oh, we're about to get to that, but first, do you need something to help you calm down? You seem a little riled up, and I don't like seeing you upset, especially if I'm the cause of it."

"Well, forgive me if I woke up on a plane only to realize that I've been kidnapped and heading to God knows what destination with a man who already has a woman but seems to be overly obsessed with me and doesn't mind killing a person in front of people for simple ass reasons!"

"Him calling you a bitch wasn't a simple ass reason, baby. But damn, am I that bad?"

I shook my head.

"Kane, even if I did need something to help me calm down, I think I've been given enough drugs for one night... or day. Wait! How long was I asleep? And what the hell did that nigga drug me with?"

"You've only been asleep for a few hours. And what he gave you is a little *concoction* of mine."

"That still isn't telling me exactly *what* chemicals are flowing inside my body."

"Just know, there won't be any traces of it if you happen to get drug tested soon, and it won't do any harm to you unless you have some health issues that I don't know about or... you're pregnant and just haven't told a nigga." He raised his brows in speculation.

"Nigga, I'm not pregnant! I'll overdose on Plan B before I become a nigga's *baby mama*!"

One Drunk Night In Miami 2

"Good thing you'll be my *wife* when we have our first child. Actually, I'm already your husband; we're just not married yet."

There was no need to go back and forth with Kane about that topic because I knew it would be a never-ending one, so I changed the subject.

"Well, I'm good on getting something to calm me down, or at least I will be once you tell me why you kidnapped me and where you plan to take me."

Kelan retrieved a bag of weed from his pocket.

"I was just going to offer you some weed."

"Still, I'm good."

"Suit yourself." He shrugged casually, then pulled out a pack of Backwoods to start preparing his blunt. "Now, are *you* ready to tell me why you're working with the fuckin' Feds?" he inquired with a quizzical expression on his face.

My eyes widened in shock at his knowledge of that, and then it hit me. When the guy called me a bitch, he also mentioned my involvement with the Feds. So, of course, if he kidnapped me for Kane, then Kane had to be aware as well.

"Kane, listen. It's not what you think," I tried to reason.

"When I first heard that, oh, a lot of shit crossed my mind. One thing is that you could've been trying to set a nigga up."

"I swear it's not that! Actually, it has nothing to do with you!"

"*Now* I know that. It has something to do with your *brother*, right?"

"Ye–yeah," I responded with a mix of apprehension and relief, realizing he was aware of the truth. Still, I couldn't shake off my curiosity about how he came to know about that deeply personal matter. To my knowledge, only a select few were entrusted with that information. "But hold on. How do you even know about that?" I further questioned.

"When I told you that I did my research on you and your

Alecia J.

family, I wasn't lying. It was listed that you had a brother, but what I found funny was that I couldn't locate the nigga anywhere. So, I had my guy do some deeper digging. Let's just say I found out that you were working for the Feds. When I approached the right person about the matter, they told me that it had something to do with your brother, but that's all they would tell me. I never got the *why*. I could've pressured it out of them by threatening to kill the nigga who I spoke with or actually killing a lot of muthafuckas until somebody told me what I wanted to hear, but I didn't know the whole reasoning behind the shit, and I didn't want to stir up no shit or anything happening to your brother because of my careless actions. So, I figured I'd ask the main source, which is you."

"Well, I thank you for not doing that. But you didn't have to kidnap me to get answers, Kane."

"Me having you kidnapped ain't have shit to do with that. This was already in play. So, are you ready to talk?"

"I... I don't know if I should be discussing this with you. Someone could be listening," I murmured.

After sealing the blunt, Kane leaned in and whispered, "Pretty Eyes, nobody is listening in on our conversation. Trust me."

I couldn't help but respond skeptically, "And how are you so sure of that?"

Kane paused briefly before replying, "Because I have a guy on my payroll who used to work for the CIA. Using one of his tools, he checked you out while you were unconscious to make sure no one had bugged you in any way that you probably wouldn't have noticed. He didn't find anything, so they obviously trusted you to keep quiet *about whatever* because most niggas would have done some spiteful ass shit like that."

"Oh," I simply replied.

One Drunk Night In Miami 2

"Now that you know that, are you ready to tell me what the hell is going on?"

I sighed deeply. Even though Kane assured me that they hadn't discovered any surveillance device on my body, I couldn't shake the feeling of unease regarding the possibility that someone was still keeping tabs on me somehow.

"Yeah. But first, I need to hit that blunt a few times."

"That deep, huh?" Kane asked, handing it over to me.

"For me, it is."

As the smoke filled my lungs, a soothing sensation cascaded over me, granting me the courage to narrate the tale of my involvement with the federal authorities.

"So..." I began after returning the blunt to him, "my brother used to be involved with drugs. To my knowledge, I was under the impression that he was making a couple thousand dollars. Turned out, he was making *hundreds* of thousands of dollars. One night, my mom called me in a panic, saying that some men in black were at their house, demanding money that my brother supposedly owed them. One of the guys, who introduced himself as the boss, got on the phone and explained that if no one could come up with the money within the next twenty-four hours, they were going to kill everyone connected to my brother, including me.

"I pleaded with him to allow me to come over and have a conversation with them before they left in order to reach a mutual understanding or work something out. Although at that moment I wasn't fully aware of what my brother had got himself into, at the end of the day, I'm my brother's keeper, and I damn sure wasn't about to let anyone kill my parents for something they had nothing to do with.

"Once I arrived at their house, I was welcomed by a group of seven men, and one of them immediately stood out as the leader. He wasted no time informing me that my brother owed him a cool one million dollars. What made matters worse is he's one of the heads of the cartel."

"Damn. Yo' brother was fuckin' with the *cartel's* money like that?"

"Apparently." I shrugged. "But again, I didn't know. I was under the impression that he was working for a plug in the city or something."

"I'll admit; I'm a muthafucka out here in these streets, and niggas *know* not to fuck with me, especially when it comes to my money. But one thing I don't believe in is killing innocent people, especially kids and women. That's where I draw the line, but those niggas... oh, they don't spare *any* lives where there is money concerned. When they come to collect, if a muthafucka doesn't have their money or dope, they're going after an entire family with no hesitation and no fuckin' remorse. Those niggas be on some *Dead Silence* type shit. You know the movie where the lady was killing all those muthafuckas, only to find out they all were related. So, she basically was killing entire generations until there were none left," Kane explained.

"Kane, I know what movie you're referring to," I acknowledged.

"Well, I'm assuming y'all came up with the money since you're still alive."

"Actually, no. Instead of resorting to violence or threats, the boss gave me an ultimatum. He seemed intrigued by my beauty and mentioned that I would be a perfect fit for his "company," which I soon realized was a euphemism for escorting. It was clear that I had no choice but to comply with his demands. Well, I had to either work for him *without* pay to settle my brother's debt, come up with the money by the next day, or else face the dire consequences, which was death for all of us. I'm still alive and working at the company, so it's not hard to guess which option I went with."

"Wait. You said he wanted you to work for him for *free*. So, you're not getting paid to do that shit?"

"I *wasn't,* but only for about two months. With that company, before clients go on 'dates' with escorts, they have the option of choosing who they'd like to accompany them. Once I came on the scene, it seemed like all the men wanted me; literally, *all* of them."

"I don't mean to cut you off, and this may be a stupid ass question, but is your boss the same nigga who went to yo' folks crib that night?"

"Yes and no. *My* boss, per se, just runs the business for him. The other guy is the CEO, who basically just collects the money, and I say that because I rarely ever see him. My boss is the one who I communicate with the majority of the time."

Kane nodded in understanding.

"So, where was I? Oh, yeah. After receiving numerous compliments and positive feedback about my work ethic, he considered putting me on the payroll to get paid, of course. Eventually, he did, but my looks, his liking for me, and the money I was bringing him in alone weren't enough to erase my brother's debt. I had to take on an additional assignment. That additional task involved cooperating with the federal authorities."

"I get all that other shit, but what I don't understand is, how the hell does you working with the Feds come into any of this shit? Surely it ain't got shit to do with you working for a fuckin' escort company?"

"An *illegal* escort company," I rectified.

Really, the only thing that made the company *illegal* was because some, hell, *a lot* of the escorts, *excluding me*, performed sexual acts with some of the clients.

Alecia J.

"But I was getting to that," I continued. "So, with the company running an 'illegal' business, they needed someone with legal connections to protect them and keep their operation hidden from the wrong people. From what has been told to me, there were a few corrupt FBI agents who discovered the illegal activities and threatened to shut the company down and send the CEO to prison.

The guy didn't like the sound of losing his top-paying business, and he damn sure wasn't trying to go to prison. So, out of desperation, he asked the FBI agents what he could do to avoid both things happening. They proposed that some of the escorts, particularly the top earners like me, go on dates with men suspected of being involved in serious crimes such as money laundering, trafficking, and drug activity. The aim was, well, is to gather as much personal information as possible from these men in order to incriminate them. Being their top earner, I'm usually the chosen one to go out with the men willing to pay top dollar, many of whom are suspected of criminal activity. So, for each arrest resulting from the information I provide, the CEO deducts one hundred thousand dollars from my brother's debt.

"And how many cases have you helped them solve so far, Undercover Agent Dior?" Kane kidded.

"Haha. But four, which has taken four hundred thousand dollars off his debt, not including the other one hundred thousand that was removed before then just by going out on dates."

"So, what was the deal before the FBI shit came into play?"

"Like I said, I was working for *free*, so hell, free labor for them."

"I'm saying, did the nigga say how long you had to work for him or what?"

"Oh. Well, each month, he'd take away fifty thousand

dollars from my brother's debt. So, me working for free for two months removed one hundred thousand dollars."

"Gotcha. So, you have $500,000 left to pay off your brother's debt?"

"Yeah," I replied with a heavy heart, lowering my head in despair.

"Do you happen to know about his current condition? Hell, do you even have some type of proof that he's alive?"

"Thankfully, he is, and he's doing well. I've talked to him, but we're only allowed to communicate with him twice a month, every other week. It could be worse; we wouldn't be able to talk to him at all, so for that, I'm grateful. He still lives a *somewhat* ordinary life. Like, he's not confined in a basement or anything, but the way he described the house they have him cooped up in, it's something we'd see in movies. And with all the security and high-tech doors they have in place, there's no way for him to leave, even if he tried, but attempting to do so would get him killed. So, the true torment for him is being unable to experience the outside world, most importantly, being separated from his family until his debt is settled."

"I can tell you miss him. Before all this shit happened, were you and your brother really close?"

"Yeah," I sniffled, on the verge of tears. "Aside from Jenesis, he's my best friend, too. That's why I'd do *anything* for him *and* to bring him home."

"Does Jenesis know about any of this?"

"No," I replied with a shake of my head. "I was scared to tell her because I didn't know if anyone had been watching or listening to me this entire time. She thinks my brother has been out of town working this whole time. He's only been away for six months, but it feels like six years. I miss him so much! I wish I had the money to just pay that muthafucka and bring my brother home!"

Alecia J.

Overwhelmed with emotion, tears began to flow down my cheeks. Kane instinctively drew closer and enveloped me in a comforting hug.

"Shh. He'll be home soon, baby. Just try to calm down," Kane assured me, his voice filled with compassion.

Once I composed myself, I pulled away from him.

"I can't believe I'm crying in front of you." I chuckled.

"It's all good. You ain't the first crybaby I done met."

I playfully hit his arm.

"Nah, but strong women cry too. It ain't healthy to hold all that shit in."

"I heard that real niggas cry, too," I poked.

"Yeah, they do, but yo' ass ain't gon' ever see me cry."

"We'll see. But now that you know why I work for the Feds, can you tell me where we're going since you made it clear that you kidnapped me because I blocked you. Oh, shit! Where is my phone? My mama, daddy, and Jenesis probably have been trying to call me! And then work!"

"Chill, Dior. I got all of that handled. You don't have to worry about going back to work for the next two weeks."

"I'm afraid to ask how you pulled *that* off."

"Some things are better left unknown." He flashed me a short smile.

"Still, my mama and Jenesis will be looking for me. They both call or text me *faithfully* every morning."

"I already talked to Jenesis, Ma Dukes, *and* Pops. They all know that you'll be out of town for some days."

"Who the hell is Ma Dukes and Pops?!"

"Your mama and daddy, girl… my soon-to-be in-laws." He winked. "We've already talked about the wedding and everything. We just gon' keep that on the hush for now, though."

"I would say you're lying, but me knowing you and the

crazy shit you've done here lately, I don't put anything past you! You have really gone crazy, Kane!"

"Crazy about you, Pretty Eyes. You should've never given that good ass pussy to a nigga like me. I ain't going no fuckin' where. Try all you might."

"I didn't just offer you my pussy. In a sense, you made me give it to you."

"I did, didn't I? The best decision of my fuckin' life." He chuckled.

"I wonder what my parents, hell, Jenesis, would say if they knew you kidnapped me to get me here because surely none of them were okay with you snatching me up!"

"They all know that I wanted to take you out of town. So, they all think we're on vacation, which *kind of* isn't a lie. But let's just keep the kidnapping part between me and you, baby, at least when it comes to yo' folks. They like a nigga, and I'm trying to get them to love me, not hate me. I'd hate to go to one of these voodoo women and have a spell put on yo' folks to make that happen, but I will, Pretty Eyes."

"At this point, I'm convinced somebody put a spell on you! I still need my phone so I can talk to them."

"Your phone is back home, but you can use mine whenever you need to."

"Where are we going, Kane?" The answer he had yet to tell me, but I was dying to know.

"It's a surprise, but I'm sure you'll like it."

"How? When you don't even know what I really like."

"I have my ways of finding out things, as you should know by now."

I rolled my eyes. "And you said we'll be gone for a few days. What am I supposed to wear? I have no clothes!"

"Be naked. That's cute enough," was his suggestion.

"Kane..."

Alecia J.

"I'm just playing, baby. Then again, I wasn't. You know I got you on the clothes tip or whatever else you need while we're on this trip. Stop trippin', baby."

"I don't know where you're taking me, but you're damn right that you got me. Had me waking up to all this crazy shit! So, I hope you brought plenty of cash with you! You gon' pay me for breaking my sleep last night, your worker breaking my vase, and for the stress you have caused me today!"

"Damn, I know a *broke* nigga's pockets hate to see you coming. Spoiled ass."

"I don't ask to be spoiled, but if my presence doesn't inspire you to treat me like the queen that I am, we won't go much further. Fair warning."

"In other words, you're saying a broke nigga can't get the time of day from you."

"Kane, how a nigga treats me holds more weight than what he can do for me. So, it's not always about money. I care more about how I'm respected. A nigga needs not to come without the money, though. I hope that answered your question."

I'll admit; I like niggas with money, and nobody would make me feel bad about it. Life is too expensive to be fuckin' with a nigga who can't do shit for you.

"I feel you. Good thing I'm a rich ass nigga. But I got you, baby."

"So, how long until we make it to *said* destination?"

Kane checked his watch. "We have about five more hours, so if you wanna take a nap, you can, or..." Kane gave me that look, indicating he wanted some pussy.

"Kane, just because I'm here with you, *involuntarily,* and you're about to spend some money on me, don't think for one second that you're about to get some pussy, nigga! Need I remind you *again* that you're in a relationship! Does Bonnie even know about this trip?"

"Yeah, she knows. Initially, this was a business trip for me. It still is, but I decided to make it a business *and* personal trip by bringing you."

"Still, I'm sure she doesn't know that I'm with you."

"Nah, she doesn't."

"My point exactly! Look, Kane, that shit we did in Miami was a one-time thing. I thought I made that clear."

"Made clear to who exactly? 'Cause I wasn't hearing none of that shit! And actually, we fucked *multiple* times that weekend. How soon you forget." He chuckled.

"Nigga, you get what I'm saying! What happened there wasn't supposed to leave Miami, and nobody damn sure was supposed to catch any feelings overnight!"

"Well, shit happens beyond our control sometimes." Kane hunched his shoulders

"Why are you doing this to your girlfriend? She seems sweet, and I can tell she really loves you."

"And that's the problem. She's too nice of a girl for a nigga like me. I need a woman with some roughness and feistiness to her... someone like you."

"So, why not just leave her?" I further questioned.

"I don't want to break that sweet heart of hers. Bonnie has been rocking with me for a while now; hell, years. She's a good ass woman. I'll give her that much. She's just not the woman for me."

"So, you *do* love her?"

"I have love *for* her. I'm just not *in* love with her, at least not anymore."

I wanted to delve deeper into that topic because I was intrigued to find out what led to the change in his feelings for her, but a yawn escaped me, a sign that I was still feeling the effects of whatever drug I was administered. So, I decided to save that conversation for another time.

Alecia J.

"I'd love to hear more about why you fell out of love with her, but right now, I *really* need to get some rest," I said as I pulled back the sheet and prepared to settle back under it.

"So, you're really not going to give me any pussy?"

"On this trip? Hell no! But maybe... if you're a good boy for the remainder of this year, I'll think about giving you some for Christmas. You can look at it as your Christmas gift," I teased.

"Pussy is not a Christmas gift. How you gon' give me something opened, used, and played with?"

I laughed.

"Well, maybe tomorrow, Kane," I said, hoping that would convince him to let me be.

"Tomorrow isn't promised. We need to fuck *today*. But I'll let you get some rest... for now."

I turned on my side with my back to him.

"Bye, Kane. Wake me up when we land at *said* place."

"Aight, but aye, two questions."

I turned around to face him.

"Yeah?"

"Is the FBI looking into Stephan? I'm just asking since you said most of your clients are FBI targets, and you were on a *date* with the nigga."

"Actually, no. Honestly, he was just a regular guy who signed up for an escort. Although he did bring up the business quite a few times. Hell, who am I kidding? That nigga talked about that shit majority of the date! That's why I was ready to get away from his ass!"

"What kind of shit was he saying?"

"Mostly talking about his position and the things he did on a normal basis. Really a bunch of nothing. He didn't mention any names or stash houses if that's what you're worried about, but he was disclosing a lot of info for me to be a stranger. So, you might want to check him about that. Of course, don't tell him that *I* told you any of this, but I could've easily been one of those other bitches and ran with that shit to the wrong nigga."

"Right. So, that was it?"

"Yep. Pretty much. However, I'm sure with the right persuasion, I could've gotten *way* more out of him. You do know that he had a lil' crush on me, right?" I taunted.

"Stop playing with me, Dior. I'll talk to him, though."

"Okay. Just make sure my name isn't mentioned. Please and thank you."

"I got you," came his reply, but I wasn't fully convinced.

"I'm serious, Kane! I don't have time to be in any shit! Somebody finding out I told you what was supposed to be confidential information could fuck with my job and my chances of getting my brother back! If that were to happen, I swear the only way you'd get this pussy again would be if you came back as a spirit from the dead, but I'll still conjure up some kind of spell to keep you away!"

Kane laughed. "So, what you're saying? That you'll kill me?"

"Damn, right!"

He chuckled again. "Look, Dior, you have my word. I know how to confront a nigga without snitching on the next person. I ain't new to this shit."

"Okay."

"Second question. What's the nigga's name who came to yo' folks' crib? The CEO, as you call him."

"His name is Emiliano Sanchez." Kane's sudden interest piqued my curiosity. "Why do you ask?"

Kane smirked. "Nothing for you to worry about, Pretty Eyes. Get some rest, baby."

Kane's enigmatic response left me wondering about his thoughts.

I found myself in a state of uncertainty as Kane took me to

Alecia J.

an unknown destination. Despite that, I found solace in the fact that Jenesis and my parents were aware of my whereabouts—well, at least they knew *who* I was with. As much as I wanted to be angry at Kane for his actions, I couldn't deny that escaping the city for a much-needed break was a relief. Recalling the days I spent with Jace out of town, I realized that it hadn't felt like a vacation at all, as I was consumed by misery throughout.

On the other hand, I was aware of Kane's charismatic nature, so I suspected that my time with him would be more enjoyable than the time I'd spent with Jace. Be that as it may, knowing that Kane had a girlfriend led me to be cautious in my interactions with him. Being *alone* around Kane, for God knows how many days, would undoubtedly prove challenging, as he was accustomed to having things his way, and the reality was that it always ended up being *his* way. I worried about succumbing to the temptation and hoped to navigate through the days without giving in.

3. Jenesis

As the soft, golden rays of morning light gently filled the room, I gradually awakened to the tender sensation of a delicate touch on my lips, rousing me from my sleep. When I fully opened my eyes, I was greeted by the sight of Kelan's lips meeting mine in a gentle kiss that swiftly evolved into a deeply intimate exchange.

"Good morning, beautiful," Kelan whispered once our lips parted.

"Good morning, my love," I returned with a smile.

Kelan's deep brown eyes met mine, and his gaze was intense, causing a chuckle to leave my lips.

"Kelan, why are you looking at me like that?" I asked, feeling a slight blush creeping up my cheeks.

"I'm sorry, baby. I can't help it. You've got to get used to me staring at you a lot now that we're together. I like admiring what's mine," he explained with a loving grin, and his eyes filled with adoration. "It's hard as fuck to believe you were single for all those years. Hell, even worse that you went without dick for that long."

Alecia J.

"Well, believe it because it's true."

"So, you're saying that you didn't talk to *any* of the niggas that I *know* tried to holla at you?"

I chuckled. "I didn't say *that*. I mean, I had conversations with some of them. Some I even went out on dates with, but it never went further than that with any of them. See, what a lot of men don't know is the dark side of pretty privilege for a woman is being lusted over but not loved. Most men just wanna say they experienced a woman, and for some reason, those were the types of men that I always encountered."

"God knew what he was doing. He was saving the best for last, which is me."

I smiled. "Well, until we're married, the jury is still out on that one. But what time is it?"

"It's time to fuck," he replied with a smack to my ass.

"Kelan, we had sex three times yesterday," I whined.

"I'm aware of that, and it would've been more than that if we didn't get a late start on the last two rounds."

"Oh, God!" I playfully rolled my eyes.

"Baby, three times isn't enough for me. I be needing about seven rounds."

"You're joking, right?" I searched his face for a hint of humor.

Kelan burst out laughing. "I'm just fuckin' with you, baby. Now, when it comes to laying this dick, yo' nigga is longwinded like a muthafucka, but I can't fuck that many times in a day. Hell nah! I have mastered five times, though, but I was drained like a muthafucka the next day. And I ain't just talking about my balls; I'm talking about physically."

I chuckled. "I bet."

Thoughts of him having sex with another woman made me bring up Melani.

"Was Melani at the house last night? You never told me. Or did you come straight here after you left the gym?"

"Nah, I stopped by there and grabbed a few things, but she was gone."

"You have any clue where she went?"

"Nope, and I really don't care."

"Kelan, I get why you feel the way you do toward her, but she's still Emmy's mama, and at some point, the two of you will have to talk."

Kelan sighed. "I know, but if she wants to talk about Emmy, then she'll need to be the one reaching out to me because it damn sure won't be the other way around. She'll swear a nigga wants her ass back or something."

"I'm not saying that you have to reach out to her; just don't count her completely out of Emmy's life."

"Now I know you're a different breed of a woman because most women, especially the ones who know that a nigga's baby mama don't like them, would be like, fuck that bitch! I'll raise Emmy!"

"And I will! The fuck?!" I giggled. "I don't give a damn about that girl not liking me, but I grew up without a mom, so I guess that's why I have a *little* empathy. Now, if it gets to where you see that she just doesn't give a fuck anymore, that's when you should start taking legal actions."

"Or *illegal* matters into my own hands," he countered.

"Be nice, Kelan. Emmy needs you. *I* need you."

"And both of y'all will *still* have me if some shit popped off. Believe that. But I'll be nice... for now. You just don't know Melani like I do."

"I'm sure I'll find out... being with you anyway."

"You're saying that like you're ready to make our relationship public already."

Alecia J.

I chuckled. "No. I didn't say all of that, but people are nosy. Not to mention, we'll be at the gym together, and you make flirting so obvious, so I'm sure people will start to pick up on something going on between us."

"Well, you know I don't give a fuck, but I'll try not to make it so noticeable when we're in public. I fuck with the lowkey shit. As long as we know what's up, we ain't gotta please the media. Just remember who you belong to now." Those words led to another kissing session.

"Oh, I meant to tell you that Kane said Dior doesn't have her phone with her," Kelan informed me after he pulled away.

Kane had shared his plans with Kelan and me about taking Dior on a trip with him to Bora Bora, a place I knew she was *dying* to visit. So, I could only imagine the look of happiness on her face once they arrived. Nonetheless, I was still curious to know how Kane planned to get her to agree to go *anywhere* with him. Like me, Dior wasn't easily persuaded when it came to certain things, especially almost anything pertaining to Kane. Kelan had talked to Kane the day before, though, and Kane told him that Dior *was* with him, so he convinced her *somehow*.

I tried calling Dior that same day, but she never answered any of my calls or responded to my texts. Kelan kept saying that maybe her phone didn't have service, but I found that to be odd since Kane's worked just fine.

"She doesn't? Why not?" I queried.

"Your guess is as good as mine. After you told me that you couldn't get in touch with her yesterday, I texted Kane and asked about her phone. He texted me back late last night and said that but you were already asleep. So, I guess you'll just have to call his phone whenever you want to talk to her. Remind me to give you his number before you leave."

I nodded.

One Drunk Night In Miami 2

"Quick question. Do you ever go visit your parents' graves?"

Kelan's unexpected question caught me off guard.

"Can you say *random*?" I said, turning away from him and positioning myself on my back.

"My bad. I know you don't really like discussing them. I was just curious."

I sighed. "It's fine. I used to visit them *a lot* with my grandma, but that was when I was younger. Lately, I've only been visiting my dad's grave, and that's usually once a year. I mean, what is there really to say to someone I barely knew?"

"Well, when was the last time you went to your mama's grave?"

"It's been years... *well* over ten years."

"Damn. Why?"

"I don't know," I lied. "My grammie always tries to get me to go with her to my mama's grave, but I always refuse. That is *one* thing I firmly stand my ground on, regardless of how much she insists or fusses at me. It usually results in her not speaking to me for a day, but she eventually moves past it."

"Do you choose not to go because of the way she neglected you for all those years?"

"Maybe," I answered, looking up at the ceiling, feeling tears welling up.

What Kelan said hit close to home. I had definitely avoided visiting my mom's grave due to the deep-seated resentment I harbored toward her for the way she treated me after my dad's passing. In my youth, I couldn't fully grasp her behavior, but as I matured and gained an understanding of depression, her actions started to make some semblance of sense. Nevertheless, as the one who had to endure those tumultuous times, my feelings toward my mom remained unchanged despite gaining insight into the complexities of mental health.

Alecia J.

"Baby, you know you can talk to me about anything. I'm always here if you need me. Even if I'm not here, I'm always a phone call away."

"I know. Thank you. I gotta get up and fix breakfast," I said as a way to end the conversation.

I pushed the covers aside and hurried to leave the bed before my tears had a chance to fall, but Kelan's strong arm swiftly grasped me, pulling me back and enveloping me in a comforting embrace.

"I meant what I said, Jenesis. I'm here for you, baby. It's not good to hold all that shit in."

My heart was so heavy with emotions that I needed to process, but I managed to hold back my tears.

"And don't worry about cooking this morning because, really, you don't have time. Well, you won't have time to cook *and* give me some pussy."

That caused me to chuckle.

Kelan flipped me over, towering over me, then pried my legs open and got between them.

"I'll make this quick since we both have to get to work," he assured while removing his boxers. I didn't have to take off anything since I wasn't wearing any panties.

After letting me know that he and Melani had been using condoms since Emmy was born, Kelan and I came to a mutual agreement that condoms would be off-limits when we had sex. I felt it was still a little too early for that, but Kelan wasn't having it any other way. He kept going on about how I was his, and he was mine, and that's how it would remain moving forward. I trusted him. At the same time, though, I told him the moment my pussy ever started randomly itching, smelling, or feeling weird, and I discovered he'd given me something, that day would be the end of us.

One Drunk Night In Miami 2

Kelan pushed my knees upward and wedged himself between my thighs.

"Mmm," we both moaned simultaneously as he rammed himself home, his body hard and primal against mine.

I could definitely get used to waking up to this every morning or every other morning.

Isla: *Where are you, girl? The meeting has started.* Isla texted me as I was getting out of my car.

Me: *Heading inside now!* I quickly texted her back as I hurriedly made my way inside the building.

Thanks to Kelan and his *overly* horny ass, we ended up pleasuring each other a little more and longer than we expected, which caused me to be late for work. I prided myself on always being on time for work, but that morning, I really didn't give a damn; they'd see me whenever I got there. The way I looked at it, the dick was worth my tardiness.

I gently tapped on the door of the conference room, waiting a moment before I stepped inside. Once I entered, the entire room seemed to fall eerily silent as if every pair of eyes swiveled in my direction, particularly Darlene's piercing gaze.

"Good morning, everyone!" I greeted them with a smile before carefully making my way over to my seat beside Isla.

"So nice of you to join us, Jenesis. I thought for a second that maybe you had called out for the day." Darlene's tone carried a subtle undertone of disapproval.

I'm sure that would've just made your day if you could come to work one day and not have to see a bad bitch like me strutting the halls because I know I'd have the best day ever if I didn't have to see your ass! That was what I wish I could've said.

Alecia J.

However, my own perspective differed substantially from Darlene's.

Darlene's snobbish demeanor was off-putting, but it was clear she had feelings of *jealousy* toward me. So, if *I* had expressed my thoughts, they would have been rooted in her behavior rather than any perceived envy.

"Oh, no! I overslept!" I fabricated an excuse.

"Hmm. Oversleeping does happen," she responded with an expression that hinted at her skepticism.

"So, what did I miss?" I asked as I settled into my seat, attempting to deflect attention from my tardiness.

"Knock, knock," I said.

After softly tapping on Isla's office door, I entered with a smile that quickly faded once I noticed her in tears. Closing the door behind me, I hurried to her side.

"Isla, what's wrong?" I asked with my voice filled with empathy. "Please talk to me!" I urged, placing a comforting hand on her shoulder.

"This... this muthafucka has taken this shit too far now!"

"Who?! Leo?" I automatically assumed.

"Yes, with his no-good ass! It's one thing to flirt with bitches in my face or even go cheat, but muthafucka, you had the nerve to go and get a bitch pregnant?!"

"Whaaaaaaaaat?" I exclaimed in dismay.

"Yeah. Mr. Leo has a baby on the way." She chuckled, but I knew it wasn't from humor.

"Well, how did you find out?"

"His little bitch just got in my inbox with screenshots of their messages, phone calls, and all types of pictures of them! Look!"

One Drunk Night In Miami 2

Isla handed me her phone, and I eagerly took a seat to read the messages, bracing myself for whatever revelations lay within. As I skimmed through the messages, my eyes widened in disbelief. "Oh, wow!" I exclaimed, unable to mask my surprise. "From the looks of it, they've been together for quite a while."

"Try two years," Isla clarified.

"Two years?" I repeated, struggling to comprehend the depth of the betrayal.

"Yeah. That muthafucka has been living a double life for two years!" Isla's voice tinged with a mix of resignation and hurt.

After reading the text that included the lady announcing the pregnancy to Leo, and he responded with an excited reaction, I decided that I had seen all I needed to. I returned Isla's phone, concluding the viewing.

"This is crazy. Like, oh, my God! Did he ever mention wanting more kids?"

"You mean, did he want a child? Because until now, he didn't have any. When Leo and I first got together, he wasn't too keen on having kids. With Imani being a teenager at the time we got married, he just wanted us to travel the world and enjoy life, which was fine by me because, truthfully, I didn't want any more kids. Imani was enough for me. Actually, she still is. But one day, a few years back, Leo approached me, saying he wanted a child. At that time, he had already started his disrespectful acts, so him asking *me* to give him a baby went through one ear and out the other. Leo has been trying for years to get me pregnant and can't figure out for the life of him why I haven't conceived a child in all these years. It's because I faithfully pop my birth control! You won't have me attached to your ass for the rest of my life!"

"Smart thinking. So, what was the purpose of her telling

you about the pregnancy? Like, is he planning to leave you for her and raise their child together? I might've skipped over that part or didn't get that far in the messages."

"Leo stated in one of the messages that he wasn't leaving me to be with her. Not so much because he loves me, but more so because *it's cheaper to keep me*. And I, for one, couldn't agree with him more. But girl... this evidence right here... oh, girl, it's gonna drain his fuckin' bank account!"

"Most definitely," I agreed like I had knowledge of how divorce settlements worked.

"As for the child, according to her, Leo still plans to be an active father. Now, how does he plan to do that while he's still married and has yet to tell me? I have no idea. But Jenesis, once Leo signs those divorce papers, he can be as active in that child's life, hell, even hers, as he wants. Hell, if I wasn't trying to take him for everything he has, I'd gladly hand him over to her *today*!"

"Okay! Well, just make sure you don't delete any of those messages."

"Girl, I'm already two steps ahead of you. I've already screenshotted all this shit just in case she tries to block me or report the chat."

I nodded.

"So, are you going to mention this to him?"

"I thought about it, then decided against it. I'ma continue to let the evidence pile up like I said. See, I'm not going to respond to her because I'm sure she's waiting for a response any minute now. I'm a woman, not to mention I have a degree in psychology, so I know how women's minds work. And if she's the type of woman that I think she is, then if I don't respond in a timely manner, give her the response she wants, or even respond at all, she's liable to blow a fuckin' gasket and just start revealing and doing all types of crazy shit. So, I'ma keep quiet and see how all of this plays out. I just can't believe this muthafucka! But it's all good. Karma is gonna be a bigger bitch than I'll ever be."

"I know that's right. But girl, don't let that shit get to you. Just be glad you're not the one who ended up pregnant."

"That part!"

"Well, I gotta go! I got tons of paperwork to do today. I just stopped by for a quick chat. Again, don't let that shit ruin your day, girl, or change your beautiful soul. Whenever I feel down or I'm in a funk, I find that listening to music or motivational speeches always tends to lift my spirits. Also, I know that Leo is your husband, but Isla, trust me when I say that nigga is so not worth you shedding any more tears over. Chin up and chest out, baby. These next few months before you can file for divorce will fly by. Now, they may be challenging, but you got this, girl. In the end, you'll end up being the one who gets the last laugh. Mark my words. And who knows... you'll probably find new love after divorcing his ass. We all have a soulmate out here somewhere, and I hate to be the one to tell you, but Leo definitely isn't yours, sis."

"Girl, you ain't telling me nothing I don't already know. But Jenesis, right now, the *only* thing I'm worried about *is* divorcing his ass. I swear that's my main focus. But I know you have to go, so I'ma stop rambling."

"Girl, nonsense! If the paperwork I had to do wasn't mandatory, I'd be ducked off in your office all day."

We shared a laugh.

"Seriously, though, I really appreciate you for listening to me vent and the advice."

"Anytime, boo! We ladies have to stick together," I said as I rose from my seat. "Now, are you good before I leave?"

"Yes, girl, I'm good. I'm about to work on a few things myself."

Alecia J.

"Well, alright. If you need me, I'm only a skip and a hop away," I let her know.

"I know. Thank you again, honey."

"Most welcome. I'll come check on you later." I tapped her desk, then exited her office.

As I made my way back to my office, I encountered Darlene at the hallway intersection. She wore a tight-lipped smile that didn't quite reach her eyes, and I offered a similarly insincere grin in return.

"Bitch," I muttered as I entered my office.

Before delving into paperwork, I remembered that I needed to call Dior and check on her. Kelan had given me Kane's number, but he didn't do so until I was heading to work. Since I was running late, I just decided to call her once I got some free time.

"Who the hell is this?" Kane rudely answered the phone.

"Um, well, hello to you too, Kane. This is Jenesis. I'm calling to talk to Dior."

"Oh, shid! What's up, sis? Kelan did say you'd be calling. But she's right here."

Moments later, Dior's voice came on the phone.

"Hey, friiiiiiiiiiiiiiiiend!" she exclaimed in excitement.

"Baby, when people get themselves a man, you don't know if they're dead or alive these days!" I joked.

"Jenesis, don't do me, boo! This isn't what it looks like!"

"Then tell me what it is, 'cause, honey, I am anxious to know how he convinced your ass to go anywhere with him."

"Jenesis, this crazy ass nigga kidnapped me!"

I burst out laughing.

"He did what?!"

"It's not funny, girl! He really did!"

"For some reason, I don't doubt that he *did*, but isn't that what you asked for not too long ago? For a nigga to kidnap you and take you out of town?"

"I did, but—"

"Then, no buts. You're enjoying yourself in *Bora Bora*, right?"

"Despite the circumstances of how I ended up here, girl, yes! But how did you know where we were?"

"Kane told us where he wanted to take you, but he didn't mention anything about kidnapping you to get you there." I laughed again.

"I swear when I get back home, I'ma find me some new friends! Here I am, telling you that I've been kidnapped, and you think this shit is funny!"

"It really is funny, though. But you don't seem like you're in any type of pain or distress, so I take it that you're good."

"I am. It's so beautiful here. Me and you gotta take a trip here one day."

"You know I'm down for that."

"I am so glad that you have met Kelan because he's slowly but surely bringing you out of your shell! I gotta personally thank him when I get back!"

I shook my head, smiling.

"Anyway, I just called to check on you. I gotta busy day ahead, so I need to get started on my work."

"Okay, but I do need to talk to you about something when I get home."

"Is everything okay?" I began to worry.

"Yes and no, but it's nothing for you to worry about. It's just something that I need to tell you that I should've been told you. But again, please don't worry because I know how you get."

"Dior, how are you going to drop some shit on me like that and then tell me not to worry?"

Alecia J.

"I know. I shouldn't have said anything. I should've just waited until I got home."

"You think?"

"Jenesis, please don't be mad, and please don't worry. I'll explain everything when I get home."

"Okay," I grudgingly replied.

"I love you, and I'll talk to you later, boo."

"I love you too. Be safe."

After the call ended with Dior, I couldn't help but wonder, *What the hell does she have to tell me?*

4. Kelan

"Now, before I start, I'ma need y'all to overlook the love marks on my back. A nigga had a good, no scratch that, a great ass night and morning. So, men, if you don't have these after a wild night, my nigga, you're not doing something right. Aight, let's get into this back workout."

I was rewatching one of my workout videos that I had recently posted on Snapchat. After taking a look at the viewers, I noticed that Jenesis had watched it, so I knew she'd be calling or texting soon. Not even a minute after that thought crossed my mind, she texted me.

My baby: *Your girlfriend is one lucky girl, Mr. Kelan.*

I chuckled. Since we were official, I had changed her name in my phone to *My Baby*.

Me: *Nah, I think I'm the lucky one.* I sent her some heart emojis following that, then added, *How is work going, though, baby?*

My Baby: *Work is work... busy as always. But I'm just*

Alecia J.

going over some paperwork right now. How has your morning been? And what are you doing?

Me: *It's been straight. Just taking a break until this next class. I can't wait to see you this evening, so I can eat that pussy.*

My Baby: *Ooouuuu! I like the sound of that. Well, in that case, let me hurry up with this paperwork so I can get off a little earlier.*

Me: *No need to rush, baby. Handle yo' business. You have full access to this tongue and dick at any given time of the day.*

My Baby: *Likewise, babe. I just have one request tonight. I wanna sit on your face while you do it.*

I smirked and ran my tongue over my lips after reading her text, picturing how that shit would turn out.

Instead of texting back, I decided to call Jenesis since I needed to rap with her about a few other things. If she didn't pick up, then I knew it had to be because she was around others. Even if Jenesis was occupied with paperwork, she'd still pick up my call.

"I was wondering when you were going to call." Jenesis chuckled after answering the phone.

"Yeah. You know I hate texting, but I just wanted to hear your voice, beautiful. I also wanted to ask you what you plan on doing for your birthday. It's in two weeks, right?"

"Yes. You remembered."

"Of course, I remembered, baby. So, what you wanna do? Is there a specific place you wanna go?"

"I really don't know."

"Is there somewhere you've never been that you wanna go?"

"Oh, my God, yes! Paris, for sure! I always said if I get married, that's where I wanna go for my honeymoon."

I mentally stored that information.

"Well, you have about a year to prepare yourself because

this time next year, we'll be heading to Paris for our honeymoon," I spoke into existence, but I was serious at the same time."

Jenesis giggled. "How are you so sure that I'm the one for you?" she questioned.

"My Pop once told me, 'If you look at a woman and don't feel anything for her, then she's not yours to keep; she's another man's blessing. Be real about how you feel and stop wasting these women's time and messing with other people's soulmates' and that shit still sticks to me 'til this day.

"Wow. Your father sounded like a wise man."

"He was. But what other places do you want to visit?"

"Let's see. Oh, I also want to visit France, Switzerland, Germany, the Dominican Republic, Italy, and Dubai. I know you might not hear a lot of women saying that they'd like to visit Switzerland, Germany, or maybe even France. A lot of women these days are more into Turks & Caicos, The Bahamas, Jamaica, or Bora Bora, like Dior. I want to go to all of those places as well, but the ones I mentioned first are at the *top* of my bucket list."

"That's what I love about you: your uniqueness. But baby, this is your world; I'm just living in it. So, *whatever* you want, I got you, and *wherever* you wanna go, I'ma make that shit happen. I don't give a damn if I have to take a whole month off to take you to all those places. Just say the word, give me a date, and it's done."

Jenesis smiled. "Where have you been all my life? You just seem so perfect that it's almost unbelievable that your baby mama would behave the way she did and practically hand you over to another *woman*."

"I'm not perfect, baby. Let me just say that. And I could ask you the same, but I've been around, beautiful. We both just had to wait for God's timing, and his timing couldn't have been more fuckin' perfect."

"Amen to that," she agreed.

"As for Melani, well, some women *and* men just don't know what they have until they lose it. It probably hasn't really hit her yet, but I'm sure it will soon."

"I'll admit, I wish we could've met under different circumstances because if it was any other man who approached me and told me that he had a woman *and* a crush on me, he couldn't say so much as *hey* to me, following that revelation. But, with you... things were different. *You* were different. So, no, I'm not ashamed to say I'm glad your baby mama didn't appreciate you or what she had. One woman's trash is another woman's treasure. But Kelan, like you, I'm not perfect either. There will be days I'll make you mad, or you'll probably want to knock my ass out," we laughed together, "but as your woman, as long as you do right by me, I *promise* to do right by you *and* Emmy. With me, you'll see what it feels like to have a real woman next to you," she professed.

"I appreciate that, baby. And with me, you'll definitely see what it feels like to have a real nigga in your corner."

"Already seeing that." She grinned.

"Likewise, beautiful. So, aight, let's get back to your birthday. Which one of those places do you want to visit first?"

"You know what? Now, thinking about it, I think I want to go back to my hometown, Ocho Rios, in Jamaica."

"Okay. You did say you were from there."

"Yeah. But I never got to really experience the Jamaican experience because I was young when I left there."

"So, is Jamaica your final answer?"

"Yep! That's my final answer!"

"Say less, baby. Jamaica it is, then." I made a mental note to book the trip that evening once I got to the crib. "So, since we're on the topic of *birthdays*, Emmy's just so happens to be two weeks after yours."

"Really?!" Jenesis shrieked.

"Yeah, my baby will be turning thirteen soon. I'm about to have a teenager," I joked.

Jenesis laughed. "Kelan, don't do my girl!"

"I'm just playin'. But nah, Daddy's Girl will be turning three."

"Aww. What do y'all plan on doing for her birthday?"

"I wanna throw her a party. I just don't know what theme to go with. You got any suggestions?"

Jenesis chuckled. "Kelan, as you know, I'm not a mom, an auntie; hell, I don't even have a God child, so I haven't the *slightest* idea about what toddlers are into these days. Maybe you should ask her mama. You are going to include her, right?"

I sighed.

"On some real shit, I'm undecided."

"Kelan... we've gone over this already. Now, I understand that her drinking problem has gotten out of hand. I get it, but as long as she still *wants* to be a part of Emmy's life and isn't causing *her* any harm, I believe you should allow her to be. Taking away Melani's rights or the chance to be in her daughter's life could potentially do more harm than good, especially if you're trying to minimize the tension."

Jenesis was right. I just wasn't prepared for what could come if Melani saw Jenesis at the party. Although Melani *assumed* Jenesis was the girl I was with, based on her seeing me talking to Jenesis at my party and seeing Jenesis at the gym when she showed up acting crazy, Melani really had no *solid* proof that Jenesis and I were fuckin' or even in a relationship. However, I was convinced that if she saw Jenesis at Emmy's party, that would be all the confirmation she needed, and I just knew that drama would follow that.

Alecia J.

"Alright, baby. I'll reach out to her," I reluctantly agreed.

"*Soon*, Kelan!" Jenesis stressed.

"I will... one day this week. Just not today."

"Fair enough. Now, as far as a theme goes, like I said, I can't really help you out too much there, but what cartoon characters does Emmy like? Is there a particular show she likes to watch?"

"She loves Gracie's Corner."

"Then there's your answer! Do her a Gracie's Corner birthday party."

"Yeah, that will be dope. I'ma hit up Kane's girlfriend and see if she can pull it off for me. Well, I know she can do it. I just hope one month is enough time to get everything together since she has other clients."

"Babe, I hate to cut you off, but someone is at my door. I'll call you back!" Jenesis words were rushed.

"Aight, baby."

After our call ended, I called Kane and asked him for Bonnie's number so I could start planning Emmy's birthday party. Bonnie assured me that she could make it happen within the time, so I sent her the $5,000 deposit via Cash App. The deposit was so high because after telling Bonnie what I wanted included in the party, she gave me an estimate of anywhere between twenty to twenty-five thousand dollars. Bonnie really wanted to waive the deposit fee, not only because she knew I was good for it but also because we were family. I appreciated that, but I didn't believe in discounts when it came to supporting people's dreams.

I was prepared to pay Bonnie what her business was worth, regardless of our family connection. Bonnie was hella talented at what she did, and the type of party I had in mind for my daughter was by no means inexpensive. I was fully aware that it would require a significant amount of time, attention, and money to bring my vision to life. Some may argue that the amount of money spent on a child's party, especially for a three-year-old, was unnecessary, but I didn't give a damn. Even if my daughter wouldn't remember it, I knew that I would, and the photos taken would become cherished memories for her. Once she got older, I wanted her to know that her daddy always made shit happen, even if her mama didn't.

Seeing that it was almost time for my next class to start, I stood from my seat and left my office, only to bump into one of Melani's ratchet ass friends.

"Tiece, what you doing here?"

"Hey, Kelan! I was just stopping through and wanted to see if I could sign up for one of your classes."

I eyed her suspiciously.

Tiece and Melani had been friends for *years,* and she'd never stepped foot inside my gym. So, I found it *very* odd that *right* after me and Melani broke up, she popped up there. What's more, I always felt like she was feeling a nigga.

"Yeah. Are you looking to join a morning class or an evening one? We have multiple times."

"Which one would you say usually has the most people in it? I need all the motivation that I can get." She chuckled, tugging at the small pudge in her belly.

"We usually have a good crowd for our 6:00 class. By then, everyone is fresh off work."

"Cool! Let's go with that one. Where do I sign up?"

"New classes start each month. The sign-up date for this month has passed. The new class started last week," I explained.

"Oh, dang," she said with disappointment in her voice.

"But... I'll make an exception for you and give you a week's discount," I offered.

"Thank you, Kelan!" she replied, with a sparkle in her eye.

As I reflected on the conversation, I realized I should have chosen my words more carefully. Tiece probably took it as me flirting with her.

"Wait right here. Let me go grab the paperwork."

After Tiece had signed all the necessary paperwork and paid her monthly fee, the signup process was concluded.

"So, when can I start?" she asked.

"Well, shid, you paid your money, so you can start today if you want to."

"I guess that was a dumb question, huh? Okay! I'll see you at six!"

I nodded.

As Tiece sashayed off, all I could think was, I gotta keep my eye on her. Something about her just didn't sit right with me.

A few days later...

"Shit, baby!" I groaned, receiving head from Jenesis. "I swear I gotta marry yo' ass ASAP! I'll be damned if you suck another nigga's dick like this! I wonder what your coworkers would think of you if they saw you in this position?"

Jenesis paused briefly to say, "You can't have morals while you're giving head, baby... good head at that. So, I really wouldn't give a fuck what they'd think or have to say. I'm sure I could probably teach a lot of them a thing or two." She winked, then went back to work on my dick.

The way she sucked and licked at my length, one would've thought my dick was like male candy to her ass.

When I felt my nut rising, I stopped her.

"Aight, baby. I gotta save this nut for that pussy."

Jenesis lifted her head in confusion.

"What?"

I chuckled. "Baby, I'm saying, I don't want to nut like this... at least not today. I'm ready to feel my pussy."

One Drunk Night In Miami 2

"Okay. So how you want it today, baby?"

"My second favorite position," I answered. My absolute favorite position was fucking her from the back. I was sure that sight and the sound of her ass clapping would never get boring to a nigga.

"Let me find out that you like me riding your dick," Jenesis teased, then straddled my lap.

"That shit should be clear as fuck since I ask you to do it every time we have sex."

Jenesis lifted her bottom, aligned her pussy with my dick, then eased herself down, taking all of my dick. I would've thought that after all the fuckin' we'd done in those last few days, that her shit would be loose, but her pussy was still *deliciously* tight.

"I think I'ma turn around this time. I'm used to riding you at nighttime. So, being able to see your facial expressions does something to me."

I chuckled.

"Aight, baby. Do you. Whatever makes you comfortable... for now, because eventually, you're going to have to get used to us fuckin' at any time of the day. I like that random shit."

"I'm noticing that." She smiled then twisted her body around and started riding me cowgirl style.

As I watched Jenesis's ass bounce up and down, I couldn't help but feel like the luckiest man in the world. Not only was my girl pretty as fuck, but her body was fuckin' sickening.

I was so into the sight that it wasn't until Jenesis shouted, "What the hell?!" then jumped off my dick and sprang out of the bed that I noticed my mama standing in the doorway of the room.

"Jenesis Dixon, I swear if you don't hop yo' ass back on this dick, me and you gon' have a *real* fuckin' problem!"

Alecia J.

I was shocked to see my mama as well, but I was more focused on getting my nut at that moment.

"But... but..."

Jenesis glanced nervously in the direction of my mama, who was standing silently, observing the situation.

"Jenesis, that's my mama," I cleared up, hoping to alleviate some of her nervousness. "But I don't give a damn about my mama being in here. I was about to nut, and I'm about to get my nut one way or another. Now come finish yo' man off. It won't take long, baby," I told her while steadily stroking my dick.

Like a good girl, Jenesis climbed back onto the bed.

"Turn around and face me, baby," I instructed when I realized she was getting back in the cowgirl position.

Jenesis made sure the sheet was secured around us both as if my mama hadn't already seen what we had to offer.

"Good. Now fuck me like it's just the two of us in here."

Jenesis started off slow, winding her hips in a circular motion. I guess me staring at her really did do something to her because Jenesis began to go crazy on the dick as if she didn't give a fuck who was watching. Hell, for a moment, I had even forgotten that my mama was in there.

"Oooooh, this dick is so gooooooooood," Jenesis cooed in a state of ecstasy with her head tilted back as she stood on her tiptoes, riding me while also pinching her nipples.

That shit was a major turn-on, and knowing that someone was watching us seemed to intensify the moment. The longer I stared at Jenesis, the more I pictured her being a mom... my future kids' mama.

Yeah, she'd make a good ass mama, I thought as I proceeded to nut in her.

"Fuuuuuuuuck!" I grunted, holding her firmly by her waist.

When Jenesis noticed that I was nutting, she tried to remove herself, but the grip I had on her waist was too strong.

One Drunk Night In Miami 2

The look she gave me let me know that she was mad as fuck, but I figured she wouldn't say too much while my mama was there.

Once I finished dropping my load off in her, Jenesis hopped off me with the quickness, then grabbed the sheet to cover her body.

"I'm going to take a shower," she mumbled with a mixture of embarrassment and anger evident in her voice. I couldn't help but chuckle, witnessing this rare display of strong emotion from her. Jenesis gathered the sheet around her and headed toward the bathroom, which required passing by my mama. "Good morning! Hello! Nice to meet you!" Jenesis hurriedly greeted my mama before scurrying off to the bathroom.

I shook my head.

"Whew! I remember those days!" my mama exclaimed after Jenesis had closed the bathroom door.

"So, you don't knock anymore, Ma?" I asked as I put back on my boxers.

"Well, hello, son. And why would I when I have a key? You have to be careful who you allow access to your home."

"Obviously," I mumbled as I got out of bed. "Still, *most* people would've waited in the front 'cause I know you heard Jenesis in here moaning and shit."

"I did! Well, I heard somebody hollering! That's why I came in here to see what was going on! I didn't know she'd be over here!" That was her excuse.

"Aight, Ma, but after you saw what was going on, you should've left. At least a normal parent would've done that."

"Well, son, you know that I'm anything but normal these days. But I do apologize."

"Apology accepted, but you need to apologize to my girl, too. I'on want her thinking that we got some kind of weird, kinky, mother and son type of shit going on."

Alecia J.

"Okay, Kelan. I will. At least now I know why the ladies are so crazy over you."

"Nah, that ain't the reason because all of them ain't had this dick. But what's up, Ma? You hardly ever come over here this early or over here at all, thinking about it."

"Well, I got out to do a quick Kroger run, and since I was over this way, I decided to stop by. I also need to talk to you, but I'll let you get dressed first. But before you go and take care of that, let me ask you something. Are you sure that girl is the one for you? She seems a bit... timid."

"Timid? Jenesis is *far* from a shy girl, Ma. If you saw the things she was just doing before you arrived, you'd have a different view of her."

"Oh, son, spare me the details of your sexual life. I've seen enough today."

"I'm just saying she's not shy. If anything, she's embarrassed. Can you imagine how she must feel, knowing that her boyfriend's mama knows what her ass, titties, and pussy look like?"

"I guess you're right, son."

"Yeah. But I'll be right back. I gotta go talk to this girl before she tries to leave my ass behind this shit."

With nothing else to say, I walked away.

Although I should've checked my mama when I first saw her in the room, I thought she would've had enough decency to leave the room once we started back fucking. But, like my mama said, she was anything but normal at times. Still, that shit pissed me off. More so because I knew I wasn't about to hear the end of that shit from Jenesis.

When I entered the bathroom, Jenesis was showering. I wanted to join her, but I knew if I got in there with her, there was a possibility that we'd end up fucking again, and I was trying to get my mama gone quick as possible. So, I was going to check on Jenesis, then head back out to see what the hell my mama wanted.

When I opened the shower door, Jenesis briefly glanced in my direction before resuming her shower.

I chuckled at her pettiness. "So, you're really not going to say anything to me?"

She paused in her showering, giving me a moment of her undivided attention.

"What exactly do you want me to say, Kelan? I'm not sure if I'm more upset about the fact that you nutted in me *without so much as a warning* or the fact that you said *nothing* to your mom about barging in on us having sex! You practically allowed her to watch us have sex! Like, what type of shit was that?! I've never been so embarrassed in my fuckin' life! Or maybe this is a norm for you! You know, letting your mama watch you fuck bitches! If this is some kind of fetish that you have, then let me know now, so I can get my shit and *never* return!"

"What the fuck?! Jenesis, my mama has *never* watched me fuck anybody! Let's get that shit straight right now! Hell, I don't know what type of shit she was on, but I can guarantee you that what happened today was a one *and* only one-time thing! I checked her ass about that shit, though! I know that shit wasn't cool, and it had to be uncomfortable, and I'm saying that from a nigga's point of view. And even though my mama said she's going to apologize to you, I want to apologize on her behalf because I don't want to lose you behind no shit like that, not this soon, anyway."

Jenesis's face softened. "I forgive you. Just make sure there's *not* a *next* time."

"You have my word, baby," I replied, but my eyes were zoomed in on her glistening body.

"Eyes up front, Mr.!" Jenesis snapped her fingers, bringing

me out of my freaky thoughts. "Now that we've gotten that out of the way, please explain to me why you nutted in me."

"Baby, on some real shit, the pussy was just too good to pull out," I admitted.

"Kelan, good pussy doesn't mean nut in it."

"Then what does it mean?" I countered.

That made her laugh.

"Can you take anything serious?" she asked.

"I'm being serious. Since it doesn't mean that, then what does it mean? Shid, put me on game. 'Cause obviously, you know something that I don't."

"Good pussy is for enjoyment, Kelan."

"Well, yours is *great*, and *great* pussy gets nutted in."

She shook her head. "Seriously, though, Kelan. We're not ready for a baby."

"We're not, or *you're* not? Because I already have a daughter, and hell, if I'm being real, I've been wanting to put a baby in you since the first day I met you.

"Kelan, you practically just got out of a relationship with someone else last week, and here I am a week later, showering in your bathroom like we've been together for years or at least months! I'm not saying that I don't want a baby, because I do… eventually. I just think it's too soon right now."

"I hear you, but look, gone and finish taking your shower. I'ma go out here and finish talking to my mama."

"I'm finished," she announced, then shut off the shower. "I'll be out in a minute."

"Aight!" I smacked her ass.

"Kelan!" she screamed, then giggled.

"I couldn't resist. You look good, baby. You look good."

"Yeah, I know," she replied, matching my grin. Our laughs filled the room as we playfully recited the chorus to one of the rapper Cartier's latest songs.

"But for real, though. I'm sorry, baby. I'ma make it up to you tonight. I'll be doing *all* the pleasuring."

"Ooooweee! It's the reciprocity for meeeeeeee!"

"Jenesis, you deserve to be filled the same way you pour into people. The smallest shit you do for me, like how attentive you are with Emmy, makes me wanna do the biggest shit for you. Just know I got you, baby." I winked and then left the bathroom.

My mama was no longer in my bedroom, so I assumed she had wandered to the front of the house. Before heading in that direction, I put on a light cotton shirt and a comfortable pair of basketball shorts. I then made a brief stop by Emmy's room to make sure she was still asleep. Satisfied that she was, I made my way to the kitchen and found my mama seated on a barstool, sipping coffee and engrossed in a TV show.

"Well, that was fast, son!" she remarked, taking in my attire.

"I haven't showered yet. I'ma wait until you leave," I informed her as I grabbed a water bottle from the fridge. "But what's on your mind, Ma?" I asked as I settled down beside her at the kitchen island.

After taking a slow sip of her coffee, she set the cup down and replied, "I'm ready to have that *talk* with Kane. I know he's out of town at the moment, but do you have any idea when he'll be back?"

"Not really. The way he was talking, he wasn't going to leave until Dior was ready."

"Dior? Who is Dior?" she interrogated.

"Oh, shit! You don't know about her."

"No, I don't! Now, who is she?"

"Dior is Jenesis's best friend."

"That still doesn't explain why she'd be with your brother, and he has a girlfriend. So, I'm guessing she's Kane's little friend, huh?"

Alecia J.

"Mama, if you only knew, but you'll have to talk to him about all of that. I don't be in his business like that," I lied. I knew exactly how Kane felt about Dior, but that wasn't my business to tell her.

"You and your brother and y'all women. I—" Mama was about to say more, but Jenesis entered the kitchen with her purse on her shoulder, which prompted me to stand.

"Where you going?"

"I'm going to the store, Kelan."

"To the store?" I retorted with raised brows.

"I'm going to get some food for this house. If you haven't noticed, you have little to none. I want to have breakfast ready before Emmy wakes up."

I felt relieved after hearing that. I just knew she was going to buy a Plan B.

"Oh. Well, if you want to, we can all just go together after I shower and wake Emmy up."

"No, that won't be necessary. I'm a fast shopper, Kelan. Well, when buying food, anyway, since it's usually just me."

"Well, that's about to change. But let me go and get you some money."

"Kelan, I got it."

"Nah. You're my woman. I'm not—"

"Kelan... reciprocity," she reminded me.

I chuckled. "Aight, baby."

I was still going to send her some money once she left because what the fuck she thought?

"I'll be back shortly. It was nice meeting you, ma'am," she told my mom. "Although I wish it could've been under better circumstances."

"So do I, sweetheart. And the name is Jewelynn," Ma formally introduced herself. "I don't feel like we've *officially* met. As a matter of fact, I don't even want to count this as our first meeting. So, how about we do an *official* meet next Sunday at my house. Every Sunday, I make a big dinner and invite my boys over. You should come."

"I'd love that. I do have to work at my other job that day, though. So, I guess it will just depend on the time."

"Well, we don't usually get started until about 5:00. Right, son?"

"Yeah. Somewhere around that time. You're usually off by then, baby."

"Yeah, I am. So, that time would work perfectly. I guess I'll see you then."

"I can't wait!" My mama smiled, and it seemed to be a genuine one.

"Be safe, baby, and call me if you need anything," I told Jenesis.

"I will. See you later!" Jenesis waved goodbye to my mama and left.

"Kelan, tell me that's not that girl's real ass?" Mama pried once Jenesis was out of earshot.

"It is, and I see that look, but *trust me,* it's all-natural."

"Hmph. That girl got a *dangerous* body. For a second there, I was almost tempted to switch to the other side and steal your girl, son."

"Ma, I love you, but I swear I'll treat you like one of these niggas in the streets if you try to fuck my girl."

"Now you know I'm just playing! She is definitely a beauty, though. And I take back calling her timid! You know, son, she just might be the one for you."

"I told you."

"Well, I'ma go. I just stopped by to check on you, son," she said as she rose from her seat. "I thought my favorite girl would've been awake, and I could've convinced you to let her

Alecia J.

come and stay with me for the rest of the weekend, but since Jenesis is here, I'm sure that's a no."

"Any other time, I wouldn't mind, Ma, but yeah, Jenesis is here, and she wants to spend some time with Emmy."

"Understandable. I guess I can share my favorite girl with her as long as she doesn't start calling my grandbaby *her* favorite girl. Then we might have a problem."

I chuckled. "She knows that name is reserved for you only."

"Well, alright. When my baby wakes up, tell her to call me."

"I will."

"Bring it in." Mama stood with her arms wide open, inviting me in for a hug. I walked over and embraced her.

"I love you, son."

"I love you too, Ma."

"I'll see myself out. Now go take a shower," she waved me off, giving me a reminder that I still had Jenesis's juices and her lingering scent on me. "Oh, one more thing before I go. I know you might be upset with me when I tell you this, but I paid Melani a visit last week while she was still here... Sunday, to be exact."

"Okay. And what exactly did you say to her?" I asked with my arms folded as I leaned against the counter.

"I just basically told her how I felt about her all the years. I told her to get her shit and be out of here by the following day. I told her to take a bath because she was really funky as hell and... I gave her fifty thousand dollars."

By the expression on her face, she knew she had fucked up.

"You did, what?!" I shouted, lifting my body off the counter.

"Kelan, it was fifty thousand dollars of *my* money."

"Ma, I don't give a damn if it was five dollars! I wanted her ass to leave here with the same thing she came with, which was *shit!*"

"I know, son. I just felt that maybe a little money would keep her away or cause less drama between the two of you."

"For how long, though? Ma, fifty thousand dollars is like five hundred dollars to a woman like Melani! I wouldn't be surprised if she has already spent all that shit!" I pinched the bridge of my nose to control my anger.

"I'm sorry, son. I really was only trying to help, or at least I thought I was."

"Look, Ma, I know where your heart was when you did that shit, but you should've run something like that by me before making that kind of decision. If you think money will keep Melani away, you're wrong."

Not many people knew Melani like I did, but I was sure they'd all find out soon.

5. Bryson

"Damn! Now that was good! Take that back; that was *great*! Actually, I think that's the best sex we've ever had! Wouldn't you agree?" Kelis gushed after I came out of the bathroom.

She was sprawled over the bed in a state of blissfulness, unaware that it would soon be shattered.

"That was my intention. I hoped to create at least one good ass lasting memory for you to cherish and remember me by," I said.

"Nigga, what?!"

Taken aback by my words, Kelis leaped out of bed, and her entire behavior transformed in a heartbeat.

"What the hell are you talking about, Bryson?!" she yelled, getting in my face.

I shook my head in irritation. That was the type of shit I had grown tired of dealing with when it came to her.

"It means that after today, I'm done with yo' ass... *for good*. Ain't no more blocking you and then getting back cool when I want some pussy or some of yo' cooking. I'm good on you, Kelis."

"But what... what have I done?" she whimpered, acting all confused.

"But what... what have I done?" I mocked her. With my finger pressed against her forehead, I retorted, "What the fuck *haven't* you done, Kelis?! Let me name a few things you seem to have forgotten! Let's start with the constant fuckin' stalking! Blowing up a nigga's phone all damn day and night! Going to other bitches' inboxes, trying to find out if I'm fucking them! Posting under my pictures and posts like we a damn couple when I've told you numerous fuckin' times to chill with that shit! But you wanna know what really did it for me? It was when you approached my mama, telling her about us and shit!"

Kelis's eyes widened in surprise.

Kelis called herself telling my mama not to say anything, not knowing that me and my mama had a close bond. So, despite her request for secrecy, my mama would've never kept something like that from me.

"Yeah, she told me all that bullshit you said about us being together and how I be hiding you from the world and doing you wrong. Kelis, when have I *ever* kept anything *less* than one *hunnid* with you?! I'll fuckin' wait!" I voiced my frustration, challenging her to dispute my honesty.

Kelis remained in a state of shock, standing absolutely motionless and unable to form a single word.

"Yeah. Then my mama said you approached her in the garden section at Walmart. Yo' ass don't know the first thing about gardening, so I find it fuckin' coincidental that the two of you *miraculously* ended up in that same damn department! How the fuck you even know what my mama looks like, considering that I've never shown you a pictured of her?! Damn, are you stalking my folks too?!"

Alecia J.

"I saw her in pictures on your Facebook page," she finally spoke.

I guess this is what Kelan meant when he mentioned posting shit on social media. Muthafuckas really do be nosy as hell, I thought.

"Still, that doesn't explain why you approached her with those lies because that's all that shit was! But I'm done talking about this shit, Kelis! It's over!" I finalized, then grabbed my phone and keys and headed toward the front door.

"You're not fuckin' serious right now!" Kelis shouted, power walking behind me, naked as hell.

"When I walk out this door, and you never hear from me again, you'll see *just* how serious I am!"

"Niggas don't leave me! I do the fuckin' leave!" she kept ranting.

I placed my hand on the doorknob, glanced over my shoulder, and said, "Well, the roles have been reversed this time," then opened the door.

"You know what... fuck you, Bryson! And make sure you lose my damn number!"

Smirking, I turned to face her and replied, "I'ma be honest. It was never saved, sweetheart."

Kelis's face was flushed with anger, but it wouldn't have been me if I didn't choose to make her *madder*.

"And as for the pussy, it wasn't even all that. It was just free, available, and convenient, and niggas love free shit!"

"Nigga, fuck you!" she yelled angrily, then shut the door in my face.

I walked off, shaking my head and chuckling.

I was lying when I said Kelis's pussy wasn't that good. Her shit was fye as hell; actually, it was one of the best that I had come across. Still, no matter how good a bitch's pussy was, it was never worth the headache when it came to me, especially since those muthafuckas came a dime a dozen. So, Kelis's ass had to go, but damn, I couldn't lie. I was going to miss the fuck out of her cooking.

I got in my whip and hopped on Facebook for a second to check out Imani's page. I was shocked as hell when she sent me a friend request, but we had no issues, so I accepted it. Once we started following each other, I made it a daily routine to visit her Facebook page every morning to see the inspiring quotes she shared, which she did consistently. However, on this particular morning, I was surprised to see that Imani hadn't posted anything. It was already close to noon, and usually, she would have already shared something by that time. I brushed it off, thinking that perhaps she was still asleep or occupied by something else.

After leaving Kelis's crib, my stomach grumbled, reminding me that I needed to eat. The hunger pangs were strong, and I craved a diverse selection of food. With that in mind, I decided to make a stop at Golden Corral. My stomach reminded me that I needed to eat.

"Hello, sir! Will this be dining in or to go?" asked the cashier.

To go, I started to say. That was until I noticed Imani sitting alone at a table.

"Dining in," I let her know.

After paying the tab and grabbing a plate, I piled all types of food on my plate, all while stealing glances at Imani, whose eyes never left her phone. I was stalling before going over to her table because I was unsure if someone had accompanied her. However, the absence of any other plates or belongings on the table led me to assume that she had come alone. Even though I wasn't entirely certain, I decided to take the risk and find out. If she was there with another nigga or waiting for one, oh, fuckin' well.

Alecia J.

"Excuse me, is this seat taken?" I asked when I approached the table, causing Imani to finally look up from her phone.

"Bry–Bryson?" Imani's eyes doubled in size, but that wasn't the only thing I noticed about them.

Her eyes seemed slightly puffy, as if she had been crying. Without waiting for an invitation, I took a seat.

"Aye, are you good? You look like you've been crying."

"That's because I have," she admitted, wiping her eyes with the back of her hand.

"You wanna talk about it? I mean, that's if you're not expecting anybody else?" I looked around the restaurant.

"No. I came here alone. I needed some *me* time."

"Oh. Well, I'll leave to give you some privacy," I said, making a move to stand up, but she placed her hand on top of mine to stop me.

"No, stay. Please. I guess I could use some company and male advice."

I raised my eyebrows. Intrigued by her request, I retook my seat.

Out of the blue, Imani started giggling. "Bryson, why do you have so much food?"

"Shid, a nigga is hungry! I should be asking you why you have such *little* food on your plate, especially at an all-you-can-eat restaurant. I'm sure if you were younger and your mama brought you here, she'd be mad as hell if she saw those tiny ass portions! You know if we eat somewhere like this, especially on a weekend day, that's all we eating that day!"

She laughed again. "You're silly, but facts! I'm really not hungry, though. Again, I just came here to clear my mind."

"So, what's going on?" I asked before stuffing my mouth with some pancakes.

"My boyfriend and I broke up today," she replied with a heavy sigh, her eyes reflecting sadness.

One Drunk Night In Miami 2

I paused mid-bite, struck by the unexpected news.

Out of all the things that could've been going on in her life, I never thought she would've said that, especially considering how much in love they seemed.

"Are you okay?" Imani asked, bringing me out of my momentary daze.

I raised a finger, finishing my mouthful of food before responding.

"My bad. I don't like talking while I have food in my mouth."

"Understandable, but are you good? It seemed like you went into some kind of trance."

"Hell, I did," I admitted. "I honestly wasn't expecting you to say that. But what that fuck nigga did?"

"What do all you men do? Cheat!"

"Hold up now. I don't have a girl and haven't had one in *years*, so any female *I* fuck with, that's all we're doing... fucking, and I let that shit be known from the gate. So, telling a female what it is upfront isn't cheating to me. Hell, that's just keeping it real. So, you can't put in me that category with your ex-boyfriend and all these other niggas."

"I guess you can't be mad at someone who's keeping it real with you."

"Hell nah. I'm one of the realest niggas around here. Ask about me."

"Oh, I have," she confessed. "But if you're so real, why don't you have a girlfriend? You can say *next subject* if it seems like I'm getting all in your business."

"Nah, you're good. I haven't had a girlfriend in almost ten years."

"Oh, wow. Are you sure *you're* not the problem?"

"Nah, she definitely was. Actually, she's the reason I gave up on all that love shit."

Alecia J.

"What did she do?"

"She cheated on me."

"Someone cheated on you?" she asked in disbelief.

"Yeah, y'all women be cheating, too... cheating y'all asses off at that, and a lot of y'all get away with doing so because you be sneaky with the shit."

"And men don't?"

"Again, I can't speak for all men, but when it comes to me, I don't give a fuck about who sees me with who. All I know is that when I'm with somebody, well, at least when I was with her, cheating didn't cross my mind. But she did more than just cheat, though. She went and got pregnant by the nigga."

"Oh, wow!"

"Yeah. That's why after her, I was like fuck bitches, get money. Well, it was always get money. You wanna know what's even crazier, though? You remind me so much of her... looks-wise."

"Really?"

"Real shit. Do you have a sister?" I had to know.

"Nope. I'm an only child."

"On your mama *and* daddy side? Assuming your parents aren't together."

"To my knowledge, yes. But you know they say we all have a twin running around here somewhere. Maybe your ex is mine."

"Like a muthafucka!" I agreed. "But look, I'on know the full story behind why yo' nigga cheated, but I will say this, yo' pretty ass better not shed another tear behind that nigga. While you're sitting here crying your eyes out and shit, he's probably blowing out another bitch's back. You're different from the females I fuck with."

"How so?"

One Drunk Night In Miami 2

"They don't cry. Those muthafuckas be wanting to record a diss track about my ass after I'm done with them!"

Imani burst into laughter.

"I'm dead fuckin' serious. Believe it or not, I had that shit happen before, and the girl was a real ass fuckin' rapper. I mean, her shit wasn't on the big stream yet, but a lot of people fucked with her music, and she had thousands of views on TikTok and YouTube."

"Oh, my God! I gotta hear this song!"

"You can't. She removed that shit when I threatened to sue her for slander."

"But don't you have to have more proof than 'she hurt my feelings' to actually pursue a slander case?"

"I see you know a lil' some, but yeah, you do, even though my feelings weren't hurt."

"So, how did you get her to remove it?"

"I told her that her lil' song was fuckin' with my reputation as a fitness trainer and that I was losing clients, which wasn't true, but that was all it took me to say to make her take the video down. However, if that shit didn't work, I was willing to commit myself to a mental institution for a couple of months and tell the judge that her song caused me to go crazy."

"You wouldn't have!"

"Oh, but I would have if that's what it would have taken. A muthafucka is not about to get famous off using my name and lying on me. Hell, if you wanna tell lies, at least give me my cut! I probably wouldn't have minded then. But, yeah, ever since that shit happened, I told myself that I'll never date another female who calls herself trying to be a rapper. Hell, *especially* a singer, 'cause those muthafuckas be too deep in their feelings. You don't have a passion for music, do you?"

She chuckled. "Absolutely not, but even if it did, it

wouldn't matter because you and I will never be, Bryson. Not a couple, not a fling, none of that."

"Damn, why you say it like that?"

"You have a little *too* many women on your roster for my liking, and I don't like to share. That's why I'm single now."

We'll see. I didn't voice those words, though.

"Well, I'm *close* to being single. I had to let one of my favorites go this morning. So, it looks like you and I are in the same boat. Hell, I wouldn't be surprised if I hear about a mixtape or see a viral YouTube video about me going around soon."

Imani laughed. "So, tell me about *this* girl. Why did you call it quits with her?"

During the next hour, Imani and I had deep conversations about various topics. In addition to discussing Kelis, I learned that Imani was twenty-five, held a master's degree in accounting, *and* was working as a tax preparer while also starting her own business, which I found to be impressive as fuck. Our discussion then took a more serious turn as she went in depth about her breakup. In turn, I found myself sharing details about my own past relationship with my ex-girlfriend, Nikki. I couldn't believe I had discussed such personal information, but I felt a need to gain a female's perspective on why women would cheat on a good man. Despite Imani's insights, that still didn't explain why Nikki had cheated on me, as her reasons didn't seem to align with my own experiences.

"Bryson, thank you for the talk. I really needed that," Imani expressed as we stood outside the restaurant, preparing to part ways.

"No problem. You really should be thanking my stomach, though. If I wasn't hungry as hell, I wouldn't have stopped here."

She chuckled.

One Drunk Night In Miami 2

"But what are you about to get into?" I asked.

She shrugged. "I'm probably about to go home and lay down for the rest of the day."

"Hell nah! That's only going to put you into a deeper depression! Look, I know you don't me like that, and you probably don't trust *yourself* around a nigga like me, but how 'bout you come to my crib and just kick it with me?"

Imani's brows rose skeptically. "Um, don't you have to work at the gym, though? Wait. Shouldn't you already be there?"

"Let me find out that you're stalking a nigga too."

Since Imani was familiar with the situation between Kelis and me, she understood what that statement meant.

"Nigga, please!"

"I'm just fuckin' with you. But, believe it or not, I'm off today. Being a fitness trainer can become stressful as fuck at times, so I took off yesterday and today to just chill."

"And you don't mind spending your off day with me?"

"Nah, I don't," I honestly answered.

"I don't know, Bryson. I enjoyed talking to you today, I really did, but I'm not trying to move on to the next nigga so fast."

"Imani, if you think I'm asking you to come chill with me because I'm trying to fuck, then you're wrong. If it makes you feel any better knowing this, I just got some pussy this morning, so I'm good for the time being. Just know, though, if I want *that* pussy," I pointed at hers, "oh, best believe I'll get it. It doesn't matter if it's a week or six months from now. I'll get it. I'm not going to lie, though; I wouldn't mind testing yours out since I'm sure it's good as fuck. So, if it ever gets to that point with us, I'll be willing to wait for it."

"Hmph," was her response to that. "So, say I did go to your house, what *would* we do?"

"Shid, whatever you want to do. I have games... board

Alecia J.

games as well as video games. I even got a karaoke machine if wanna pour your feelings out into a song."

She smiled.

"But if you just wanna chill and watch movies all day, we can do that too. Just know, whenever you're around me, you'll never have a dull moment."

"I'm starting to notice that. So, do you have the latest 2K?"

"Do I? Hell yeah! What? You trying to match me in it?"

"Well, I wouldn't ask if I wasn't."

"Okay. So you trying to get your ass whooped? That's basically what you're asking for, huh? A good ol' ass-whooping?"

She chuckled. "Nah. I'm trying to see *you* get your ass whooped by a girl!"

"One thing I hate is a capper."

"Two things I'll never 'cap' on is my pussy and my excellent gaming skills."

"Well, let me be the judge of both of those. But come on. You can follow me to my crib. Let's see if you can back up all this shit you're talking."

"Lead the way."

I couldn't believe I had displayed that level of kindness toward Imani. Normally, I wouldn't have invited any chick over to my crib to just 'chill,' but there was something about Imani that drew me to her beyond her looks. More so, I was highly attuned to energy, and she let off a good vibe. While I wasn't trying to make her my girl or anything, I was open to seeing where things could go with us.

6. Dior

"I can't believe I'm saying this, but I really enjoyed our time together. Thank you for that much-needed trip," I expressed to Kane as we exited his jet.

"You don't have to thank your soon-to-be man for anything, baby. The pleasure will *always* be mine. Hell, if you weren't ready to come back, we'd still be there. Real shit."

I rolled my eyes at Kane calling himself my man. I had gotten homesick, so I was ready to return to the States. More than anything, I was ready to see and talk to my best friend. Although Jenesis and I chatted here and there throughout the trip, we couldn't speak freely due to either Kelan being around her or Kane attached to me like flies on shit.

"Kane, for the *I don't know how many times* we are *not* together, and we damn sure won't be as long as you have a girlfriend."

"I told you I'm handling that."

"That's the problem, Kane... it's *not* handled! Kane, I'm not one of these desperate women who will gladly *and* proudly parade around with you in another country as your side bitch! Hell, the only reason I went on the trip was because you *forced* me to!" I asserted.

"I didn't force you. You could've jumped out of the jet if you really didn't want to go."

I cocked my head in disbelief at his comment. However, I wasn't entirely surprised. That was typical of Kane, making such remarks even if he didn't necessarily mean the shit he said.

"And you're saying all that, but did I force you to *fuck* me all those days?" he added.

I fought hard to resist temptation while spending time with Kane, but my resolve crumbled on the third night. The atmosphere was filled with alcoholic drinks, hookah smoke, and the lingering scent of weed. As the night wore on, I found myself drunk and high, far beyond my usual limits. In that state, one thing led to another, and for the rest of our time together, we found it impossible to resist each other. As I sat on the plane returning home, I couldn't help but dwell on the regrettable choices I'd made. I even found myself shedding tears as I sought forgiveness from God, for I had surely sinned. I had *way* too much fun that week with another woman's man. The way I was fucking and sucking on Kane, one would've thought he was mine indeed.

"Nah, you didn't force me, but that's neither here nor there. This cannot happen again, Kane! The kidnapping stops here!" I stated firmly.

"I was going to be a *gentleman* and ask if you wanted to join me on the trip. That was until I found out you had a nigga blocked. In all honesty, the kidnapping only happened because you blocked my ass, which I've already told you. So, you really have yourself to blame for that."

"Ugh! Kane, listen. We had fun. Whew..." I paused to

briefly reminisce about the wild and freaky shit we did to each other, "a *lot* of fun," I continued, "and I swear if I wasn't a woman who didn't believe in karma or had any morals for myself, I'd continue playing this lil' game with you." I enclosed the space between us, and in a lascivious tone, I whispered, "If you think this pussy gets wet for a nigga who doesn't belong to her, imagine how wet she'll get if your dick was hers. Kane, I love your type of freakiness because it matches mine, and a bitch wouldn't mind waking up to that kind of loving every morning, but I want *full* custody of that dick, not just visitation rights. So, if I can't have *all* of you, then I don't want any of you." I pulled away, leaving him in his thoughts.

When the singer Betty Wright mentioned that "having a piece of man is better than having no man at all," I instinctively turned down the volume because I disagreed with that sentiment.

"I guess I can't do nothing but respect that."

"Yeah, I've heard that before," I mumbled, assuming Kane didn't hear me.

"From who? Not me. 'Cause until now, I ain't never told you no shit like that. You must got me confused with another nigga. But I'll give you your space."

"Yeah, but for how long, Kane?"

"However long you need. I'ma have my driver take you home. I just need you to do one more favor for me."

"That depends on what *said* favor is. Does it require me to open my mouth or legs?"

He chuckled. "Nah, girl. I just need you to ride somewhere with me real quick."

"To where, Kane? I'm exhausted, and I'm ready to give my pillows some much-needed head! I know they miss me because I surely miss them."

Alecia J.

"Say what?"

"I was being sarcastic, Kane. I'm ready to go to sleep," I clarified.

"Oh. I assumed you got enough sleep on the plane."

"I got *some* rest. I'm really just ready to get in *my* bed."

"And you will *soon*. I just need you to take this ride with me."

I blew out a breath of exasperation.

"Okay, Kane," I inevitably agreed.

"Kane, where are we?" I asked when we pulled up to a huge house that I assumed wasn't his since he lived in Miami.

"At an old friend of mine's crib. Come on. I'll get the door for you."

"Thank you," I expressed to Kane as he assisted me out of the vehicle. Once outside of it, I smoothed my hands over my clothing. "I just want to know why I needed to come here with you?" I further questioned.

"You'll see, baby. Now, less questions and more walking."

I complied without any talkback. Walking alongside us were a couple of Kane's men, who had arrived in separate cars.

As we reached the doorstep, my anxiety spiked. I couldn't pinpoint the reason for my nervousness. Perhaps it was the uncertainty of why Kane had brought me here, or maybe it was the unmistakable presence of guns on all the men, including Kane, leaving me on edge, unsure of what could transpire. As the door swung open, a burly man dressed in a snug-fitting shirt, black jeans, and sturdy black boots emerged, his earpiece signaling his role as a security guard. His bald head and imposing physique reminded me of the wrestler and actor The Rock.

Addressing Kane in a deep voice, the man said, "I assume you're Mr. Anton Rich," while scrutinizing the other men around Kane.

"I am," Kane simply replied.

His admission caught me off guard, and I couldn't help but look at him with a puzzled expression.

What the hell? I wondered silently, keeping my thoughts to myself.

The guy looked down at his watch with a displeased expression.

"It appears that you are ten minutes late, Mr. Rich, and Mr. Sanchez does not tolerate tardiness."

Mr. Sanchez? That name piqued my interest.

"Seems like he and I have *one* thing in common, but in my line of business, as long as a muthafucka shows up, *sometimes* that's all that matters to me, so surely, he ain't trippin' about a nigga being ten minutes late. But I don't give a damn if I was an hour late, I'm here."

Kane's blunt response conveyed a lack of regard for punctuality. Be that as it may, his *bossiness* was such a turn-on.

The man stood there, visibly seething with anger, as if he wanted to say more or even harm Kane. Instead, he abruptly walked outside and proceeded to pat Kane down, catching him off guard.

"Aye, muthafucka!" Kane angrily shouted.

"It's protocol," the guy informed him.

"Yeah, but you touching my nuts and shit ain't. Now, I'll let you take my gun... for the time being, since I'm a business man myself, and I know how this shit goes, *and* because I really ain't come here on no killing shit, but you can't have my dick. It's spoken for," Kane glanced over at me and winked. "Now, back the fuck up!" he barked at the guy.

"You're welcome to come in, but if your men aren't willing

to put their guns away, then they won't be allowed inside. Boss's orders." He shrugged.

"You see, that's the thing. These are *my* men, which means *I* fuckin' pay them, not *your* boss. So, unless his other men, which I'm sure it's well over twenty niggas in that muthafuckas, protecting his ass, put *their* guns away, then my men ain't doing shit, and you can tell him *I* said that. So, since he doesn't allow guns belonging to others inside, then tell him we can have this meeting outside if that works better for him, but we're having this meeting one way or another."

"Wait here," the guy said. He went inside and closed the door behind him.

"Kane, what the hell is going on?! Your damn name isn't no fuckin' Anton!" I muttered nervously, my eyes scanning the area to check for any potential surveillance devices.

"Calm down, Dior," Kane chastised in a hushed tone.

"I'm just saying, you could've at least given me a heads up so I could've played my part!"

"Well, now you know for future reference."

"And who is this Sanchez nigga you're meeting, anyway? Please tell me this isn't the same nigga who is my boss's boss?"

"Dior, chill. You'll find out soon." That was his way of telling me to shut up. I did... for the time being.

After a short wait, the guard returned and announced, "Mr. Sanchez will see you now."

"Damn right, he will," Kane said with an air of confidence. "Let's go, baby." Kane took my hand and escorted me inside.

As we entered, we were greeted by a familiar voice, "Well, I'll be damned. If it isn't Kane Masters."

My gaze followed the sound to find my boss's boss at the top of the staircase. He was dressed in a sharp black suit, holding a glass of what appeared to be champagne, and had a puzzled look on his face, mirroring my own confusion, nervousness, and frustration.

"Sanchez," Kane responded, addressing Emiliano by his last name.

"You know, when my guy Joey here told me that the asshole outside was giving him a hard time, I never expected that asshole to be *you*." He chuckled.

"What kind of *hard* time did he say I gave him? Because the way he rubbed on my nuts, I would have assumed he got some type of pleasure out of touching a big ass dick."

"Joey? Having a thing for men?! No! He's married to a gorgeous woman, and they share three children!"

"Married men are at the top of the DL list. But fuck all of that. Let's get to this business."

"Very well. So, to what do I owe the pleasure of this *very* unexpected visit, Kane? I mean, it really is a surprise."

"I'm sure you were expecting to have a meeting with *Anton Rich*, right?"

"Actually, I was, but seeing you here, I'm guessing he doesn't exist."

"He doesn't. Just think of him as my *alter ego*. But off the record, I took you to be smarter than that, Emiliano. You really didn't look into this Anton guy before agreeing to a meeting with him? The Sanchez I *knew* would've never let a stranger into his home."

"Well, this *Anton* guy came highly recommended, and being that he, who I now know is you, paid me an *exceptional* amount of money for this last minute meeting, I assumed *he* was a standup guy and about his business, so I didn't see a need to do any further research."

"Maybe it would be wise to do so the next time you agree to a *sudden* meeting with a *new* client," Kane advised him.

Alecia J.

"No worries. I will... personally. I will say this, though, if you were a snake, a poisonous one, you damn sure would've bit me." Emiliano laughed off before handing his glass to Joey and descending the stairs. Once he approached us, his gaze locked onto me.

"You... you look familiar. Do we know each other?"

Before I could respond, Kane stepped in.

"Actually, she's the reason I'm here. Is there somewhere the three of us can talk... in private?" Kane's request was met with hesitation as Emiliano's narrowed eyes remained fixed on me.

"Yes, there is. Follow me," Emiliano finally spoke, giving Kane his attention.

We approached two closed double doors guarded by stern-looking soldiers. One of them produced a key, then swiftly unlocked and swung open the doors, granting us entry into a vast, pristine white room. The room was absolutely breathtaking, and every detail was impeccably white. It exuded an air of opulence and importance, with even a well-appointed bar area nestled within its confines. It was clear the room was seldom used, and when it was, it was reserved for significant meetings—much like the one we were about to have, although I had yet to find out why Kane had taken me there.

"Oh, where are my manners? Can I offer either of you a drink?" Emiliano inquired graciously.

"Ye–" I almost accepted, but Kane quickly shut that down by replying, "Nah, we're good," while shooting me daggers.

"Okay. Suit yourself." Emiliano shrugged, then moseyed over to the bar and treated himself to a drink.

"Kane, I could use a drink right now! I'm not a little girl, and you're not my daddy!" I murmured, fussing.

"When I'm in that pussy, I'm daddy. But seriously, when we leave here, I will get you as many drinks as you'd like. As for now, you need to remain sober as hell."

One Drunk Night In Miami 2

I huffed.

"So, let's have a seat and talk, or do you prefer to stand?" Emiliano asked Kane when he returned.

"I prefer to stand. This shouldn't take too long."

"Very well then. Now, although I'm *very* curious about why you're here, I wasn't under the impression that we had any ongoing issues, and I'm certain that any debts we had are squared away. Unless there's something I'm missing."

"While all of our debts *have* been cleared, her brother's hasn't." Kane pointed at me.

Emiliano, puzzled by Kane's statement, looked at me more closely and recognized me.

"Wait a minute. You're Lance's sister," he realized.

"I am," I confirmed.

"And you work for my company. You're actually my top girl," he further inquired.

"I do, and I am," were my simple responses.

"Wow! I can't believe I didn't recognize you right off the bat. Let me just say I'm absolutely impressed with your work ethic. Keep up the good work." He quickly transitioned back to the purpose of our meeting. "Well, given that I know who you are *now,* let's address the real reason you're here. It's regarding your brother, I assume."

Kane chimed in, "Yes. This meeting has *everything* to do with her brother."

My eyes became moist, not only at the mention of my brother but also because I suspected that Kane was about to take a significant step, and I was prepared to marry him if my hunch was correct. At that point, Bonnie and I would have to become sister-wives and share that nigga.

Emiliano picked back up his drink and took a sip.

"Kane, as I'm sure you're aware, especially since you're here, her brother owes me a *significant* amount of money."

Alecia J.

"A significant amount, like *five hundred thousand dollars?* Which really isn't a lot of money to a nigga like you, *is it*, Emiliano? But I understand that business is business."

"True. So, of course, you know I can't just *let* him go without *something* in return." His eyes flicked over to me, laden with suggestion.

Kane stepped forward and declared, "Nigga, she's not for sale! Not now! Not ever!"

Emiliano slowly retreated with his hands raised in surrender.

"Kane, by now, I know you're not a man to cross. I had no idea that you two were..." he said, gesturing with confusion between us, attempting to discern the nature of our relationship.

"A couple? Yeah, this my woman," Kane fibbed, pulling me closer to him. "So, like I said, she's off limits."

"I know now. So, back to her brother. What are you proposing?" Emiliano swiftly shifted the conversation back to the matter at hand.

"To let him go... immediately," Kane commanded.

Emiliano chuckled devilishly. "Kane, you wanna know what I've always admired about you... your sense of humor."

"What the hell is so funny about what I said, though? Shid, I wanna laugh, too." Kane stood with his arms crossed, his stern face betraying his frustration.

Emiliano quickly shifted his demeanor to seriousness as he noticed Kane's change in expression.

"Look, Kane, I have no beef with you. So, I'm willing to have your lady reunite with her brother tonight. I just need the rest of the money that I'm owed."

Kane stepped to him and gritted, "I think it's fair to say that me, along with my brother and Pop, paid her brother's debt some years ago, or must I remind you that the three of us are the reason your ashes aren't floating around in some ocean right about now or you're not six feet under!" he finished then gave them some distance.

Emiliano paused for a moment. His hand trembled slightly as he lifted the glass to his lips, savoring the taste of his drink. "I'm well aware of what you did for me that night, Kane, and I'll *never* forget it."

Kane leaned forward, his gaze piercing. "And what were the last words you said to me and my brother that night before they wheeled our ass off to jail?"

Emiliano took a deep breath as if the weight of the memory was heavy on his chest. "That I am indebted to the both of you for saving my life."

"*And?*" Kane pressed for further clarification.

"And as long as I have breath in my body, if either of you ever needs *anything,* no matter what, I'd always assist you in any way I can."

"So, I need you to hold up to your word by releasing her brother... *now.*" Kane's tone left no room for argument.

"But how... how will I see him tonight? I don't even know where he's at," I chimed in, my voice tinged with a mix of joy and a bit of sadness.

Kane faced me.

"Baby, your brother never left the city," he revealed.

Taken aback, I stammered, "Wh–what?"

"Yeah. After you told me about the situation with your brother, I had my IT guy do me a huge, short-notice favor, and I found out that your brother had been here in LA the entire time. They've been holding him captive in the house next door. *Right,* Sanchez?"

Emiliano looked away and replied, "Yes."

I collapsed onto the floor, overwhelmed by a torrent of tears. My brother had been near me that entire time, and I didn't even know it. I was so overjoyed that I'd finally get to see him again after six long months. To some, six months may not seem like an extensive period, but the separation from a loved one for that duration, coupled with the ability to only communicate once a month, made the passing time feel like an eternity.

Kane knelt beside me, his strong arms tenderly cradling me. "Please stop crying, baby. I promise I'll have him home tonight," he assured me. Turning to Emiliano, Kane instructed, "Call one of your men and have them bring over my brother-in-law... now!"

Emiliano adopted a serious yet playful tone and replied, "Do you not trust *me* to go get her brother, Kane?"

"Sanchez, I fucks with you the long way, but when it comes to business and personal matters, which this is both, the only nigga I'll ever trust is my brother. So, I hope that answered your question. Now, make the call," Kane firmly ordered.

I peered up and saw Emiliano reach into his pocket to retrieve his phone. He dialed a number, and as the call connected, Kane issued a cautious warning.

"Again, I *like* you, Sanchez, and I value our relationship, but I swear I won't hesitate to kill yo' ass if I so much as *think* you're on some funny shit. I know you're Mexican, so avoid contacting someone who solely understands or speaks Spanish, and refrain from using any coded language." Kane further demanded that Emiliano put the person he was calling on speakerphone.

Emiliano's expression revealed his discomfort at taking orders from another man, especially when he was a boss himself.

The guy who answered the phone greeted Emiliano with a respectful, "Boss."

Emiliano swiftly instructed, "Bring Lance to the house... now."

"On it, Boss," the guy replied with nothing further to say.

Once the call ended, the room fell into an eerie silence as we awaited my brother's arrival. The anticipation felt like I was meeting a long-lost sibling after *years* of separation. Suddenly, the doors to the room swung open. My brother stepped in first, with handcuffs secured around his wrists and ankles, like a true prisoner. Other than his increased physical build, a noticeable growth of facial hair, and a desperate need for a haircut—that a simple visit to the barbershop could fix—not much had changed about him since we'd last seen each other.

"Sis," Lance said once our eyes met.

"Lance!" I sprang off the floor and rushed over to him. As I reached him, I embraced him tightly, wrapping my arms around his shoulders. "Oh, I have missed you so much!" I cried.

"I've missed you too, sis, but what's going on?" he whispered.

"You're free, bro! You can finally come home!"

"Huh?" he asked perplexedly.

"I'll explain everything later," I told him, then turned to Emiliano. The words, "Take these damn handcuffs off my brother! He's no longer your prisoner!" erupted from my lips with a sense of urgency and determination.

The man who had escorted Lance inside turned to Emiliano, seeking his approval. With a nod from Emiliano, Lance was finally freed from the restraints. As soon as the handcuffs came off, Lance embraced me in a tight, grateful hug, expressing his relief, love, and gratitude.

"So, Kane, does this conclude our meeting?" Emiliano asked as if he had more pressing matters to attend.

Kane chuckled. "Not quite. There's *one* more thing we need to clear up."

Alecia J.

Lance leaned in close and asked, "Who is that nigga?" referring to Kane.

"He's the *nigga* you should thank when we get out of here. It's because of him that you're free," I spoke through my teeth.

Lance nodded.

Emiliano continued. "What else is there to clear up? Lance's debt is no more, and he's going home. That's what you wanted, right?"

"Yeah, but before her brother leaves this house, I want to have him examined," Kane explained.

"Examined?" Emiliano's brow furrowed in confusion, and I noticed the same perplexed expression on Lance's face.

"I want to have him *thoroughly* checked for any bugs or tracking devices. After he leaves here, I want to be sure there's no way for any of you to keep track of him *ever* again," Kane adamantly stated, his eyes scanning the room as if daring anyone to challenge his assertion.

Emiliano nodded thoughtfully, his brow furrowing in contemplation before replying, "I have no problems with you doing that. Once a deal is sealed, it's sealed. However, how do you plan to do that *here*? I don't have that type of equipment just lying around here."

"Being a boss... you should," Kane advised him. "But no worries; I came prepared. I brought along a specialist. He's out front. As you should know, the process doesn't take long. Once he's cleared, we'll be on our way and out of y'all lives forever. Well, *probably*."

Like Kane said, the procedure didn't take long, and thankfully, no tracking device was detected on my brother during the process.

"Well, it looks like we're good to go," Kane said with satisfaction. "Oh, one more thing. Surely, you don't think she's returning to your company to work, but if you did, I want you to know that this is her *zero*-day notice. Yeah, I meant to say *zero* instead of two weeks' notice because she won't be returning to that job after today. I know you might lose a lot of people with her no longer being employed with you, so I'm prepared to compensate you for your loss."

Kane held out his hand, and one of his guys handed him a black duffle bag, which Kane handed to Emiliano.

"There's enough money in there to hold you off until you find another girl, although I know none of them will compare to my girl. I also gave you a little extra... for your troubles. So, do we have an understanding on everything? Is there anything else I need to go over?"

"Nope! I think this concludes our meeting," Emiliano responded.

"Well, you know a deal isn't official until we shake hands," Kane remarked.

When Kane extended his hand, nostalgic images from a scene in the movie *Django* flashed through my mind. I couldn't help but feel a sense of unease, hoping that Kane wasn't about to resort to violence. I was in good spirits, and any such act would have definitely ruined it.

Emiliano cautiously reached out and shook Kane's hand.

"*Now*, this meeting is concluded," Kane finalized. "You gentlemen have a good day. Sanchez, be good, my boy."

"You do the same, Kane. Tell your brother and mom I said hello."

"Will do." Kane nodded, and then we all exited the house.

And just like that, I had my brother back.

"Sis, how the hell did you manage to pay him back all that fuckin' money? 'Cause I know he didn't just let me go like that?" Lance asked, seemingly curious.

"Again, *I* didn't. He," I motioned toward Kane, who was

Alecia J.

swaggering in our direction, "worked his magic and made it happen."

"So, are you ready to introduce me to my brother-in-law?" Kane asked, flashing a charming smile as he joined our conversation.

"Brother-in-law? Sis, you done went and got married? Damn, was I gone that long?" A perplexed expression crossed Lance's face as he tried to comprehend the situation.

I chuckled. "Lance, I'm not in a relationship or seeing anyone. So, no, I'm not married. Kane, this is my brother, Lance, as you now know. Lance, this is Kane, and he's... just Kane."

"Oh, so now I'm *just* Kane, huh? But the other day, I was daddy—"

"Kane..." I warned him because I knew he was about to run out.

"Yeah, aight. But what's good, man?" Kane slapped hands with Lance.

"Shit, just glad to be leaving this muthafucka. As a matter of fact, let's get away from here."

As we headed to the cars, Kane informed us, "One of my men is going to make sure y'all get back home safely. I gotta head back to the strip to head home."

"Head home? You're not from around here?" Lance asked.

"Nah, bro. I live in Miami."

Lance looked at me and Kane questioningly. "Damn, so y'all really ain't together?"

I giggled. "No, Lance, we're not." I stopped in my tracks once we approached the vehicles. "Look, bro, it's complicated, but we'll talk about all of that later. Let me talk to Kane for a minute."

"Aight. But I gotta ask. If you and my sis ain't together, why did you go through all this trouble to get me home?"

One Drunk Night In Miami 2

"Believe it or not, it was actually *no* trouble at all. I mean, I had to make a few calls here and there, but trouble? Nah. Sometimes, it's all about who you know or who owes you a favor," Kane answered.

Lance nodded in understanding.

Kane continued, "As for me and your sister, we're not together *yet,* but we will be... *soon.* So, you'll see me around more often, *brother.*"

"Well, I appreciate whatever you did to get me the fuck out of there, man. Y'all might not be together, but only a real nigga or family would do what you did, so welcome to the family, bro," Lance gave Kane some dap.

"No problem, man. *Anything* for your sister." Kane smiled, looking at me.

"Aight, I'ma let y'all talk." Lance then stepped over to the side to give us some privacy.

I faced Kane. "Kane, I'm literally struggling to find the words to express my appreciation for what you did for me tonight. There are *countless ways* to bring a smile to my face, yet what you've done... it surpasses them all." As I peered up at the sky, I fought back tears. "To me, what you did was one of the best things that anyone could've ever done for me. I know it wasn't *priceless,* but to me, it was."

"I told you that I got you, baby, and although I mean that, you owe me now." He smirked.

I reared my head back in confusion.

"Excuse me?"

"You. Owe. Me. Baby," he reiterated.

"I should've known this was all too good to be true!" I shouted after realizing there was an ulterior motive behind his previous kindness. I wished I could've retracted the speech of gratitude I had spoken.

Alecia J.

"Although my actions were from the heart, I feel like you can repay that favor."

"By doing *what* exactly, Kane?"

"You belong to me now. Which means that pussy belongs to me too. So, when I call or text you, I expect you to answer and respond in a timely manner. If I tell you I want some pussy, I expect you to give that muthafucka to me with no backtalk and damn sure no excuses."

"In other words, this whole 'getting my brother back for me' was basically me selling my soul to you for his freedom! Just great! Fuckin' great!" I grumbled.

"I wouldn't say all that. How about this... if you don't fall in love with me in the next three months, I'll leave you alone... for good," he proposed.

"For *good*?" I questioned, trying to gauge the sincerity in his voice.

"Yep," he verified with a resolute nod.

I studied Kane's face in search of any flicker of dishonesty, but his stern expression revealed nothing, making it all the more challenging to read him.

"Deal," I affirmed, reaching out my hand. He shook it, finalizing our agreement.

"Now *that* was you making a deal with the devil. From here on out, I need you to think about me 23/7. You can get one hour for yourself."

"Nigga, what?"

"You heard me, baby. So, I'll advise you to use your *one* hour wisely. Most importantly, *don't* give my pussy away, Dior. I'll be back for it and you, too. And take me off the fuckin' block list and make *sure* you answer my calls and texts," he stressed.

"And what will happen if I *don't*?" I taunted in a challenging way.

Kane let out a mischievous chuckle.

One Drunk Night In Miami 2

"The next time you think it's wise not to respond to my texts or before you *intentionally* miss one of my Facetime calls, picture this: you're stuck in a dark, smelly, trashy alley in the middle of nowhere. For days, you call out for help with no food, no water, and no source of communication. It's just you, the dark alley, and the rats running around until I feel like you've learned your lesson and decide to come and get you."

My imagination ran wild, and the thought of that scenario becoming a reality terrified me.

"I wish like hell you would!"

"Pretty Eyes, by now, you should know that I'm capable of doing the craziest, most irrational, maybe even unheard-of shit ever. So, if you want your wish to come true, all you gotta do is, *fuck around and find out*, but I'll advise you to heed my words."

The sense of danger that surrounded Kane was undeniable, and it was clear that he was not someone to be taken lightly. That night, I witnessed just a glimpse of his intimidating presence. I was aware that going against his wishes could lead to severe consequences, and I had no intention of finding out what those might be. In order to remain in his good graces, I was willing to do *whatever* it took.

When I woke the next morning, I found myself in the familiar surroundings of my old bedroom at my parents' house. Earlier, Lance and I had made our way there after leaving Kane's place. We stayed up well into the early hours of the morning, engrossed in conversation.

Once I gathered myself, I left the room and made my way across the hallway to check on my brother, who was also staying in his old room. As I gently pushed the door ajar, I found him snoring blissfully. Understanding that he probably

Alecia J.

hadn't experienced such undisturbed sleep in the past six months, I chose not to wake him and quietly closed the door before heading downstairs, where I was greeted by the distant, soothing notes of low music playing.

Good morning, Mother," I sang cheerfully as I strolled into the cozy, sunlit kitchen.

She turned with a warm smile. "Good morning, baby, and what a splendid morning it is."

"Indeed, it is," I replied as I settled into my seat at the table. "Well, it looks like we're about to eat good on this Sunday!" I exclaimed hungrily as I observed the abundance of fresh greens, sweet potatoes, black-eyed peas, ingredients for home-made mac and cheese, a generous portion of chicken wings, as well as the fixings for cornbread and chicken dressings, and an assortment of dessert items neatly laid out on the table.

"Well, your brother is back, so I thought I'd cook him a nice home-cooked meal since I'm sure he hasn't had one in a while."

"Well, he's been eating something as buff as he has gotten," I joked.

"You have a point there." She laughed. "So, what do the two of you have planned today? I'm sure y'all are going to do *something* together."

"Actually, we don't have anything planned *together*. Although your son did mention *getting him* some today."

"Getting him some?" My mom whipped her head in confusion as she finally faced me.

I chuckled. "Ma, your son hasn't been with a woman in six months, so go figure."

"Oh, Lord! I wish that one of you would just go ahead and give me a grandbaby already. At this point, I don't care who gets you pregnant or who Lance goes out and has a baby with. I'm just ready for me a grandbaby."

I sighed.

One Drunk Night In Miami 2

"Well, Ma, you'd be better off putting your luck on Lance giving you your first one because I'm not just about to have a baby with any nigga."

"What about *Kane?*" She grinned.

"What about him? Ma, I already told you that Kane and I are *not* a couple. I still can't believe he convinced you that we were. Then again, Kane has a way with words to persuade a woman to do or believe anything."

"That, he does. But after all that he has done for you, one would beg to differ about you two being a couple."

"Ma, the day I post a man on social media is when you'll know I have a man, one that I'm serious about, anyway. I also never told you this, but Kane has a girlfriend. *That's* the real reason we're not together," I revealed.

My mom's eyes bulged, and she clutched her hand against her chest as if that was the most startling, unexpected news she'd ever heard.

"What?" Her disappointment was palpable in her voice and expression.

"I'm sorry that I had to be the one to break it to you, Ma, but yes, Kane has a girlfriend... a *gorgeous* one at that. Of course, he wasn't going to tell you or Daddy that, being that he wants to be in y'all good graces."

"But why try to pursue you and go through all of this if he has a girlfriend?"

"These men don't care, Ma. I can't really just say that about Kane, though. Kane claims that their relationship has run its course. Yet, he doesn't want to leave her in fear of hurting her. If that's the case, in my opinion, there will never be a good time to leave her. I don't know what the future holds for us, or even them, but as of right now, we're just *friends.*" I wasn't being totally honest.

I avoided telling my mom about Kane expecting me to be at

Alecia J.

his beck and call. I knew if I had, she would've definitely viewed Kane differently. For some reason, she *and* my dad loved his ass, despite only having two encounters with him, and they probably still would, even after becoming aware that he had a girlfriend.

"Well, if he does the things he's done for you just being your friend, I can only imagine what he'd do if you were his *girlfriend*." She winked. "So, since your brother will be getting his freak on today, what do you have planned today?" She changed the subject.

I pushed my chair back and stood up, stretching my arms above my head.

"Well, I haven't seen my best friend in almost a week, so I'ma go spend some time with her for a lil' while. Oh, but I will be back for a plate, and she probably will, too."

"Tell my daughter Jenesis that I said hey. You are talking about her, right?"

"Ma, be for real. The one and only."

We laughed together.

"I know, baby."

"But where is Dad? I'ma go see him before I head home."

"Please do. You know he'll have a fit if you leave here without speaking to him. But he's upstairs in his office reading, honey."

"Okay. Well, I'll be back later. If I'm not back before you finish cooking, call me when you're close to being done, and tell Lance to call me when he wakes up. I love you."

"Will do, baby. Oh, wait! So, I know lately that you've been thinking about switching up a few things in your life… your job being one of those things. So, I have a friend down at the DHS office, and she said they're in need of caseworkers. I meant to bring this up to you yesterday, but I got distracted when I saw your brother at home. I understand that you may not have much experience in this field, but it's a standard eight-to-five office job, and they are willing to provide training and financial assistance for further education if you decide to pursue this path. Take some time to think about it, and if you're interested in exploring this opportunity, I can provide you with her contact information."

"Thank you, Ma. Since I'm down to one job now, I might just have to look into that," I kidded. "But I'ma go talk to Daddy, and then I'm gone. I love you!"

"I love you more, and tell Kane he gon' have to see me!"

I giggled. "I sure will."

"Friiiiiiiiiiiend, I missed you!" Jenesis squealed when she opened her front door and saw me. She then proceeded to hug me tightly.

"Obviously, not *too* much since you had me out here ringing the doorbell for over five minutes! I started to break a window to make sure you were okay, And, eww... go put on some clothes!" I scolded playfully.

Jenesis was casually strolling around in a bright pink sports bra and a black thong.

"Don't come to my house thinking I'ma be dressed. You're the guest, boo, not me. But I'm good, girl. Kelan just wouldn't stop fucking me until he got his nut," she murmured.

"He's here?!" I asked in the same surprised, low tone.

"Yes. He's in the shower washing off my goodies."

"You just had to let that part be known. But y'all are really serious, huh?"

"Yes, girl. We have a *lot* of catching up to do."

"Yes, we do. That's why I came over. Well, I planned on us talking here, but since Kelan is here, we can go out some-

Alecia J.

where. Besides, I'ma need a drink for the shit I need to talk about."

"I second that. But let me go put on some clothes, and I'll be back."

"Yeah, you do that. If y'all just finished having sex, yo' ass should've hopped in the shower with him."

"Well, maybe I *would* have been able to if I didn't have to answer the door for yo' ass."

"Touche, bitch. Well, you can go now. Maybe that was you who I was smelling when I walked in," I kidded.

"Eat my pussy, hoe!" Jenesis patted her kitty before turning around and heading toward the back.

"As pretty as it is, I just might after you clean it up!" I yelled, leaning over the couch.

I was joking about the *eating her pussy* part. Jenesis did have a pretty kitty, but a girl couldn't do shit for me but give me some head and *maybe* a couple of orgasms. A freak like me needed more than that when it came to pleasing me. I needed me a man with a big and good ding-a-ling to keep me thoroughly satisfied—a nigga like Kane.

Approximately fifteen minutes later, Jenesis returned to the front room fully dressed, with Kelan following her.

"What's good, Dior? Did you enjoy your trip?" Kelan asked.

"Heeeeeey, Kelan, and yes, I did. Your brother showed a girl a *really* good time. Even though he felt like he had to kidnap me to do so."

Kelan chuckled. "You gotta be careful with that nigga. He doesn't play fair."

"If I didn't believe it before he pulled that stunt, trust me, I do now!"

Kelan's lips curled into a smirk before he turned his attention to Jenesis. "I'll be back later, baby. I gotta go take care of a few things." Going into his pocket, he retrieved his wallet and handed her a card. "Here. Go spend some time with your girl today. Y'all go shopping, get y'all nails done, or whatever girly shit y'all do. And before you say no about taking this card, just know I ain't talking no for an answer today, or hell, any other day for that matter. Jenesis, you're my girl, so you might as well get used to a nigga spoiling yo' pretty ass. From here on out, you won't have to go into your pockets for shit unless you choose to be hard-headed and stubborn."

I know that's right, Kelan! I applauded silently as I observed how effortlessly he catered to Jenesis. Though I yearned to express my thoughts, I abstained, not wanting to interrupt them.

"Kelan, for once, I'm not going to go back and forth with you about *your* money," Jenesis smiled. "As a matter of fact, I won't say anything moving forward."

"That's what I like to hear. Now, give me a kiss before I go, baby."

As they kissed, I sat there, gazing at them with admiration, a wide smile lighting up my face. Knowing all that my friend had been through with Sincere, I couldn't help but feel overjoyed that she had found a good man. Jenesis truly deserved all the happiness life had to offer.

"Aww! Don't they make such a cute couple?!" I playfully teased as their kiss came to an end.

"Girl, come on!" Jenesis said, and with that, we left the house.

"So, what's the tea, honey? Between my *exhilarating* trip with Jace and my unexpected 'kidnapping,' we haven't had much time to talk lately," I joked as I settled into my seat at the restaurant, ready to indulge in great food, exquisite drinks, and some much-needed conversation.

"Girrrrrrrrrrl, where do I start? Speaking of *kidnapping*, let's just say I've been *dicknapped* these last two weekends," Jenesis said.

"*Dicknapped?*" I laughed and questioned for clarity.

"You know when you have things to do on the weekend, but your man entices you with food, affection, attention, and dick, so you never make it out of the house."

"Whew! I remember those days! But girl, what I would give to have a man like Kelan! Does he have another brother, other than Kane, who's single?"

"I hate to disappoint you, but no, ma'am. But even if he did, Dior, you know damn well Kane is not about to let you be with another nigga, especially a brother of his."

"Why did the crazy one have to fall for me?"

"Those are your types, right?" Jenesis chuckled. "Kane is the true description of *if a man wants you, he will literally come get you.*"

Even though Jenesis and I didn't talk much while I was away, I did find a moment to share the story of my kidnapping with her, and she was just as shocked as I was when I woke up to that discovery.

"Girl, tell me about it, but don't sit here and act like Kelan is all innocent, boo! That man showed up to your house with food just *days* after meeting you!"

"Yeah, thanks to *you* giving him my address."

"Look at the bright side... he turned out to be your man and not some creepy stalker."

"The difference between my situation and yours is Kelan was checking on me because I was sick, not because I blocked him, but now that we're together, oh, I know for sure that he'll pull the fuck up at my house, my job, hell, anywhere. Kane's definition of 'pull the fuck up' is on a different level of craziness."

"Jenesis, you have no idea, girl. Crazy is an understatement when it comes to that nigga. But we never got around to talking about what happened with Melani and Kelan," I brought up a new topic.

Over the course of the next fifteen minutes, our drinks arrived, and as we drank, Jenesis provided me with a detailed account of everything she knew about Kelan and Melani's situation.

"Damn, that's crazy," I exclaimed after she finished. "Has Kelan heard from her since?"

"No. I would hope that she's somewhere getting some help," Jenesis answered while softly massaging her neck as if she were experiencing discomfort.

"Jenesis, what the hell is wrong with your neck? You've been messing with it every five minutes, it seems like," I asked out of concern and curiosity.

"You remember that pose I did the first day at the workout class?"

"Hell, who could forget?" I countered with a hint of amusement.

"Anyway, Kelan wanted to try it this morning, and let's just say my neck hasn't been right since."

I smiled in approval. "It looks like Kelan seems to be bringing out the freak in somebody."

"I've been a freak, boo. I just haven't had a nigga to be freaky with lately," she quipped.

"Oh, well, excuse me, honey! But Jenesis, you're one of the most flexible women I know, so that should've been a breeze for you."

"Performing the pose itself, yeah. However, I've never been *fucked* in that position."

Alecia J.

"Ouch! You got a point there. But I'm sure all that good dick you received was worth the pain you're enduring now. Amen!"

"Gul!"

We laughed together, but it ceased when the waitress approached the table.

"Are y'all ready to order now?" Since we had our drinks, she was returning to get our food orders.

"Let me get..." I paused because I quickly remembered that my mom was cooking a big dinner that evening, so I didn't want to overdo it at the restaurant.

"Can I just have some spinach dip, please?"

"Spinach dip?" Jenesis queried, raising an eyebrow since I had expressed my hunger before arriving.

"Girl, Mama is cooking a big meal today, so I'm trying to save my appetite. Well, *most* of it," I explained.

"Well, in that case, let me have the same because I'm definitely stopping by to get me a plate. You know I love your mama's cooking!"

The waitress chuckled.

"Don't I know?" I acknowledged with a smile. As I handed the waitress the menus, I made it known, "We'll both have the same, and my good friend will be treating me today, so you can put everything on her tab."

"Girl, for a second, I thought that was Kelan's mom," Jenesis mumbled, looking over at some woman, which prompted me to look in that direction.

"You've met Kelan's and Kane's mom?" I asked in surprise.

"Oh, that's right! I didn't tell you what happened yesterday! I knew it was something I had to tell you!"

Jenesis vividly described the comical yet humiliating moment when Kelan and Kane's mom unexpectedly burst into the room while they were in the middle of having sex. I couldn't help but erupt into uncontrollable laughter after she finished.

"Dior, it's not funny! Girl, I was so fuckin' embarrassed. Actually, I still am a little!"

"I'm sure she meant no harm. Kane did tell me that she hasn't been with a man since their dad died some years back, so maybe she needed some excitement in her life."

"Well, she got an *eyeful* that day."

"I bet. But you said his mom has a key to his house? What if his baby mama still does, too?"

"His mama *had* a key to his house. Kelan took it from her the next day. As for his baby mama... hmm. That's a *damn* good question. I'm going to ask him about that."

"You better, girl, before y'all fuck around and have some real-life *Lifetime* stalking shit going on."

"Right. But what I would *really* like to know is, what is this *big* secret you had to tell me when you were with Jace?"

"I never said it was a *big* secret, although it is, well, was. But that's really why I wanted some privacy. If I knew Kelan was going to be leaving, we probably could've stayed at your house. Then again, I needed this drink. But here goes."

"Jenesis, say something!" I urged.

She had a dumbfounded look on her face after I finished disclosing the story of my brother's capture, his subsequent rescue, and Kane's role in it all.

"Girl, give me a moment! I'm trying to process all this shit!" Jenesis finally spoke, punctuating her disbelief with a sip from her margarita. Another minute ticked by before she found her voice again. "Dior, that's some crazy, hell, scary shit."

"I know, right? So, imagine how I've been feeling these last few months. There were so many times I wanted to tell you what was going on, but I was just too afraid."

"I get it, boo. What's understood doesn't have to be explained, at least not to me. If I had a brother, I would have probably kept quiet about it, too. As long as he's doing well, that's really all that matters."

"Yeah, he's good, girl. He's packed on some muscles as well." I raised my brows suggestively. "You sure you don't want to trade Kelan for my brother?" I kidded.

Lance used to have the *biggest* crush on Jenesis before, during, and even after her relationship with Sincere. However, like most men, pretty women were his weakness, and he seemed to have no self-control when it came to entertaining and fucking them. Therefore, I strongly advised against the two of them ever getting involved.

"I'm almost certain he doesn't have more muscles than *my* man, though," Jenesis remarked before sticking her tongue out in a playful manner.

We shared a laugh.

"But, sis, you tried it! You know that brother of yours is a hoe! With his fine self," she included.

"Mm-hmm. I'll make sure to relay the message that you called him *fine*." I grinned.

"I love you, friend, but I'm not trying to have to fight you or fall out with you because Kelan killed your brother."

"Girl, you know I was just playing. I *love* Kelan for you. *Seriously*. I'm sure my brother will find his soulmate one of these days if he gets his shit together."

"So, what does he plan on doing for work now? Surely, he's not thinking about getting back into the drug business?"

"Jenesis, after the shit I've been through these last six months because of him, *I* will hold my brother hostage if he ever mentions getting back involved in that lifestyle again, or hell, I'll have Sanchez come pick his ass back up!"

"You wouldn't?" Jenesis countered in disbelief.

"Okay, no, to the last part. You know I love my brother too much to be away from him that long again, but I'll definitely have Kane get one of his men to drug his ass and chain him up in my guest bedroom!"

We laughed together.

"But no, we talked last night, and he's *adamant* about not getting back in these streets. He's actually thinking about getting a nine to five."

"Good for him. You can never go wrong with one of those. Then again, you can. Oh, I never told you this, and it honestly slipped my mind, but do you know that bitch Darlene had some videos of me from Kelan's party when I was drunk as hell?!" she murmured.

"Say what? How? Hell, why?"

"My point exactly! The bitch 'claimed' that an anonymous person sent them to her. I called the bullshit as soon as she showed me she had them in her possession."

"That's weird as fuck. I don't trust that bitch! I'on even know her like that, but just based on all the shit you've told me about her ass, I don't like her! You want me to whoop her ass, friend? You know I'll do it for you with *no* hesitation 'cause a muthafucka ain't about to keep fuckin' with my friend! I'll even make it so clean that she'll never know you had any involvement in it. That way, you can keep your job and laugh at her ass when she shows up to work with raccoon eyes!"

Jenesis bent over in laughter.

"Gul! Surely, she wouldn't come to work with two black eyes! But fuck that bitch! She's trying her best to get an ungodly reaction out of me, and one of these days, she's going to get that ass whooping she's been asking for... by *me*."

Alecia J.

Jenesis really was the sweetest person that anyone could ever run across, but unless someone saw her go slap the fuck off, they really didn't know her. That muthafucka there was different.

"But enough about her irrelevant ass. So, do you feel guilty for being with Kane all that time, knowing he has a woman? And before you say it, no, I'm not judging. I'm the *last* person to judge anyone in that kind of situation, although our situations are damn near similar."

"Whether I feel guilty or not, Jenesis, what was I supposed to do? Just sit on a plane for six days?"

"Well, you could have," she kidded.

"Girl, I wish the fuck I would have! And then we were at the number one place on my bucket list that I wanted to visit!" I twirled my straw in my glass and added, "I do feel bad for sleeping with him."

"Do you really?"

"Now? Yes. While it was going on? No. I enjoyed every *stroke* of that dick," I shamelessly admitted. "Ugh! Why is dark-skinned dick so good? They must put their meat on the grill."

Jenesis cackled.

"Girl, I swear you just say the craziest shit at times! But seriously, where do you and Kane stand after all of this? I mean, what he did was..."

"Very thoughtful. Very kind. Very *demure*," I repeated, recalling the popular phrase that had been circulating on social media.

"Don't you start saying that. I see it enough on Facebook."

"I had to say it, friend. As for where me and Kane stand," I released a frustrated breath and pondered our situation, "I don't know, Jenesis, but after last night, I started to see him in a different way... a good way. I mean, I already knew he was a real ass nigga; he let that be known from day one, but niggas don't just do what he did for *random* females."

"Well, we both know that you are *far* from a random chick when it comes to Kane. But come on, girl. Let's go spend some of this money that Kelan gave *us*." Jenesis grabbed her purse and rose from her seat.

I raised a finger as I savored the last sip of my margarita.

"You ain't said nothing but a word, friend," I responded, finishing my drink and following her lead.

Despite the temporary tranquility that came with my brother's return home, past experiences led me to ponder how long this peaceful period would last before chaos once again found its way into my life.

7. Kane

The sound of my name being called startled me out of a deep sleep. Dazed and disoriented, I struggled to discern between the realm of dreams and reality.

"Kane!" the voice called again, more urgently that time, forcing me to open my eyes. It was Bonnie, standing next to the bed with her hands planted firmly on her hips.

"I'm awake, baby. What's with all the yelling?" I groggily replied.

"Kane, I called your name like ten times!" she yelled with annoyance and concern heavy in her tone.

"Damn, for real?" I asked, picking up my phone to check the time. It was a little after one o'clock in the afternoon, and I had slept the morning away, exhausted from my recent trip.

"Yes. You must've had a *really* good time on your trip. You went to bed as soon as you got here last night, which was still pretty early, and you never sleep in this late on any given day."

"Yeah, that trip drained me," I replied, thinking about how my *nuts* had gotten drained from all the fucking Dior and I had done.

One Drunk Night In Miami 2

While taking a look at my missed calls and texts, I noticed Dior had texted me. I didn't want to disrespect Bonnie by replying to Dior's message while she was standing right in front of me—even if she didn't know who I was texting. So, I put my phone away for the time being and gave Bonnie my full attention. "But what's good, baby?"

"Aside from me coming to make sure that you're okay, I came to ask what you wanted to eat today. I was about to head out and do a little grocery shopping."

"I—" I was about to respond, but my business phone rang, interrupting me. "Hold on, baby," I said.

Bonnie rolled her eyes in response.

"Yo!" I answered Marlo's call.

"Aye, boss. I got somebody who wants to holla at you," Marlo said.

"Somebody like who, nigga?"

"Jazmin, Angelo's baby mama."

"Jazmin? What the hell does she want?"

"She didn't say. She just showed up at my crib and said she needs to talk to you. She said it's important."

I peered up at Bonnie, and her irritated expression didn't go unnoticed. Our jobs usually kept us occupied throughout the week and even on Saturdays, so Sundays, we usually set aside as our dedicated time together unless one of us was out of town. I hated to leave, but Bonnie knew what my line of work consisted of, so when someone deemed a conversation important, I had to prioritize it.

I sighed because I hated disappointing her.

"Can it wait? At least until tomorrow? You know that Sundays are my rest days, and I like to keep the sabbath day as holy as *possible,* with the exception of cursing. So, if it involves me having to kill a muthafucka, tell her to come back tomorrow."

Alecia J.

"Again, I don't know what it's about, but she said you'll want to hear this, so I guess not."

"Look, tell her to stay put. I'll be there in the next hour."

"Bet," he said, then hung up.

Bonnie angrily stormed out of the room.

Sitting on the edge of the bed, I ran my hand down my face, feeling the weight of the impending conversation with her. I knew I had to end things with Bonnie. I didn't want to lead her on or, worse, hurt her. It pained me to imagine her feeling trapped in a relationship with me, unable to fully embrace happiness and life. Despite my tough exterior, I was deeply committed to keeping the Sabbath day holy, as I had explained to Marlo. My upbringing in a world of street life had not overshadowed the influence of my mother, who raised Kelan and me in the church. Despite our divergent paths in life, God remained central to our existence, a guiding force in our successes. As I picked up my phone again, my thoughts turned to Dior's text, a momentary distraction from the weight of the situation with Bonnie.

Dior: *Good morning, Kane. Mama said that she wants to see you ASAP. Her words, not mine. Lol.*

I chuckled.

Me: *Good morning, Pretty Eyes. That doesn't sound good. What I do? Lol.*

I didn't wait for her reply because I needed to get up and get dressed to go see what was so important that Jazmine pulled up on Marlo, but before I did that, I wanted to check on Bonnie. When I left the room, I couldn't find her. Upon peeking through the double doors leading to the patio, I spotted her outside, lost in her own world, vibing to the music. Not wanting to disturb her peaceful moment, I quietly retreated to the bedroom to prepare for my day.

Thirty minutes later, I was showered and dressed. When I

One Drunk Night In Miami 2

made it upfront to leave, Bonnie was lying on the couch, wrapped in a blanket, and watching TV.

"Bonnie," I said with a pang of unease, "when I get back, we need to talk."

She slowly sat up and responded, "Yes, we certainly do."

Her words caused my anxiety to escalate, and I could feel sweat forming on my forehead and underarms. I assumed that maybe she had found out that Dior had gone on the trip with me. Despite my complicated feelings for both Dior and Bonnie, Bonnie was my girlfriend, and I dreaded her finding out about my ongoing involvement with Dior from someone else. My emotions were tangled, and I was torn between my attachment to Dior and my desire to spare Bonnie emotional pain.

"I just want you to know that I'm going home to Belize next week for a few days. I just got a lot on my mind, and I need to clear my head."

I was sure her reason for wanting to do that was closely tied to our issues, whatever those may have been, so I swallowed my immediate response and simply replied, "Okay."

"That's all you have to say?"

"What else do you want me to say, Bonnie? I know you have no family here. Hell, I don't either, and I know sometimes you get lonely here. So, whenever you want to visit them because you miss them or even if you just need to get away, I'll never stand in the way of that. Whatever makes you happy. Just as long as you keep in touch with me while you're gone and you bring your ass back, we'll be good."

"I will," she commented, wearing the smile I was waiting to appear.

That was one thing I loved about Bonnie—her forgiving nature. She didn't hold grudges for too long, which I appreciated, although I tried my best not to give her many reasons to be mad at a nigga.

Alecia J.

"Well, aight, I'ma go see what this nigga talking 'bout, and when I get back, you'll have me for the rest of the day."

"How long do you plan to be gone? I'll try to start cooking or at least make sure the food is ready by the time you're on your way back. Although, you still haven't told me what you wanted to eat yet."

I glanced at my watch. "Give me 'til about four o'clock. I should be back no later than that. And don't worry about cooking today. Take today off. Prop your feet up. Watch those Lifetime movies you love. Hell, drink you some wine and just relax, baby. I'll just stop by somewhere on my way back and grab us something."

"Well, you don't have to tell me twice." She chuckled, then sank back into the couch.

"I love you," I told her before leaving.

Her response was soft but sincere. "I love you too, Kane."

I knew with a heavy heart that despite the love we shared, the path forward was uncertain. I steeled myself for the difficult choice, bracing for the possible pain it would bring to her.

"What's up, Jaz? You looking good." It was a genuine compliment, not on no flirting type shit.

"Hey, Kane, and I appreciate that." She glanced over at Marlo and smiled.

I wasn't the smartest nigga in the world, but I knew when two people were secretly fucking or had an attraction to each other. I made a mental note to ask Marlo about that shit, but first, I needed to address why she needed to see me so urgently.

"So, what's good, Jaz? I ain't trying to rush you, but I gotta get back home to my girl. I'm not sure if Marlo told you, but I usually don't conduct business on Sundays unless it's a *dire* emergency, so I hope whatever you have to tell me is worth me leaving the crib for."

"It is."

I took a seat on Marlo's couch.

"Okay, then. So, talk."

"So, a few nights before Angelo died, he had stopped by my house."

"He stopped by your house? I thought you and him had no dealings, not even with the baby?" Marlo interrupted with a frown. He seemed upset, but he asked the same question I was curious about.

"We didn't, Marlo," Jazmin explained.

Oh yeah, they're fucking.

She continued, "He only came over to tell me to stop calling him about Gabby. While Angelo was there, someone called him. He said it was important, so he took the call. Me being nosy, thinking it was another bitch who had called him, I followed him. Angelo went outside on the back and was dumb enough to put the phone on speaker, and that's when I overheard him talking to some guy. I couldn't hear every detail, but from what I did get from the conversation, they were planning to rob someone, and not a small robbery either. Days later, when Angelo showed up dead, I immediately assumed it was behind that."

"More than likely," I said as if I wasn't the one who had taken his life. "Now, back to the nigga he was talking to. Did Angelo ever mention his name during their conversation?"

"He did. He called him Stephan."

"Stephan?" I repeated to make sure I heard her correctly. "Are you *positive* that's the name he said?"

"Yes, I'm positive."

"You said Angelo had the nigga on speaker, so you heard his voice, too, right?"

Alecia J.

"Yes."

"Did he sound like an older cat?"

"Definitely older."

I nodded and clenched my jaw in anger at the thought of Stephan trying to rob me.

"I appreciate you for that info. I just have one question. Why tell me this now if you been knew?"

"Well, I had known Angelo to be involved in all types of shit, so him robbing someone wasn't a total surprise. It wasn't until last night that one of my friends mentioned it was *your* stash house that he robbed, and according to her, you hadn't found out who'd done it, so I thought that information would be valuable."

"It's more valuable than you know. But again, I appreciate you for bringing it to my attention."

"No problem. Well, I'ma go. I just stopped by to tell you that."

"Aight. I'll walk you outside," Marlo volunteered.

"Take care, Jaz," I said.

"See you later, Kane. Oh, and Kane?"

"Yeah?"

"You wouldn't happen to be the person who gave me the *very* generous donation, would you?"

"What money?" I smirked.

"I never said it was *money*." She smiled and then left the house with Marlo trailing behind her.

I wanted to be nosy and see what they were talking about or had going on, but I decided to check my phone, hoping for a message from Dior. Instead of texting Dior back, I decided to call, but she didn't answer.

Me: *I see you're already disobeying orders, Pretty Eyes. I wouldn't do that if I were you.*

One Drunk Night In Miami 2

Not even thirty seconds later, her name lit up as a Facetime call on my phone.

"I was going to give you another thirty seconds."

"Kane, I only missed your call because I went inside Jenesis's house to use her bathroom, and I left my phone in the car, so please don't trip!"

I smirked, appreciating her commitment to our agreement.

"I'm not trippin', baby. As long as you called back. But what Ma Dukes wanna see me for?"

"Oh, she's *very* upset that you didn't tell her that you had a girlfriend."

"And let me guess, you told her?"

"Well, she kept pressuring me about us being together, so yeah, I did."

"I don't know why you just didn't tell her we were. Hell, we're going to be *soon*."

"Whatever you say, Kane."

"Nah, that's whatever I *know*. As a matter of fact, the next nigga who asks you if you're single, let 'em know you got a nigga and that he's knocking the Mario coins out of that pussy! I know a lot of muthafuckas there, Dior, so be careful who you try to entertain."

"Okay, Kane."

"Why do you keep commenting all dry and shit?"

"Because, Kane, at this point, it does no good arguing with you or going against anything you say. You're going to always be right. Things have to always go your way. So, it's whatever you say and want. You win."

"I—" I was about to respond by telling her that my world revolved around whatever she wanted, but Marlo stepped back into the house. "Aye, baby, I'ma call you back, aight?"

"Okay."

Alecia J.

After I ended the call with her, I stood from the couch, prepared to leave.

"So, how long y'all been fucking?" I came straight out and asked Marlo.

He chuckled. "Dawg, how you just assume I'm fucking her?"

"'Cause I ain't no dumb nigga, *nigga*. So, either y'all fucking or will be soon. Which one?"

"I'm definitely hitting that pussy," he confirmed my suspicions.

"Shid, I already knew that. Yo' ass just better not be with her because she's a millionaire now."

"Hell nah, man! We've been kickin' it for about three months now."

"So, you was hitting the pussy before Angelo died?"

"Hell yeah!"

"That's why yo' ass didn't mind beating his ass that day or me killing him."

"I didn't give two fucks. That nigga wasn't doing shit for his daughter anyway. The way I looked at it, you eliminated one more deadbeat ass nigga from walking around here not taking care of his responsibilities."

"All I'ma say is, don't be like that nigga and fuck over a good woman. Jaz is a good woman. So, do right by her, or I'll be coming after yo' ass next."

"Man, you ain't even gotta worry 'bout that. We locked in fa sho!"

I nodded. "That's what's up. Well, I'm about to dip. You can call yo' girlfriend and tell her that she didn't have to leave on my account." I chuckled. "But I'll holla at you tomorrow, nigga."

"Already." Marlo and I slapped hands again, and then I left.

One Drunk Night In Miami 2

I was about to head to the crib, but that shit Jaz dropped on me about Stephan possibly being the nigga behind the robbery had me wanting to pay him a visit right then.

"Aye, Carlos, change of plans. Instead of heading to the crib, take me by that nigga Stephan's crib. I need to holla at him real quick."

My driver swiftly executed a U-turn and redirected the car toward Stephan's residence without asking any questions.

"Kane! Oh, my God! How are you?" Stephan's wife, Lisa, greeted me with a hug after answering the door.

Yeah, that nigga had a wife, a beautiful one at that, yet he was spending money to go out on dates with escorts. I never understood that shit.

"Hey, Lisa. I'm doing well, and yourself?"

"Sweetheart, who was at the—"

"Door?" I finished Stephan's sentence as he stood there, completely at a loss for words upon seeing me, as if I were a ghost.

"Oh, honey, it's Kane! Were you expecting him?"

"No, I wasn't, so I'm just as surprised as you are," he said with his eyes never leaving me.

"I apologize for dropping in so unexpectedly, especially on Sunday, since I know those days are usually reserved for family time, but I need to have a quick word with Stephan. I promise I'll have him back inside before dinner starts." I faked a smile.

"Oh, of course! Would you like to come inside?" she kindly offered.

"We can just—" Stephan began.

"Actually, I would," I insisted, rudely cutting him off.

Alecia J.

It had been at least a year since I'd to his crib, so I wanted to see if he had *upgraded* since my last visit.

"Come in," Lisa welcomed me.

The scowl on Stephan's face made it clear he wasn't pleased with the invitation, and I couldn't help but wonder why. However, as soon as I stepped inside, the reason became immediately clear.

My eyes were immediately drawn to the multitude of moving boxes scattered throughout the rooms.

"Are y'all moving or something?"

"Yes, we are!" Lisa shouted in excitement.

"Is that so?" I asked, attempting to conceal my anger as I glared at Stephan, who purposely avoided making eye contact.

"Yes! We're moving to Naples!" she further explained.

"Two hours away, huh?"

"Yes, I thought Stephan would've told you by now!" Lisa exclaimed, seemingly surprised that I was unaware.

"Nah, he didn't. Now, *I'm* the one surprised."

"Honey, why didn't you tell your *boss* that you were moving? You know they have to know these things."

"Yeah, Stephan, why *didn't* you tell your *boss* that you were moving?" I emphasized, reminding him of my authority.

"I was going to tell you," was his reply.

"When? *After* you moved? I mean, I'm glad you're moving on up, but moving on up without informing your boss gives *moving funny* vibes to me."

"Honey, can Kane and I talk privately?" Stephan asked his wife.

"Of course, honey! Kane, I'm cooking oxtails and rice if you'd like to stay for dinner."

"That sounds real good right about now, Lisa. Unfortunately, though, I can't stay for dinner. I gotta get home myself, but I'll *definitely* take a plate to go if you don't mind."

"Nonsense, Kane! You're like family! Without your family, we wouldn't have any of this, and my husband wouldn't be in the position that he's in!"

That's for damn sure, I wanted to say, but I didn't want to come off as cocky in front of Lisa since *she* was the one who made the comment.

"I'll get that plate for you."

"Lisa, I'm not trying to be greedy, but if you don't mind, can you make it two plates? I told my girlfriend that I'd bring her something back to eat, and she loves oxtails, so I definitely can't go home with one plate."

"You most certainly cannot! You'll never hear the end of that!" She chuckled. "But I'll be right back! It's so good to see you, Kane!"

"Likewise, Lisa."

Once Lisa had disappeared around the corner, Stephan spoke.

"So, we're doing pop up visits now, Kane?"

"I do them every once in a while, just to check in on my employees *and* other times when *deemed necessary.*"

"So, what's good?" he asked.

"You tell me, Stephan."

"What is that supposed to mean?"

"Shid, just what I said. Is there *anything* you want or feel the need to tell me. Speak now or forever hold your peace." Because if he didn't tell me what the fuck I wanted to hear, he'd be forever holding his peace in hell soon.

"Nah. Business is good. There's nothing to tell on my end."

I observed the area once again.

"From the looks of it, it's doing *damn* good for you. Stephan, I just have one question, and then I'll be out of your hair, as you older people say," I taunted because he swore he was younger than his age. "Where were you the night that stash

Alecia J.

house got robbed? The stash house, as in the one we've had yet to find the muthafucka *or* muthafuckas who did it."

Stephan ran his hand over his bald head.

"That was the night before your birthday party, right?"

"Mm-hmm." I nodded.

"Shit, nephew, that's... that's been well over a month ago, so I can't really say where the hell I was at that specific time. What you getting at, though? Surely, you don't think I had shit to do with that, do you?"

"Nah. Nah. It's just protocol. I'm asking all employees, so don't feel singled out," I lied, watching for any sign of relief in his expression. If he showed any, that would indicate guilt to me.

"Oh, well, shid, I honestly can't remember. I probably was here getting it in with Lisa, if you know what I mean." He nudged my side.

"Here you go, Kane!" Lisa returned with the food wrapped up in a bag.

"I appreciate you, Lisa. I'll let y'all get back to your day. I'll be in touch, Stephan. Oh, and congratulations on the move."

"Thank you! I can't wait to move into my dream home!" Linda exclaimed excitedly.

That's exactly what it's gonna be... your dream home because if I have anything to do with it, y'all won't be moving any fuckin' where. Again, I kept those thoughts to myself.

After exchanging a few more words, I departed the house.

I meant to address him about the shit Dior told me about him running his damn mouth about the business, but I figured that conversation could wait another day.

When I got in the whip, I called my IT guy, Frank.

"Kane, my guy! I'm not used to hearing from you on a Sunday. This must be important."

One Drunk Night In Miami 2

"It is, Frank. My bad if I'm taking you away from your family, but I need a favor... a huge favor."

"Anything."

"I need copies of my employees, Stephan and Angelo's phone records from the last three, no, six months."

I didn't have to provide their last names because he had a list of all my employees' information, including their addresses, phone numbers, and even social security numbers.

Stephan was a more calculated man than Angelo, so if they had indeed robbed me, I was certain it was *well* thought out and planned rather than a spur-of-the-moment decision. More so because they were aware that they weren't stealing from just an ordinary nigga, but from *me*.

"Okay. How soon do you need this information?"

"I don't need it by the end of today, but as soon as possible. If you can have it to me by tomorrow evening or at least within the next two days since I know you have other clients and this is a last-minute request,"

"I got you. I do have a few assignments tomorrow, but I'll try my best to get this over to you no later than tomorrow night."

"I appreciate you, my guy."

"No problem. I'll be in touch with you tomorrow."

"Sounds good."

I really needed Frank to get a rush on those records. The quicker I connected Stephan with Angelo, the sooner it would be lights out for his ass, but patience was key in that situation.

Angelo was already dead, so his involvement really didn't matter at that moment, although I would've given him a harsher death had I known at the time, but Stephan... that nigga was supposed to have been like family. So, if he was the nigga who had robbed me, his death would be anything but easy and sweet.

8. Jenesis

"Good morning, everyone! Please gather around," I announced to my dietary team as I entered the kitchen. "I want to take this moment to express my appreciation for the outstanding work you all have been doing. Your commitment to getting the meals out on time, ensuring the food is at the right temperature, and accommodating the needs of both the staff and residents has not gone unnoticed. I would like to give a special thank you to our morning chefs, Ms. Mary and Ms. Louise," I gestured toward them with a smile, and they reciprocated with appreciative nods. "I'd also like to express my deep gratitude to our other morning shift chefs, Gwen and Theresa, who I hope are enjoying their well-deserved days off.

"Although I'm not able to be present for every meal service, and it may seem like I'm *always rushed off my feet*, please know that I see and admire the effort and dedication each one of you brings to our kitchen. Your hard work truly makes my job so much more manageable. In light of this, as a token of my deep appreciation, I'll be throwing you guys a little appreciation party this Friday in the dining area. We'll have door prizes that you'll have to be present to receive, personal gift cards, and some other fun things. Now, regarding the menu for the party. I know y'all are used to pizza being given out around here as a celebratory gift, but not this go-round. The food will be catered and consist of soul food and seafood options. Yep, all that.

This entire party will be sponsored by me and courtesy of me only, so it's only right that I go out for y'all. The facility is aware of what I have planned for y'all, but they're not contributing to anything. So, yeah, we gon' switch things up a lil' for the norm around here. When it's over, we'll probably have people wishing they were a part of the kitchen crew."

The room erupted in laughter.

"I knew you was banking, Ms. Jenesis!" one of the younger employees stated.

"I'm blessed," I commented with a smile.

The idea to do something special for my employees had been on my mind for a while. When I shared my plan with Kelan, he insisted on taking care of all the expenses. Kelan was truly remarkable in every way—from his looks and charm to his generosity to that *big* and *exceptional* masterpiece that hung between his legs. Let's just say he was quite gifted in more ways than one. I swore Kelan had to have been in the batch of the top five best men that God had created because he was truly everything any woman could desire.

I wanted to say that him doing all the things he did for me was a gift *and* a potential curse—one that would come back to bite me in the ass. Thankfully, I wasn't one of those women who depended on or needed a man financially, so I always had my own money to fall back on if we happened to not work out. However, I didn't see us breaking up anytime soon, but… if so, I also didn't see Kelan as the type to throw what he'd done for me back up in my face.

Alecia J.

"Will this just be for the morning shift?" Someone inquired.

"Oh, no. This will be for all shifts. So, yes, I have to make this *same* announcement when the evening crew comes in. Now, as I mentioned, y'all will have personal gift cards gifted to you. So, on one of these sheets of paper," I held up a clipboard, "I need y'all to write down places that y'all like to eat or stores y'all like to shop at. If any of you are off on Friday, make sure y'all stop by at around 3:00 to grab you a plate and your goodies. Again, thank y'all for everything y'all do."

The news was met with excited murmurs and expressions of joy and gratitude that rippled through the room.

"Y'all are most welcome, and I love y'all more! Now get back to work!" I jestingly encouraged. "And don't forget to fill out these papers for your gift cards! Once y'all are done, just set them in the basket over there, and I'll get them when I return." With those words, I exited the kitchen and crossed over to the dining area, where I spotted Isla smiling all in the maintenance man's face.

Well, would you looka here?

As soon as Isla noticed me, she playfully waved and said, "Hey, girl! I'll be in your office in a minute!"

"Okay!" I responded, channeling Craig's mom from the movie *Friday*. Although the actress's response was meant to be in a nice, nasty way, I added a light-hearted touch to mine.

My office was conveniently located next to the kitchen, allowing me to be easily accessible in case any of the kitchen staff needed me. After getting comfortable in my office, I took a moment to call my grandmother. I realized that it had been a few days since our last conversation, and I wanted to check in with her.

"Well, hello, my beautiful granddaughter. I was going to

give you another day before I showed up at your house or job to see why I haven't heard from you." She chuckled.

"Hey, Grammie. I'm okay. Life has been... *eventful* but in a positive way."

"Oh, really? Well, do tell me more," she urged in an intrigued tone.

I went on to update her on the recent developments in my relationship with Kelan.

"Well, I must say I wasn't expecting to hear *that*. Now, Jenesis, you know I love you, so you know I'm going to always tell you my honest feelings. I do have reservations about the timing of your relationship with him, as he just got out of another relationship. Be that as it may, I also know that love knows no boundaries, and I've always encouraged you to live life to the fullest with absolutely *no* regrets. So, baby, if you're happy, then I'm happy for you."

"I am, Grammie. I really am. Kelan makes me *so* happy. I honestly think I'm living in a fairytale and that one day, I'm going to wake up and realize I was dreaming the whole time because everything just seems so perfect. *He* seems so perfect, but I know the perfect person doesn't exist."

"No, they don't. But let me give you this piece of advice. When things are going well in your life, don't worry about how long it will last. Don't downplay it. Don't brush it off. Don't sabotage it. Just embrace it, even if it won't last forever. Baby, you're acting like you don't deserve true happiness."

As I sat in contemplation of my grandmother's words, a gentle knock echoed through my office before Isla stepped inside.

Raising a finger to signal that I was on the phone, I mouthed, "Hold on."

"You're right, Grammie, but one of my coworkers just came into my office, so I'll have to call you back later. I love you."

Alecia J.

"I love you too, baby. Have a good day."

"You too, Grammie."

After ending the call, I redirected my attention to Isla.

"Whatcha doing, girly?" she asked, her face adorned with a broad smile.

With a grin on my face and my arms folded, I retorted, "I should be asking what *you* were out there doing."

Isla appeared clueless and asked, "What did I do?"

"Don't try to come in here acting like you weren't just out there flirting with the maintenance man!"

"*Flirting?* Girl, is *that* what you thought you saw? No, ma'am!" She chuckled. "Not to be mistaken, I like Curtis. I mean, he's cool, but he's *far* from my cup of tea, honey! Aside from that, he's a married man, and me flirting with a *married* man while going through this shit with my no-good-ass husband is the last thing on my mind. Curtis was just telling me how he'll be moving soon, and they need a replacement for his job. They don't want to give it to any of the men already here because they be at odds with each other already. So, they're looking at hiring an outsider. Do you happen to know someone with relevant experience?"

I pondered for a moment, and then a specific memory surfaced. I recalled Dior's brother, who had dabbled in carpentry. Despite Lance never fully capitalizing on his carpentry prowess, he possessed an unmatched skill for maintenance and fixing things.

"You know, I just remembered. My friend's brother is actually in search of a job. I'll definitely talk to Craig about it today."

Craig was the administrator who had a small crush on me, but our friendship was strong. So, I was confident that he would willingly help me secure the position for Lance with no problem, given our close relationship.

One Drunk Night In Miami 2

"Well, alright, girly. I would stay longer, but I have another busy workday! You wanna go out for lunch, though? My treat."

"Girl, you had me at 'my treat.' I'll never turn down a *genuine* free meal."

"*Never* any strings attached. Just good food, good company, and good drinks." Isla's voice dropped to a low, almost conspiratorial tone as if she feared eavesdroppers. Although we *never* indulged in drinks while on the job.

"Right. But just let me know when you're ready," I told her.

As Isla was leaving, she replied, "Will do, hun. Don't work too hard!"

I couldn't help but mumble, "That's easier said than done," as I glanced wearily at the mound of paperwork on my desk. "<u>Push through, girl, regardless of how you feel, because feelings don't pay pills</u>," I motivated myself, feeling utterly exhausted and dreading the busy day ahead of me.

"What the hell?" I mumbled when I stepped outside.

I was startled by the sight of a suspicious, rusted, and grime-covered older model Honda with blacked-out tinted windows parked in front of my house. The car stuck out like a sore thumb in my neighborhood, which added to my growing sense of unease.

"Who's there?!" I called out, hoping for a response, only to receive a blink of the headlights in acknowledgment. The partially rolled-down window obstructed my view, leaving me unable to make out the individual's features. Fearing for my safety, I swiftly retrieved my phone and prepared to dial 911.

"I don't know who you are, but you need to leave my property before I call the police!" I warned assertively, brandishing my phone to emphasize my point. In response, the window ascended, and the car sped away, leaving me with a pounding heart and a rush of adrenaline.

Rushing to my car, I hesitated a moment before driving off. Despite the unsettling encounter, I headed to the gym, finding comfort in the thought of Kelan as a source of security in that moment.

Panicked and breathless, I burst into Kelan's office, interrupting his phone call.

Kelan looked up from his phone, wide-eyed, and immediately wrapped up the conversation. He hurriedly pushed his chair back and rushed over to me.

"Baby, what's wrong?! Talk to me!" he urged with concern in his voice and worry etched on his face.

"Before... before I came here, someone was parked outside my house, in an unknown car, watching me, more like stalking me! It felt like they were waiting for me to come out, or as if they knew I'd be leaving at that exact time!"

"Why the fuck didn't you call me, Jenesis?!" Kelan barked angrily, his voice echoing with frustration.

"I was too shaken up to call anybody! Not to mention, by the time I realized I should have, they had left! And since I was coming here, I just decided that I'd wait to tell you face-to-face!" I responded, my voice quivering with anxiety.

"Did you get a good look at the person's face?" Kelan asked in a softened tone.

"No, the car was tinted. Oh, God! What if I have a stalker?!"

Kelan gently cupped my chin, his touch tender yet firm. "Jenesis, baby, calm down. I want you to listen. As long as I have breath in my body, I'm not going to let *anybody* hurt you. I don't care if we have to go against *your* wishes about us living together before marriage. I'll move in with you or have you move in with me if that's what it will take to protect you." Kelan's voice was steady, filled with determination and reassurance.

"Thank you, Kelan. I'm so scared," I confessed as he enveloped me in his arms, offering a sense of safety and warmth that I desperately needed.

"Don't be. I got you, baby." Kelan's words wrapped around me like a protective barrier against my fears.

During the next ten minutes, Kelan skillfully eased my worries by providing reassurance that gave me some peace of mind and convinced me that everything would be okay.

"Are you good now?" he asked, his eyes searching mine for any traces of unease.

"I'm not good, but I'm *better*. Thanks to you."

"If you're not feeling up to it, you can skip class today. Actually, I would prefer it if you do. I don't want you to leave, though, 'cause you're not leaving until I do, but you can definitely sit this one out."

"I think working out will give me a little distraction from all of this, even if it's temporary."

"Aight. Well, I need to call my brother. Class will start in a few, so gone out there and get ready. I'm sure Dior is looking for you if she's coming."

"Oh, she's here. She's been the one blowing my phone up with calls and texts. But I'll let you go so you can talk to your brother. I'll see you when you come out. Tell him I said, hey."

Kelan nodded, then said, "Jenesis, are you *sure* you're okay?"

I chuckled at his caring nature.

"Kelan, I'm good. I promise," I assured him. "*Please* stop worrying."

"Jenesis, you're my woman, and as your man, I'm supposed to be worried when shit like this happens."

"I appreciate that, but *your* woman needs you not to be... at least for the time being. I don't want you taking your frustration out on the class when you go out there. They'll pick up on it and sense that something is wrong."

"You're right, and I won't. I'll just take my frustration out on that pussy tonight."

I chuckled.

"Why my girl gotta get a beating for something she didn't do?" I laughed.

"Nah, I'll be gentle with her, baby, and you too," he voiced sexily while tugging at my shorts and licking his lips. "But gone out there before I start something that I *will* finish."

"On that note, I'ma go 'cause when you say shit like that, you're serious."

"Dead ass, baby. Now gimmie me a kiss," he requested.

After our kiss, I departed his office.

When I stepped out into the open, a sense of relief washed over me, but the lingering uncertainty of the unidentified person outside my house still weighed heavily on my mind.

Once I spotted Dior, I made my way over to her.

"Hey, boo!" I greeted her.

"Jenesis... so nice to see you. But just answer this for me. Since when do we come into the building without each other? More importantly, when do we ignore each other's calls and texts? I'll wait!"

Shaking my head at Dior's dramatic display, I couldn't help but chuckle at the over-the-top nature of her complaint.

"Dior, some crazy shit happened not too long ago, but I'll fill you in later." I'd hoped with those words that she'd caught the hint that I didn't want to discuss it right then. However, knowing Dior's persistence, I knew she wasn't going to let me off that easily.

"Please don't tell me that Kelan has fucked up already, and he was in there giving you some apology head or dick?"

"Girl, no! And I would never come in here after I finished fucking without washing my ass first! You got me mixed up with some of these women who come in here!"

I've always been baffled by the fact that some women show up at the gym without taking a shower first. It was understandable that you'll work up a sweat during your workout and need to shower afterward, but it would be considerate to at least cleanse your main areas with soap before being around other people. During an individual workout, someone might be able to overlook a bit of body odor. However, in a group fitness class, we often found ourselves in close quarters, and any unpleasant smell could completely disrupt the atmosphere. It's hard to focus on exercising when you're trying to dodge a bad odor and keep your nose in the air the whole time.

"Yeah, like the bitch over there who's been staring in my face since I walked in this muthafucka. Actually, both of their asses be staring like I'm fuckin' their niggas or something."

I glanced over in the direction that she was looking in.

"You're talking about the new girls?" I questioned.

"Hell, I guess they're new," she replied with a nonchalant shrug.

The previous week, Kelan had introduced a couple of fresh faces, and the two girls in question were among them. However, Dior was out of town, so she missed that announcement.

"But I know one of them personally, and she's known for walking around the city with stank pussy!" Dior's expression contorted into a look of disgust.

I chuckled.

Alecia J.

"I'm serious, Jenesis! Then, she's a CNA. Like, how you around here wiping other folks' ass, and your own ass stinks? And have the nerve to call herself a bad bitch! Thou shalt not walk around with smelly pussy while thinking thou is cute! Take a bath, bitch!"

I chuckled. "You must be talking about the one wearing the black? Because the other girl seems to take pride in her appearance."

"That's the *exact* one I'm talking about. So, I'm puzzled how the two of them are even friends *if* they are, but surely they're not."

"She looks like she is messy."

"Messy and miserable, friend!"

"What's her name?" I pried.

"Tiece! Look at 'em. I'm sure they're over there trying to find a flaw and probably mad because they can't! It bothers bitches when they can't call you a bum or hoe. I'm so glad these niggas around here can't sit and discuss me sexually."

"Okay!" I concurred.

"But if she is on some messy shit before she opens her mouth to gossip about *anyone,* she needs to rub her coochie first and then sniff her hands. Sis got bigger fish to fry!"

I quickly diverted my attention and stifled my laughter by burying my face into Dior's shoulder. If I hadn't, they would've undoubtedly caught wind of our conversation and probably figured out we were discussing them if they hadn't already.

"Dior, you've gotta be stopped," I said once I straightened up, trying to contain my laughter. "And remind me to never get on your bad side because who knows what you might say about me."

"Jenesis, there's nothing about you that I haven't already told you myself, so hearing it from someone else wouldn't surprise you," she mentioned blatantly. "But really, there's nothing wrong with you except for being stuck in your stubborn ways sometimes. I still love you, though," she added as she playfully nudged me.

"Yeah, yeah. But as for those two, let them continue to talk and stare, honey. When you're her, you never worry about them."

"Jenesis, I will braid the grass before I worry about why a bitch don't like me, and you know that. But, fuck them! What is your *man* in that office doing? He'll usually be out here on our asses about stretching. As a matter of fact, let's get to it!"

"He's on the phone with his brother. Or at least that's who he said he was about to call," I answered as I began to do my stretches.

"You still didn't tell me what y'all were *doing* in there," she further inquired.

"Nosy are we?" I chuckled.

"*Very!*"

"Well, if you *must* know, he was eating my pussy," I fibbed just because she was so curious.

Dior paused her stretching routine and blinked erratically, her eyes reflecting a sense of confusion or surprise.

"I thought you said he wasn't?"

"I lied. Sue me." I struggled to suppress a smirk and uphold the facade of my deceit.

"So, that's the type of freaky shit you're on these days? Getting your coochie ate in the office while there are *hundreds* of people on the other side of the door. Well, there are not hundreds of people *here*, but you get what I'm saying. But okay, friend! I ain't mad at you! Let me add that to my list of freaky shit to do!"

I laughed. "Girl, Kelan was *not* eating my pussy; we were just talking, although he did want to, and maybe I should've let him. Maybe that would've calmed my nerves a little more."

Alecia J.

"*Calm your nerves?* Okay, all jokes aside, what's really going on, Jenesis? And don't say you'll fill me in later. Fill me in *now* because later, I'll probably be the one walking around here with high blood pressure from trying to figure out what's going on with you! So, let's hear it, ma'am!"

Realizing that Dior wasn't going to let it go, I decided to share with her the details about the unfamiliar car that was posted outside my house.

"What the hell, Jenesis?! Why didn't you call me?! Hell, *anyone* for that matter?!" she scolded me in a voice above a whisper. Dior's concern and tone mirrored Kelan's, but with a touch of maternal protectiveness as if she were my mom.

"Kelan asked the same. At the time, all I could think about was getting here to Kelan as fast as possible. That's why I didn't wait for you outside," I explained.

"I understand. Do you think it was..."

"Sincere?" I finished looking around cautiously, making sure no one heard us.

"Yeah."

"The thought of it being him crossed my mind."

"Did you tell Kelan?"

"Girl, no! I haven't even told Kelan about the possibility of him getting out soon. So that thought went away just as fast as it came, especially since I don't believe shit Myeisha says. If anything, I figured it was someone Sincere probably had watching me."

"Could've been. And you know I don't believe shit that comes out of that bitch's mouth! Still, you *need* to tell Kelan, *just* in case that bitch *is* telling the truth."

"I will."

"I'm serious, Jenesis."

"I will, Dior. I promise."

"Okay. But I know that had to be some scary shit. I'm just

glad that you're okay. What's up with these niggas stalking women, though? Considering you do have a random nigga stalking you."

"Or female," I interjected.

"True, 'cause some of these bitches run around here like they're *cuckoo for cocoa puffs*! Speaking of stalkers, though, tell me why Gavin's ass hasn't stopped staring at me since I got here either," she murmured.

Dior told me his name after she mentioned he had shown up at her job one night.

"Girl, Gavin is harmless." With a hand wave, I immediately dismissed the idea of him being a stalker or weird ass nigga.

"Or at least he *seems* to be," Dior countered. "You can never be too sure of these men, friend. I hope he just has a staring problem because I already have too many crazies in my life."

"That, you do," I concurred, leaning forward to do a stretch. I couldn't help but giggle as Bryson came around us and nosed about like an inquisitive little dog. "Bryson, what are you doing?" I quizzed.

"Listen, somebody in here is smelling hella bad," Bryson grumbled. "And I ain't talking about musty! One of these bitches walking around here with some sour pussy! So, I'm trying to find the suspect."

"Are you serious?" I asked in disbelief. More so because Dior and I literally *just* had a similar discussion pertaining to that.

"Hell yeah!"

"Well, what you sniffing around Dior and me for? Our shit is good!" I bragged.

"Can't rule anybody out!"

Dior playfully hit his shoulder. "Bryson, get yo' ass on!"

Alecia J.

"I'll be back!" Bryson left the room and moved through the space with the precision and grace of a true Inspector Gadget.

"That boy is something else. You know, he and Imani have been talking a *lot* more lately," I mentioned.

"Is that so?" Dior responded in a surprised tone.

"Mm-hmm. He's been walking her to her car after class and everything."

"Damn, I've just been missing all the tea around here!"

"Trying to take trips and be fast will do that," I kidded.

"I was taken against my will, and I'm standing firm on that!"

"What about the trip you took with *Jace*?" I playfully teased.

"Now, see... that was different."

"Mm-hmm."

"But Jenesis, why you had to bring him up?! Ugh! I was doing good not thinking about his ass!"

"Have you talked to him since you left from around him?"

"Girl, hell no! When I blocked Kane's ass, he was next. Actually, he was the reason I blocked Kane."

"What did he have to do with you blocking Kane?"

"When one nigga irritates me, I take it out on all their asses! One band, one sound!"

I chuckled.

"And you see what blocking Kane led to. So don't be surprised if Mr. *Jace* pulls that same move."

She waved me off. "Girl, please! Jace doesn't have the balls to do no shit like that. He's too *soft*. Knowing his ass, he's probably been at home crying or going around the bar, looking for me."

"When do you plan to go back to work anyway? At the bar, that is?"

"Next week, and I dread it. Then again... I probably *won't* be returning there."

"Why not?"

"So, yesterday, Mama told me that one of her friends who works at the DHS office mentioned that they have a few job openings for caseworkers. So... I gave the lady a call today, and she set me up an interview next week."

"Really?!" I exclaimed excitedly.

I had no idea that Dior had thoughts of working at a desk job, but the excitement written all over her face painted a clear picture of her aspirations.

"Yep!"

"Dior, oh, my God! I'm so happy for you, friend! You've practically got that job already! It's in the bag. We're claiming it right now! But seriously, I'm so happy for you."

"Thank you, friend. But it's time, ya' know?"

"Well, speaking of work, you and your brother both may be landing new jobs next week. So, one of our maintenance guys, actually, he's the maintenance supervisor, is leaving and they're looking for someone to fill his position. Lance has a lot of experience in that department, right?"

"Girl, yes! He let all that schooling and good talent go to waste."

"Well, maybe not *entirely*. The person who's in charge of hiring would be my supervisor, and we're pretty close. In fact, he has a crush on me, so he'll pretty much do *anything* for me. All I'll have to do is tell him about Lance, and I'm sure he'll make sure he gets the job. He wasn't at work today, but I'll speak to him tomorrow and take it from there."

"I appreciate you, Jenesis, and I'm sure Lance will, too."

"Dior, we're more than friends... we're family, and family has to look out for one another. I got you, boo. Always."

"Likewise. But back to Bryson and Imani 'cause I swear we

Alecia J.

got *way* off topic. But if ol' girl knew like I *know*, she'd run far away from his worrisome ass!"

"Bryson isn't *that* bad," I said in his defense.

"Nah, he isn't. He's cool. She just seems like a sweet girl, and I'd hate for him to hurt her."

"Especially with her being Isla's daughter," I included. "I mean, we aren't best friends, but we work together, and I do consider her a *friend*... now, at least. So, I don't want to bring a wedge between us since I'm the one who practically pushed Bryson on her daughter."

"You just make sure little Ms. Isla *remains* just a friend. No need to go adding any other titles to that."

I chuckled at Dior's slight jealousy.

"Oh, look! There goes your *honey!*" Dior pointed out Kelan.

A spark ignited in my eyes as if it were the first time I'd seen him.

"Good evening, ladies and gentlemen!" Kelan addressed the class. "My apologies for running behind. I had a little emergency that I needed to take care of, but I appreciate y'all patience. I hope y'all have gotten a good stretch in because we'll be working on multiple areas of the body today."

The room buzzed with a mix of complaints and eager determination. Dior and I found ourselves among the complainers.

"I know, but trust me, the end result will be greater than the pain you'll have to endure. I'll give y'all about five more minutes, and then we'll get started," he concluded, then headed in our direction.

Dior leaned over and whispered, "Looks like he's making his way over here. You know, sooner or later, people are going to start wondering about you two."

"If they haven't already," I retorted.

One Drunk Night In Miami 2

"Hey, Kelan!" Dior spoke to him when he approached us.

"What's good, Dior?" Kelan returned, then quickly focused his attention on me. "Baby, let me talk to you for a second," he requested, then gently guided me to the side.

"Is everything okay?" I asked with concern.

"Yeah. So, I got you some security set up outside your house."

"You... you do?'

"Yeah. You'll have six men watching the house twenty-four hours a day."

"Six?"

"They won't all be present at the same time. Three will be on duty during the day and three at night. Do you want more or feel you need more? Although when I'm there, you won't need nobody but *me,* beautiful."

I blushed. "No, I think that should be plenty. I am curious to know how you were able to pull that off so fast, though."

"Jenesis, you must've forgotten what my brother does for a living? Hell, what I *used* to do. I may not be in the game anymore, but I still have connections... a *lot* of them, with my brother being the biggest one. So, whatever resources I lacked, Kane most definitely can, and he gon' always make happen whatever I need him to make happen. So, yeah, Kane has a lot of his men down here as well. In case some shit pops off with me or Mama, they'll already be nearby. So, just like him, I want to make sure when I'm not at your crib that you're good... at *all* times. I don't need you around here worrying about shit."

For a moment, I was on the verge of kissing him, lost in the intensity of the moment. Then, as the reality of our surroundings hit me, I quickly took a step back, creating some distance between us, and cleared my throat. "So, when will they be arriving?"

"They should be heading to your crib now. When class is

Alecia J.

over, I'll trail you home to make sure everybody is in place and everything is good."

"Okay."

"I got you, baby. Don't worry." He winked and then diverted his attention to the class.

"Alright, class! Let's get started!"

As Kelan took charge, I found myself gazing at him in admiration and silently expressing my gratitude to God for bringing such an exceptional man into my life.

Dear God, this man you sent me... thank you.

9. Miracle Foster

"That bitch looks like she just got the best dick of her life," Tiece muttered with envy laced in her tone as she glowered at Jenesis.

Frustrated by Tiece's presence, I rolled my eyes inwardly. I yearned for her to move the hell from by me. Whether she was aware or not, her lack of personal hygiene didn't go unnoticed, and I didn't want anyone to mistake her poor habits for mine.

The other reason was due to her tendency to annoy the hell out of me, which she had succeeded in doing since our first day starting there. *Strangely*, we both started the class on the same day. My primary reason for being there was, at Melani's request, to keep an eye on Kelan. At the same time, there were a few areas of my body that needed a little improvement. So, I kind of was killing two birds with one stone. However, Tiece's presence puzzled me. I had even mentioned it to Melani, who was equally unaware of her motives for being there. Let Tiece tell it, she signed up because she wanted to get her body in shape and lose a few pounds—says the person who had a *nice* shape. So, of course, I instantly called her bullshit. In all honesty, I *always* had my doubts about Tiece when it came to trusting her.

Hell, how could anyone begin to trust someone who didn't even prioritize good hygiene?

"I wonder what they were doing in his office or if they're together for real?" Tiece continued with her investigation. "I've been following her page, and she hasn't posted anything about being in a relationship," she admitted.

"You've what?" I retorted.

According to Melani, Tiece had no idea that I was there doing an *observation* on Kelan. Although what Tiece said about her snooping on Jenesis's page came as a shock, I maintained my facade of disinterest in Kelan and Jenesis's relationship, pretending that I was only there to work out.

"Melani told me everything about her and Kelan's breakup, and, if you don't know, that's the girl with whom she suspected he was cheating. At the same time, Melani has no actual proof that it's her because Kelan never came out and told her the girl's name. That's just what she *speculated* since she saw the girl around Kelan twice."

Despite being privy to that information, I refrained from correcting Tiece or sharing my perspective so as not to raise suspicion.

"Maybe Melani was wrong about it being her. I mean, I see them talking all the time when I'm here, but like I said, there's nothing on her Facebook page that indicates she's involved with anyone."

"Maybe she's just a private person," I pointed out.

"Maybe. But if she is with him, she won't be for long. I got my dibs on that."

"Say what?"

"You heard me correctly, and before you say it, I care

nothing about the fact that he's Melani's baby daddy. At this point, that's all she is to him."

This trifling ass bitch! I knew it was a reason I never really liked her!

"Aside from the fact that he's her baby daddy, Melani is your *friend*, Tiece!" I emphasized in a low, intense tone.

"Correction... *was!* I don't know what that bitch is to me now! She's been moving funny lately, and I don't have time for all that *wishy-washy* behavior. And I don't care about you relaying this message to her! Melani had a *good* ass nigga; one she didn't deserve! Do you beg to differ?"

"No. I *wholeheartedly* agree with you on that. Still, that doesn't make it cool for *you* to go after him."

"Miracle, from day one of meeting Kelan, I found myself crushing on him, but... out of respect for me and Melani being *friends,* I kept my feelings at bay when around him. But I'd be lying if I said I haven't been *waiting* for the day when he left her ungrateful ass, so he can get with a real bitch."

"And that *real* bitch is supposed to be you?" I sniggered, much to Tiece's annoyance, as she glared at me with malice.

"It will be," she replied, sounding confident in her capabilities. "Miracle, one thing I have *no* problem getting is a man."

Their sense of smell must not be functioning properly when they approach you in order for them to find you attractive. Maybe eventually their full senses return, and that's why you can't 'keep' a man, I thought.

"So, if little Ms. Jenesis is with him, they won't be together for too much longer. Not if I have anything to do with it."

I had always *heard* tales of fake friends, but the encounter with Tiece was unlike anything I had ever experienced. I couldn't wait to tell Melani about her ass.

Out of the blue, Bryson, the other fitness trainer, interrupted us with a disapproving "Goddamn!"

Alecia J.

It was clear from his scrunched-up face that he wasn't expressing attraction to us. Judging by his reaction, he seemed bothered by something, possibly Tiece's body odor.

Directly addressing Tiece, he asked, "Is that you smelling like that?" with unabashed honesty, leaning in to confirm the scent.

Tiece, visibly offended, retorted, "Excuse me?" Her hands were assertively placed on her hips, highlighting her indignation.

Bryson wrinkled his nose in revulsion as he vigorously waved his hand back and forth over it, trying to dispel the unpleasant odor.

"Look, I'm not even about to repeat myself. For one, I *don't*, and secondly, you heard *exactly* what the fuck I said. You should also know *exactly* what I'm referring to. Now, since this is my place of employment, and I kind of need this job, I'ma say this in the most *respectful* way that I can. You gon' have to bounce, smelling like that. I don't know if you got some kind of medical condition going on, but you gon' have to get that shit looked at or handled before you can come back in here. You're fuckin' up the vibe and people's senses. Let me give you some free game, though. If you want a nigga to eat that pussy like groceries, you gotta wash that thang like dishes, Ma. As for you," Bryson turned to me, "if you were any type of *real* friend, you wouldn't have her in here like this."

I wanted to tell him that bitch wasn't my friend.

"What smell is he talking about, Miracle? Do you smell something on me?" Tiece asked as if she was oblivious to her own body odor or possibly immune to it.

"Tiece, if you have a change of clothes, why don't you go shower and then come back?" I suggested, "I mean, you did come straight from work, and you do work at a chicken factory."

One Drunk Night In Miami 2

"More like *Captain D's*," mumbled Bryson, eliciting a soft chuckle from me.

Tiece discreetly sniffed her clothing and nodded. "Yeah, maybe you're right. I was just rushing to get here. I do have a change of clothes, though. I'll just go shower in one of the showers out there. Just let Kelan know I stepped out for a second," she said hastily, leaving her scent lingering as she hurried off.

"Damn. Walking around smelling like that should be a sin and added to the ten commandments," Bryson said, shaking his head in disbelief, then he focused on me. "Myra, right?"

"*Miracle*," I corrected him.

"Well, shid, I was close, but what's up with you? Maybe you and I can make our own little *miracle* tonight," he flirted.

I scoffed. "Excuse me?"

"I ain't talking about a baby if that's what you got from that. I'm talking about some *Miracle Whip,* if you get what I'm saying. Shid, then again, they say birds of a feather flock together, and with you having a friend like her, some shit smelling and looking like tartar sauce might come out of you. So, nah, I'm good. You cute, though," He winked, then swaggered off.

I wanted to curse his ass out, but there were more important matters that required my attention. The act of betrayal by Tiece toward Melani continued to occupy my thoughts, evoking a profound sense of concern and disturbance. Regardless of the status of their friendship, the fundamental virtue of loyalty should *never* waver. The unspoken rule was clear—ex-boyfriends, particularly those who share children with a person, were strictly off-limits, and Tiece was fully aware of that boundary.

10. Melani

"That bitch really said that shit?" Miracle told me what Tiece had said to her about having a crush on Kelan and trying to get with him.

Given Miracle's history with men, I had assumed *she* would've been the one to pose a threat to my relationship with Kelan. However, it turned out that my *best* friend had been lusting over my man damn near the entire time we'd been together.

"Girl, yes. She didn't hold back anything... confessed it proudly and shamelessly," Miracle explained.

Upon hearing that, my immediate reaction was to pull up on Tiece. Unfortunately, I had more important things on my agenda that day to tend to. So, beating her ass would have to wait another day.

"Bitches ain't shit, but thanks for letting me know, boo. I'ma handle that ass; not today, though. You know I'm going to see my dad today, and right now, that's the *only* thing I need to focus on."

After giving it a lot of thought, and with Miracle's consis-

One Drunk Night In Miami 2

tent encouragement, I ultimately made the decision to go and visit my dad, deliberately choosing not to inform him in advance. The mix of emotions and the uncertainty surrounding his reaction to seeing me after such a prolonged period made the experience deeply moving and intense.

"Right. Are you sure you don't want me to ride along with you, or well, take you? I don't necessarily have to go inside with you, but I can keep you company along the way," Miracle kindly offered.

"I appreciate that, but this is something I need to deal with on my own. The drive there will give me some thinking time and an opportunity to carefully plan out what I intend to say to him," I stated, then glanced at the time on my phone. "Actually, I need to get going. It's a two-hour drive, and I want to be back before it gets dark. I'll call you once I make it," I shared, then grabbed the keys and headed for the door.

"Alright, take care of my baby. She's my pride and joy," she said with a grin, referring to her car that she occasionally lent to me for running errands. Despite Miracle's initial reluctance about letting me use her car, she understood the importance of my visit to my dad, so she didn't mind me using it for that particular trip.

While I had the means to buy my own car, I kept that information to myself. I was willing to rely on her generosity until I got myself settled. Plus, I had a feeling that the money Jewelynn had given me would come in handy for something else soon.

"I'll treat her like she's my own. I'll be back soon!"

With that, I set off, mentally preparing for the two-hour drive that would likely stretch into three hours due to my driving style, anxiety about seeing my dad after so long, and my tendency to get motion sickness. It was a challenging combination, so I anticipated making several stops along the way.

Alecia J.

The warm afternoon sun cast a soft glow as I sat in the driver's seat of my car, parked outside my childhood home. I repeated the words, "Get out of the car, Melani," over and over in my mind, but my nerves kept me immobile. I had mentally rehearsed what I would say to my father once I faced him, yet the thought of getting out of the car made my heart race.

With the window down, I breathed in the familiar scents of the neighborhood –the fragrance of freshly cut grass mixed with the cool afternoon breeze. I reminded myself that the visit was necessary and that turning back was not an option after driving all those hours. Summoning my courage, I finally exited the car.

As I stood on the doorstep, preparing to ring the doorbell, a whirlwind of doubt and anxiety engulfed me. "Why am I so nervous to see him?" I murmured under my breath.

In a sudden panic, I turned to retreat to the car, but the creak of the door opening halted me in my tracks.

"Me-Melani? Is that you?"

Hearing my dad call out to me from behind, I stood frozen in place, unsure of how to respond. Slowly, I pivoted on my heels to face him. My dad's eyes were glistening with happiness and tears.

I swallowed the lump in my throat and replied, "Yes, it's me, dad."

Tears gushed down his face, and I found myself mirroring his emotional outpouring. The unexpected surge of emotion revealed just how much I had missed him.

"Come," he beckoned, opening his arms wide. I enclosed him in a heartfelt embrace, holding on as if trying to make up for lost time. "Melani, I've missed you so much!"

"I've missed you too, Daddy," I confessed, my tears flowing

uncontrollably. After we both regained our composure, he ushered me inside. "Come in. We have a lot to catch up on."

As I stepped past the threshold, I took a moment to soak in the familiar surroundings of my childhood home. Memories, both joyful and painful, flooded back, though the happiest ones prevailed.

"Can I get you something to eat or drink?" my dad offered, his baritone voice filling the spacious, tastefully decorated foyer.

"No, thank you," I replied, my eyes taking in the opulent surroundings of the house—the polished marble floors, the exquisite artwork on the walls, and the warm, inviting ambiance.

"Very well, let's head to the living room and have a chat," my father suggested, leading the way with an air of ease and familiarity.

"So, tell me, what's been going on with you lately? How has life been treating you?" my father inquired, his eyes conveying genuine concern and interest.

"Well, until a few weeks ago, I was living a life of luxury. I was fortunate to have a *great* man who spoiled me with more than just materialistic things but also love. I had the pleasure of not ever having to fill out an application for employment if I never wanted to. Most importantly, I had my daughter," I paused.

The fact that I hadn't seen or talked to Emmy since I separated from Kelan weighed heavily on me, and Kelan's silence spoke volumes. He hadn't reached out to me, likely waiting for me to make the first move. I hadn't contacted Kelan due to my uncertainty about his reaction. Despite my apprehensions, I couldn't bear the thought of Emmy growing up with doubts about my love for her, and I knew maintaining distance from Kelan could potentially fuel his pursuit of sole custody of

Alecia J.

Emmy, given my recent disappearing acts, so I knew I had to get in contact with him as soon as possible.

"Emerald... that's your daughter's name, right?"

"Yes. But we call her Emmy for short."

He nodded with a gentle smile on his face.

"Yeah, Candice tells me about her all the time and shows me pictures of her. She's so beautiful. Just like you," he complimented.

Candice, my cousin, was the one I mentioned who maintained regular contact with him.

"Thank you, Dad." My voice wavered as my thoughts momentarily drifted to my daughter.

"Candice has been keeping me in the loop with your life, as I'm sure you know, but I want to hear about it from your perspective. But first, I want to know what brought you here today. Not to be mistaken, I'm glad you came. I'm even happier to see you, but it's been five years, Melani. Have you held a grudge against me for all these years?"

"I have, Dad," I honestly admitted. "But... I came here today to try and make amends and to see if we can leave the past in the past. But that would require some much-needed answers to a question that I'm hoping you can *finally* shed some light on. Why did you have Sincere sent to prison all those years, Dad? I just have to know."

My dad tilted his head upward and released a heavy sigh.

"I'll tell you the truth. The question is, will you be able to handle the *outcome*?"

"Dad, I've waited *five* years to have this conversation with you. In that time, I've tried to consider every possible reason that could explain your actions, but I always come up empty. I've spent countless hours thinking, and I'm tired of thinking. It's time that I hear the truth from you."

"And I intend to give you that. However, I can assure you

that the reason I have in mind is not one you've considered. I need a moment to gather my thoughts. I'm going to get a drink. I'll be right back." My dad stood, then glanced over at me, and suggested, "Maybe you could use one too."

"I'm fine," I replied.

He nodded, then excused himself and left me in my thoughts.

As I awaited his return, I sat there nervously, nibbling on my nails, tapping my feet, and rocking back and forth, desperately trying to unearth the elusive 'why.'

After about five minutes, I started to worry that my dad might not return, but he eventually reappeared.

"So," he began after retaking his seat, "before I tell you why I did what I did, I need you to know that Sincere has been released from prison *if* you're not already aware."

The fuck?!

That was news to me. I knew Sincere mentioned that he was getting out *soon*, but I had no idea that he had already been released. What angered me even more was the fact that he hadn't reached out to me. Be that as it may, I didn't want my dad to know that I had any knowledge of his release, so I pretended to be confused and unaware.

"Re-released, but I thought—" I started to say, but my dad cut me off.

"Yes, he was meant to remain in jail for a *long* time, potentially for life, but I managed to get his charges removed by using some connections."

Well, you are the judge who unjustly added false charges to his case, making it relatively easy to have them removed. Rather than voicing my inner thoughts, I managed to articulate, "A few things still aren't adding up. Why would you go to such lengths to imprison him for all those years, only to have a change of heart after so much time had passed?"

Alecia J.

"It was because of you. I knew that your resentment all these years stemmed from him, so I thought that if he was free, you would eventually come home, even if just for a visit. It seems my plan panned out."

"To be quite honest, I had no clue that he would be released... at least not this soon," I murmured almost inaudibly.

My dad scrutinized me with a stern gaze as he asked, "Have you... have you still been in communication with him?"

"What would that matter?" I found myself replying in a more confrontational tone than intended. "And how else did you expect me to *know* he was getting out if I wasn't still in touch with him?"

"Through the grapevine, Melani!" he bellowed, rising from his seat with visible anger. "But you really want to know why it matters so much?! It matters because he's your fuckin' brother, Melani! There's the answer you've been waiting for all these years! Are you happy now?!"

I felt a sudden rush of emptiness, as if all the air had been sucked out of the room when those words escaped his lips. I found myself sitting there, completely devoid of speech, as a whirlwind of emotions swept through my veins, and a myriad of perplexing thoughts clamored for attention in my mind.

"Did you... did you just say that he's my brother?!"

"Yes, Melani. He's your half-brother. A few years before you were born, I cheated on your mom with his mom, and he was conceived," he confessed in a softer, remorseful tone.

"Oh, God! You're... you're lying! Please tell me that isn't true?!" I whimpered.

"I wish I wasn't. That's why after I saw you with him that day, I knew I had to do whatever in my power to keep you from him. I'm so sorry, baby."

I leaped from the sofa.

"Sorry?! You're sorry?! I don't even know how this shit will affect me moving forward! Regardless of if you told me after you met him, this is something I should've known about *years* before that, Dad! I could've had a baby by this man; hell, even married him, and all you can say is you're sorry!"

"That's why I did what I did, sweetheart! The way you spoke about him and how close you two were the day he came here with you, it seemed like you were getting *really* serious, so I did what I had to do!"

I chuckled, but not from humor. "No, you didn't do what you had to do. You did what you knew you could get away with! Wow! You learn something new every day. My brother... my fucking brother. You were right when you said *that* thought probably never crossed my mind because *that* shit sure the fuck *never* did! How could you, Dad? How could you?" I repeated in an incredulous tone. "And don't you dare try to say that you wanted to tell me or tried to because I asked you *so* many times before I left here, and you never tried to tell me *shit*, at least not the truth!" I was deeply hurt and in shock.

"Melani, I—" he started to explain, but the sound of the front door opening and closing interrupted his sentence.

Moments later, a tall, beautiful woman with short hair entered the room, and her gaze immediately fell on the two of us.

"Dean, what's going on?" she questioned him.

Confusion hung heavy in the air as my dad made his way over to her. His embrace revealed their close connection.

"Geneva, this... this is my daughter, Melani, who you know about. Melani, this is my wife, Geneva," he introduced.

The word "wife" landed heavily on my heart.

"You're... you're married?" I finally managed to voice, trying to process the news.

"Yes. I remarried three years ago," my dad confirmed.

Gathering my thoughts, I approached Geneva. "Wow! I'm

just finding out all types of shit today, huh? You want a little advice? Leave before he cheats on you like he did my mom. So, years later, you won't—"

"Melani, that's enough," my dad sternly warned in a calm yet firm tone.

"You're right, it is. I think it's time to go because I've obviously overstayed my welcome. This time, you won't have to worry about when you'll see me again because I'm letting you know now that I won't *ever* be back. Good riddance, *Daddy!*"

"Melani!" He called my name repeatedly as I hightailed it out of the house.

Tears cascaded down my cheeks, each drop a testament to the anguish I felt in that moment. The hurt I felt was indescribable. Not to mention the disgust from knowing that I had fallen in love with my *brother*. Once I was in the car, I wasted no time peeling out of the driveway. Despite knowing there were more details omitted that would've given me a better understanding of the situation, I couldn't bring myself to inquire about them at that moment. My priority was to create as much distance as I could from my dad.

"I hate him! I hate him! I hate him! How could he not tell me that?!" I repeatedly shouted while fiercely striking the steering wheel with my hands.

I maneuvered recklessly through the streets, darting through traffic as if I were the only car on the road. My distress clouded my judgment, causing me to carelessly run a stoplight, resulting in a jolting collision with another car.

"Fuck!" I cursed aloud, feeling the weight of the situation crashing down on me—*literally*.

Not only had I just learned the shocking truth about Sincere's relationship to me, but I also had to prepare myself for the fallout with Miracle about the damage to her car.

What a day! What a fuckin' day!

11. Bonnie

"Hey, Ms. Wendy," I greeted Elias's mom once I approached her.

She was tending to her vibrant and colorful flower beds in the front yard. Their splendor and liveliness were exactly how I envisioned my future dream house's landscape.

"Bo-Bonnie?" she exclaimed, her face lighting up with surprise and joy as she struggled to rise from her gardening chores.

Swiftly, I hurried over to lend her a helping hand.

"Thank you, sweetheart," she expressed gratefully once on her feet. "I must say I wasn't expecting to see you return here so soon, that is. You usually just come to visit every few months or so."

I always made it a point to visit Elias's parents' house whenever I traveled to Belize. It was my way of staying connected with them.

"I just needed a break from Miami. Last time I was here, I was caught up with my dad's party, and then the following day,

Alecia J.

I headed back home. So, I didn't really get to enjoy myself aside from that," I elaborated.

"Mm-hmm. So, this trip is more of a *personal* one, huh?" Ms. Wendy inquired with a knowing smile.

I couldn't help but chuckle. "I suppose you could say that."

"Would *Elias* have anything to do with your quick turn-around?" she pursued the topic with a smile.

"Mayyyyyyybe," I dragged, feeling a slight blush creeping up my cheeks.

"I wish the two of you would've worked out. I always just knew you'd be my daughter-in-law. The crazy thing is, I still have hope that one day you will be," she shared, her voice filled with unwavering optimism.

As I reflected on the past, I couldn't help but envision a different present.

"Ms. Wendy, if Elias hadn't made the decision to leave, I'm almost *certain* that we'd still be together, perhaps even happily married with children. The whims of fate continue to amaze me. In other words, life has a way of surprising us."

"Yes, it does. Well, I hope you're included in Elias's future," she beamed.

"Even if we're just friends, I will be," I assured her. "I actually stopped by to see if you knew where he was."

"Oh, he's inside."

"Oh, really?"

"Yes. I take it that he's not expecting you."

"No. I wanted to surprise him."

"Well, he'll be surprised, alright." She chuckled. "But you can go on inside, baby. I'ma stay out here and finish up this gardening."

"Ms. Wendy, one of these days, you're going to have to teach me how to plant. I aspire to have a beautiful garden like this one day. I attempted once but failed miserably."

One Drunk Night In Miami 2

"You simply lacked the guidance of a *skilled* mentor, that's all," she bragged with confidence, followed by a smile. "But sweetheart, it's not as hard as many people think it is or put it out to be. Whenever you're ready to get some of *Ms. Wendy's* teachings, just let me know, and I'll be more than happy to help you get started."

"I'd appreciate that, and I'll probably be getting those lessons real soon. Now let me go in here and see what that son of yours is up to. It's good to see you again, Ms. Wendy."

"It's always good to see you too, sweetheart."

Once I crossed the threshold of the house, I swept my gaze across the familiar setting. My frequent visits during my and Elias's dating days had etched every corner and crevice of their home into my memory. After a thorough search of the front room, I started to believe that Elias might not be home. However, the sound of music emanating from a nearby room caught my attention, and I followed it to his old room.

Approaching the door cautiously, I was determined to surprise Elias. Gently peeking through the slightly ajar door, I caught a glimpse of him sitting on the bed with his back turned to me. Elias appeared entirely unaware of my presence as he fixed his attention on something displayed on his phone. It became clear to me that he was looking at my recent post on Facebook. To add another layer of emotion to the moment, the song "Residuals" by Chris Brown, one of the most heartbreaking songs I could think of, was playing at that moment. Seeing Elias staring at my photo while that particular song played, I couldn't help but assume that he was reminiscing about our past relationship.

Out of the blue, tears began to overflow from my eyes, stirred by the realization that despite leaving Belize and being back home, I hadn't stopped thinking about him. He had been on my mind since I departed Belize. Leaning against the wall

Alecia J.

just outside his bedroom, I released a prolonged, wordless cry, dreading the prospect of Elias catching me in that emotional state. As the song's final notes tapered off, I gathered my emotions, preparing to greet him with an unexpected surprise.

"Knock, Knock." I carefully tapped on Elia's bedroom door, causing him to hastily turn around.

"Bonnie?" Elias's eyes widened as he recognized me, mirroring the shock on his mom's face when she first saw me. However, it seemed like he was even more taken aback by my unexpected presence.

"It's me." I smiled.

He rose from his bed and met me at the door.

"What are you doing here?"

"Oh, I was just in the neighborhood, you know?" I said, casually moving around his room and letting my hand graze the bed where we had shared countless intimate moments. I quickly pushed aside those bittersweet memories.

"Girl, stop playing. What you doing here for real, Bonnie?"

"I wanted to talk to you."

"I gave you my number the last time you were here. You didn't have to come all the way here just to talk to me."

I met his gaze. "Well, let me rephrase that... I wanted to see you."

"I guess you're ready for me to uncomplicate things in your life."

I chuckled. "I didn't say all of that. Actually, you being back has made things *more* complicated in my life."

"Is that so?" He smirked as if that was music to his ears. "Why don't we talk about this *complicated* situation on a trail walk? You down?"

"Oh, my God, yes! I haven't been on one in so long!" I shrilled in excitement.

Trail walks used to be our signature activity, and if I knew

One Drunk Night In Miami 2

Elias as well as I thought I did, he would take me on the one that held the most sentimental value for us both.

"Aight. Let me just piss right quick, and I'll be ready."

I nodded.

Elias excused himself momentarily, leaving me alone in the room.

While Elias went off to handle his business, I found myself unable to resist the urge to peek around, hoping for signs that would've tied him to being in a relationship.

"You know what they say about curiosity, right?" Elias jested, startling me as he appeared behind me.

I quickly straightened up from my perusal of some papers on the nightstand, unaware that he had returned. His teasing remark caught me off guard, leaving me red-faced at being caught in the act.

"I wasn't prying," I fibbed, attempting to disguise my curiosity as nonchalance.

"Let you tell it. But, you ready?"

"Yes, I am."

As we exited the house, the soft caress of the warm sun greeted us, casting a golden glow over the charming garden his mom was still tending to. She looked up as we approached, her face adorned with a friendly smile.

"Where are you two off to?" she pried.

"We're just going on a lil' trail walk, Ma," Elias answered.

"Trail walk, huh? Well, okay. Be careful. Oh, and Bonnie, I'm cooking s*tew beans and rice* for dinner. You should come over. I remember that to be your *favorite* by *me*," she coaxed.

"It still is, so yes, ma'am, I'll definitely be stopping by to grab a plate."

"Sounds good. You two have fun on your little adventure. Don't get too lost… in each other, that is," she playfully added, evoking a shared chuckle among all of us.

Alecia J.

"Aight, Ma. We'll see you later."

"See you later, Ms. Wendy!"

"Let's go embark on a new, well, *old* journey, beautiful." Elias took my hand and guided the way.

Noticing the familiar direction we were heading, I inquired, "Since you mentioned an *old* journey, I take it that we're going to our favorite area?"

With a charming smile, he confirmed, "We are."

Elias was so damn handsome. He had such a resemblance to the actor *Lance Gross* that it seemed uncanny. The only noticeable difference was Elias had a slightly taller stature. He also possessed dimples and a deeper shade of brown in his eyes.

"Your mom must've known I was craving some stew beans and rice," I said, making conversation.

"*Craving?*" Elias looked at me suspiciously.

Amused, I clarified, "Elias, I'm not pregnant. So, no, not *that* kind of craving."

"Oh." Prompting further, he asked, "Well, since we're on that topic, do you have any kids?"

Surprised by his question, I responded, "What? No!"

"Shid, I'm just asking. I mean, we're really just now catching up, and a lot of shit can change or happen in a person's life in eight years."

"Very true. But I could guarantee you if I had a child, your mom would've informed you by now."

"Yeah, you're right about that. So, do you still want the seven kids you mentioned having?" The corners of his eyes crinkled with humor. Although that statement was true, they harkened back to a time *years* before when I expressed a genuine desire for a large family.

"Ooooooh, no." I chuckled. "Maybe if I started a little earlier, yeah, but now, I'll be satisfied with two, or even just one if that's what God has in store for me. What about you? Do you have any little *Elias Juniors* or *Ellas* running around here?" I joked.

"No, not yet, at least," he replied with a suggestive glance in my direction, as if he was implying the possibility of *us* having children in the future. "But back to my mama," he smoothly transitioned the conversation. "Earlier, she said that she wasn't cooking shit. Now that you have shown up, she's suddenly in the mood to cook... your *favorite* at that."

"You know your mom loves me," I boasted.

"On some real shit, she does, though. You know you were supposed to be her daughter-in-law, as she says."

"Trust me, she never fails to let me know that every time I see her, and I already got my reminder today." I smiled. "But, nah, your mom knows that my love for stew beans and rice is out of this world, so she knew I'd never turn down that meal. So, I'm guessing her agreeing to cook that was her way of convincing me to come over."

"I'm sure."

"So, what do you plan to do now that you're back for good? Are you back living with your mom? Or do you have your own place?"

"I'm staying with her for the time being. I love my mama, but living with her *permanently,* at the age I am now... hell nah! I'm actually going house shopping tomorrow. You wanna join me?" Elias's lips curled into a seductive smirk, revealing his irresistible dimples that had the power to enchant any woman. He continued, "No pressure, but I figured since you're here, and we haven't kicked it in a while, maybe we can while you're here. I mean, it ain't like you gon' have shit else to do, anyway."

We exchanged laughs.

"How you just gon' assume that I don't have anything planned?"

My sole purpose for going to Belize was to see Elias and

hopefully get to spend as much time with him as possible, so of course, I didn't mind accompanying him.

"Lucky guess. So, will you?"

"Sure. I don't mind."

"Issa date then, my beautiful Bonnie."

Each time he called me by that name, it tugged at my heartstrings, knowing that it was a name he exclusively reserved for me. At the same time, I couldn't help but wonder if Elias had ever given another girl a similarly affectionate or personalized nickname.

"So, let me hear about this new nigga in your life who's been getting all of my love since I've been away," he joked, referencing the Chris Brown song.

Despite Elias's light-hearted tone, I detected a genuine interest in his inquiry. In that moment, I considered questioning him about looking at my photo, but I opted against it, choosing instead to let him revel in his moment.

"His name is Kane. He's a year older than me. I started talking to him a year after you left here. I met him through a mutual friend while he was in prison. Once he was released, we became an 'official' couple and have been in a relationship ever since," I shared.

"What does he do for a living?" Elias asked, wanting to know more details.

"If I tell you, you probably wouldn't believe that I'm with someone like that, but... he's one of the most notorious drug dealers in the state of Florida, more so, Miami."

"You're fucking with a drug dealer?"

"See! I knew you'd have that reaction!"

He chuckled. "I'm just saying. Yo' shy ass and a drug lord don't mix, baby."

"I'm starting to realize that," I sadly said.

Kane and I had yet to have that 'talk,' the one we were

supposed to have when he returned home that day. Oddly, I felt it pertained to our relationship. I wasn't going to bring it up to him because I didn't want to look suspicious or even end up telling on myself. Unbeknownst to Kane, I had become aware that he was still seeing Dior on the side. I had gone through his phone and stumbled upon their messages. It was the night before his supposed 'business trip,' during which I suspected Dior had accompanied him since we didn't talk as much as we normally would when he'd be away. That was one of the reasons that prompted me to plan another trip to Belize. At the time, I wasn't trying to be on some 'get back' type of shit. My real intention was to spend quality time with Elias in person rather than catching up with him over the phone.

Elias paused our stroll and gazed at me with a penetrating look.

"Bonnie, it's clear as fuck that you're not happy with this nigga, so why won't you leave him? Is that muthafucka putting his hands on you?" he seethed.

"Hell no!" I cursed before I knew it, which was something I rarely did.

"Shid, I'm just asking. Don't shoot the *concerned* guy, baby," he kidded, lightening the conversation.

"But no. He's never put his hands on me... ever. Kane is a good dude. He makes sure that I'm *always* good, but..." I faltered, struggling to put my thoughts into words.

"But what, Bonnie?"

"The love just isn't there anymore. When you asked me why I won't leave him, I found myself wondering the same thing about him. I mean, this man could have any woman he wants, yet he chose me, well, *chooses* me to be his girlfriend."

"Well, you can't blame the nigga for that," Elias remarked, giving me a once-over. "But what do you mean by 'he chooses

Alecia J.

you as his girlfriend'? Y'all have an open relationship or something?"

I wasn't prepared to divulge that significant part of my life to him, nor did I ever think I would. Additionally, I wasn't about to tell Elias that my man was clearly in love with another woman, at least not right then. I felt that it was important to have that conversation with Elias *after* Kane and I had a chance to speak first.

"No, nothing like that. All I will say is, the love I once had for him, emotionally, doesn't exist anymore," I confided.

"What about the love you had for me?" he inquired, his voice filled with a mix of hope and uncertainty, causing me to take a few nervous steps back.

After a moment of hesitation, I admitted, "Believe it or not, it really never left," baring my true feelings.

In response, he pointed at his chest and said, "That's good to hear because you've always remained here."

Elias's words stirred something deep within me. With a sense of relief, I commented, "That's good to know," with a small smile tugging at the corners of my lips. "But let's keep moving. We still have a little way to go." I reached out, grabbed his hand, and pulled him along.

As we journeyed along the trail, I couldn't resist asking Elias the burning question that had been on my mind: "So... did someone special catch your eye while you were away?"

Elias's expression shifted noticeably at my question, with a fleeting shadow of sadness passing over his face.

"Yes," he confessed honestly.

A momentary pang of jealousy coursed through me at that admission.

"Oh. Well, are the two of you still together?" My heart raced with anticipation, yet I was also apprehensive of his response.

"No. She passed away last year."

"Oh, no! What happened?!" My heart was heavy with genuine empathy.

Elias went on to describe the girl and her passing, exuding a mix of pain and love in his narrative. As he recounted how they met in the army and how she fell unexpectedly ill and passed away, I felt the weight of his sorrow in his words and voice.

"I'm so sorry, Elias," I offered sincerely.

"Thank you. I'm good now, though."

As we continued our walk, Elias opened up about his time in the army and the strained relationship with his late father, who had also passed while he was away. Despite being aware of his father's struggle with alcoholism, I was completely oblivious to the extent of the abuse his mom endured. It was that harrowing situation that led Elias to make the difficult decision to leave Belize. He simply couldn't bear to witness his father's relentless mistreatment of his mom any longer. What made it even more unbearable was her steadfast refusal to leave him. My guess is that her fear of the father held her back. We also conversed about my career as an event planner, and I noticed the admiration in Elias's eyes as he listened intently to my experiences.

"I'm proud of you, Bonnie," Elias congratulated me on my success.

"Thank you, Elias. I'm proud of you, too, although I hate you had to leave, but it seems like something good came out of you going there."

"And that is?"

"It seems like the army made a man out of you," I replied, gazing at him with wistfulness.

Alecia J.

"What? Girl, I was a man before I went in there. You better act like you know, or *maybe* I need to give you a reminder," he teased in a flirtatious and somewhat provocative tone.

Oh, I know all too well. Those were my inappropriate thoughts, but I chose to keep them to myself.

"Whatever." I chuckled, trying to downplay the swirl of emotions inside me.

"But, nah, if you don't go in there, a man, you'll definitely leave there as one," Elias added with a hint of seriousness. His eyes grew distant as he momentarily immersed himself in memories of his time in the army.

I observed the surrounding area with awe. "You know, I just realized we made it!" Exhausted from the long walk, I was relieved to finally have a moment to rest. Pointing at a nearby tree, I exclaimed, "Oh, look!" Elias followed my gaze, and we both made our way over to the tree, where our initials still stood proudly etched into the bark. "I find it so amazing that it's still visible after all these years. We did this *well* over ten years ago," I said while marveling at its beauty.

"Yep, and I remember it like it was yesterday. But I heard they can last for decades," Elias informed me.

Lost in thought, I wondered aloud, "Hmm. I wonder how many people have passed through here and seen this?" As I traced my hand over our names, memories of the day we carved them resurfaced.

"Ain't no telling," Elias replied.

The gentle breeze rustled the leaves as I stepped back from the sturdy oak tree. Before me lay a vast area dotted with trees, their branches swaying gently in the wind. The air was filled with chirping birds, carrying with it the scent of freshness and natural beauty. As I took in the tranquil scene, I found myself saying, "The beauty of this place will never cease to amaze me.

There have been so many times when I've wanted to return and make this my home once again."

"Then why won't you?" Elias challenged as he closed the space between us. "I mean, you do have a *good* ass reason now. That good ass reason being *me*."

"Elias..." I tensed up when he cradled my face and guided me to lean against the tree.

"My beautiful Bonnie, do you believe in destiny?"

"Wh-what?" I stammered, confused by his sudden question.

"Had my ex not passed away, I would've never returned here, at least not this soon, nor for good, anyway. So, with you going through what you are with your current nigga, and me losing my ex, me coming back here had to be fate, right?" Elias tenderly brushed the back of his hand over my right cheek.

"I... I guess. I don't know!"

"Well, I do. Bonnie, even with me being with ol' girl, I've never stopped loving you," he confessed, his words carrying a weight of longing and affection. "The way you're nibbling on your bottom lip and how your breathing has hitched lets me know that you're turned on right now." Elias leaned forward against my neck and whispered, "Remember, that was one way I could always tell when you were ready for this dick." His warm breath gently caressed my skin, ushering a soft exhale from my lips.

A man who learns a woman's body is a dangerous muthafucka. Not only can she not hide anything from him, but when it comes to pleasing her, he's going to get her right every time.

Unexpectedly, Elias hiked my dress up, ran his hand along my thigh, and then gripped my right booty cheek.

I gasped, caught off guard. "Elias, wh-what are you doing?"

"What does it look like I'm doing?" he replied while tugging at my panties.

Alecia J.

"Elias, we can't do this!" I murmured. "Especially not here! What if... what if we get caught?!" I fretted.

"Let them watch. Shid, we're on an adventure, so we might as well do some adventurous shit. You only live once."

"Still, Elias, this... this isn't—"

He silenced me with a sweet kiss.

"It's been eight years, my beautiful Bonnie. Eight *long* ass fucking years since I've been in this good shit. Are you saying you don't want this dick as bad as I want his pussy?" His lips grazed mine again.

"Ye-yeah," I moaned breathlessly.

"Yeah, what, baby?" he continued to tease while toying with my nipples and placing sweet kisses on my neck. "I need you to tell me that you want this dick. I need to hear those words."

"I... I want that dick," I succumbed to my temptation.

"Bonnie, if we go here, there's no turning back... absolutely *none*," he cautioned. "Once I get back in this pussy, I'm the *only* nigga who will have access to it moving forward. So, again, I ask, are you sure this is what you want to do?"

Without a moment's hesitation, I affirmed, "Yes."

Elias grinned in satisfaction after hearing that I was fully committed to our daring endeavor.

After letting his shorts and boxers drop to his ankles, he swiftly lifted me in his arms, pinned me against the tree, pushed my knees up, and wedged himself between my thighs. My wetness was ready to receive him. Then, slowly, he slid into me.

"Elias," I moaned in blissfulness.

Hunger met hunger when our bodies came together.

Elias filled me better, more fully than any other man had. Sex with Kane was *great,* but I had a deeper, more profound connection with Elias, which made the experience more fulfilling.

"I love you, my beautiful Bonnie," he professed while slow stroking my pussy.

"I love you too, Elias. I love you, too," I repeated.

I wasn't eager to have sex with Elias just because I missed him and wanted to see what that dick was still hitting on. Hell, I was horny from not being fucked in over a week by my own man, and a girl had needs, and those needs were going to be met that day. Did I feel bad about sleeping with Elias? Not one bit! It was the best sex I had in a long time! What heightened the experience was the setting where it took place. Kane was a freak, but he would've *never* agreed to anything like that, at least not with me. I was sure while I was away that he would use that opportunity to spend some time with Dior. Was I a bit more upset? Nope. Because I was going to spend just as much time and equally fun with Elias.

In our relationship, Kane and I had agreed that it was okay to see others—from time to time—but we always made sure to communicate honestly with each other, if or when we'd do so. However, Kane broke that trust when he started sneaking behind my back and seeing Dior without telling me. It was clear to me that she wasn't just a casual fling for him. I suspected that he was deeply in love with her, but I was prepared to reciprocate in kind.

What's good for the goose is good for the gander, right?

12. Jenesis

"Babe, you were supposed to go in that store for one thing, and you came back with all of this stuff," I told Kelan as he put the bags in the backseat.

"Well, you know how that goes," he replied with a chuckle.

We were heading to his mom's house for the 'meet and greet' dinner, but we ended up stopping by the store to get her something she needed. Kelan asked if I wanted to go inside with him, but I declined. I was still sticking to my rule about us not being out in public together, particularly in that city, since his breakup from Melani was still fresh.

"What are you doing with all of those smell-good items?" I asked in amusement and confusion as I noticed at least two bags filled with wax melts, air fresheners, and Plug-Ins. "Let me find out that you be couponing on the low," I jested.

Kelan waited until he got in the car to respond.

"Nah. Some of them are for the crib, and you can grab some for yours if you want, but I really got all that shit because Bryson told me that somebody was funky as hell in one of the classes the other day."

One Drunk Night In Miami 2

I burst into laughter, cutting into his talking.

"I'm dead ass serious, baby," he continued. "I can't have that kind of shit happening. So, I'll be prepared tomorrow. Hell, moving forward."

"Oh, I know you will, and he wasn't lying either," I said once I had composed my laughter. "It was some girl named Tiece," I snitched.

"You know her?"

"Just from the class. Dior knows of her personally, though. She was the one who put me on game about her hygiene. Then, after Bryson finished his investigation, he later came to tell us that she was the culprit." I chuckled.

"That's Melani's homegirl. Actually, that's her best friend."

I leaned back in surprise. "Really?"

"Yeah."

"How long has she been one of your clients?" I quizzed, peering at him with narrowed eyes, trying to gauge his reaction.

"Not long. She literally just started right after Melani and I broke up," he responded, his eyes flickering away from mine.

"And you don't find that odd?" I pressed, a sense of suspicion creeping into my tone.

"I did when I first saw her there, and I still do."

"Hmph," I muttered, then diverted my gaze outside the car window, lost in contemplation.

There were so many thoughts swirling in my mind, clamoring to be voiced, but I chose to hold them back for the time being. Shifting in my seat, I turned to face him, deciding to steer the conversation in a different direction.

"So, what advice can you give for 'officially' meeting your mom? Like what are the dos and don'ts around her?"

"Just be yourself," he simply stated. She's perceptive, like the nigga from Jeepers Creepers: she can pick up on fear, and if she senses you're intimidated, she'll see you as weak, and weak

Alecia J.

women are a turnoff for her. She thought you were shy when she saw you at the crib, but I had to let her know that my baby was far from that."

"Shy? The word 'mortified' might be more accurate." We chuckled together.

"I told her that too, except I said the word *embarrassed,* but don't worry, I had your back, baby. I'll always have your back." He picked my hand up and kissed it. I smiled in response.

"Before we head to Ma's crib, I gotta stop by and pick my granny up. She usually goes over there with me and Emmy."

"Okay. Where does she stay?"

"Just around the corner from Ma's crib. Trust me; Mama ain't gon' be too far from her."

I nodded.

"I never asked, but does she ever remember you when she sees you? I know you told me that she has mid-stage dementia, and while most individuals at that stage do recognize their family members, it's not always consistent," I mentioned, drawing from my experience as a nurse.

"There are days where it takes her a little while to place me, but for the most part, she usually remembers. I've always been her favorite, so maybe that's why. Don't tell Kane I said that."

"When people say that, they're usually lying," I joked.

"Real talk. If you think I'm lying, just ask her when you get around her."

"Oh, I will."

"Are you ready for your birthday trip?" Kelan grinned while lightly gripping my thigh.

"Yes," I beamed.

We were leaving for Jamaica in the following two days, and I couldn't be more excited.

"Baby, I promise to treat you like the queen that you are

while you're there, but you may as well get ready to get yo' back blown out every night."

"*Every* night?"

"*Every* night," he confirmed.

"That means you won't be getting any for the next two days then because this kitty will need a break in between."

"I'm still full off that good shit from last night, so I'll give you a two-day break. Enjoy it while it lasts."

"Since we're talking about birthdays, have you reached out to Melani about Emmy's party?"

The look on his face let me know he hadn't.

"Kelan..."

"I'm going to tomorrow. I promise, baby. We're having a good day, and I don't want to ruin it by calling her, and I damn sure don't need you mad at me about something like that. I'ma call her tomorrow. I promise."

One aspect of Kelan that truly captivated me and distinguished him from my ex was his non-confrontational nature. He made a conscious effort to steer clear of arguments, unlike my ex, who seemed to thrive on picking fights over trivial matters. Kelan's demeanor was like a breath of fresh air, and he embodied a whole new level of maturity.

"Okay," I replied and decided to let the conversation go and simply relish the remainder of the ride.

"Hey, Granny." Kelan greeted his grandmother with a tight hug as we entered the cozy living room. She was comfortably seated on the sofa, engrossed in watching *Who Wants to Be a Millionaire?*

"Hey, baby." She beamed at Kelan.

"Hello, Melani. How are you today?" she spoke.

Alecia J.

I glanced behind me, attempting to discern who she was referring to. *Perhaps Melani is standing behind me,* I thought. However, as I turned my gaze back toward her, I realized she was addressing me. It was important to bear in mind that she was battling dementia, causing her to mistake me for someone else. Kelan chuckled and pulled me closer to him.

"Granny, she's not Melani. This is my new girlfriend, Jenesis. Jenesis, this is my granny, Lizzie."

"New girlfriend?" His grandmother looked at me with astonishment. "You certainly aren't her. You're much prettier," she complimented me with a warm smile.

"Well, thank you, ma'am. Kelan tells me that he's your favorite."

"He is, but don't tell his brother that," she whispered as if Kane was nearby.

"Told you," Kelan said.

"Whatever," I responded, then looked around in search of her caretaker, who Kelan told me was a nurse, but I didn't see her anywhere.

"Um, babe, where is her nurse?" I whispered.

"That's a good ass question. Granny, where is Andrea?"

I was about to ask Kelan how he knew her name, but I quickly remembered him saying that he and Kane were the ones who had hired and paid the nurses.

"She's—" his grandmother began.

"I'm right here! Hey," Andrea's words trailed off as she noticed me. It wasn't because I was a new face but because we were already acquainted. I couldn't tell who was more surprised to see the other: me or her.

"Jenesis."

"Andrea," I replied, my tone dry and unfriendly.

"You two know each other?" Kelan asked, clearly taken aback.

"Well, we—" Andrea started.

I rudely interrupted with a loud "Unfortunately," drowning out her words.

Andrea and I used to be close friends until she did something incredibly hurtful. As a result, I found it difficult to be civil toward her.

Completely oblivious to the underlying animosity, Kelan let her know, "She's going to go with us over to my mama's house. By the time we get back, your shift will be over, so you can go ahead and leave."

"Okay. Well, I'm sure she'll enjoy that outing."

I discreetly rolled my eyes at Andrea, not so much the comment she made, but just her fake ass.

"She always does," Kelan countered.

"Well, I'm going to go and fill out my timesheet to give to you, and then I'll leave."

Kelan nodded. "What was that about?" he muttered once she was out of earshot.

"I'll tell you about it later," I said, not wanting to say what I really felt out of respect for his grandmother being in our presence.

"I don't like her, grandson," Kelan's grandmother said, her voice fraught with disapproval.

I couldn't help but assume she was referring to me.

"Who you don't like, Granny? My girlfriend?" Kelan asked the question that I was curious to know as well.

"No, baby. That nurse," she replied in a low tone, pointing in the direction Andrea had gone to.

"Why not, Granny? Did she do something to you?" Kelan questioned with urgency and rage creeping into his expression.

"She... she curses at me, and I have to wait a long time to get my food sometimes," she explained with a touch of sadness in her voice.

Alecia J.

Kelan's expression quickly transformed from concern to anger, as if a switch had been flipped. In an instant, he went from looking like an innocent, caring grandson to a raging bull, ready to charge.

"How often does she do this?" Kelan asked.

"Um... quite often," she hesitated before responding, not due to concern about Andrea overhearing the conversation but rather because she struggled to recall.

With Kelan's grandmother battling dementia, it was challenging to determine the credibility of her statements. Be that as it may, Andrea was always known for being a bitch and having a nasty attitude. That was one reason I found it surprising that she was employed as Kelan's grandmother's nurse. People can put on a convincing facade, so I suspected she presented a grand front to secure the job.

"Okay, here you gooooooo!" Andrea reentered the room with a radiant smile and presented a neatly folded piece of paper to Kelan.

Before I could anticipate what transpired next, Kelan sprang from the sofa with an impulsive energy, grabbed Andrea by her neck, and pinned her against the wall with her legs dangling from being lifted. I suddenly felt rooted to the spot, stunned by the unfolding scene. Not only was I shocked by the rapid escalation of the situation, but I was also taken aback by Kelan's uncharacteristic behavior. Though he casually mentioned how he used to get down in the streets before he went to prison, that was the first time I had observed such raw emotion from him. As I watched in shock, I couldn't help but fear for Andrea's well-being more than she appeared to fear for herself.

"Bitch, what's this shit my granny is saying that you've been cursing at her and taking yo' time with her meals and shit?" Kelan bellowed in anger.

One Drunk Night In Miami 2

"I..." Andrea grasped at Kelan's shirt, struggling to speak.

Shock held me in its grip, rendering me unable to speak.

"Talk, bitch!" Kelan's demand for her to talk came out as a harsh command, his relentless hold on her neck tightening. It was clear that she was in immediate danger. As a nurse, I couldn't stand idly by while he killed her because that was sure to be the outcome. So, I knew I had to intervene to save her.

I stepped to Kelan and placed my hand on his shoulder.

"Kelan, please, let her go," I spoke calmly. "You're going to kill her, baby. I understand that you're upset, but this isn't the way to handle it, especially not in front of your grandmother," I implored. "Think about everyone who cares about you, who would be devastated if you end up in prison: Emmy, your brother, your mom... and me," I found myself confessing my blossoming feelings for him without actually uttering the words.

Kelan's eyes swept back to his grandmother, who was seated with a deep furrow of worry etched across her face before turning back to me with a softened countenance. With a deliberate, almost hesitant motion, he finally loosened his grip on Andrea's neck, and she tumbled to the ground, her body collapsing like a discarded sack of potatoes. Kelan cast a look of revulsion downward at Andrea's fallen form.

"Be lucky that I am a changed man and that I got some people who I care about enough to not want to live the rest of my life in a jail cell. Had my girlfriend not been here, though, yo' folks would've been arranging your funeral tomorrow. You see, it's a lot of people that I don't play about, and that lady over there is at the top of that fuckin' list! I might didn't kill you, but don't think this shit is over. Once my brother gets word of this shit, it's lights out for yo' ass. He's a kill first and *maybe* ask questions later type of nigga. So, if I were you, when I'd leave this house and go live it up for the remaining time I have on this

Alecia J.

earth, although I don't think you'll be around long enough to do much of anything because he's gonna have you killed *soon* if he doesn't do it himself. Fair warning. Now get the fuck out of my granny's house and don't bring yo' ass back around this neighborhood, and don't be expecting a paycheck. If I see you around here, or anywhere, for that matter, I might be liable to finish what I started today," Kelan concluded.

Andrea scrambled to her feet. After grabbing her bag off the sofa, she hurried out of the house.

"Let's go, baby," Kelan said calmly as if he hadn't just almost killed someone in front of me.

What the fuck just happened? I wondered.

"Baby, you good?" Kelan asked me as he gently guided me back into the bathroom, closing the door behind us.

"Yeah, babe. I'm good. Are *you* good?"

"Yeah, I'm straight. I just came to check on you to make sure you're not in here looking at a nigga differently after what happened at my granny's crib or stressing out about this dinner. I know my mama can come off as a little intimidating sometimes."

I straightened myself up from leaning on the counter. "I'm not going to lie. You did scare me back there, maybe because it happened so unexpectedly. However, you did warn me a little about your past behavior, so I wasn't completely surprised. As for your mom, I don't know what kind of girls you're used to bringing around your mom or how she and Melani got along, but I'm not her or any of those other females, so no, she doesn't intimidate me. But I'm letting you know *right* now, if she steps out of line, I'ma check her," I stated firmly. "Fair warning, like you told Andrea. But trust me. I can handle her."

Kelan held his hands up in surrender.

"Aight, baby, but I never said you couldn't handle her. With the way you just handled me with your words, I'm sure you can."

"I can, baby," I assured him with confidence. "So, don't worry about me. I really came in here to clear my head for a minute. That shit with Andrea really did blow me, maybe because I knew her before going there today. Did you tell your mom?"

"Yeah, I told her, and she's fuckin' pissed. She wanna go kill her ass, something I should've done, and probably would've done if you wasn't trying to be—"

"Don't even say it. I wasn't trying to be Captain-Save-a-Hoe." I chuckled.

"Well, I'on know how you knew I was gon' say that, but yeah, that."

"What did you expect me to do, Kelan? I just couldn't sit there and do nothing. Then again, I probably *could* have, but Kelan, as a nurse, I have a deep sense of compassion, and witnessing someone in need would have contradicted everything I stand for and love about my profession. So, yes, I'm glad I was there, or you might have killed her."

"Possibly, but what was the deal between you and her? I sensed the animosity."

"Andrea and I have history that goes all the way back to my nursing school days. We were classmates and close friends. To give you the full story, I asked her to join me, my ex, and her then-boyfriend for a night out. We had a double date, to plainly put it. Months later, I found out she and my boyfriend had fucked, and she was the one who came on to him."

"Damn," Kelan said.

"Yeah. She's the reason I don't trust bitches now or call any of these hoes my friend; well, aside from Dior."

Alecia J.

"Did you tap that ass, baby?" He chuckled.

"*Did I?* That bitch is well aware of the damage these muthafuckas are capable of doing," I referred to my fists holding them up. "That's why that hoe looked like she had seen a ghost when she saw me."

"Let me find out that my baby is a lil' gangsta."

"I wouldn't say I'm a gangster. Like, I don't just go around starting fights or picking with folks, but I'll definitely take it there if need be."

"I feel you, baby. Oh, and don't think I overlooked when you said that you love a nigga. You love me, baby?" Kelan approached me, wearing a lopsided grin, then enfolded me in his arms.

"I'm *falling* for you, Kelan," I spoke those words, careful not to reveal the depth of my emotions.

Though I suspected I was in love with him, I hesitated to give voice to the extent of my love. I hesitated to reveal my feelings, especially since he hadn't expressed them first.

"I'll take that. Just know that the feelings are mutual, baby," he said, then planted a kiss on my lips.

Bang! Bang!

"Y'all, come on out of there! The food is ready!" His mom announced, banging on the door. "And you better not be in there fucking!"

"Aight, Ma!" Kelan said, drawing back from me. Once we figured she'd left, we burst into silent laughter. "Are you good now?"

"Yes, Kelan, I'm good."

"Good. Because I'ma have to go back on my word about not getting any of that pussy tonight. This shit has stressed me out, and you know that gold mine between your legs is my top stress reliever. So, I'ma need that when we leave here, baby. I'll make it up to your girl tomorrow."

One Drunk Night In Miami 2

"By doing what for her?"

"By leaving her alone for *one* day."

I giggled. "You never do right, but come on. I don't want your mama looking at me with her nose turned up the entire evening because she thinks I was disrespecting her house by having sex with you."

"Well, shid, it wouldn't be the first time."

"With *me,* it will be. Now, come on."

"So, my son tells me that you're a dietitian and an RN," Kelan's mom, Jewelynn, began her interrogation as she sat across from me at the table.

The five of us—me, Kelan, Emmy, his mom, and grandmother—devoured the meal she had prepared. Jewelynn had lovingly prepared a feast of smothered pork chops, white rice, creamy mac and cheese, tender cabbage, yams, and perfectly sweet cornbread. From the first bite, I fell in love with her cooking. She probably was a bitch, but she could definitely throw down in the kitchen.

"That's correct," I confirmed with pride.

"Impressive," she remarked in admiration. "Well, if you're a dietician, then I assume you know a lot about food, which means you can cook well... *our* kind of food, that is," she said, seemingly trying to be condescending.

That was the side of Kelan's mom that he had warned me about, the side that would make me tell her a thing or two. When she mentioned 'our kind of food,' I understood that she was referring to black folks' food."

I smoothly cleared my throat and delicately set my napkin down, preparing to gently burst her bubble. "Jewelynn, there's hardly a dish I haven't mastered," I confidently asserted. "And

Alecia J.

for the rare unknown, TikTok and Pinterest are my trusty guides. So, if Kelan wants *our* kind of food one night and prefers Chinese, Italian, Japanese, Mexican, or Jamaican," I playfully switched to a Jamaican accent, "the following five nights, I can effortlessly whip up one of those meals with ease," I added, punctuating my words with a wry smile.

Jewelynn's expression shifted to one of humiliation as I finished, but Kelan's face radiated pride as I stood my ground against his mother.

"Hmph. Well, it's good to know that he has a woman who can cook because that baby mama of his... whew!"

"Ma..." Kelan warned her since Emmy was present at the table. She was over Jewelynn's house already when we arrived.

"Oh, I forgot that my favorite girl was at the table," she quickly apologized, "but she has her headphones in, so she can't hear us. But back to what I was saying. With you being a *top chef*, I won't have to slave over the stove every other day to ensure that he and my grandbaby have a homecooked meal."

"Be for real, Ma. You don't have to cook for us, hell, for yourself as much as you do. You just choose to," Kelan called her out. "I know how to cook, remember?" he included.

"I know, son, but a man is supposed to provide, and you leave the cooking and cleaning to the woman. Well, most of it, anyway. At least that's how I was raised."

Well, times have changed, ma'am. I felt the urge to chime in and share my thoughts, but I decided to keep them to myself.

"Besides, no woman should be going around proudly bragging that she can't cook."

"I have to agree with you on that," I couldn't help but express my opinion on that statement.

"Since you're a dietitian, do you eat healthy all the time?" Jewelynn probed further.

"*Majority* of the time, not all the time. I have my cheat days, like today. So, yes, I still eat soul food and other sweets that I crave. I just don't overdo it. Sometimes, it's not what you eat. It's all about the portion size," I explained.

Over the course of dinner, we managed to sway from talking about my personal life to talking about theirs. We laughed about funny stories from when Kelan and Kane were younger, which allowed me to see her humorous side.

"Jenesis, do you mind if I have a little private chat with you for a second?" she asked after we finished cleaning the kitchen area—which she was totally against me helping, but I insisted.

I looked over at Kelan, and he seemed initially against it, but then he nodded in an approving way.

"Um, sure," I begrudgingly agreed.

"Ma, make it quick. Emmy has school tomorrow, so we need to be getting home."

"What I have to say will only take a few minutes. I just wanna have a quick woman-to-woman talk. Come," she gestured toward the outside patio.

Once we were outside, I was about to take a seat, but she said, "There's no need for that. Like I told my son, this will be brief."

"Okay."

"I want you to know that I like you, and coming from me, that's a compliment when it pertains to my boys. Now, I'm not the type of mom who tells them who they can and can't date, but I do voice my opinion if I feel a certain woman isn't for them... Melani, to be exact. I'm not sure if you've met her, but that girl is a piece of work."

"So, I've heard *and* seen."

"Mm-hmm. Well, I said that to say, be careful. Women like Melani are unpredictable. Like I've told Kelan, I had to deal with her kind plenty of times back in the day. Now, I don't want you to come into this relationship with my son, having to fight for your love for him every day, but I want you to be prepared for what may come."

"I'm prepared, maybe not mentally or emotionally, but physically." I held up my fists.

She smirked. "And sometimes, that's all you need to let a bitch know that you mean business. But thank you for coming today. I enjoyed talking with you and getting to know about you. I really like you for my son, and I think the two of you can make it. Again, I'm not the mom who interferes in her children's personal affairs, but... I will if need be. I really just want the best for both of my sons. That's all."

"Understandable. Kelan deserves the best, and I am the best, so..."

"You know what... I think I'm going to end up liking you... a *lot*." She smiled.

"Well, I would surely hope that we can get along because I don't plan on breaking up with your son or seeing us breaking up *anytime* soon."

"With that mindset, yeah, you're definitely the one for my son. But let's get back inside so y'all can get my grandbaby home. I'll get your number from Kelan, and maybe we can have us a girl's day soon. Just me, you, and Emmy."

I chuckled at the fact that she included Emmy, but Kelan did say that she was her pride and joy, and usually, when you saw one, you'd see the other. That showed in how much time Emmy spent at her house and their close bond.

"Sounds good."

"Oh, and who is this girl Dior that I've been hearing has been spending time with Kane? Kelan said she's your friend."

"She is. She's my best friend," I verified.

"So, what exactly do the two of them have going on? Because I'm obviously the last one to know about everything. Does she know that Kane has a girlfriend?"

"Their situation is just as, if not more complicated than me and Kelan's, when he was with Melani. So, yes, she's aware that he has a girlfriend, just like Kane is aware that he has a girlfriend."

I started to develop a genuine fondness for Kelan's mom, and I was determined to maintain a positive relationship with her. However, I wasn't about to let her come for my friend like she was a hoe while she acted like her son was *blameless* in their situation.

"Hmph. Okay," she replied, leading us back inside the house.

To my surprise, the dinner turned out better than I expected. Like Kelan, I preferred to avoid confrontation, but I refused to tolerate disrespectful behavior. While I cherished my relationship with Kelan, I wasn't willing to endure a situation involving a mama's boy or a man whose mom controlled his life; it was a major relationship red flag for me. I was hoping that all it took was that one time standing up to Jewelynn, and she would know her place and *keep* it moving forward. Maybe I should've done the same to Melani when she called herself popping off at the mouth at the gym that day. I wasn't sure how Melani would act in the future, especially after Kelan spoke to her. However, as I had told Jewelynn, I was prepared. If Melani approached me about Kelan, their daughter, or our relationship, I hoped she would come correct and with respect. I was a lady, but I could be a bitch if necessary.

13. Melani

"I bet you'll think twice before you try to go after any nigga I've been with! Stanky pussy bitch!" I yelled at Tiece after I had just finished whooping her ass.

My chest heaved as I stood there, watching her sprawled on the ground, whimpering in pain, with a torn shirt and bloodied nose and mouth. No, Kelan and I weren't together, but it was the principle of the matter, and what she had done cut deep. Adding to that, she was my best friend. Tiece knew things about us that I hadn't shared with anyone else; hell, we even discussed positions that me and Kelan tried. The whole time I was trying to put her on game on how to spice up her sex life, she was probably envisioning doing the shit with my man.

"Melani!" I heard my name called from behind me.

As I turned around, I couldn't help but roll my eyes when I saw that Miracle had pulled up on the scene.

"What the hell is she doing here? Hell, how did she even know I was here," I murmured frustratedly under my breath.

Despite Miracle's caring and concerned nature as a friend, there were times when I wished she would just mind her own business. Without missing a beat, Miracle rushed out of the car and over to me.

"Melani, what are you doing?! Do you know you're all over Facebook right now?! This lil' fight of yours has gone viral! That's how I knew where you were, if you're wondering! Look, you need to come home now before the police show up!" She chastised me like she was my mama.

Despite wrecking Miracle's car, which fortunately the damages were fixable, she still allowed me to stay at her house. I just knew when she found out about her car, she'd put me out the same day. However, after I explained the complicated situation regarding my supposed brother, Sincere, for whom I lacked concrete proof, she showed some sympathy toward me.

"I guess I can leave now. My work here is done," I said, the faintest hint of a smile playing on my lips as I cast a final glance at Tiece's bruised body.

As we made our way to the car, I made it clear to Miracle that I wasn't in the mood for conversation. Despite her probable urge to reprimand me, she honored my request, and we drove home in silence. During the ride, I used the time to comb through the Facebook profiles of Jenesis, Kelan, and Sincere, something I'd been doing for days.

Kelan's timeline was filled with gym-related posts, giving no indication of his personal life. Jenesis, on the other hand, occasionally shared quotes but hadn't posted a single photo in a few weeks, let alone one featuring her and Kelan, leaving my suspicions about their relationship intact. Meanwhile, I couldn't shake off the shock of Sincere's unannounced release from jail and his subsequent lack of contact with me. Perhaps my dad's message had been premature, as surely Sincere would have reached out if he had truly been released. At least, that's what I hoped for.

Upon arriving at Miracle's house, I hastily made my way

Alecia J.

into the room I occupied and turned on the shower, eager to wash away the day's events and the mounting stress I had been dealing with. But just as I was about to step into the bathroom, my brief moment of respite was interrupted by the ringing of my phone. To my surprise, it was Kelan calling, the last person I expected to hear from. Without hesitation, I answered the call before he could hang up.

"Kelan!" I exclaimed, feeling a mix of emotions.

"Why are you doing all that yelling?"

"I'm... I'm sorry. I just wasn't expecting you to call," I said in a calmer tone.

"I'm sure you *were*... eventually, anyway. I just called to let you know that I'm throwing Emmy a birthday party next weekend at the house at around four o'clock, and I'm extending an invite to you," he said, his tone making me feel like a distant acquaintance rather than Emmy's mom.

Shit! I cursed internally at the realization that I had forgotten about my own child's birthday.

"You didn't forget that her birthday is next week, did you?" Kelan asked as if he could perceive my thoughts.

"No, Kelan, I didn't," I replied unconvincingly, hoping he wouldn't pick up on my fib.

"Yeah. Well, I ordered some T-shirts, and I got you one. You ain't got to pitch in on shit; I just need you to show up. Well, I don't *need* you to, but it would look good if you'd be there for your daughter's special day."

"I'll be there, Kelan. How... how is she?"

"Do you mean the daughter that you've seemingly forgotten you had? Oh, she's fine, but you should know that. She has been asking about her mama, though."

A smile crept onto my face. "She... she has?"

"Stop asking dumb shit, Melani. Despite you being a shitty ass mama to her, she somehow never picked up on that shit.

Hence, she still loves your ass," Kelan said, making me feel worse than I already did.

"If she's been asking about me, then why haven't you let her call me?"

"Melani, ask yourself why *you* haven't called to check on your daughter. *That's* the real question. But I'm not about to do this shit with you today. I just called to give you the details about the party. It's up to you if you come or not, but whether you do or don't, a party will still be had."

"Okay, but wait!" I hurried, sensing that he was about to end the call.

"What is it, Melani?" he retorted in an irritated tone.

"What about us, Kelan?"

"Shid, what about us, Melani?"

"You gave up on us so easily. It's like you didn't even try to fight for our relationship."

"It's because I spent over a year fighting for your love and for you to get your life together. Eventually, I felt like I was in the ring fighting alone, and as you know, that gets old real quick. If you really wanted our relationship to work or cared about your daughter as much as you claim, I shouldn't have had to remind you to be a good mama or girlfriend. That should've come naturally to you, but it's obvious you don't have what it takes to be either. I gotta go. I'll see you next Saturday, or maybe not."

The next sound I heard was the dial tone. Kelan had hung up on me. So, of course, I called back *three* times, but he didn't answer. However, he did send me a text.

Kelan: Stop blowing up my damn phone, Melani. I'm around my girl now, and I don't need her thinking no shit. I would hate to block your ass, but I will.

As if I were caught in a loop of familiar yet unsettling sensations, I flung my phone across the room in a sudden, unex-

Alecia J.

plainable impulse. The device smashed against the wall, shattering into pieces once again.

"What the fuck, Melani?!" I cursed myself. That was the second phone I had broken in less than a month for the same reason.

Before I could gather my thoughts, Miracle abruptly entered the room.

"Melani, what's going on?" she inquired, her eyes scanning the scene of my latest misfortune.

"I dropped my phone, and it broke. It's fine, though. I'll get another one in the morning," I replied, masking the truth with a seemingly convincing lie.

"Ah, dang. Well, okay," she relented, retreating from the room as quickly as she had entered. I was relieved that she didn't press me further, perhaps swayed by the fact that her bare floors provided a harsh landing for any tumbling device, making my story seem plausible. I appreciated her understanding, as I wasn't in the mood to face any admonishments at that moment.

Instead of taking a shower as I had planned, I went into the bathroom and turned the water off. I then went back to the bedroom to get ready for bed. Before getting into bed, I took a few Percocet pills from my purse. I knew the right amount to take without harming myself, but I also knew how much to take to get the high I craved every day. I had experimented with cocaine, which gave me a better high than pills, but the side effects were too much for me. I didn't want to *look* like a drug addict, so I stopped using cocaine and stuck to pills. I went to the kitchen to make a sandwich, and shortly after, I felt the effects of the drugs. I curled up in bed with my pillows and shed tears. Eventually, I fell asleep and slept through all my troubles, only to wake up and start the cycle all over again.

One Drunk Night In Miami 2

"What are you doing here, Melani?" I found myself standing outside Sincere's mom's house, questioning my presence there.

That morning, thoughts of my father and Sincere consumed my every waking moment, particularly the nagging suspicion that Sincere could be my brother. The need to uncover the truth was insatiable. Reluctant to involve Miracle, who had been driving me around since I wrecked her car, I took an Uber to get there.

Before Sincere was sent to prison, he and Jenesis lived together in a house, the location of which was always a mystery to me. However, Sincere once pointed out his mom's house while we were traveling, and the location of that house remained in my memory. Since he and Jenesis were no longer together, and assuming Sincere had been released from prison, it was logical to think he might have returned to his mama's house. Even if he wasn't living there, I hope she'd be generous enough to provide me with the information on where I could find him.

"Well, I can't stay out here all day. Eventually, someone is going to notice me out here, so here goes."

Mustering up my courage, I moseyed up to the front door. Once near, I pressed the doorbell and shuffled my weight from one foot to the other as I waited for an answer. After a moment, the door creaked open and revealed a woman who I immediately recognized as Sincere's mom.

"Hello. How may I help you?" she inquired, her voice warm and inviting.

Although Sincere had met my dad, I'd never met any of his relatives. However, I'd seen pictures of his mom, so I knew exactly who she was.

Alecia J.

"Hello. I was wondering if Sincere is home. He lives here, right?" I played it off.

"It depends on who's asking?" she cautiously scrutinized me.

Well, obviously, me if I'm on your doorstep, asking about him. I refrained from voicing my thoughts, knowing that getting the truth wouldn't be easy.

"I'm Melani. I'm a friend of his, and I haven't seen him in a while. That's all." I plastered on a fake smile.

His mom looked at me with a piercing gaze. "Well, if you truly consider yourself a *friend* of his, you'd be aware that he's been incarcerated for the last five years."

Realizing I had been caught, I decided to come clean. "Okay, I'll be honest with you. I used to be in a relationship with your son, and I heard that he was no longer in jail. I *really* need to speak with him on a serious matter!"

"I don't know where you're getting your information, but my son is serving a long sentence in jail, so he won't be getting out *anytime* soon."

What the hell is going on? Is she lying, or did my dad lie?

"Okay. Well, maybe you can help me!" I pleaded, my voice quivering with desperation, as she stood at the doorway, poised to shut it.

With an irritated look, she turned to face me and said, "Little girl—"

"I have reason to believe that he may be my brother!" I blurted, cutting her sentence short.

She arched her brow. "What did you just say?"

"Before your son went to prison, I was seeing him on the side. That's the truth. Fast forward five years later, I find out from my dad that Sincere is, or could be, my brother."

As I spoke, she stepped out onto the porch, her face growing increasingly grim.

"You're... you're Dean's daughter, huh?"

My throat felt dry as I answered, "I... I am."

Her eyes stretched, and she stepped backward into the house.

"I need you to leave... now!"

Confusion and desperation welled up inside me. "But... but..."

"I can't help you!" Her tone was firm.

"But you can!" I insisted, my voice rising in frustration. "I just want the truth, that's all," I entreated, softening my tone, hoping to sway her to reconsider.

"If you got that information from the horse's mouth himself, then that's all the proof you need!"

After uttering those final words, she closed the door with a sense of finality. Her parting statement provided me with the answer I had been seeking, although it was not the one I'd hoped for. Resigned to the situation, I began the journey back home on foot. While I could have easily called Miracle for a ride, I welcomed the opportunity to mull over the perplexing questions that coursed through my mind.

Why did my dad say that Sincere was out of jail when he may not have been? Or maybe his mama lied to me?

The uncertainty gnawed at me, demanding an explanation.

14. Dior

I stood in front of my floor-length mirror in my bedroom, taking a moment to appreciate my reflection. Beast at the gym; beauty in the mirror. I couldn't believe I was funny, fine, and thick. Like, Lord, where does it end?"

That day was a big day—I had my interview coming up, and I wanted to make a good impression. I wanted to strike the right balance between professional and fashionable, so I opted for a simple yet stylish look. I wore a crisp white collared shirt paired with khaki dress pants. To complete my outfit, I added some gold accessories—earrings, a bracelet, a watch, and a necklace. Just as I was lost in my thoughts, my phone rang, interrupting my moment of self-admiration.

When I saw my brother's name on the screen, I couldn't contain my excitement and quickly answered the call, yelling, "Hey, bro!"

"What's good, sis? What you got going today?"

"Actually, I'm headed to that interview I was telling you about the other day."

"Oh, yeah. Well, shid, it looks like we're both on a getting-money mission today."

"What do you mean?" I asked with my phone wedged between my shoulder and ear while slipping on my heels.

"I got an interview today, too," he announced.

"Really? Where?"

"At Jenesis's job. They called me yesterday."

"Oh, yeah! That's what's up, bro, but you know you got this!"

"'Preciate that, sis, and the same for you. But what you doing after that?"

"I have to work at the bar tonight, so I'll probably just come back home and rest up. I would've been doing something with Jenesis with it being her birthday, but she's out of town with her boyfriend."

"*Boyfriend?* Since when did she get a boyfriend? Without my permission?" he joked.

"A lot has happened since you've been MIA, bro."

"Shid, I see. Well, when you talk to her, tell her I said Happy Birthday. I gotta get my wife something."

"Lance, bye! My friend is *happily* taken and will probably soon be happily *married*."

"Damn. I guess I gotta finally move on, huh?"

"Yeah, you do," I chuckled at his silliness. "Well, bro, I hate to cut our call short, but I gotta get out of here."

"Same here. But look, if I don't talk back to you today, stop by my crib tomorrow. I need to holla at you about something."

"Is everything good?" I was headed out the door, but I stopped in my steps.

"Oh, yeah, everything good, sis. Just some I wanna show you."

After getting him out of the sticky situation, I was both

Alecia J.

curious and a bit cautious about what he had to show me. With limited time to spare, I replied with a simple, "Okay."

After saying our goodbyes, our call came to an end.

Although I kind of figured I had the job secured, the prospect of stepping into the unknown both excited and daunted me. As if it were a confirmation from God, "You Will Win" by Jekalyn Carr filled the car as I turned on the ignition. The passenger's door wasn't closed, so I peeked my head outside the car, peered up toward the sky, and said, "Thank you, God. I know this opportunity is because of you."

I was sitting in my car outside the DHS office, waiting to go in for my interview. Since I had a little time to spare before the interview start time, I decided to call Jenesis and wish her a happy birthday.

She didn't pick up my call after I called her twice. She was with Kelan, though, so I didn't worry too much. Whatever Jenesis was doing, I knew she'd call back when she got the chance.

With some extra time on my hands, I decided to get on Facebook and give Jenesis a birthday shoutout. After selecting some of our most memorable and my favorite recent photos together, I compiled them into a post and shared it. I kept the shoutout brief, as most people were already aware of our strong bond. As I continued browsing through Facebook, I stumbled upon a fight. My natural curiosity led me to click on it. However, what truly caught me off guard was the identity of the two individuals involved in the dispute.

"Why the hell are they fighting, and how do they even know each other?" I quizzed as I watched Melani whoop the dog shit out of Tiece. "I gotta admit, that short, pretty bitch can fight," I acknowledged her impressive fighting skills. Be that as it may, she was no match for Jenesis, and I said Jenesis instead of me in case she ever tried to come for my girl. She wouldn't stand a chance against me either.

After finding some amusement in watching the scene a little while longer, I eventually closed the app and prepared to make my way inside. However, right when I was about to exit the car, two individuals caught my attention.

"What the hell are they doing coming out of there? Together anyway?" I muttered, surprised to see Tavaris and his baby mama leaving the building.

I wondered if they were there to apply for assistance programs like food stamps.

Nah, both of them wouldn't be needed for that, I thought.

Then, upon closer observation, I noticed that although they exited the building at the same time, they went their separate ways, each getting into their own cars, which led me to consider other possibilities.

Perhaps they're no longer together, and she's seeking child support, or maybe he had doubts about the child and requested a DNA test.

Despite those curious thoughts, I quickly refocused on my own purpose for being there. I made sure to wait until they both had driven away from the parking lot before stepping out of my car. While I couldn't have cared less about being seen by his baby mama, I knew that if Tavaris had spotted me, he would have approached me, disregarding my previous requests for him to leave me alone—although he might have assumed those requests only applied to interactions at the bar.

Once I entered the building, I immediately sensed all eyes focused on me. It was never my intention to come off as conceited, but I've always been confident in my appearance, and I could tell I was turning heads. After providing my name

Alecia J.

to the receptionist, I turned around to search for an available seat. The room was packed, and for a moment, I worried about finding a place to sit. However, I considered myself lucky as I eventually spotted an open seat in the middle of the room.

I turned to the girl who sat next to me and initiated the conversation with a casual, "Hey."

The girl greeted me back with a friendly "Hey, girl," as if we were already acquainted. She then expressed her dislike for interviews, stating, "Ugh, I hate interviews! Just hire me; I stand on business!"

"Okay!" I couldn't help but chuckle in agreement. I noticed she was dressed similarly to me, so I asked, "What position are you interviewing for? If you don't mind me asking."

"I don't. But for one of the caseworker positions. You know they have multiple spots available."

"So, I've heard. I'm here for the same reason," I informed her.

I thought our conversation would've lasted a little longer, but a staff member called her to the back.

"Well, good luck to you, girl! What's your name, by the way?" she randomly asked me.

Why is that important? I wondered.

"Dior," I finally answered, a little skeptical.

Taking note of my name, she introduced herself as India, adding optimistically, "If all goes well, maybe we'll be seeing each other around here."

Smiling, I confirmed, "I'm sure we will," almost as if I were speaking our potential future job encounters into existence. "Good luck to you as well."

After her departure, I surveyed the waiting area to see if I saw any familiar faces. I didn't need anyone in there thinking I was doing that bad. While I would never knock a woman who had children and could benefit from the services, I didn't have kids, so my situation would've looked like I was there out of desperation.

As I continued my search, a woman displaying 'ghetto-fabulous' features entered the building. It was clear from her body type that she had undergone a Brazilian Butt Lift (BBL). I was intrigued by her presence and found myself discreetly listening in on her conversation with the receptionist.

"How may I help you?" the receptionist asked her.

I didn't even have to try to eavesdrop, as her response was loud and unrefined, just as I had predicted.

"Yeah, where y'all food stamp applications?" she asked, her voice carrying through the room as she energetically chewed her gum and tapped her long, elaborate, colorful, manicured nails on the counter.

Coming to the DHS office to apply for food stamps and rocking a BBL is insane, but like the influencer Shemar said, "But hey, I'ma stay out it."

I put my focus on my phone, went to my messages, and noticed that I had a text from Kane that I somehow missed. Thankfully, it had only been ten minutes since he sent it because I didn't feel like hearing his mouth.

Kane: *Good morning, Pretty Eyes. Good luck on your interview, but you already know you got this, baby.*

I smiled at his thoughtfulness. Kane was certainly a handful, but beneath that tough exterior, he truly had a heart of gold.

Me: *Thank you, Kane.* I felt like fucking with him that morning, so I also sent: *Whenever I see you again, you gotta eat what my mama made.*

Since my mom owned a bakery, he probably thought I was talking about a dessert or something.

Kane: *What she made, baby?*

Alecia J.

Me: *Me.* I sent followed by a smiley face and some laughing emojis.

I noticed that he was responding, but I didn't get the chance to see his reply right then because my name was called. After I put my phone away, I rose from my seat and prepared for the best.

Here we go.

"Friend, I'm so proud of you! Yasssssssssssssss!" Jenesis congratulated me on my new job. She had called me back during my interview, so I returned her call as I was leaving the building.

"Thank you, my love! Your girl is about to be sitting behind a desk instead of standing up at a bar!"

"Yaaaaaaaassss! So, when do you plan on leaving the club?"

"I'm not sure yet. Then again, I work nights there, so *maybe* I'll still work there on the weekends to keep a little extra money in my pockets. I'll just have to see how my schedule goes with this job. I'ma talk to my boss tonight and let him know I can't work during the week anymore."

"Do you think he'll work around your schedule with your new job?"

"Girl, yes! He loves me, and I'm his best bartender, so he'll do anything to keep me there. But if, for whatever reason, he won't allow me to cut my hours, I'll just quit. But I'll cross that bridge when I talk to him tonight. Enough about me; it's your birthday, and I'm raining on your parade!"

"Dior, birthdays come around every year. Job opportunities don't. Just know when I get back, we're going to celebrate my birthday *and* your new job."

"Another trip, maybe?" I hinted.

"Another trip?" she retorted, giggling.

"Well, you're all up in Jamaica, living it up, and I'm here, so yeah, I'm a lil' jealous, and us taking a trip together would make me feel better."

Jenesis chuckled.

"As if you weren't just up in Bora Bora 'living it up' with Kane not too long ago."

"Yes, girl, I was living the good life," I reminisced.

"Speaking of him, what's going on with you two?" Jenesis pried.

"Same ol' same ol'."

"Have you two made plans to see each other again?"

"*Plans?*" I scoffed. "Girl, Kane isn't the romantic type who plans a nice dinner that you can prepare for. He's more of a *spur-of-the-moment* type of nigga. The kind who kidnaps bitches when he wants to see them."

Jenesis went into a fit of laughter.

"Girl, what am I going to do with you?!"

"I'm serious, Jenesis."

"But you're still stuck on that?" Jenesis asked once she got her laughing under control.

"Hell yeah! And I'ma remain stuck on it! The type of shit that happened to me isn't heard about in real life. That's the kind of shit you read about in one of these urban fiction books! Hell, I might need to reach out to an author because I got a story to tell."

"Don't we all, girl," Jenesis agreed.

"I am curious to know when he's going to make his way back here, though. One thing I can't deny is that nigga got some good ass dick. I don't think no nigga can stir my macaroni like him... and then he adds a lot of milk to it."

"TMI, bitch!"

Alecia J.

"They're facts, though, boo. But anyway, did you see the post I made for your birthday?"

"I did, and I responded. Thank you so much, friend."

"Always, boo. Are you going to post pics of your birthday trip?" I was curious to know.

"Girl, Kelan asked the same, but both of you know how I feel about us being in the spotlight right now. I think I'm going to post pictures, but the ones with him in it, I'm going to block his face."

I playfully rolled my eyes because I didn't think people still did that.

"Really, Jenesis?"

"Yes. Either that, or I won't include him at all. You know I don't like drama, so if I have to cover his face for the remainder of the year, that's what I'ma do."

"Well, no judgment zone over here, boo. Do what you feel is best for you and your peace of mind. As long as *I* and y'all know the real, that's all that matters. Oh, I meant to tell you. So how 'bout Tiece and Kelan's baby mama are all over Facebook fighting, friend!"

"What? Why? According to Kelan, they're best friends."

"Best friends?" That was news to me.

"Yeah. I thought you would've known that since you told me you knew her."

"Yeah, I know of her, like from high school and around the way, but not as in. I keep up with her on Facebook or anything. But if they're supposed to be best friends, I can guarantee you that after that fight, they aren't anymore."

"Why were they fighting? Or do you know?"

"Are you ready for this? So, according to the people in the comments and from what I heard Melani saying to Tiece while she was beating her ass, Tiece told Melani's other friend, Miracle, the one who is also in the workout class, that she wanted

Kelan, and had been wanting him the whole time Melani and Kelan were together."

"Damn. That's probably why she joined the class," Jenesis said.

"Right."

"When Kelan told me that she was Melani's friend, I told him that something didn't sit right with her joining the class when she did. I would ask why she's fighting over a nigga who's no longer hers, but I guess it's the principle of the matter."

"Right. Fighting over a man in general is crazy, but if he's mine, a hoe better tie her shoes tight! Baby, *John Wick* killed over four hundred muthafuckas over a *dog,* and you think I'ma play about my nigga? Tuh!"

Jenesis laughed. "Okay! Well, boo, you know I love our talks, but my man is waiting for me. We're about to go water horseback riding."

"Ooouuuu! That sounds fun! I'm serious about us going on a trip together, excluding the brothers. I told you that I'm trying to be outside as much as possible before I find my husband!"

"Girl, you already found yo' husband. You know Kane ain't about to let you marry another nigga."

"You know what... I'll talk to you later. While you're down there, make sure you do anything that I *would* do."

"I surely will."

"I love you, friend. Enjoy your birthday, although I'm sure Kelan is going to make sure you do! And make sure you send me *lots* of pics, especially the ones you plan to post, so I can approve them. We gotta post the ones that's gon' ruffle a few feathers."

Jenesis chuckled. "I will, boo. I love you, too. Bye."

I tossed my phone over in the passenger seat and prepared to head home to rest up for work later that night.

Alecia J.

"Damn, you're beautiful as fuck, Ma. I know a nigga got that ass stamped," some guy sitting at the bar complimented me.

I was about to tell him that I was single as fuck until I remembered Kane's words.

"You're right, I do have a man, and he's knocking the Mario coins out of this pussy every time he gets the chance!"

"Damn! Well, I can't compete with that, but you can't blame me for trying." As he stood, he placed a generous fifty-dollar tip on the counter. "You be good, Ma."

"You be good, too, and thank you for the tip," I mumbled, watching him walk away as I tucked the money into my pocket.

The guy wasn't bad looking at all. Under different circumstances, I might have considered giving him my number. However, my fear of Kane sending someone to catch me off guard and test my loyalty kept me from taking that risk. Suddenly, Kourtney rushed up behind me with excitement in her voice.

"Girl, do you see that fine man down there?!"

I rolled my eyes before turning to see who she was talking about, although I wasn't particularly interested.

"*That's t*he man you're talking about," I gestured in the direction that Tavaris was sitting in.

I hadn't even noticed him there, maybe because he wasn't sitting in my section. I assumed, since he was sitting on that end, that he took heed to my words about leaving me alone.

"Yeah. He's fine, isn't he?"

"He's alright," I answered, not wanting to give him *that* much credit for his good looks.

"You know him, right?"

I twisted my face up in confusion at how she had knowledge of that. "Nah, I don't," I lied. "But why do you figure that?"

"Oh. Well, he came in here the other day, looking for you while you were on vacation."

"Looking for me?"

"Yeah. He asked if you were working that night, so I just figured you two knew each other."

"Kourtney, you know, there's such a thing as people knowing you but you not knowing shit about them, right?"

"Well, dang! I was just telling you! Why do you always have to be so aggressive all the time? Ugh!" she grumbled.

"And why do you always have to come and tell me something about these men in here? I ain't studding them, and they ain't studding *you*!" I responded in a harsh and unkind tone, although it was the truth.

"That's cold, Dior," she bitterly said.

"Those are *facts*, though, Kourtney. At least I'm keeping it real with you."

"Yeah, aight," was her response, then she walked off with a visible attitude.

I glanced over at Tavaris, feeling an intense glare forming on my face. What happened next caught me completely off guard. Kourtney leaned in close across the counter and said something to him. Initially, I suspected that she might have been being a hoe by shooting her shot, but when she withdrew, Tavaris subtly shifted his glance in my direction.

What the fuck? Did that bitch mention me to him? I wondered. I was about to go and check both of their asses, but the sound of Jace's voice halted my steps.

"Long time no see, beautiful."

Shit!

I slowly pivoted on my heels, my expression tightening into a forced smile.

Alecia J.

"Jace! How are you?"

"Well, I'm good now that I see you're good. I was worried about you."

"No need to worry about me. I'm doing just fine."

"Clearly. So, what's going on with your phone? Have you blocked me?" he chuckled.

"No. It's actually broken," I fabricated.

"Well, do you need the money to get another one?" He pulled out his wallet, prepared to give me some money.

"Oh, no. I've just been lazy. I plan to get another one tomorrow." I had my phone in my back pocket, and I was hoping and praying that it wouldn't ring while he was in my presence.

"Well, where have you been? Since I couldn't get in touch with you, I've been coming up here to see you."

"I've been out of town," I vaguely replied.

"Another business trip?"

"No. This one was more... personal and unexpected."

"Mm-hmm," he responded in a dubious tone.

"Well, I don't want to take up too much of your time. I just wanted to see you. How about we have lunch tomorrow? My treat, of course," he offered.

"How about not, Jace?" I finally voiced.

The look on his face was of extreme shock.

"Excuse me?" His response was a mixture of surprise and hurt.

"Jace, look, you're a nice guy, and I'm sure any woman—*any woman other than me, I wanted to say*—would be ecstatic to go out with a man like you. What we had was fun—*until it wasn't, I wanted to add*—but we're just two different people who want different things out of life. I like you, Jace, I really do, but this isn't and will never work between us," I explained.

"Well... I wasn't expecting to hear that tonight or ever, if I'm being honest. I have to know, what brought on these feelings? I thought we had something good going on."

"Jace, again, you're a nice guy, but you're still technically married. The other reason I really can't just put into words. It's just for the best." Quickly remembering that Kane could've had someone watching me, I included, "It's for the best. So if you value your life, you'll just leave me alone... for good."

"Whoa! Okay! Forgive me, but I'm just puzzled by all of this."

"Jace, I wish I could help you better solve the puzzle, but I am at work, and I have people waiting to be served. Look at it this way. It was good while it lasted."

That was even a lie. That nigga had the worst stroking game ever.

Without waiting for a response from him, I went to assist one of the awaiting customers.

An hour later, I was in serious need of a break, so I took one, only to step outside and be approached by none other than Myeisha.

"Happy National Pet Day to the bitch who stays barking but never bites. How may I help you, Myeisha?"

"Cute, Dior. Very cute." Myeisha simpered.

"*That*, I am. Now tell me something I don't know, girl," I quipped with a tilt of my head.

"Oh, shit. This is the Dior who Tavaris left to be with you?" her friend, who resembled a stud, said. So, for all I knew, maybe that was her 'lover' friend.

The look on Myeisha's face was one of embarrassment. It was like she wanted to whoop ol' girl's ass for saying that shit.

"For the record, *I* do the leaving when it comes to these niggas, which included Tavaris. So, no, sweetie, nobody *ever*

Alecia J.

took a nigga from me. Yo' friend probably got fucked, though. Actually, Tavaris is inside if you need that confirmation."

"Myeisha, I thought you said—"

"Brit, chill! Damn!" Myeisha obviously tried to stop her from telling me what I had already suspected she told her, which were *lies*.

"Yeah, aight." The Brit chick dropped it and then stepped over to the side to give us some privacy.

"What do you want, Myeisha? I'm not in the mood for your bullshit tonight, but if it's an ass-whooping you're looking for, I'll always make time to give one of those out."

"Chill. I come in peace... well, concerning you, that is. I'm just here to deliver a message from my brother for you to pass on to your friend Jenesis."

"Which is?" I snarled and stepped toward her, prepared to knock her the fuck out if she said anything out of the way.

She took a step back.

"He just wants her to know that... he'll be paying her a visit *soon*."

Before I could control my hand, it wrapped her around her thick ass neck, and I harshly pushed her up against the brick building. I didn't give a fuck who was watching or if I lost my job that night. I would never let anyone disrespect my friend or play in my face concerning her.

"What you thought because all these muthafuckas are out here that I wouldn't say or do shit to you?! Bitch, I'm really 'bout that life if you haven't noticed yet! Do I need to give you a reminder of who the fuck I am and who the fuck I *don't* play about?! Asking me to relay threatening ass messages from your punk-ass brother to my friend is a death wish on both of y'all end! Bitch, I will kill you out here and sit in jail proudly for doing it!"

"What the fuck?!" I heard coming from Myeisha's friend,

who ultimately came to her rescue. "Aye, yo, chill, man!" the girl tried to persuade me. By then, a whole crowd had formed, taking in what was happening.

"Nah, I love seeing this bitch at my mercy. This kind of shit makes my pussy wet." A wicked smile crept on my face as I watched that bitch take what I hoped would've been her last breaths.

"Damn," came from her friend. She wasn't seemingly concerned about Myeisha's well-being. Instead, she was more focused on lusting over me.

At that moment, my boss called out, "Dior!" and his voice jolted me into releasing my grip on her neck. Myeisha was left desperately gasping for breath, her hand clutching at her throat and her eyes fixed on me with a malicious expression.

"Find you somebody to play with, bitch, because I ain't the one, the two, and damn sure not the muthafuckin' three, but you knew that! But if you didn't, you should now!"

"Man, let's go! You out here starting shit and can't even fight!" her friend said, shaking her head.

"Fuck you, Brit, and find you a way home! Maybe you can ask that bitch to take you since you were so busy fantasizing over her than trying to help me!"

I started to go after Myeisha for that 'bitch' comment, but Thomas held me back, shaking his head, telling me no.

"This shit ain't over, bitch! I got yo' ass! Believe that!" Myeisha called herself threatening me as she got into her car.

I *really* wanted to get at her ass then, but Thomas gave me that same stern look.

"Alright, everybody, you can either go back inside or home," Thomas ordered. "There's nothing left to see out here, and I don't want to see any of what just happened roaming around social media! I meant it, or I'm coming after you!" he warned everybody.

Alecia J.

Thomas was a very popular and well-known guy throughout the city, and a lot of people respected him, so I assumed no one would go against his words.

"Dior, what are you doing, sweetheart? You're messing up already. We just had a talk about you getting a new office job, and you're out here doing things like this?" he scolded me, but not too harshly.

"Thomas, she was out here trying to play in my face about my friend, and you know I wasn't going for that, especially when she's not here to defend herself."

He chuckled. "You've always been a feisty one, just like that mama of yours." That was another reason Thomas liked me; he had a crush on my mama for *years*. "But listen, I'd never tell you to let someone *blatantly* disrespect you or someone you love, and you just let that shit ride; however, in certain situations and in certain areas," he gestured outside of the club, "we have to learn to control our emotions because you know that people live for drama these days and they love to see a muthafucka's downfall. Hopefully, no one will post what happened here tonight, and you'll be in the clear. Dior, I love you like you're my own daughter, so of course, I always want the best for you. You're on the right track, and I want you to stay on that. With that said, still beat a muthafucka's ass, but *only* when necessary."

"I'll *try* to keep what you said in mind. But no, seriously, thank you for the talk, Thomas."

"Anytime, baby girl. Now, let's go. You know those girls act like they can't run that bar without you."

"There's no acting; they can't."

We shared a chuckle and headed inside.

I took into account what Thomas said. At the same time, Jenesis was my friend, and there was nothing I did or said that night that she wouldn't have done if the roles had been

One Drunk Night In Miami 2

reversed. I wanted to call and tell her about the shit that Myeisha said, but since it was still her birthday, I didn't want to ruin any moment of her day or time while she was away, but best believe as soon as she let me know she made it home, I would waste no time telling her that shit.

15. Kane

"What's good, baby? How was your trip?" I asked Bonnie as she settled into the car after I picked her up from the airport.

"Hey, babe! It was great! I had a *really* good time!" she responded cheerfully, wearing her stylish shades and sporting a big ass smile.

The way she was cheesing had me looking at her sideways; it was the same smile she'd display after I just got done dicking her down, and we hadn't fucked in over a week, so surely she wasn't still smiling from our last time having sex. Not only that, but she also showed no type of affection: no hug or kiss, and that was something she'd usually give when we hadn't seen each other in a while.

"Is that so?"

Maintaining her smile, she replied with a soft "Mm-hmm," as if the happy expression was a permanent fixture on her face. "But what have you been up to since I've been gone?"

"You know, just slicing and dicing muthafuckas around

here. Nothing too major." I shrugged casually like killing muthafuckas was a normal thing—well, it was for me.

For the remainder of the ride home, we had small talk. However, Bonnie didn't talk much about her trip, which was unlike her. Usually, I could never get her to stop talking, especially when it came to her trips to Belize, so my curiosity about what she did while she was there was piqued.

When we parked at the house, Bonnie turned to me and announced, "Kane, I think I want to move back home to Belize."

That shit caught me completely off guard.

I leaned back in my seat, confused as hell. "Say what?"

Bonnie removed her shades, revealing the sincerity in her eyes.

"Damn, you're serious? Well, surely you know *I* can't move there with you with all the shit I have going on here. So, this must gon' be a solo thing?"

"It's just a thought for now, Kane."

"Just a thought or not, Bonnie, we've been together for seven years, and you're just now getting homesick?"

True, Dior was the one I really wanted to be with. Still, I was mad as hell hearing that shit. Maybe because the announcement was unexpected.

"No, I'm not homesick, but I'm glad you brought up how long we've been together. Kane, we've been together for seven years, and not *once* have you ever mentioned marriage to me. Has it ever crossed your mind? Hell, do you ever want to get married?"

"Is that what this is about?! Us not being married?! Shid, do you want to get married?"

"One day, Kane, yes, but no, this isn't solely about marriage!"

Alecia J.

"Then what is it?! You had some kind of *epiphany* while you were there or something?!"

"No. That neither," her voice lowered.

"Well, the only other thing I can think of is you being unhappy, and I really don't understand how you can be that, with me anyway, because I do *everything* to make sure that you're always good. So, what is it, Bonnie? Are you not happy here? With me?"

"Kane, it's..." Bonnie's words trailed off as if she wanted to say something but had to think it through first. After a brief pause, she continued. "Like I said, it's just a thought for now. But since we actually have the time to talk now, what is it that *you* wanted to discuss with me the other day when you brought me those oxtails home? We never got a chance to have that conversation."

Bonnie sat with her arms folded, wearing an expression that hinted at hidden knowledge, or perhaps she was just waiting for me to speak. I found myself unprepared to broach the topic of Dior with her, but I felt trapped, realizing that it was either confess then or never.

"Bonnie, I–" As I began to speak, my phone suddenly began to ring.

Saved by the phone, I thought. I couldn't help but feel relieved by the timely distraction. I was thankful for Marlo calling at that very moment as I really wasn't in the right frame of mind to have that conversation with Bonnie.

"Yo!'" I answered.

"Boss, you have some deliveries," he spoke in code.

"Good shit! I'm on the way!"

I heard Bonnie kiss her teeth.

After finishing the call with Marlo, I faced her.

"Bonnie, I..." I began, but she cut me off.

"Kane, what's understood doesn't have to be explained,

especially not to me." She opened the door and exited the car. "If you don't mind, could you just bring my luggage in when you return?"

"I'm your man, Bonnie. Of course, I don't. I got you. Do you want me to bring you back something to eat? Or is there anything else you need?"

"No, I'm good. I'm tired from the flight, so I'm about to shower and crash."

"Okay. I won't be gone too long. I love you."

"Love you too," she replied, then closed the door.

Something was off about Bonnie, even the way she said she loved me. I was used to the sweet and innocent Bonnie, but the Bonnie who returned from Belize seemed like a completely different person—more carefree and nonchalant. I couldn't shake the feeling that something was off.

Bonnie had a unique birthmark on her hip, and I was going to make it my business to check if it was still there when I got back home because there was no way the Bonnie I knew just flipped on me like that. I wasn't about to be on no Deborah Cox shit. Wasn't no stranger about to be living in my damn house.

When I made it back home later that night, Bonnie was knocked out. I wanted to check for that birthmark, but there was no need. Bonnie had a distinct snore, one that could separate her from anyone and one that I always joked with her about, so I knew that was indeed her. Throughout the night, I couldn't sleep. I couldn't get Bonnie's odd behavior off my mind, so the following morning, I called the only person I trusted to shed light on what might've been going on.

"What's up, bro?" Kelan said after answering the phone.

"Look, I know you're on your *honeymoon* and shit, but I need to rap with you about something real quick."

Kelan chuckled. "Nigga, ain't nobody on no damn honeymoon; I'm just in Jamaica celebrating my baby's birthday with

Alecia J.

her. Now, next year around this time, you might catch us in Paris somewhere, but what's up, nigga?"

"Bro, something is up with Bonnie."

"Something like what?"

"She came home yesterday from Belize, and she's been acting different."

"Different like what?"

"Shid, just different... behavior-wise. Like, we're barely communicating around this muthafucka today. Hell, I even tried to get some pussy, and she claimed her period just came on this morning!"

"Shid, maybe it did."

"I don't believe the shit! It just miraculously came on the day she came back from outta town, knowing I would want some? Hell nah!"

"Bro, I ain't no woman, but shid, that's mother nature for you, but if you really have your doubts and the shit is bothering you that much, just have her to show you. Hell, that's what I'd do."

"If we were talking about Dior, hell yeah, I'd tell her to do some shit like that, but this is Bonnie, nigga. She hasn't given me a reason not to trust her."

"Until *now*, obviously," Kelan added.

"You think she probably done met a nigga there?"

"What? Bonnie? Cheating? Hell nah! Look, bro, what you're experiencing or what you *think* might be going on is probably your own guilt or *karma*. I mean, you have been fucking Dior while you're still with Bonnie."

"Listen at the pot calling the kettle black, nigga."

"Yeah, but I let Melani's no good ass go."

"Shid, finally! But Bonnie ain't shit like Melani, so it ain't that easy as it should've been for yo' ass. If Melani was my girl, I would've been handed her ass back to the streets. But back to this situation with Bonnie. I don't know what the fuck to do."

"Well, you gotta figure out what you *wanna* do, bro. I mean, both of them are good ass women, but you know you can only have your cake and eat it too for so long."

"True," I sighed. "I'ma figure this shit out, bro. I 'preciate the talk and the advice. I'll let you get back to making me another niece or nephew."

"I don't know how you knew, bro."

"Nigga, because I know yo' horny ass." Right then, my dogs started barking.

"Nigga, where the hell you at?"

"I'm at home, nigga."

"Since when did you get some dogs, or is that shit on TV?"

"Since yesterday. They were Stephan's dogs; they're mine now."

"Bro, what?"

I briefly explained to Kelan about the shit Dior had told me about Stephan running his fuckin' mouth about the business, his moving situation, *and* how and why I had his dogs. I wasn't going to kill Stephan right then, and even when the day came, I still wouldn't; I was going to make sure his *dogs* did.

"Damn, bro," was all Kelan could say afterward. "Well, if shit goes how you plan, that's gon' be a ruthless ass death."

"And that's exactly what I want... ruthless and messy. But I ain't gon' hold you up, bro. I'll holla at you later. Bring me back a souvenir or some shit."

"Aight, nigga."

"One."

Talking about my brother, shid, I was in need of some pussy my damn self. Since Bonnie was being stingy with hers—or if she really was on period—I hit up Dior. I hoped that she wasn't on her period, too, but even if she was, that would've been cool. I just really wanted to see her ass.

"Yes, Kane," Dior answered the phone dryly.

"Aye, I told you to stop answering the phone like that."

"Like what, Kane?"

"Like you don't be wanting to talk to a nigga. But real quick, are you on your period?"

"What? No. Why?"

"The less questions, the better, baby. But I need you to rest up tonight because tomorrow, I'm fucking you for a few hours."

"Then again, I did think I saw a lil' blood down there earlier, and my stomach has been aching a lil in this last hour."

"Dior, cut the bullshit before I have that muthafucka cramping for hours while you're in labor with my son! I already told you this one time before. Now, I'ma be down there tomorrow to see you."

"Who's to say that I don't already have plans for tomorrow?"

"*Me.* The only plans you have usually involve work or something with Jenesis, and you're off tomorrow, and Jenesis is out of town on her honeymoon with my brother, so I know you're not doing anything with her."

"Honeymoon?! What do you mean, *honeymoon?!* Did they go down there and elope or something?!" Dior sounded livid.

"Nah. That's just some shit I've said to you and Kelan. They're on her birthday trip for real. But fuck all of that. Do you own a trench coat?"

"What? Yeah, I do. Why?"

"I told you to stop asking so many questions, Pretty Eyes. Leave some shit for your imagination. But that's how I know you're a freak; all freaks own a trench coat. I want you to wear that muthafucka tomorrow. I would tell you to come with nothing underneath, but I want to see yo' sexy ass in some lingerie. I'll text you the address and time tomorrow, baby. Don't be late."

After solidifying plans with Dior, I felt a little relief, but my unresolved issue with Bonnie continued to gnaw at my thoughts. Uncertain of the duration of my stay in LA, I recognized the imperative need to distance myself from Miami—if only for a few days—in order to gain mental clarity. I figured being away from Bonnie might provide the space I needed to contemplate our relationship. Although my feelings for Bonnie ran deep, if she was genuinely unhappy, I was prepared to let her go, a decision I knew I would eventually have to make regardless.

16. Dior

"Hey, bro. I'm sorry it took me a while to get over here. Work drained me last night, and I *had* to get some rest," I explained to Lance after I entered his home.

"You good, sis. I ain't been too long got back to the crib anyway. But yo' ass has been sleeping a lot more than you did before that shit happened with me. Let me find out you don' let some nigga knock you up."

"Boy, please!" I waved off that ridiculous thought.

"Yeah, I hear you. I won't keep you long, though. I want you to get back home so you can rest. You gon' need all the sleep you can get before my nephew or niece gets here," he joked.

I playfully hit his shoulder. "Bro, stop jinxing me like that! I swear if I end up pregnant in the near future, I'ma go into hiding, have the baby, then leave it on your doorstep in hopes that it turns out looking like you so you can think it's your baby by one of these women you've been messing with around here."

"If somebody else said some shit like that to me, I'd think they're playing, but yo' crazy ass would definitely do some shit like that."

"Bro, I've been known to do some wild ass shit, but I wouldn't do that. My child? Someone *I* birthed? Nah... especially with the mama and daddy we have. I wouldn't hear the end of that if the truth ever came out."

"You damn sure wouldn't, but come on." He led me to his bedroom.

As we entered one of the bedrooms, I couldn't help but exclaim, "Whoa!" I was completely taken aback by the sight that met my eyes.

The California king-size bed was adorned with money and duffle bags—that I suspected were filled with even more money—giving it an almost surreal appearance.

"Wh–what is all of this, Lance? Where did you get all this money? Oh, God, please don't tell me you're back into this shit! I swear—"

"Sis, calm down. This is drug money, but it's *old* drug money. I had this money before they took me away. I kind of figured they were on to me, so I had someone to hold it until I came back, well, *if* I returned. But... if I didn't, after a year of not hearing from me, or if I ended up dead, I told the person to give this money to you," he explained.

"So, wait." I chuckled bitterly, the sound lacking any humor. "Are you telling me that I went through six months of *all* that bullshit, and you *had* the money to pay him the whole time?!" I seethed with anger.

"I never considered the possibility that he would come after y'all because of *my* debt."

"That man is part of a fuckin' cartel, Lance! What did you really expect? With you being in the drug business, you

Alecia J.

should've done your background on them, and you would've known how they get down when it comes to their money! But you *turned* what you owed him into a debt, Lance. Judging by what I see here, it didn't have to be! You clearly have well over a million dollars on this bed alone, not to mention what's in those other bags! So, why didn't you just pay him?!"

"Greed," he shrugged and answered with startling honesty. "That kind of money is addictive as hell."

"Yeah, well, being *greedy* led to your family having to make sacrifices for you! Damnit, Lance!"

I loved my brother, and I knew he'd never *purposely* do anything to harm our family. At the same time, I couldn't help but express my frustration with him.

"I'm sorry you had to go through all that shit, sis. I swear I am," Lance expressed, reaching out to touch my shoulders as a gesture of sincerity. Taking a seat on the edge of the bed, he continued, "Like I said, I honestly didn't expect any of that shit to go down like that, and I damn sure didn't think he would've made you work for him."

I joined him on the bed. "Still, Lance, we talked while you were away. Surely, one of those times, you could've told me where the money was, and I would've gone and got it for you."

"And by doing that, you would've possibly had an innocent person or *people* killed. I never told you this. Well, I couldn't tell you while I was there, but our calls were recorded. So, whenever we talked, somebody was *always* listening in on the conversation. That was why sometimes when you'd ask me certain questions, I'd get silent, or I'd bring up another topic."

"Yeah, I kind of sensed that. That's why I stopped asking *certain* kinds of questions."

"Yeah. So, if I told you that kind of info over the phone, they would've located the spot where I had this stashed, and not only would they have taken all of my shit, but I'm almost certain they would've taken the nigga's shit who was holding this for me, too, and I didn't want that."

"Understandable." I nodded, feeling a little relieved with a clearer understanding.

Despite that, I couldn't help but still feel a bit of anger toward my brother for his selfish behavior, which had caused all the chaos. If only he had paid the man, we could have avoided all of that. So, he wasn't *completely* off the hook in my eyes.

"I appreciate all you did for me, sis. Real shit. So, as a token of my appreciation, I want to give you this," he said and handed me one of the duffle bags.

At first, I thought he was gifting me a new designer bag with a few goodies inside since it was a different brand and color from the others, but as I took it from him, I noticed its weight... it was heavy, really heavy. I cautiously unzipped the bag and was stunned to find it filled with stacks of one-hundred-dollar bills.

"Lance, what is this?"

"It's money, girl." He chuckled.

"I know that, but why are you giving me this much, or *any* for that matter?"

"Did you think I wasn't going to find out that you were the one keeping up on the bills around here and keeping my shit cleaned while I was gone?"

That was true... *somewhat*. I took on the responsibility of managing my brother's finances, with some support from our parents, who graciously covered all my expenses during the initial two months. Subsequently, I stepped up to the plate and volunteered to take over as I was earning more than enough income to manage both my own household expenses and his.

I always used to ask my brother why he wouldn't have a house built, considering his good credit and decent income. His current house was fine, but I knew he could afford something

Alecia J.

better. He'd always tell me he wasn't ready for that kind of responsibility. However, the night he came home, he admitted to me that he was actually renting that particular house to maintain a low profile for the time being. Again, I had no idea that he was bringing in nearly as much money as Emiliano revealed or what I saw on the bed that day.

For those last four months, I *faithfully* paid all his utility bills, phone bills, life insurance, and car insurance. I also made it a point to visit the rental office and discreetly pay his rent. They never questioned my relationship with him during the time I showed up there. For all they knew, I could've been his girlfriend. I was sure it didn't matter much to them, though; hell, they just wanted their money. Thankfully, both of Lance's cars were fully paid off, so we didn't have to worry about that bill. Additionally, I dedicated a day out of each month to thoroughly clean the interior of his house, but I hired someone to handle the outside maintenance.

I smiled. "Guilty. However, I can't take all the credit. Mama and daddy took care of everything for the first two months, so make sure you thank them. But remember, I told you that I didn't start getting paid from Emiliano until two months after I started working for him, and I was making *damn* good money."

"Hell, to be able to pay your bills and mine, you had to be."

"Yeah. That's one thing I will miss about that job... the money. But the money I spent on your bills isn't anything near this amount." As I peered into the bag, my brow furrowed in an attempt to estimate the amount of money it contained. "How much money is in here?"

"It's one million dollars," Lance responded casually.

My jaw dropped in disbelief. After recovering from my initial shock, I protested, "One million dollars! No, Lance! I can't accept this!" I attempted to return the bag to him, but he gently pushed it back toward me, insisting, "Nah, sis, you earned that."

"Regardless, Lance, this is money that I'm sure you worked hard to get. So, keep it. I didn't do what I did to get compensated a larger amount. I did it because I'm your sister, and I know you would've done it for me."

"In a heartbeat, sis. That's why I want you to take this money as a reminder that I *always* got you like you got me. So, *please,* take it."

I smiled, looking at the money. "Well... since you *insist.*"

"Yeah, I do. Go shopping. Travel the world. Start you a business. It's yours to do whatever you want. Just know, there's plenty more where that came from.

"Obviously," I said as I admired the bountiful display of money spread across the bed.

With a mischievous grin, I picked up one of the bands of money and began to playfully fan myself with it. "In the timeless words of Future, 'Drug money, it can buy you what you want,'" I half-rapped, half-giggled, to which Lance nodded in agreement.

Lost in a reverie of the endless possibilities that the money could bring, I was suddenly jolted back to reality by an incoming text message. It was from Kane, notifying me of his arrival in LA and providing an address where he wanted me to meet him. Urging me to hurry, he emphasized that I had thirty minutes to reach him.

"Thirty minutes!" I shouted, quickly forgetting that my brother was near me.

"You good, sis?"

"Yeah. Yeah. Look, bro, I appreciate this more than you will ever know, but I gotta go... like now!" I said, hoisting the duffle bag onto my shoulders.

"Aight, sis, but are you *sure* you're good?"

Alecia J.

"Yeah. It's Kane, and we have this little agreement. I'll explain it to you later! I love you! See you later!" Rushing through my words, I swiftly leaned in to give him a quick kiss on the cheek before darting out of the house and making a beeline for my waiting car.

As I hurriedly drove home, the daunting challenge of timing loomed over me. It was going to be a race against the clock. I estimated it would take me a solid ten minutes to reach my house. Once there, I still needed to factor in the time it would take to shower and get dressed. To add to the pressure, I hadn't even checked the distance or estimated travel time to the address he had given me. It was clear to me that Kane wasn't playing fair. It seemed as though he wanted to test my limits, but little did he know how fiercely competitive I could be.

"Ah, come on!" I yelled and grumbled while impatiently tapping my fingers on the steering wheel as I waited in the standstill traffic.

Time was ticking, and I had a mere five minutes to make it to Kane if I wanted to be on time. The other cars on the road seemed to conspire against me, adding to my frustration. Out of desperation, a thought crossed my mind of getting out of the car and walking to him. Maybe then Kane would've at least seen the effort I put in to make it to him on time, even if it meant arriving a few minutes late. As I impatiently waited for the traffic light to turn green, a text message buzzed through on my phone. It was from Kane.

Kane: *You have five minutes to get your ass here, or this just might be your fate come tomorrow.*

The chilling message was accompanied by a video of a

woman in a dimly lit alley, her distressed appearance matching the ominous warning from Kane.

This nigga is crazy, I thought. Crazy or not, I skillfully and hurriedly maneuvered through traffic to reach him on time. Upon arriving at the given address, I found myself parking in front of a lovely house nestled in the shadows of the night. The darkness obscured most of its features, but my focus was solely on reaching that doorstep within the dwindling minute I had left.

After hastily grabbing my purse and the overnight bag I packed, just in case, I rushed out of the car.

"Fuck!" I cursed when I realized that one of my heels had snapped while I was running. As soon as I reached the doorstep, I pounded on the door until it swung open, revealing Kane on the other side. He was dressed down, wearing a plain white T-shirt, a pair of basketball shorts, Nike socks, and slides.

"Right on time, Pretty Eyes. Right on time," he repeated with a grin, clearly impressed by my punctuality.

"You know, with all the money you have, you could've just sent for me if you were so worried about me being on time!" I fussed as I brushed past him and into the house.

Kane shut the door behind us and chuckled, finding my sass amusing. "I could have, but I wanted to see how much effort you'd put into getting here. I also knew that you'd make it here on time. I was tracking you," he revealed as he held up his phone to show me. I had no clue how he had gained access to track my phone, but then again, that was Kane. "So, you didn't have to rush to get here as long as you got here.

"Really, Kane?!" I shrilled, my frustration bubbling to the surface. "So, what was the purpose of the text?!"

"To throw you off."

"Nigga, I broke my heel trying to make it to you on time! Do you know how much I paid for these shoes?!"

Alecia J.

"My bad, baby. I'll buy you another pair. Hell, ten if you want."

"And I expect them by the end of this week," I made my demanded firmly.

"You got it, baby. But fuck all of that," Kane said as he took a seat on the sofa with a relaxed smile. "Come here." He motioned with his finger.

As I walked over to him, I took in the details of the living room.

"Whose house is this, Kane?" I inquired as I stood in front of him with curiosity in my voice.

"It's mine. It's my home away from home, I guess you can say. So, you ain't got to worry about no shit popping off here. Now, let me see what you got on under there." He pointed at my trench coat.

With no hesitation, I removed it and revealed the sexy black lingerie underneath.

"Damn, Pretty Eyes. That shit is sexy as *fuck* on you. And that's my favorite color," Kane said while massaging his dick through his shorts. "I'm tired of looking. It's time for some action." Kane lifted his bottom, retrieved a condom from his pocket, then secured it on his dick. "Shid, you already know if I'm in this position how I want that pussy."

I removed the trench coat completely, straddled his lap, and then placed his tip inside me.

"Damn, Dior, I ain't even in the pussy good, and you 'bout to make a nigga nut." He groaned while gripping my ass cheeks.

I smirked. "Buckle up for a rollercoaster ride of feels that's guaranteed to have you smiling, moaning, tearing up, and definitely leave you wanting more when it's over," I whispered in his ear, doing a lil roleplay.

"As long as this ride don't kill me, I'ma enjoy this mutha-

One Drunk Night In Miami 2

fucka all night long. I might be a lil dizzy when it's over, but I'm sure it will be worth it," he said in humor.

"Mmm," I moaned softly as I eased down on his dick, taking all of him in.

"I think you should be fine. I got you strapped in *real* good." My pussy clenched and rippled around him, causing him to toss his head back in ecstasy.

It's safe to say a time was had that night.

17. Jenesis

"Good day!" I cheerfully waved to the security guards as I left for work.

Although I appreciated their presence, I couldn't help but feel that their protection was unnecessary, especially when Kelan was at the house. I felt like his protection was all I needed.

The journey to work was accompanied by a disturbing lack of clarity as I attempted to process the information Dior had shared with me the night before. Her account of the club incident involving herself, Myeisha, and the alleged message from Sincere tugged at my thoughts incessantly. I found myself wrestling with restless sleep, my mind consumed by the implications of Sincere's supposedly imminent release despite the myriad charges against him. It wasn't until I sought solace in prayer that a semblance of peace settled over me. While I suspected Myeisha of stirring up mess, I couldn't dismiss the possibility of Sincere's release, especially since she had mentioned it *twice* within those last two months. So, I remained vigilant and cautious of my surroundings.

One Drunk Night In Miami 2

Knock! Knock!

"Come in," I said to the person on the other side of my office door.

Moments later, Lance entered my office.

"Lance! Oh, my God! Hey!" I rose from my chair and greeted him with a heartfelt hug.

"What's good, Jenesis? I'm glad to see that you missed a nigga. You're smelling good," he complimented while slyly flirting.

I playfully tapped his chest as I drew back from him. "Same ol' Lance, huh?"

"Ain't nothing changed. You know you gon' always be my wife in my mind."

I shook my head and then retook my seat.

"I know. So, what's going on? I see that you're rocking the company shirt, so that means you got the job. Okay! When did you start?"

"Yesterday. I came by to thank you for putting in a good word for me, but they said you were still on vacation."

"I was. I actually came back the day before yesterday. I needed a day to recuperate before coming back here."

"I feel you. I see you're doing your thing these days, Ms. *Boss Lady*. Your office gives off *excellence* with all these degrees," he complimented while observing my office.

I smiled. "Well, thank you."

"Nah, for real, this shit is impressive as fuck. But I heard you done went and got married."

"*Married?*" I chuckled. "Did Dior tell you that?"

"Nah, I'm just fuckin' with you. She did say you have a man now, though."

Alecia J.

"I do," I verified proudly while blushing, thinking about my baby.

"He's a lucky ass man; that's for damn sure. The way you're smiling, it won't be long before he's your husband. All I ask is for y'all to put me in the wedding somewhere. I ain't gotta be the best man. I'll settle for a groomsman."

I laughed. "I'm sure when or *if* the time comes, we'll be able to fit you in *somewhere*."

Another swift knock echoed through the room, and without waiting for a response, Isla peeked her head inside.

"Oh, I didn't know you had company! I'll come back!" she said.

"Nah, you can come on in," Lance assured her. "I'm not staying long."

After seeking my confirmation, Isla entered the room.

"Isla, this is my friend Dior's brother, Lance, whom I mentioned to you before. He's the new maintenance supervisor. Lance, this is my *beautiful* coworker, Isla," I introduced the two. I added the 'beautiful' part to ensure that he took notice of her.

Isla shot me a brief look when she noticed what I was doing. I raised my eyebrows, silently telling her to pay attention to him.

Isla turned to Lance and said, "So, you're Lance."

"I am," he confirmed, and I noticed that he hadn't stopped smiling or taken his eyes off Isla since she entered the room.

"Well, it's nice to meet you, Lance. I've heard a *few* things about you."

"I hope those *few* things you heard were good," Lance replied, his eyes locked onto hers.

"They were," she affirmed, never breaking eye contact.

Observing the interaction between the two, it was clear that they were undeniably interested in each other.

"Well, I'll let you ladies be," Lance said, breaking their intense eye contact. "Jenesis, I appreciate you for looking out for me. I owe you."

"Lance, if you don't take your butt out of here, talking about you owe me. We're practically family. *Anything* for the family. You know that. Just don't have me out here looking bad and regretting getting you on."

"Never that, Jenesis. I'ma make you proud." Lance chuckled, infusing his words with a hint of jest, yet his determination was evident as he shifted his attention to Isla.

"It was nice meeting you, Isla. I'm sure I'll be seeing you around."

"Ye–Yeah, I'm sure we will. It was nice meeting you, too."

As he turned to leave, Lance paused and directed his gaze back at Isla. "Oh, and Isla, you have a beautiful name. It suits that beautiful face of yours." He winked playfully before adding, "You ladies have a fantastic day," and sauntered off, leaving Isla in a pleasantly flustered state.

"Well, it looks like somebody has eyes for *somebody*." I grinned.

"Oh, stop." Isla dismissed my comment and took a seat opposite me. "He was just complimenting me. What's the harm in that?"

"Well, I suppose there's no harm unless *you* also find him attractive," I teased.

"Girl, he is!" she leaned across my desk and exclaimed.

I chuckled. "He's single too," I hinted.

Isla leaned off the desk, and her demeanor quickly changed. "Well, too bad I'm not."

"How are things going at home with you two?" I was curious to know.

"Same ol', same ol, girl."

"Have you heard back from the 'supposed' baby mama?"

Alecia J.

"Surprisingly, no. I think it's because he's been spending more time with her lately."

"Wait, what? What do you mean by that?"

"He's been staying out a lot of nights, and even when he's home, it feels like we're complete strangers. He doesn't show me any affection. He doesn't even look at me the same way. It's like I'm invisible to him. Like damn, have I lost my attractiveness?" Her voice was filled with so much pain.

When Isla mentioned that, I immediately got up from my seat, sensing that she was on the verge of a breakdown.

"Oh, no, ma'am! We're not even going there!" I knelt next to her and said, "Isla, you pick your head up right now! Do not give that man the satisfaction of seeing you weak!"

When Isla lifted her head, her face was covered in tears.

"Jenesis, my marriage was supposed to last."

"Or maybe it wasn't, Isla. Perhaps Leo is just supposed to be a temporary presence in your life. Isla, listen, sometimes things fall apart so that better things can fall into place. I've never told you about my ex, and one day, I'll go into depth with you about how we ended, but the day we broke up was one of the most painful days in my life. I didn't think I would ever be able to move on or even love again, but look at me now. I have a *great* man." I paused just to reflect on how good of a man Kelan was. "Yes. Whew, girl, I have a great man," I had to say it again. "And one day you will too. It may not be next year... It might take five more years like it did for me."

"Five years?!" Isla shrilled in appalment.

"Girl, yes. It took me five years to find my prince charming."

"So, you hadn't been with a man *sexually* in five years?"

"Nope."

"Oh, girl! Yes, we do have to talk soon! What about this

weekend? Drinks? Or is this your weekend to work at your other job?"

"It *would've* been my weekend to work there, but I took off. My boyfriend is throwing his daughter a birthday party, and I'm helping him with a few things. Raincheck?"

"Of course, girl! But honey, I can't wait to meet this man who has been making you so happy!"

Although Isla and I had become very close, confiding in each other about many things, she was unaware that Kelan and I were actually a couple or even that we had an intimate relationship before becoming official. She did become suspicious once when Kelan visited me at work, but I quickly came up with a cover story, telling her that he was just dropping off food for me since Dior couldn't make it. That still had her side-eyeing me, but she never brought the topic back up.

I had actually planned to reveal our secret during the *spur-of-the-moment* cookout I wanted to host, but the cookout never took place, so Isla remained in the dark about our relationship. I did plan to tell her soon, though.

"You will... soon. Isla, just know, he's *everything* I've ever wanted in a man."

"You must've said Ciara's prayer," Isla joked.

"Girl, no! If anything, he said *Russell's* prayer because I'm the prize!" I chuckled. "I'm just kidding; he is too. Maybe I was just specific about what I wanted in a man like Ciara. When I talked to God, I told him what I desired in a *husband,* and it's like as I was talking to him, he was creating that man just for me, and once he was ready, he sent him my way."

"Well, after my divorce, I'll be doing the same. But girl, we still gotta talk because I want to hear all about your trip to Jamaica! I see you have even gotten you a lil tan. Okay!"

"Girl, yes!"

"Well, I want all the *deets*!"

Alecia J.

"I got you, girl."

"All jokes aside, Jenesis, thank you for being the beacon of support that I need going through this *pre-divorce*. I really don't think I would've been as level-headed as I am now without your encouraging words. I'm so grateful for our friendship. And yes, we are considered friends! As a matter of fact, when I take all of this nigga's money, me, you, *and* your friend Dior are going on a girl's trip. I think it's time that me and her get acquainted."

"Listen, I'm all for that, but fair warning, Dior doesn't like to share. *However,* she's not opposed to meeting new people. Actually, she mentioned me and her going on a trip soon, so maybe you won't have to wait until next year to meet her; just join us on this one. Although I don't know where we're going yet."

"I'm down, honey! Just let me know the dates so I can take off, and I'm there!"

"Okay. I'ma run it by Dior first, though, since it was *her* idea to take a trip. You know how some people get when you invite others to something without their knowledge, especially when *they* planned it."

"I do, so I understand."

"But again, I'm sure she won't have a problem."

"Okay. Well, just let me know. Let me get to my office so I can look like I'm doing some work." She chuckled. "I'll see you later, my girl."

"Alrighty."

After Isla left, I took the time to leisurely go through the wonderful photos and videos that Kelan and I had captured during our time in Jamaica. These precious memories had already been shown to Dior for her 'approval,' but I had held off on sharing them on social media.

"Fuck it!" I mumbled as I gathered the chosen videos and

pictures that I wanted to put out there, and then I crafted a catchy headline and hit the "post" button.

While I decided against displaying Kelan's face or disclosing his name in the post, I was confident that when I revisited my page later that day, I would still have received numerous likes and comments because people are naturally curious. Nevertheless, it had been a long time leading up to me being in a relationship, so my followers had best be prepared to be sick of me because I was going to constantly be shouting, "My man! My man! My man!"

"Bonnie, I have to hand it to you, girl, you absolutely nailed it with this party. I don't think I'd have the skills or patience to pull something like this off. It's absolutely beautiful," I praised as I gazed around Kelan's backyard, taking in every meticulous detail of the Gracie's Corner-themed decorations. From the cake to the delectable desserts, the tablecloths, and the colorful balloons, everything exuded Bonnie's creativity and hard work.

Although Bonnie and I were introduced at Kane's birthday party, we hadn't really had the chance to engage in a *meaningful* conversation. Since Kelan was engrossed in a chat with his brother, cousins, and homies from the neighborhood, who had brought their children, and Emmy had found her own playmates—which gave me a much-needed break—I decided to take a seat. That's when Bonnie joined me. However, I felt like I wouldn't get to enjoy too much time to relax, as Emmy would surely come back to whisk me away for more exploring.

"Thank you so much, girl. I have to admit it takes a lot of hard work and dedication to bring my client's ideas to life. But I can't take all the credit; there are a few people who help me along the way. Yes, the ideas are mine, but it's a team effort."

Alecia J.

I nodded.

I tried to keep our conversations brief and straight to the point. I didn't want to do *too* much smiling in her face, knowing that her man was fucking my best friend. The last thing I wanted to be labeled as was 'fake' to anyone.

"So, I hear that you and Kelan are a *couple* now," Bonnie sparked a new conversation.

"Who told you that?" I chuckled, trying to deflect her question.

"No worries; y'all secret is safe with me. But I kind of overheard Kane talking to Kelan about it. I take it that's why you're here," she said with a mischievous sparkle in her eyes as she sipped her tea.

"Okay, yes, we're a couple, and you're right, not many people know. Well, probably everyone here knows now. Leave it up to Kelan."

Despite my desire to keep our relationship on the low, most of the people at the party were close to Kelan, so whenever he introduced me to someone, he addressed me as his girlfriend.

Bonnie chuckled. "How is Dior?"

My brows rose in confusion. I didn't expect Bonnie to ask about Dior.

"Um, she's good."

"I see how hesitant you were to answer that, but I'm also sure, with you two being best friends, that she told you about our time in Miami."

"Oh, yeah. I heard it was a *memorable* night."

"Yes, it was," she wistfully said as she recalled their time together that night.

"I'll definitely let her know you asked about her."

Bonnie nodded, and then her attention shifted to her phone. Her face lit up with a radiant smile as she tapped away at her screen. I stole a quick glance at Kane, only to notice that he hadn't reached for his phone, so I suspected little miss Bonnie was keeping a few secrets of her own. Just as I thought that was confirmation enough, her phone chimed, and that same beaming smile returned. However, it quickly vanished as she abruptly stowed away her phone upon Jewelynn's approach, who was clearly irritated and vocal about something.

"I hate when those bad ass muthafuckas come to events! They act like they don't have any home training! Then again, they don't!" Jewelynn complained.

I chuckled. "What's going on, Jewelynn?"

"My sister done brought her bad ass grandbabies here, and they're tearing up every damn thing! I know they're not used to shit like this because their sorry-ass grandma or mama won't do shit for them, but you're not about to come here taking over *my* grandbaby's party and ruin it! Oh, no! That's *not* gonna happen!"

Jewelynn was visibly agitated. If there was one person I knew she didn't tolerate any nonsense about, it was Emmy. "Got my favorite girl over there crying and shit!"

When Jewelynn said that, I reflexively turned my gaze across the yard in search of Emmy. I soon spotted her with Kelan, who was tenderly holding her, and it appeared that he was wiping her tear-streaked face.

"Oh no, I need to go over there."

"I'm coming too," Jewelynn declared. "Bonnie, you might want to go check on your inflatables. I think those little rascals have put holes all in them."

"Oh, goodness!" Bonnie exclaimed, then hurried off in that direction.

"I'm surprised to see you and her talking." Jewelynn made conversation as we headed over to Kelan and Emmy.

"I mean, I wouldn't say we're friends, but why wouldn't I talk to her? I have nothing against her."

Alecia J.

"I'm just saying most friends follow in their friends' footsteps when it comes to disliking someone."

"Keyword... *most*, not all, but who said *Dior* disliked Bonnie?"

Woman if you only knew. Those two have been up close and very personal with each other, I wanted to say.

"Besides, I'm not that kind of person who hates someone who hasn't done anything to me, and Bonnie hasn't given me a reason not to like her."

"Well, it's obvious your friend and my son have *something* going on that no one cares to share with me. I want to meet her... soon. Please relay the message."

"Will do."

Right then, we approached Kelan and Emmy, and it pained me to see her with tears in her eyes.

"Aww. What's wrong, Emmy?" I said, trying to sound comforting.

"They were mean to me," she sniffled in a sweet, innocent voice.

"Who was mean to Gigi's favorite girl? Tell Gigi who did it," Jewelynn cooed in a gentle tone, brushing the hair out of Emmy's face.

Emmy pointed over to where some boys were playfully splashing water on each other.

"I'll be right back, baby." Jewelynn excused herself. However, before she left, I overheard her mutter, "Don't nobody mess with my grandbaby."

I let out a small chuckle and turned to Kelan. "Your mom is so protective of her."

"Baby, you have no idea. She's going to be the same when it comes to our baby." He winked. I couldn't help but smile and shake my head.

"You haven't heard from..." I hesitated to say Melani's name and gestured toward Emmy, but I was sure Kelan understood who I was referring to.

"Nah, I haven't. I called and texted her, but I'm not going out of my way to make sure she's at her daughter's party." Kelan's demeanor quickly changed.

"Okay," I simply replied. "So, when are you going to cut her cake?"

Kelan looked at Emmy with a loving gaze and asked, "Are you ready to cut your cake, princess?"

"Yes, Daddy!" she squealed with joy, her eyes lighting up at the prospect of her special moment.

I was overwhelmed by the heartwarming bond between them. In that moment, I couldn't help but envision a future where Kelan and I would have a family of our own.

Suddenly, an undeniable urge to use the restroom hit me.

"Babe, can you hold off on cutting her cake? I really want to be there, but I have to pee," I said to Kelan in a hushed tone, hoping he would understand my predicament.

"Yeah, baby. Go handle your business."

"I'll be right back!"

"Jen! Come back!" Emmy started to cry.

I quickly turned around. "I'll be right back, pretty girl! Don't cry! I just need to tinkle, okay?"

"Okay." Kelan chuckled. "And you say I got her spoiled?"

"Hush! I'll be right back."

Finally reaching the nearest bathroom, I quickly stepped inside and closed the door behind me, seeking some much-needed privacy. As I sat down on the toilet, I swiftly dialed Dior's number, hoping for a moment of peace to talk.

"Hey, boo!" Dior's cheerful voice filled my ear.

"Hey, love! I just called to tell you that your *soon-to-be mother-in-law* requests your presence soon," I playfully teased.

"Mother-in-law?"

Alecia J.

"Kane's mom, girl. She said she wants to meet you."

"For what?" I had already informed Dior that Kane's mom knew about her and Kane, so she was aware of that.

"She wants to know what you and Kane *really* have going on since none of us will tell her."

"Well, no need for her to depend on me being the snitch. The only way she'll *formally* meet me is *if* me and her son somehow *miraculously* end up together. I'm not every getting introduced to a man's family as a *side chick*. The fuck?"

I burst into laughter.

"I'm serious, Jenesis. I know if it was to ever come to light about us that people would look at me as one. Not that I give a fuck what muthafuckas think because I know the real, and so do you and Kelan. Y'all know I was *forced* into this situationship with that nigga!"

"Anyway, girl, I really called to tell you about Bonnie. Well, first of all she asked about you, and not in a negative way. She pretty much just told me to tell you hey."

"Oh, well in that case, tell pretty Bonnie that I said hellooooooooo! I just hope she's not trying to *nice* her way back between my legs 'cause honey what happened between me, her, and Kane was definitely a one-time only thing."

"Nah, I think it was genuine. Besides, I think somebody else has her attention."

"Somebody like who?"

"Another man!"

"What?! Get out of here, girl!"

"I *may* be wrong, but I kind of caught her looking at her phone and smiling a lot, while texting at that. Again, I could be wrong, so I don't want to accuse her of cheating."

"You may be wrong about that one, friend. She just seems so quiet and to herself."

"Dior, as we both know *or* should by now anyway, looks can be deceiving.."

"Those are facts! When I first laid eyes on Kane, all I saw was a fine ass, dark-skinned ass nigga, who looked like he had some dope ass dick. That last part turned out to be true; hell, better than I imagined, but never in a million years did I think some pussy, even mine, would have a nigga this fuckin' crazy."

"You've had a stalker before, *remember?*" I chuckled, reminding her.

"Yeah, but he was nowhere on Kane's level of craziness."

"Well, I don't think it's your pussy that made him crazy, maybe *crazier,* but according to Kelan, Kane already had a few loose screws before y'all met."

"Well, all those bitches must be gone now!"

I laughed.

"You're still at the party, though?" she asked.

"Girl, yes."

"Well, since you called me while you're still there, I assume Emmy's sorry ass mama hasn't shown up yet or didn't show up at all."

"Girl, no! That shit is pathetic. Like how dare you not show up for your own daughter's party, especially one that you didn't have to put a dime on?"

"Hell, a penny. Bitches like that make my ass itch!"

"Right."

"Jen!" I heard from the other side of the door coming from Emmy's light toddler voice.

"Oh, shit! That's Emmy! I gotta go! I'll call you when I leave here!"

"Okay, boo, and make sure you do!"

After washing my hands, I opened the door and saw Kane and Emmy walking up the hallway.

"There you are!" Emmy said.

Alecia J.

"Aww. Did I take too long?"

She nodded, causing me to chuckle.

"I'm sorry, but I'm all done now." I turned to Kane. "Let me guess, she asked you to bring her in here?"

"Nah, Kelan was about to bring her, but I was coming in here for something, so I just told him I would."

I nodded, and then a thought hit me. "Um, Kane, where is my birthday money? Yeah, Kelan told me that you were going to break me off with something when you saw me?"

"I got you, sis," he said as he went into his pocket and pulled out a wad of money. "As you can see, money ain't never a problem. Now, choose your birthday gift," he said, extending the money to me.

"Choose my birthday gift?" I asked, puzzled.

"Take whatever you want. If you just want a couple hundred, take that. If you want it all, take all that shit!"

"Uncle Kane, you said a bad word!" Emmy said, prompting laughter from all of us.

"You can't say shit around that girl... literally not *shit*," Kane whispered to me.

I chuckled.

"Uncle Kane, it's my birthday! Can I have some money, too?" Emmy asked with a pout.

"Uncle Kane just bought you all those toys out there."

"You know what..." I took all the money from Kane's hand. "I'll just take it all, and Emmy and I will split it. Thank you, Uncle Kane," I joked, and Emmy joined in, saying the same.

"Yes, thank you, Uncle Kane." That little girl was too smart for her own good.

"Yeah, y'all welcome."

"Alright you two, let's head outside so we can watch the birthday girl cut her cake!" I playfully tickled Emmy.

The three of us exited the house together, but as I caught

sight of the scene before me, I wished I'd stayed inside a little longer. Melani had arrived, and it seemed like she and Kelan were in a heated argument.

Oh, shit!

"Mommy!" Emmy's voice rang out, grabbing the attention of both Kelan and Melani.

The glare that Melani shot my way made it clear that my presence was unwelcome, and I braced myself for the inevitable confrontation that lay ahead.

18. Kelan

"Hey, Kelan! Where's my baby?" Melani walked up to me and asked.

I had to do a double take at her, not at what she said but at the way she came there dressed. She had on some skimpy black shorts that barely covered her ass cheeks and her pussy print was visible. And let's not talk about her top, if one could call it that. It was more like a sequined bralette, something similar to what a stripper would be seen wearing.

"You can't be fuckin' serious right now, Melani!" I gritted, trying to keep my voice low to not draw too much attention.

"What are you talking about, Kelan?" she giggled, playing dumb.

"Melani, not only are you well over an hour and thirty minutes late for your daughter's party, but you come up in here dressed like this!"

"Well, I'm late because I don't have a car anymore, Kelan, so I had to find a way here! Or did you forget that when you broke up with me, you made sure that I left the same way I came... with nothing?!"

One Drunk Night In Miami 2

I stepped to her. "Yeah, I did, but my *mama* made sure you were straight," I asserted, my words hitting her with surprise. Melani's eyes widened at my knowledge as unease flickered across her facial features.

"Okay, but what's wrong with what I have on, though?" Melani deflected as if she was blind and someone else had dressed her.

"You really want to do this right now, Melani?"

"Kelan, I just want to see my daughter."

"Well, you won't see her looking like that!" my voice rose a little.

Before the tension could escalate further, Mama stepped in with her commanding presence and addressed Melani directly. "What in the world is going on over here? And, Melani, what the hell are you wearing? You do realize that this is your daughter's *birthday* party?" Mama's disapproval of her attire was clear in her tone.

"Hello to you too, *Jewelynn*, and yes, I'm *well* aware that this is my daughter's party. Hence, the gifts I brought," Melani retorted, holding up the bags she was carrying as if to prove a point.

"Then why in the hell are you out here dressed like an attention-seeking *slut*?" Mama bluntly asked her, not one to mince words.

I interjected with a cautionary, "Ma..." in an attempt to defuse the growing conflict.

"Well, it's the truth, son. I'm just saying what you probably didn't tell her, and what someone with sense should've told her before coming here dressed like that. But hey... I'll stay out of it." Mama held her palms up and backed away.

The sound of "Mommy" carried through the yard as Emmy called out.

Alecia J.

"Fuck!" I mumbled under my breath as I caught sight of Emmy with Jenesis. I knew Melani was about to have a fit.

"Is that... is that the same bitch who was at your party, as in the same bitch who was at the gym that day—"

"You got your ass knocked out for talking crazy like you are now?" I finished. Melani looked at me like she couldn't believe I said that. "Yeah, that's the same girl. I'm surprised you even remember seeing her at the gym that day, seeing how high or drunk you were, but if you call my girl a bitch again, her friend won't be the one knocking yo' ass out. I'ma give her the honor of doing so."

Melani rolled her eyes, but her lips curved into a smile when Emmy rushed over and wrapped her tiny arms around her leg.

"Mommy!" Emmy's voice echoed with excitement.

"Hey there, Mommy's little sunshine!" Melani scooped Emmy up in her arms, peppering her face with sweet kisses.

Overcome with emotion, Melani couldn't hold back her tears.

"Why are you crying, Mommy?" Emmy asked, concerned.

"Because Mommy missed you so much!" Melani explained, holding Emmy close.

"I missed you too! Where have you been?" Emmy's innocent curiosity rang out, joined by the eager gazes of Mama, Jenesis, and even Kane, who had come over with Jenesis and Emmy.

"Mommy... Mommy has just been a little busy these last few weeks," was the bright answer she came up with.

"This girl!" Mama scoffed throwing her hands up then walked off, clearly having heard enough.

"Well, are you going to stay for my party? I am about to cut my cake!"

"You are?! Well Mommy can't miss that!"

One Drunk Night In Miami 2

You done missed damn near everything else, I wanted to say.

"I'll be back! I have to go tinkle! Jen, can you take me to tinkle?" When Emmy asked Jenesis that instead of Melani, Melani's face turned red.

"Mommy can take you to the bathroom, Emmy," Melani said with a slight quiver in her voice, making sure to emphasize her title in Emmy's life.

Emmy, sensing Melani's unease, insisted timidly, careful not to hurt Melani's feelings, "But I want Jen to take me."

"Emmy," Jenesis, known for avoiding unnecessary drama, started to intervene, likely about to tell Emmy to let Melani take her, so I stepped in.

"Baby, take Emmy to the bathroom. I need to talk to Melani," I told Jenesis. She nodded in understanding.

Emmy gently eased out of Melani's arms and went over to Jenesis, and together they left. As Melani watched them go, she glared at Jenesis.

Finally unable to contain her curiosity, she turned to me and asked, "So, you and her really are together, huh?"

With a calm assurance, I confirmed, my arms crossed in front of me, "Yeah, we are."

"Wow! So how long have the two of you been fucking? Obviously a while for Emmy to seem to be so close to her."

"How long we've been fucking is not important. Even if I answered that and told you the truth, with your mindset you probably wouldn't believe me because you'd swear they didn't create a good bond within that short amount of time, so it's pointless to tell you. But, again, that's irrelevant."

"All I know is you better not be letting Emmy call her Mama! That's my child, Kelan and I'm the only mama she'll ever have!"

"What the fuck, Melani?! Did you hear Emmy call her Mama? She *clearly* called Jenesis, by her fuckin' name; well,

Alecia J.

Jen, as she calls her! But hell, if she does decide to call her mama, the way you're moving, I'll definitely allow that shit! You haven't talked to your daughter in weeks, and then you show up to her party, looking like you came to the wrong fuckin' party! Melani, you might've pushed her out of your pussy, but that shit doesn't give you the title of being a mother. Just how they call these deadbeat ass daddies out here sperm donors, well I look at you as Emmy's egg donor," I told her straight up.

Tears filled Melani's eyes as she spoke. "That's not cool, Kelan."

"Nah, what's not cool is you thinking this shit you're doing is cool! It's like you don't realize you're the one pushing your daughter into another woman's arms, opening that window for her to look up to Jenesis as a mama! You're doing that shit; no one else! So, if you want to blame anyone for what's happening, look in the mirror, Melani! With that said, if you want to be a part of Emmy's party, you're changing fuckin' clothes, and that's that!" I stated with finality.

"What the hell am I supposed to put on, Kelan?!"

"Shid, you should've thought of an appropriate outfit before throwing that shit on. *Luckily,* I have you a shirt, *remember?* If you just pull those fucking shorts out your ass, maybe you'll look a little decent!"

Melani began to tug at her shorts.

"Man, come on."

She and I went inside the house, so I could grab the shirt for her.

"Here. Here, you can go to the bathroom and change," I said as I handed it to her."

"Thanks."

"Yeah. When you come outside, we'll cut Emmy's cake."

I turned to walk away, but she called out, "Wait!"

I stopped and faced her. "What is it, Melani?"

"Look, I'm not hating or anything, but I think you should be careful with that girl."

"What girl? Jenesis?"

"Yeah, her. I don't know if you know or not, but her ex-boyfriend is in prison or was. If he hasn't gotten out, he will soon, and from what I heard, he's coming for her. I also heard there's a possibility that the two of them could still be talking."

"Yeah, I know about her ex-boyfriend, but I'm curious who *you* got that information from."

"The streets talk." She shrugged.

"I know the streets talk, but why the hell were they so comfortable telling *you* that shit?"

"Because I asked, Kelan, okay?! I had a suspicion that she was the girl you were talking to, and I wanted to know about the lady who'd be around my daughter. So, yeah, I did some digging on her. Whether they're still communicating or not, I don't know how accurate that is because you know how messy some people can be."

"Yeah, I do," I said, referring to her and hoping she caught on to it.

"I'm just looking out for my daughter *and* your wellbeing."

"Yeah. Well, gone and get dressed, and I'll meet you outside."

With that, I walked away without giving her the opportunity to respond. I could've thanked Melani for the info she gave me, but I wasn't one hundred percent sure that what she said was even true. At the same time, I wasn't the type of nigga to brush off something major like that without looking into it myself. I realized the only way to uncover the truth was to confront Jenesis. Her reaction alone would give me my answer.

"Daddy, we've been looking for you," Emmy said as I stepped outside and came across her and Jenesis.

Alecia J.

"Yeah, where were you, *Daddy*?" Jenesis asked, her face initially lit up with a smile, but once she noticed that I didn't reciprocate that smile, hers faded, giving way to confusion.

"Emmy, Daddy was talking to your mama, but now he needs to talk to Jen for a second. Can you go over there with your Gigi until I get back?"

"Yes, Daddy, but when are we going to cut my cake?"

"As soon as Daddy gets back. I promise." I kneeled down and pinky-swore her, which brought a smile to her face. "Now, go over there with your Gigi."

"Yes, Daddy!" She ran along, and once I saw that she made it to Mama, I turned to Jenesis and instructed, "Come with me. I need to holla at you."

"Um, okay," she replied in a puzzled tone.

Once we were inside the house, I pulled her into the closest bathroom and locked the door behind us.

"What's going on, Kelan?" she asked.

"I'ma ask you something, and I need you to be straight up with me."

"Okay. What's up?"

"When is the last time you spoke to your ex?"

"My ex? As in Sincere?"

"Yeah, the nigga in prison."

"It's been five years. I told you that. I told you the last time I spoke to or even saw him was when he accused me of snitching on him, and I've had no communication with him since then. Why do you ask, though?"

"According to Melani, he's getting out soon, or maybe he's *already* out, and from what she's saying or heard, y'all two still been talking."

"You're not serious right now, are you? Of course you are! I don't know if I'm more stuck on the fact that you'll believe or even *come* to me with some bullshit that a bitch who clearly doesn't like me said, *or* that you'd think I'd go back to a nigga who's had me living in fear for my life these last five fuckin' years! Did you take any of that into consideration before approaching me with this bullshit?! I'm not talking about the part about him being released soon, but me talking to him still! Like, *really*, Kelan?! Is this what our relationship is going to consist of? You running back, telling me *lies* that your baby mama has told you! Because that's exactly what that shit is!"

Jenesis was livid. It was then that I knew I had fucked up.

"Baby, calm down. I was just telling you what she said."

"No, fuck that, Kelan! I'm not calming down, shit, because you weren't just asking; you practically accused me of the shit! If you were 'just telling me,' you would've said some shit like, "Baby, guess what Melani's stupid ass gon' say?" Or some shit like that! Instead, you came off strong, basically repeating what the bitch said as if you believed the shit, or even *somewhat* did!" Jenesis took a breather, then chuckled lightly and added, "You know what... maybe it's best that I—"

I inched closer to her, encircling my hand around her throat. "That you what?" I asked, my voice firm. "That you need to leave here, or leave *me*? Although my touch was gentle, most women would have shown a *bit* of fear in their eyes—but not Jenesis.

I chuckled and flicked my nose. "Jenesis, listen to me, baby, and listen to me *real* good. The only way you won't be my girlfriend is if you're my fiancée, and the only way you won't be my fiancée is if you're my wife, and the only way you won't be my wife is if I'm a widower, but even then, you'll still technically be my wife. As a man, *your* man, I apologize, baby. I'm sorry for even thinking you'd move like that, when that's not even your character. Now, we had a lil misunderstanding. I apologized, and we gon' move on from this shit 'cause ain't no breaking up... ever. So, if you were even *thinking* about leaving a nigga, you can dead that shit. But if that thought is still twirling inside that brilliant mind of yours, let me give you a reminder on what you'll be missing out on if you try to leave a nigga."

Without giving Jenesis time to react and with my hand still attached to her neck, I swiftly turned her around to face the mirror, dropped my jeans and boxers, lifted her dress, pulled her panties to the side, and then thrusted my dick inside her pussy.

"Oh, shit!" A soft whimper escaped her lips, not borne of pain, but rather of pleasure. At least, that's what her expression seemed to give off.

Her pussy was so wet and good that for a second, I wanted to take it easy on her ass, but I needed Jenesis to understand the severity of the situation. I wasn't letting her leave me, not that day, the next, or *ever*.

19. Melani

After I put on the shirt that Kelan had given me, I took a moment to adjust and make sure everything looked presentable for my daughter's party. Once satisfied, I stepped out of the bathroom. However, before heading back outside, I felt the urge to do a bit of exploration around the house. I began with Kelan's bedroom, the very room we once shared. My curiosity led me to wonder if anything had changed since my departure. Upon opening the door, I was met with a sight that was all too familiar. The room appeared exactly as it did when I left. The bed was impeccably made, the air was fresh, and there were no clothes thrown about. It was spotless, but then I remembered that Kelan had always been a bit of a neat freak. Satisfied with my findings, I gently closed the door to his room and made my way down the hall to Emmy's room. Her princess-themed space mirrored the cleanliness of Kelan's, save for the numerous toys scattered about.

As I prepared to leave the house, a distinct sound caught my attention. It was the sound of two people fucking. Intrigued, I followed the moaning until I traced it to one of the

Alecia J.

other bathrooms on the opposite side of the house. Sure enough, my suspicions were proven true. Two people were indeed fucking: Kelan and Jenesis. I'm talking about getting it in.

"You want another woman calling me daddy?" *Smack!* "You want another woman saying she love this dick?" *Smack!* "You want another bitch to wake up every morning, getting this good shit?" *Smack!*

After every question, Kelan delivered a slap to her ass. I was so taken aback by how loud they were, as if they were there alone and others couldn't walk in and hear them. Nonetheless, the entire time, I couldn't help but imagine what her backshots looked like.

"Jenesis, talk to me while I'm in my pussy, baby!" Kelan slapped her ass again.

"No, baby! I don't want any of that!" Jenesis finally managed to speak, after being speechless for some time.

I had a quick flashback of one of me and Kelan's sex sessions, and I felt myself getting horny just from the thought. I knew how good that nigga's dick was, so I knew the exact pleasure she was receiving, which angered me. If I didn't envy her before, I did after witnessing that. Approximately three minutes later, they were done. Kelan could usually go long rounds without getting tired, so I assumed he was just giving her a quickie due to the ongoing party outside.

"Kelan, if you keep nutting in me, I'm going to end up pregnant," I heard Jenesis say in a joking way.

This nigga is nutting in her already? Damn, how long have they really been fucking? I wondered.

When I told Kelan the made-up story about Sincere and him coming back for Jenesis, I intended to have the two mad at each other during the party. It seemed like it brought them closer together—literally.

One Drunk Night In Miami 2

"Shid, that's the whole point. I've been wanting to get your pretty ass pregnant from day one of getting in that good pussy."

Realizing that the door could've opened at any second, I hurriedly made my way outside, angry and all. Once outside, I stood close by the door that I knew Kelan and Jenesis would have to come out of to enter the backyard. I waited there for what felt like an eternity until they finally exited the house, radiating with smiles.

"Kelan, are you ready to cut our daughter's cake?"

Jenesis snickered and then rolled her eyes.

"Yeah. We can do that. Alright, everybody, let's get ready to sing happy birthday to the birthday girl," Kelan announced loudly, commanding everyone's attention.

As we all gathered around to sing happy birthday to Emmy, I noticed how Jenesis allowed me to stand on one side of Kelan while he held Emmy and Jewelynn stood on the other side. During the gift-opening, it was just Kelan and me next to her, so I appreciated that she respected the boundaries. Throughout the party, I found myself keeping a close eye on Jenesis. There were times when it seemed like I paid more attention to her than to my own daughter.

What bothered me was how unfazed Jenesis was. Every time I glanced her way, she had a contented smile on her face, even when Kelan wasn't around. She could've been that way because of that good dick that Kelan had dropped off in her, though. I knew that feeling of pure happiness all too well. After getting that good shit, I used to have a smile on my face the remainder of the day or night.

I was also surprised to see Jenesis engaged in multiple conversations with Jewelynn and Bonnie. It was less surprising with Bonnie, given her genuinely friendly nature. Jewelynn, on the other hand, was *not* very receptive to people and was generally hard to please despite my efforts to win her over,

Alecia J.

while with Kelan, I failed to do so. However, the sincere rapport between her and Jenesis was palpable, and it didn't seem like she was putting on an act just for the sake of the party.

The party had just ended, and as Kelan and I stood in the backyard chatting, I gathered the courage to ask, "Can Emmy spend the night with me? I promise to have her back here tomorrow in time for her bedtime, since she has school the following day."

"Spend the night with you? Hell no, Melani! Not only have you not been an active parent in her life these last few weeks, but I don't even know where in the fuck *home* is for you!"

"I'm staying with my friend Miracle," I informed him.

"You're throwing out her name like I'm supposed to know who she is! Who the fuck is she?! One of your lil' ghetto friends?!"

"Miracle isn't ghetto. She works at a bank," I quipped as if I believed her personality should be in line with her job title.

"Females that work in banks or any professional settings be ghetto as hell too."

"Well, she's not. She's one of your clients, so you should know she's nowhere near ghetto," I slipped up and revealed.

Fuck! I cursed at myself.

"What do you mean she's one of my clients? Oh, wait! Damn! There is a girl who started not too long ago named Miracle. As a matter of fact, her *and* your other lil' friend Tiece be talking an awful lot in class."

"That bitch Tiece is no longer my friend," I enlightened him.

"I would ask why, but I really don't give a fuck. But you

One Drunk Night In Miami 2

know, now that I think about it, both of them joined on the *same* day. Now that shit *can't* be a fuckin' coincidence."

"Them joining the class on the same day is *definitely* a coincidence. I knew Miracle planned to join, but when she said Tiece had too, on the same day as her, that shit shocked the fuck out of me."

Miracle wanting to join the class, aside from me asking her to, was true, so that kind of played in my favor.

"Mm-hmm. Let me find out you got some shit up your sleeves. I promise you'll never see Emmy again."

My emotions swirled as a lump formed in my throat, and a wave of despair washed over me at the terrifying prospect of never being able to see my daughter again. Although I didn't have Miracle doing anything malicious when it came to keeping an eye on Kelan in class, I knew Kelan very well and his words were his bond. The expression on his face let me know he meant business. If he had discovered that Miracle was spying on him for me, he could have used it to his advantage, jeopardizing my relationship with Emmy forever.

"I had nothing to do with either of them joining your class, Kelan. I swear. That was their own doing."

"Mm-hmm," he replied in an unconvinced way. "Still, I don't know this Miracle chick, and I'm damn sure not about to send my daughter with you to some stranger's house."

"So, what is it going to take for you to let me get her one weekend?"

"For you to act like you fuckin' care about your daughter, Melani! Damn! It's that simple!"

"I do care, Kelan!" I tried convincing myself more than him.

"You think showing up here today with gifts and taking pictures with her, that I'm sure you're going to post on Facebook to have people thinking you're the world's best mom, is

Alecia J.

going to cut it? Those muthafuckas on social media might not know the real you, but I do! Melani, I've told you this before, and I'ma tell you again, and probably for the last time, I need consistency from you! Not just you popping up here and there and damn sure not just for special events. That shit is not going to be acceptable to me, not for too much longer at that. Yes, Emmy is young, but she's smart too. So don't think your disappearing acts go unnoticed by her. *Hence,* her asking you where the fuck you've been lately.

"Look, I'm tired, and I've had a *long* fuckin' day, so we'll have to revisit this conversation another day. I will say this, if you can show me that you're *trying* to get your shit together, by calling to check on your daughter more frequently, getting a place of your own, and hell, getting a job or even a car so that you'll have transportation to come see her or meet us somewhere, I'll *consider* letting you get her for a weekend, but *only* if I see that you're putting in some type of effort to be in Emmy's life. But even if none of that was the case, Emmy is about to leave with my mama and as you know, Mama always look forward to spending time with her, so the answer would've still been no."

"Alright, Kelan," I voiced in sadness.

It was clear that he wasn't going to let me have Emmy for the night, so I decided not to push the matter further. My desire to spend time with her wasn't driven by any malicious intent; I genuinely missed my daughter. However, I also understood Kelani's perspective. I needed to pull myself together, but it was challenging to do so while witnessing his affection for another woman.

Kane ended up taking me to Miracle's house after the party. I simply couldn't get over the fact that Kelan had moved on–so soon at that. It was heartbreaking. Unable to contain my curiosity, I went on Facebook to check out their profiles. When

One Drunk Night In Miami 2

I landed on Jenesis's page, I wished like hell that I had just taken my ass on to bed. I was greeted with photos from her birthday trip with Kelan. Even though his face was hidden, his body shape and tattoos were unmistakably his. My heart sank as I read her post captioned, 'Good men still exist, because one of them is mine. I pray we work out forever; I don't want anyone else. #birthdaytriptoJamaica.' Even though she didn't tag Kelan, I immediately checked the comments to see if he had discreetly replied, and he did, using a series of emojis that essentially confirmed they were locked in for life.

After noticing that she had shared pictures on her Facebook page, I quickly checked Kelan's Snapchat to see if he had posted anything. Since it was Emmy's birthday, I was certain he had, and I was right. Kelan's Snapchat stories were filled with numerous photos from Emmy's birthday party, many capturing shots of Emmy wearing her Gracie's Corner birthday tutu outfit. Amongst the snaps were pictures of Kelan with Jenesis. There was even a picture of the three of them together. Initially feeling a surge of anger, I was about to call and curse his ass out until I clicked further and saw that he had thoughtfully posted a picture of me, him, and Emmy. While I was still a bit hurt that he had placed their picture before ours, I couldn't help but feel grateful that he had included me, even though I felt undeserving as Emmy's mother.

However, nothing could have prepared me for the last video he had uploaded. It was a video of him and Jenesis making a public announcement of their relationship. The video was short but poignantly expressed their love, which concluded with them sharing a kiss.

"Ugh!" I screamed in anger.

I almost threw my phone across the room again, but I quickly remembered what happened the last two times I did that stupid ass shit.

Alecia J.

I desperately needed something to help me cope with the overwhelming emotions caused by what I had just witnessed. Frantically, I retrieved my purse and reached for what I had labeled my emergency therapy—the illicit pills I had obtained since I no longer had any prescribed medication. After taking a few, I turned to the bottle of vodka on my nightstand, knowing full well that combining the two was a dangerous choice. Nonetheless, I needed a temporary escape from the tormenting thoughts in my mind.

Amidst the haze of my altered state, a realization struck me. I still had a key to Kelan's house. It wasn't a desire to cause harm; rather, it was an eager need to catch a glimpse of his life without me in it. Hastily, I donned a black hoodie, snug black leggings, and a pair of my pink, white, and black Nike Dunks. I snatched up my phone and purse before hurriedly leaving the room.

"Shit!" I exclaimed with frustration as I realized I didn't have a way to get to Kelan's house.

The only way I could see myself getting there was if *Miracle* gave me a ride, but I knew that was highly unlikely. It was well past midnight, and she was probably in a deep sleep. Additionally, Miracle was not one to involve herself in messy situations. Truthfully, she had only accompanied me to Kelan's party because Kelan and I were together at the time. Given that we were no longer together, I knew she wouldn't want to get involved. Recalling that Miracle always kept her keys hung up by the door, I quietly made my way to the front door, hoping to find them in their usual spot.

"Yes!" I muttered under my breath when I spotted them.

1 swiftly grabbed the keys, set the alarm, and then cautiously left the house. As I made my way to Kelan's house, I drove with utmost care. This was not only due to the fact that I was under the influence of both liquor and pills, but the car I

was driving was a rental car, which Miracle had obtained after the accident and was expected to return it on the following Monday. So, it was imperative that I avoided getting pulled over or getting involved in another accident.

The journey from Miracle's house to Kelan's took approximately twelve minutes. Rather than parking directly in front or nearby, I opted to park around the block and cover the remainder of the distance on foot.

"This must be meant to happen," I murmured, observing that Kelan had left the garage open. It was clearly an oversight, as he consistently prided himself on ensuring its closure every night.

I tossed my hoodie over my head, masking my identity like a seasoned fugitive, as I stealthily approached the house. With careful precision, I timed my movements to make sure I remained unnoticed. Despite the multitude of cameras surrounding the property, I managed to keep my face out of view, especially in case Kelan decided to review the footage. As I reached the door leading inside, I desperately hoped that Kelan's recent preoccupations had prevented him from changing the locks or the alarm code. My silent plea was answered as I gained entry without encountering any obstacles.

Once inside, the house felt cool and exuded the comforting scent of fresh cotton. Despite the darkness, my familiarity with the layout spared me from the risk of stumbling into the unknown. The door to Kelan's room stood wide open, a stroke of luck that played in my favor. Had it been locked or closed, my entire mission would have been rendered futile, as I would've never dared to attempt to open a closed door.

As I cautiously entered the room, I made an effort to move quietly and not make a sound. Upon seeing Kelan and Jenesis nestled closely together, a pang of jealousy, anger, and malicious thoughts came over me. It appeared that she was completely naked, leading me to believe that he was as well. With both of them snoring loudly, I doubted that either would wake up at that precise moment. However, I wasn't about to be a fool and take any risks and find out. I also wasn't ready to leave. I felt like some action would unfold that night, so I sought refuge in the nearby closet outside the room. The slanted doors allowed a partial view outside, while the dim glow of the night lights in the hallway provided me with a faint glimpse of my surroundings, preventing complete darkness.

I was grappling with drowsiness for that next hour as the alcohol and pills began to kick in. Just as I considered leaving, I overheard Kelan asking, "Baby, where are you going?" Assuming Jenesis was getting out of bed, she replied, "To the bathroom. I'll be right back."

"Give me a kiss before you go," he sweetly demanded.

"You're so spoiled." She chuckled.

I rolled my eyes as I visualized them sharing a kiss.

A few moments later, she emerged from the bed—naked as I predicted—and entered the bathroom, which was connected to the bedroom and within my line of sight.

"Damn, she has a nicely shaped ass. Hell, body," I muttered.

I didn't anticipate Kelan getting out of bed as well. Instead of joining Jenesis in the bathroom, he left the room. His big dick having ass was naked as well, and it was just the swinging as he walked. After a while, Jenesis exited the bathroom and returned to bed, I presumed. Curious to see more into the room, I moved over a bit and accidentally bumped my head on something, creating a noise.

"Babe, are you okay?" Jenesis called out to him.

I silently prayed, *Shit! I hope this man doesn't come to this closet!*

A few moments later, Kelan returned to the room with a

glass in his hand. I couldn't quite make out what was in it. "What you mean, baby?" he asked.

"I thought I heard something out there. Like you bumped into something."

"Nah, baby. It wasn't me. Do you want me to check it out?"

"No."

"Are you sure?"

She said no, Kelan! Damn! Leave well enough alone! I thought.

"I'm sure, but thank you. Is this for me?" I assumed she meant whatever was in the glass.

"Yeah. You know I don't drink milk, but I know you love yours before you go to bed, and I don't recall you drinking any tonight."

"You're right; I didn't. Thank you, babe. I see that you be paying attention. Brownie points."

"You're my woman. It's my duty to pay attention to you."

I rolled my eyes at his affection toward her. I used to get the same from him; I just wasn't appreciative enough.

"Well, my grandmother actually started the tradition... for me, that is. She used to make me drink a glass every night." She chuckled. "It's been a routine that has stuck with me since my childhood. Aside from that, drinking milk at night has several benefits. Milk contains calcium, which is essential for bone health, as it helps strengthen bones and prevent osteoporosis. It also contains tryptophan, an amino acid that can promote better sleep by increasing the production of serotonin and melatonin. Additionally, the combination of calcium and casein protein in milk can help boost your metabolism. Lastly, if you didn't know, the protein in milk can help repair muscles after an intense workout, and carbohydrates can replenish energy stores," Jenesis explained knowledgably.

Alecia J.

"Baby, I'm a fitness trainer. Of course, I knew about the protein in milk." Kelan chuckled.

Well, I didn't know any of that.

It's said we learn something new every day. I guess something positive came from sneaking into the house that night because I got a whole lesson on the benefits of drinking milk at night.

"Are you done?" Kelan asked.

"Yes."

"Good, because I'm about to fill you with my milk now," he told her, which meant they were about to fuck.

"Nah, you've already filled me with your milk today, *twice* at that. Right now, I feel like *drinking* it."

"Oh, that's what you're on?"

"Mm-hmm," she voiced in a salacious tone.

Seconds later, Kelan's pleasured groans filled the room and the hallway from Jenesis giving him head.

I cringed and cried simultaneously while listening to them pleasure each other and as he made love and professed his love to her. I guessed that was my karma for taking a good man for granted.

"Shit!" I muttered a curse as I awoke in the closet, having fallen asleep for hours.

It was almost 6:00, and the sun was just rising. Kelan never got up that early, especially not on a Sunday; however, I was unsure about Jenesis's sleep schedule. Refusing to hide in the closet for another minute *or* day, I took a risk and stepped out. When I peeked into Kelan's room, I saw him and Jenesis still soundly asleep with their backs turned to me.

Thank goodness! I thought before dashing out of the house.

One Drunk Night In Miami 2

I managed to make it back to Miracle's house in one piece, but I was in for a rude awakening once I stepped inside. Miracle stood near the door, dressed in a long, thick, pink robe and a matching bonnet, her arms folded across her chest, wearing a clearly displeased expression.

"Really, Melani? You stole the car?! What the fuck?!" she fussed.

"Miracle, I can explain."

"Well get to explaining!" she urged. "And this shit better be good!"

Miracle's voice reverberated through the room as she screamed, "You did what?!" in utter disbelief after I finished recounting my 'break-in' at the *Masters'* residence.

"I know it was a dumb move, and I feel even more dumb now," I admitted.

"Ya think?! But as you should! Melani, what were you thinking?!? If Kelan or that girl had woken up and saw you standing over them or just saw you in the house, period, they had *every* right to kill you!"

"I know. He loves her already. Can you believe that?" I said as the memories of Kelan's heartfelt words to Jenesis flooded back, causing me to choke up. "I lost count of how many times he expressed his love for her; that was just how many times he told her. Although she never reciprocated the words, I know she loves him too."

"Melani, I shouldn't have to remind you, as I've already mentioned before, but you had a wonderful man, and now he's with a woman who truly appreciates him. This is just something you'll have to come to terms with eventually."

"What? Seeing him love another woman?"

Alecia J.

"That *and* seeing him happy with her. Melani, I advise you to take your loss and leave well enough alone while you can by refraining from interfering further in his new relationship. Your primary focus should be on your daughter and setting yourself on the right path, that's all," Miracle concluded with a tone of concern.

I listened carefully to Miracle's words and considered every point she made. Nonetheless, as long as Kelan and I shared a child, I knew I had the upper hand, and that alone gave me a glimmer of hope that one day we'd get back together.

20. Jenesis

"New hair! Who is *she*?!" I gushed when Dior entered my office, flaunting a new hair color. Instead of her signature fiery red hair, she had opted for a sophisticated maroon shade.

"It's me, friend! I just toned it down a bit," she said, embracing me with a smile.

"So, before we get into this new look, why didn't your butt tell me you were coming here?"

"Well, I was going to *call* you to show you the reveal, but then Lance asked me if I could stop by to grab him some breakfast since he didn't have time to stop by anywhere before coming to work. Of course, you know I couldn't tell my brother *no*. So, I figured I'd just kill two birds with one stone."

"So, I need to hear the story behind this transformation, honey, 'cause you were adamant about keeping your red hair."

"I knooooooow... ten years strong, but I thought, 'new job, new look,' *maybe* 'new me.' I just didn't want to feel out of place there by standing out too much with my bright red hair. I want

Alecia J.

to present a *professional* image and make a smooth transition into my new career."

"And there's nothing wrong with that. I'ma just have to get used to seeing you with this color. I still love it, though."

"Thanks, boo, but it was time for a change. Now, if you see me back rocking my red, that means I done quit because one of those bitches pissed me off."

I laughed.

"I'm serious, Jenesis."

"So, have you shown *Kane* your new look?"

"No, and I kind of dread it. He loved my red hair. It's just something he'll have to get used to."

"Don't be surprised if he kidnaps you again and forces you to dye your hair back that color." I chuckled.

"Jenesis, at this point, *nothing* that man says or does surprises me. That nigga is definitely in a league of his own."

"So, how is Lance liking the job so far? I'm just asking you because I know you and him talk more than me."

"He said he loves it. He said it's laid back, and he gets along with his co-workers."

"Sometimes it's not where you work. It's who you work with. Having likable co-workers is always a win."

"I wholeheartedly agree with you on that, boo, 'cause that bitch Kourtney at my job be making me want to knock her ass out *every* night!"

"The same here when it comes to Darlene's ass! Ugh!" I expressed my disdain for her.

"You know what? When I gave Lance his food, he was all in some woman's face. Take that back, I think she was in his, and for some reason, I believe it was the woman, Darlene."

"Was she wearing all white and some red lipstick?"

"Yep!"

"Yeah, that was that bitch. She walks around her and flirts

with all these male workers, thinking that people don't know. That's just one bitch I wish would quit, retire, or get fired." Suddenly, a thought popped into my mind.

"Dior, do you think that Lance would fuck her?" I whispered.

"Girl, what?! And why?!"

"Something about her has always rubbed me the wrong way. I feel like she's not as perfect as she tries to come off to be. I need some dirt on her, just something. Anything. Maybe if Lance can get close to her, he can get something up out of her or discover something about her from just spending time with her."

"I don't know about that, Jenesis. No doubt, my brother *loves* women, more so pussy, but I don't know if he'll go for that. Now, if you just wanted him to flirt with her here and there, I'm sure he'd be down to do that, but fucking her? Nah, friend. You may have to get somebody else to do that."

"Well, how else will he get close to her?"

"You're right, but again, I know Lance, so he might not be down for that. He likes you, though, so he *might* do it off the strength of *you* asking him to, but I'll let you run that by him."

"I will."

Desperate times called for desperate measures, and I could've been reaching, but I was determined to bring Darlene down at any cost.

"If that plan doesn't work, I'll have to figure something else out. All I know is, I gotta get her ass some kind of way before I leave here."

"Leave here?"

"Yes. Girl, I don't plan to work here forever. Yes, I love my job and the pay, but I want to be my *own* boss, and I can't make that happen working for other people. Aside from that, I have a man now, and I be wanting to enjoy my weekends with him and Emmy, but when I have to work at my other job, I really can't, so I'm definitely thinking about letting that one go."

"Jenesis, you have a rich ass nigga, one who doesn't mind spoiling yo' ass! Girl, I would've *been* said *adios amigas* to that nursing job, and probably this one too!"

"Again, I happen to love what I do at *both* of my jobs. I just want *one* job where I can put both of my skills to use if that's possible."

"Well, if there's anybody who can make *anything* happen, it's you, friend. As long as you don't try to move away, I'll support all your dreams."

I chuckled. "If that thought ever comes to mind, just know you'll be moving right along with me."

"Unt, unt! I don't like being a third wheel!"

"As if you haven't before." I threw a jab, referring to the threesome she had.

"Touche, bitch!"

"I'm just playing, but if I decide to move with Kelan somewhere, and you wanted to come along, you'd be fourth wheeling. Kelan comes as a package with Emmy."

"With her pretty self," Dior complimented. "So just imagine how y'all babies are going to look."

I was about to respond to her, but a text message came through from Kelan. My face brimmed with happiness.

"I guess I spoke him up," Dior said.

I nodded as I viewed his message.

Kelan: *Damn, baby, I'm already missing you.*

Me: *I wish I was kissing you instead of missing you.* I sent a sad emoji.

Kelan had left the night before to head to Miami on a business trip, and of course, he was going to spend some time with Kane while he was there. That trip held significant importance as Kelan aimed to fulfill a longstanding dream of opening a gym in Miami, marking a significant milestone on his bucket list. However, Kelan found himself in quite a predicament as he attempted to figure out how he would handle the new venture, especially considering he was already juggling two other responsibilities—the two gyms he already owned. Be that as it may, he was determined to see his vision through. Recognizing that the construction process could take some time, Kelan said he'd cross that bridge when the time came.

Kelan: *How does my pussy feel this morning? Is she sore from yesterday?*

Before Kelan left, he had fucked me like he'd never get the pussy again.

Me: Yes, but it's a good sore. I added a few emojis.

Kelan: Good. So, every time you take a step, you'll feel it and think of me while I'm gone. Remember who that pussy belongs to, baby.

Me: You never let me forget. Lol. You just remember who you belong to while you're away.

Kelan: I know who I belong to, baby. That's the least of your worries.

"Girl, Kelan and I are going to have a serious talk when he gets back," I told Dior as I put my phone to the side.

"About what?"

"Dior, I think my man is a nympho! Like, he wants sex *all* the time!"

"And what's wrong with that?" her freaky ass asked.

"Friend, my mouth and pussy need a break! I know they be mad at me when I give in to that nigga. Even on the days my period is on, he wants daily head."

Dior laughed. "And you give it to him, right?"

"Uh, yeah, bitch! I'm not about to give him the opportunity to cheat, although if a nigga wants to cheat, he will."

"Facts, but, girl, I don't think Kelan has a sex problem.

Alecia J.

Maybe he's just addicted to *yo'* ass," she pointed out, then stood.

"Leaving so soon?" I playfully pouted.

"Unfortunately, yes, friend. I have to head to work."

"Shoot! I forgot that quick that you had that job, and we were just discussing it, but shouldn't you be there by now?"

"The lady who I was training with won't be in until ten o'clock today, so they just told me to come in at that time."

I nodded. "Well, have a good day, boo, and don't be a stranger," I joked.

"I'll call you later, girl."

When Dior left, I thought over the conversation I had with her about Kelan. I was serious about talking to him. I loved sex just like the next person. Well, maybe not as much as him, but before it became an issue, I wanted to address it, although I didn't expect that conversation to go too smoothly.

21. Kelan

"Kelan, are you really going to sit there and not bother to touch me or fuck me?" Jenesis asked as I sat on the couch, and she stood in front of me, wearing a sexy ass red lingerie that had all her womanly parts on full display.

"Jenesis, I haven't had any pussy in a week, mainly because your period was on the last couple of days, but those other three days after I got back home, you were on some straight bullshit, and now I'm just supposed to give in because *you* want some?"

"Kelan!" she pouted, then took a seat next to me. "You're taking this *way* out of proportion. I just needed a break, babe. That's all. It was becoming too much having sex every day or even every other day, especially with my work schedule."

"Well, if you've gone this long without some dick, you can go another day or two."

"So, you're *really* not going to give me any?"

"Nah. I'm tired and not in the mood."

Jenesis scoffed, then ran her hand across my hard dick and

said, "Your dick says differently. When you get out your feelings, you know where to find me."

As she sashayed off, I couldn't help but stare at her ass that jiggled harder with every step she took, or maybe she did it purposely. When Jenesis slammed the bedroom door, I knew she was pissed.

I was sexually frustrated and needed to get away for a while before I ended up giving in to her demands, although I knew eventually I would. I wasn't going to make Jenesis wait too long; I just wanted to give her a dose of her own medicine. Since we still weren't on speaking terms later that night, I called up Bryson and told him to take me somewhere so I could clear my head. There I was, trying to go somewhere to get a distraction from sex, and that nigga took me to a damn strip club. Not just any strip club, though, the one where Dior worked. If bad influence was a fuckin' person, Bryson's ass would be him.

"Damn, you're fine. Forget you nutting in me. Hell, you look so good that *I* want to nut in *you*," some chick came over and flirted with me in my section.

"'Preciate that, but I'm taken, love. As a matter of fact, my girl is at home waiting for me right now to give her some of this dick."

"Lucky girl. The good ones *and* good-looking ones are always taken," she said in despair and walked off.

I wanted to say more regarding her comment, but I decided against it. Besides, I wasn't there to entertain any hoes. I probably was mad at Jenesis's ass, but I would never cheat on her.

"Not you over here cheating on sis because she's holding out on the pussy!" Bryson approached me, laughing.

"Man, hell nah!"

"I was about to say!"

"Say what? Ain't yo' ass the one who brought me here, nigga?"

"Yeah, so you could unwind, nigga. Now, nothing is wrong with looking at a different set of ass and titties from time to time. You can window shop; just don't touch the merchandise, and damn sure don't buy it."

"You ain't telling me nothing I don't know. But, aye, did I see you over there talking to Kelis?"

"Yeah."

"I thought you broke shit off with her?"

"Cuz, sometimes the pussy be so good that you just have to tolerate a muthafucka."

I chuckled.

"But nah, that was her. I was telling her ass to leave me the hell alone, though. When I said I'm done with that crazy ass broad, I'm done with her."

"Speaking of crazy, the girl who just left from over here told me to forget about me nutting in her; she wanted to nut in me."

"Damn! Which direction she went in again?" Bryson's stupid ass said, scanning the club. "I'm serious, cuz. I ain't never had that happen! I'm trying to see what that's like for real!"

"Well, let me know how that turns out because yo' ass will definitely find out before me."

Right after saying that, some chick walked up to Bryson and started touching all over him.

"Bryson, stop being stingy with the dick. At least let me pet him," she begged, all up in his space.

Desperation is at an all-time high in this muthafucka, I thought.

"Jamie, the dick God gave your husband must be small or smelly because you stay begging for mine."

I chuckled under my breath.

"Whatever, Bryson! Don't worry about me asking for it anymore!" she said and stormed off.

Alecia J.

"Shid, I won't. I've been waiting for you to get the hint that you'll never get it!" he yelled after her.

"Damn, these women are wild and bold tonight," I said, shaking my head.

"Man, what? I had this cougar come up to me right before I came over here, saying her coochie so wet it'll wash all my sins away. Now, cuz, I ain't gon' lie, I got her number because I'm kind of in need of a cleansing and some redemption."

I laughed. "Fuck all these hoes, though. The real question is, what the hell is up with you and Imani? And I know y'all got something going on the way y'all be under each other in class."

"Have we *fucked*? Not yet, but she's cool as hell. She's like a nigga's homie and best friend. She stays coming over to my crib, whooping my ass in 2K. At first, I thought it was just luck, but her ass can really play. I haven't beaten her yet. On some real shit, though, between you and me, I could definitely see me and her on some boyfriend, girlfriend type shit."

"She must got a nigga?"

"Nah, she's single... now."

"Then what's the problem?"

"It's me, bro. This shit with her resemblance to my ex bothers the fuck out of me. If I stare at her for too long, I be thinking sometimes that she is Nikki and that she had a few surgeries done so she can look a lil' different, just so she could come back into my life. But you know how I feel when it comes to talking about her, so next subject. Back to you. Cuz, you got a baddie *and* a *good* ass woman, not to mention she's successful. Get yo' ass out of here, go home, and make up with yo' girl, because I can guarantee you, the majority of these hoes in here just want a come up off a nigga like you; hell, me too. So, go home and cater to the woman who makes her own money, and don't ask you for shit."

"Look at you trying to preach to me."

One Drunk Night In Miami 2

"I learned from the best, cuz." He popped his collar.

"But you right. Jenesis is a diamond in the rough. I'd be a fool to mess up what I have with her, fuckin' around with these hoes."

"Cuz, you'd be a *damn* fool, and I will tell you that shit to your face if it ever happens!"

"It's not, but I'm ready when you're ready, nigga. I'm on your time, remember?" I said, reminding him that I rode there with him.

"Oh, shit! Let's ride! Imani had just texted me anyway, saying she wanted to come over to the crib."

"Look, Bryson, if you're feeling Imani, and you wanna pursue something with her, you gon' have to put away yo' fear of her being yo' ex or connected to her somehow. The worst thing *you* can do is let her go, and she ends up with another man and the whole time, she's probably your soulmate."

"Soulmate? I'on know about all that, but I hear you, cuz. Look, before we go, though, I gotta find this woman who approached you not too long ago. I'm trying to see what that feels like by the end of this week!"

While Bryson went off in search of that woman, I decided to shoot Jenesis a text.

Me: Baby, I'm sorry about earlier. I'm about to come back over so we can talk. I can't go to sleep with this shit on my mind. I'll understand if you don't want to, but I just want you to know that I don't want to lose you over something as little as that shit. I love you, girl.

Jenesis didn't respond before I made it to her crib, nor did she read the message, so I *assumed* she was asleep. For her sake, she better had been.

22. Jenesis

"Do you want me to go check his ass, friend? Because you know I will! I ain't about to let him play in your face like that, well, *my* face! He's also been throwing money at the strippers!" That was Dior. She had called me, going off when she saw a girl in Kelan's face at her job.

I chuckled. "Dior, boo, it's fine. He's just a little upset right now. Now, if you see a bitch grinding on him or some shit like that, don't hesitant to call me or check his ass, but I don't think we have to worry about that. Oops! He just texted me, apologizing as we speak," I said, viewing his message.

"Girl, what do you have between your legs?" Dior quizzed.

"The power of the pussy, friend. The power of the pussy," I repeated.

"Well, alright. I just called to tell you what was going on. You know I got you."

"I know you do, friend, and I appreciate you for always having my back. Now, get back to work. I love you.

"I love you too."

One Drunk Night In Miami 2

Seeing that Kelan was headed back over to my house, I hurriedly got out of bed and went to unlock the door so he'd be able to come in without me having to get up. I wanted to play a trick on him. Kelan didn't like for me to have sex toys; he felt like he was all I needed for my sexual satisfaction, which was true. So, I went to grab my rose and dildo from the closet and then laid them next to me in bed. Once Kelan arrived and saw them on the bed, I knew he'd automatically assume I had used them to pleasure myself.

As I lay there with my eyes closed, I could hear Kelan calling my name loudly, trying to wake me. I couldn't help but smirk as I feigned sleep, listening to him getting more and more frustrated. After a while, I decided to give up the act and rolled over onto my back, rubbing my eyes as if I had just been roused from a deep slumber.

In a groggy tone, I asked, "What is it, Kelan?"

"Why in the hell did you have these in the bed?" he asked, referring to my sex toys.

"Kelan, is that what you're raising hell about?"

"Damn right!"

I burst into laughter. "Kelan, I just put those out for display to see your reaction. I never used them, well, not tonight, at least."

"You play too much. You know how I feel about these things."

"Are you worried that I'd get more pleasure from them than you?" I taunted.

"Jenesis, find you something safe to do before your cherished lil' toys find themselves a new and permanent home inside your fireplace." Though Kelan's tone was light, I sensed an undercurrent of seriousness in his words.

As Kelan spoke, he removed his shirt, unveiling his chiseled abs, an array of intricate tattoos adorning his skin, and the well-defined muscles of his arms and chest, a testament to his commitment to fitness.

My mouth salivated at the sight.

If this nigga doesn't fuck me tonight, we're going to have a problem.

Kelan came over to the opposite side of the bed and took a seat next to me.

"I'm not sharing you with nobody or *nothing,* including those damn toys. I'm the only nigga, and my dick is the only thing that's gon' feel that good shit. The only way you'll enjoy this," he held up my rose, "is if *we* enjoy this."

Kelan set the rose on the nightstand, pulled the cover back, hopped behind me, and then spooned me. All I had on was a gown, so, of course, his left hand went straight to my pussy.

"I know I already texted you and said it, but I'm sorry about that shit from earlier. I never took the time to take your feelings or *pussy* into consideration."

We chuckled together.

"Nah, seriously, I heard you, baby... loud *and* clear. I ain't gon' lie, though; I'm addicted to this pussy *and* you," Kelan confessed what I already knew as he glided his fingers across my clit, heightening my horniness. "But I'ma give pretty mama a break every now and then."

I snickered at the nickname he gave my kitty.

"Damn, she's *wet, wet* tonight," Kelan said as he pleasurably fingered me.

"She drips a different kind of wet when she loves you," I tossed over my shoulder.

A smile tugged at the corners of Kelan's mouth.

"You love me, baby?" he asked, removing his finger from my center and allowing me to turn on my back.

"I think..." I paused because it was time for me to be truthful about my feelings. "No, I do."

"Well, I don't have to tell you that the feelings are mutual because, by now, you know how a nigga feels about you."

"Since we made our relationship public now, tonight I went on Facebook and took down the photos that had your face blocked and replaced them with the real ones."

"For real?"

"Yes. Kelan, you're too good of a man. Hell, too fine of a man to keep hidden. I want to show you off to the world as much as possible."

As I stared deeply into Kelan's face, I couldn't escape the sense of a man who had gone unnoticed and unacknowledged for far too long. I found myself perplexed by Melani's actions, constantly contemplating why she would open that door and allow another woman to sweep in and claim her man—especially when he was a man of great quality and virtue. I gently swept my hand across his face, feeling the warmth that emanated from him as I poured my heart out.

"Kelan, if Melani never spoke these words to you, let me be the first to do so. You are more than enough. You are truly amazing. As a father, you excel beyond measure. Your skill as a fitness trainer is unmatched—you truly are the best, as you set the standard for excellence. Kelan, you are the answer to my prayers. You are the reason my smile has returned. You evoke emotions in me that defy description. You are mine... every sexy inch of you." I affectionately tapped his nose. "I love you."

"That's love, baby. That's love. I love you too," he replied, followed by a kiss on my lips, which led to a night of pure *fucking* blissfulness.

23. Bryson

"I won! Give me my money!" Imani said, perfectly imitating Smokey from the movie *Friday* as she playfully demanded her winnings with her hand outstretched.

"You what?" I continued to play along.

"Nigga, I *won*! This ain't no Friday, and you damn sure ain't Debo!"

We both bent over in laughter.

That was the homie/best friend relationship I had explained to Kelan. I had never met a girl like Imani. She was like the girl version of me, and whenever we spent time together, the good vibes and good energy were always present.

"Here go yo' funky twenty dollars, girl." I placed it in her hand.

"See, why it gotta be funky? Had you won, I would've given you your money without all the extra lip talk!"

"Yeah, yeah. But what you about to get into?" I asked her, lounging back on the couch as I idly flipped through the channels on the TV.

One Drunk Night In Miami 2

"Bryson, do you not see the time? It's almost four o'clock in the morning! I'm going home!"

I lifted myself from the comfortable embrace of the couch, my attention shifting from the television to Imani.

"Stay," I told her.

Imani's playful demeanor had suddenly been replaced with a look of confusion and timidity.

"Wh-what do you mean *stay*?" she hesitantly asked, tucking a few stray strands of hair behind her ear.

During Imani's visit that night, my mind was preoccupied with the recent conversation I'd had with Kelan about pursuing her. Reading Imani's emotions was always a challenge, but there were a few times I caught her ass looking at me with lustful desire. However, she'd quickly revert to her nonchalant self once she realized I had noticed her.

I rose from the couch and towered over her small frame. Despite the uncertainty of her response, I took my shot anyway.

"I want you to stay," I repeated, hoping she would understand my intentions.

"Stay? But... but why?"

"Come on, Imani! We've been kicking it all this time, and you're going to tell me you haven't noticed that I've been feeling you even a bit? Or that you haven't been feeling me?"

"Bryson, I honestly didn't think you felt *anything* for me besides a genuine friendship. I thought you just looked at me like one of your homies."

"I do, but I also find you attractive... *very* attractive." I removed a piece of hair from her face. "That's one difference between you and my homies."

"What's... what's the other?" she anxiously asked.

"I can't *fuck* them, nor do I want to."

Her breathing hitched.

Alecia J.

"Bryson, I like you, and yes, I find myself thinking about you *a lot* when I'm not around you, but I'm not sure if we're ready or even meant to be a couple. I just got out of a relationship, and you... you got all your women."

"I don't have any women. I'm trying to make *you* my woman. But if you're talking about the females I *fuck*, if you tell me that this is what you want, *us*, even if you want to take this shit slow, I'll text every one of them *right* now and tell them to lose my number. Simple. I got rid of the one who I considered my favorite, so getting rid of the rest would be a breeze. The ball is in your court, though, Imani. Like I said, we can take this shit however fast or slow you want to. I just need to know how you're feeling right now."

Imani appeared deep in thought, nibbling on her bottom lip, taking her time to respond. The fear of rejection gripped me, as I had never been turned down by any woman before. Not one to be very patient, I chose to give Imani a glimpse of why we should be together before letting her speak those fateful words.

Without giving her a warning, I gently placed my hands on Imani's face and met her lips with mine, something I had been wanting to do since the day we first met. Imani's lips proved to be just as I had imagined—luscious and velvety, added with the scent of mint gum that lingered on her breath. I expected Imani to pull away, but to my surprise, she instead held onto the back of my head, intensifying the kiss. I lifted Imani into my arms and carried her to the bedroom. After placing her gently on the bed, we both stripped out of our clothes. I thought Imani had a bad ass body with her clothes on, but the clothes did no justice to the sight that was before me.

"Impressive," she complimented me before I could compliment her. Imani was gawking at my dick like it was the biggest dick she'd ever seen, up-close, that is.

One Drunk Night In Miami 2

"Shid, likewise," I returned, referring to her sickening ass body that I couldn't wait to get a hold of.

"And he's big, I know, but he'll be gentle with you since you're a first-timer." I winked and went to my drawer to grab a rubber.

When Imani started playing with her pussy and making all kinds of sexy ass moans, my anxiety peaked. It was like I couldn't get the fuckin' rubber on fast enough, maybe because I was trying to focus on her and its security at the same time.

"Finally," I said once I had the rubber placed to my liking.

"She's all ready for you," Imani announced, patting her pretty pussy.

"Shid, you ain't got to tell me twice!" I wasted no time getting in the bed and crawling between her legs.

"Damn, did you squirt? 'Cause that muthafucka is *wet, wet*!"

Imani smirked. "No. This is a normal *wet* day. So, if you're not used to driving in the rain, you might want to be careful when you get on the road. It's *very* slippery when it's wet," she teased.

"I'm a skilled driver, baby. I can handle *all* road conditions, but I prefer a *rainy* day over a sunny day *any* day. Now, although I'm enjoying this lil' roleplay, let's get down to business."

I toyed with Imani's clit, coating the rubber with her wetness.

"You're not playing fair, Bryson! Stop teasing me! Put it in!" she practically begged.

"Aight."

I opened Imani's thighs a little wider, then swiftly, I plunged into her wet heat that instantly gripped the fuck out of me.

"Shit!" I gave her pussy a few strokes, but I had to pause for a second, not only to process that shit, but I felt like I was about to nut.

"You good?" Imani chuckled.

"Shid, I'm good! This pussy, though... *great!*"

When I went to lift Imani's legs to get deeper in that shit, she pressed her hand against my chest to stop me.

"What's wrong?" I asked in an almost disappointed tone, assuming she wanted me to stop.

"When we get done, I'ma need you to get in your phone and handle that business with those other females. From here on out, I'll be the *only* one getting this dick.

"You got it, ma."

I ain't gon' lie, those next fifteen minutes that we went at it were rough on a nigga. I never in my life wanted to hold off on nutting when fucking a bitch, but my dick had plans of its own that day. Once I felt my nut approaching, I gently wrapped my hand around Imani's throat, feeling the rapid rhythm of her pulse beneath my fingertips. Our eyes locked, and in a split second, the familiar contours of Imani's face morphed into Nikki's visage. I furrowed my brow, attempting to dismiss the unwelcome figure, but Nikki's features lingered, superimposed over Imani's.

Gradually, I became aware of the increasing pressure of my grip on Imani's neck, matching the intensity of my fixation. As I struggled to regain control, I realized that my hold on Imani's neck had subconsciously tightened. I strained to catch Imani's voice amidst the chaos, but the raw, stinging sensation of scratches deeply etched into my arms and chest by her was felt. It was as if all the pent-up rage from the day Nikki hurt me had resurfaced, prompting me to unleash it upon Imani.

As I was lost in thought, I was abruptly shaken back to reality. When I glanced down, instead of Nikki's face, I saw Imani's. Quickly, I withdrew my hands, recognizing that I had not only caused Imani physical harm but also deeply affected her emotionally. Her appalled expression mirrored my own shock as she struggled to comprehend what had transpired and fought to catch her breath.

"Nigga, are you fuckin' crazy?!" Imani roughly pushed me off her, got off the bed, and proceeded to put her clothes on. "You almost fuckin' killed me! Did you not fuckin' hear me telling you to stop!"

"Imani, I'm so fuckin' sorry! I... I don't know what happened! It's like I blanked out!" That was the truth.

"Blanked out from what, Bryson?! Surely not from the pussy! So, what the fuck were you *really* thinking about?! You know what? At this point, it doesn't even matter! I'm about to get my shit and get the hell out of here!"

After slipping on her slides, Imani's hurried footsteps echoed as she made her way up to the front, her posture radiating frustration, hurt, and disappointment. I followed her, desperate to explain.

"Imani, wait!"

She spun around to face me, her eyes flashing with a mix of emotions. With her finger pointed in my direction, her voice trembled, "Stay the fuck away from me, Bryson! I mean it! I don't know what just happened in there! I don't know if that's a fetish of yours, but that shit was not cool! You... you could've killed me!" Tears began to flow down Imani's cheeks. I reached out to comfort her, but she backed away, her expression filled with fear and distrust.

"I hope you made good of the pussy you got today because, so help me, God, you'll never get it again!" Imani picked up her purse and concluded, "Lose my number, Bryson! Don't you ever, and I mean *never*, contact me again!"

I felt the urge to chase after her, to find the right words to explain what had happened, but I found myself immobilized. I remained rooted in the living room, still naked as hell, trying to process the sudden turn of events.

"Fuck! What if she tells her folks what I did?! What if she finds my mama and tells her about that shit?! I'll never hear the end of that shit! Hell, they might take away this condo! Fuck! Bryson, why the fuck did you do that, nigga?! What the fuck were you thinking?!" I muttered to myself, my head repeatedly colliding with my hands as I paced back and forth in distress.

"I gotta get the hell out of here! I gotta get away from this city! That's my only option!" Leaving town seemed like my only viable choice. I rushed to the back to pack some clothes, but before I could even begin that task, I stepped into the bathroom to dispose of the condom, only to discover that it had burst.

"Fuuuuuuuuuuuck!" I screamed with my head tilted back.

Neither Imani nor I had apparently paid attention to it at the time because we were so focused on the other issue. I didn't see hardly any nut on my dick, so the majority of it had to have gone inside her. *If* she miraculously ended up pregnant from us fucking that one time, I'd hope she'd still keep the baby. If not, I would've understood that, too. Imani looked like a responsible girl, so it was possible she was on birth control.

I didn't have time to worry about the *what-ifs* concerning that situation. My primary objective was to escape the city for a while. After packing a few bags, I left the crib and headed to the unknown. I realized I would have to tell Kelan –if no one else– what happened, considering we were partners, and he relied on me to be at the gym. I just hoped he'd understand that I needed to take some personal time off, so I could clear my head from all that shit.

How did a good ass night turn out so fuckin' bad?

24. Dior

"You see, this is why I hate coming to the emergency room! They take too fuckin' long!" I complained as Jenesis and I sat in the cold room, awaiting my test results.

For three days, I had been battling a relentless illness, experiencing bouts of violent vomiting, overwhelming nausea, and a high fever that left me shivering uncontrollably. Despite Jenesis's best efforts to care for me as a nurse, my symptoms only worsened, leaving us with no choice but to seek urgent medical attention at the emergency room.

"Dior, calm down. I'm sure they'll be here soon. Do you need another blanket?"

"No, I'm fine, friend. Thanks. And thank you for coming here with me *and* dealing with me these last few days. I know I've been a headache. I don't know what I'd do without you."

"I don't either," Jenesis playfully quipped. "Oh, I meant to tell you... Lance agreed to my plan."

"Really? Then again, I told you he probably would since it was *you* who asked for the favor."

Alecia J.

"Well... I kind of had to do something for him too."

"Something like what?" I quizzed.

"He wants me to get him a date with Isla."

"Isla? As in your coworker, the one whose daughter you tried to hook Bryson up with, and the one who's in the same workout class as us?"

"Yes, *her*." Jenesis chuckled.

"But isn't she married? Or at least I think I remember you saying that."

"She is, but girl... that's her story to tell."

"You're saying that like me and her talk."

"Well, maybe y'all will get the chance to become acquainted when we go on our girls' trip."

"Girls' trip? What girls' trip?!"

Jenesis laughed. "It's not one that me and her planned to take together. I was actually going to ask you if it would be okay if she joined us on the trip that we were talking about taking soon. I know you don't know her that well, and you don't like going places with random people. That makes two of us, but she's cool, and if I say that, then you know it's the truth. Besides, she doesn't have many friends, *like us*, and she could *really* use this trip, Dior."

"Hell, we all could," I said. "But okay. She can come. And since I got me a *lil'* money, I'll pay for the entire trip."

Jenesis was aware of the money that my brother had given me, and she was the *only* person I told.

"Not you being all generous!"

"Don't do me, friend! You know I have a heart of gold!"

"You do. And who knows? She could very well end up being your *sis-in-law* in the future."

"With my brother's hoeish reputation..." I scoffed. "I doubt that. Then again, *maybe* she could be the one to make him consider settling down. Of course she'd have to be *divorced* first."

"Right."

"But yes, we can all go out of town or the country together. I think that would be fun. As long as she knows that I'm the best friend."

Jenesis playfully shook her head. "She and *everybody* else knows that, Dior."

"Then, we should be good then. I would like to hang out with her first before we start making vacation plans, though."

"Fair enough."

"So, when is their *date?*"

"I haven't talked to Isla yet, but I will soon."

"What about the bitch Darlene and Lance?" I asked.

"Oh, well, according to Lance, *they* have a date *next* weekend. I can't wait to hear about it!"

"I can't believe she fell for him so fast."

"*I* can," Jenesis retorted. "Girl, Darlene is a fuckin' cougar. She loves men younger than her. Not to mention, you know your brother is a *charmer*."

"That, he is. I must say, it runs in the family," I boasted.

Jenesis and I shared a laugh, but it abruptly ceased when the short, Asian-looking doctor entered the room. With anticipation, I perked up in the bed, eager to uncover the cause of my sickness.

"Well, Ms. Curry, it turns out that you have the flu," the doctor informed me.

"The flu?" Jenesis and I exclaimed in unison, obviously surprised.

"I know. You don't typically see too many people walking around with the flu during the summer season, but it's possible," the doctor explained.

"Well, I guess this news is better than you telling me that

Alecia J.

I'm pregnant. As bad as I've been feeling, I thought for a second that my dildo had gotten me pregnant somehow," I jokingly remarked, although the doctor didn't find that too amusing.

"Um, so, the thing is, we tested your urine, and it turns out that you *are* pregnant."

"Wait, what?" Jenesis blurted out in disbelief. Her reaction mirrored my own, but I was too stunned to form a coherent response. It felt like my ears were playing tricks on me.

"Come again?" I finally spoke. "If my *ears* served me correctly it *sounded* like you said I was *pregnant*."

"You're not hearing this by mistake, Ms. Curry. We double-checked for accuracy, and both of yours came back positive. So, yes, you are indeed pregnant. Congratulations are in order!" he said with a smile, though there wasn't much to smile about.

"Jenesis, do you hear this?"

"Yeah, friend. I'm sitting right here with you, and I'm *just* as shocked as you are."

"Ms. Curry, along with your other findings, it appears that you're slightly dehydrated, so I want to start you on some IV fluids, which I'll have a nurse come in to administer shortly."

"Oh, no!" I quickly objected. "I don't want any of the nurses here putting in my IV! The last time I allowed one of the nurses here to put in an IV, my parents thought I had been using drugs because of the marks on my arm! So, no!"

"Ms. Curry, I understand your frustration, especially after just finding out about your unexpected pregnancy, but it's crucial for both your health and your child's that you receive some fluids."

My child. That sounded so unreal.

"I never said I was against getting it, but if I do, I want her," I pointed at Jenesis, "to administer it. She's a nurse, and at least I know she knows what she's doing."

"Well, that's really not how that works here."

One Drunk Night In Miami 2

"Sir, you have a nurse out there who is familiar with my friend's work ethic, and she can vouch for her since I obviously can't. She can even be in here while she's administering. The entire team of doctors and nurses from this facility can be present, if necessary, but none of your colleagues will touch me."

After receiving a positive recommendation from the nurse who worked there, careful consideration, and them agreeing on a team of nurses supervising Jenesis while she administered the IV and fluids, they finally allowed it.

"I still can't believe you managed to persuade those people to let me do that," Jenesis said as she helped me settle into bed, carefully avoiding close contact to prevent catching my illness.

"Girl, I can damn near convince anybody to do anything," I wheezed. "Ugh! I hate feeling like this... and why did this have to happen right when I'm starting a new job?"

"Just call them on Monday, boo. I'm sure they'll understand. Shit happens; hell, *life* happens."

"I'll call, but if they're on that bullshit talking about it's too soon for me to be taking off, I'ma just show up there dressed how you are now," I weakly quipped, trying to inject humor into the situation.

Jenesis was steadfast in her commitment to remain healthy. She was fully outfitted in her yellow PPE gear, including an N95 mask she had obtained from her nursing job, which she kept in the trunk of her car for situations like those.

Jenesis laughed. "So, are you ready to address the elephant in the room?" she prodded.

"Elephant? What elephant?" I glanced around, puzzled by her cryptic reference.

Alecia J.

"Dior, when do you plan to tell Kane that you're pregnant?"

I rolled my eyes, knowing that conversation was inevitable.

"I don't know. But knowing him, he probably already knows. Hell, he probably planned this shit, too, or got me pregnant while I was knocked out on that plane! The muthafucka didn't even ask if he could be my baby daddy. He just nutted in me!"

Jenesis chuckled. "Well don't just go making assumptions, Dior. The condom could've broken one night, and y'all just didn't know it."

"You're..." I coughed. "You're the one who is supposed to be pregnant, not me. Lord, I'm pregnant by a man who's not even my man! This would happen to me." I tossed my head back on my headboard.

"Well, all I will say is, if you have *any* thoughts of getting an abortion, count me out from going with you. I love you, sis, but I'm *not* trying to feel Kane's wrath, or Kelan's for that matter. As a matter of fact, let's just get off that subject."

"And here I was, thinking you loved me and *always* have my back. I guess it is true when they say you see people true colors during the worst time of your life."

Jenesis bent over in giggles. "Girl, I am not about to do this with you tonight! But seriously, don't wait too long to tell him, Dior."

"I'm not. Actually, he'll be here tomorrow. He said he has to go to his mama's house for something first, and then he'll come over here later. So, I'll tell him then."

"I can't wait to hear about his reaction. Do you need anything else before I leave?"

"Just a hug." I pouted.

"On *any* other day, I'd give you *plenty,* but not today. I love you, though."

One Drunk Night In Miami 2

"Okay. I'll give you a pass *today*."

"Well since you don't need anything else, I'm going to go shower and head to bed. If you need *anything*, ring your bell."

Jenesis had kindly volunteered to spend the night at my place to take care of me, and she even went the extra mile by gifting me a bell for easy assistance. She truly was amazing.

As I bid her good night, my throat felt a bit sore, but I managed to whisper, "I love you! Goodnight! And thank you for everything!"

Replying with equal warmth, Jenesis said, "I love you too! Goodnight, and you know you're always welcome!"

After she closed the door, I reclined on my pillow and gently touched my belly, which didn't show any physical signs of pregnancy yet, but I knew there was a baby growing inside. When we returned from the hospital, Jenesis went out and purchased a pregnancy test for me. As soon as I was home, I used it, and the result was positive. I couldn't understand for the life of me how I ended up pregnant when Kane and I always used protection. Our lil situationship was already complicated, and the prospect of introducing a baby into the mix was only going to create further complexity.

"Where is Jenesis with my soup?" I muttered as I anxiously scrolled through my call log, preparing to call her.

Two days before, she had made some delicious homemade chicken soup for me, which I finished in one day because it was so damn good. Jenesis had mentioned that she had a little left over that she planned to bring to me, but hours had passed, and she still hadn't shown up. Just as I was about to call her, the doorbell rang. I knew it couldn't have been Jenesis because she had a key and always invited herself in.

Alecia J.

I hesitated to get up from the sofa, feeling comfortable and still a little under the weather. The next day, when I woke up, I wasn't completely recovered, but I felt much better than the night before. Of course, *Nurse Jenesis* advised me to stay in the house for a few more days, so I followed her orders. I assumed the person at the door was Kane, as he had mentioned that he left Miami hours before. I wasn't quite ready to have the conversation with him about my pregnancy, but I knew it would have to happen sooner or later. So, if not then, when? However, when I opened the door, I was shocked to see the last person I expected standing on my doorstep.

"Gavin? What the hell are you doing at my house?!" The greeting was far from friendly. I glanced over his shoulder to see if he was alone.

"I need to talk to you," he said then rudely brushed past me and invited himself into my home.

I whipped my head at his audacity. "Excuse you, negro! I didn't invite you in!" I yelled, slamming my door, which at the time, I didn't realize I had done it and should've kept it open.

"What do you and my brother have going on?" He cut right to the chase.

"Your brother?! And just who the hell is your brother?!" I replied, feeling a sudden sense of confusion and disbelief as he revealed, "Jace."

"Jace? As in Jace Waters? Because that's the only Jace I know!"

"Yes, him."

What the fuck?

"And you two are brothers? Like, *real* brothers?"

"Yes. We have the same parents," he answered.

"Wow!" I shook and scratched my head in disbelief. "This... this is crazy."

"Not crazy; just a small world."

"Obviously! Still, what does my relationship with him have to do with you showing up on my fuckin' doorstep uninvited and unwelcomed?!"

"Why he is stalking you?" That question blew me because his guess was as good as mine.

"Stalking me?! What the hell are you talking about?!"

"Every night he's parked outside of your house!"

"Well, it's not because he be in this muthafucka with me! Furthermore, the better question is, how do you know that your brother is *supposedly* stalking me? Are you stalking him, or are you stalking *me*? Which one?"

"I started off following you a bit after I saw you at the club that night. When I saw you talking to my brother there one night, I started following him, and he led me to your house," he admitted in a casual tone as if stalking a person wasn't considered a crime.

"So, both of you have been stalking me?! Now, when it comes to Jace, I kind of understand why he would be stalking me. Then again, it's never okay to stalk someone. But you... What the fuck is your excuse?!"

"Since the day I saw you walk into that gym, I've wanted you."

"Eww!" I said with a look of disgust on my face, not caring if I hurt his feeling.

"You do know that he's married, right?"

"Yes, I do, and I don't give a fuck because we have nothing going on, at least not anymore! Now, Gavin, I don't what's with the sudden infatuation with me or why you thought it was safe to come to *my* house, with this bullshit on today of all days, but I need you to leave, and this is me asking you nicely."

"I'm not going anywhere until I get what I came for." After he pulled out a gun, I realized why he said that so boldly.

"Wh–what do you want?! If you came here for money, then

you're assed out of luck because I don't have any!" As I spoke, I instinctively began to step backward, aware of the dangerous situation unfolding before me.

I cursed myself for not keeping a gun up front. I had two in the house, but neither were within my reach.

Gavin chuckled wickedly. "Oh, no, beautiful lady. What I want is worth more than money... at least to me it is. I want your treasure box."

"Treasure box?" I asked perplexed.

"That treasure box between your legs!" He waved the gun downward toward that area.

"Gavin, if you think for one second that I'm about to freely give you some of *this* pussy, then you're sadly mistaken! Now you need to leave, and that is my last time telling you!"

"Why can't I get a piece of the pie? I mean, you're around here giving it to everybody else, including our *other* brother."

"Your other brother?" My mind instantly went to Kane because he was the only nigga I was fucking.

"Yeah, but he's irrelevant, though. But I know about the two of you as well."

"Look, Gavin, I don't give a fuck what you know or think you know. Get the fuck out of my house!" I yelled, kicking him backwards. The kick was so forceful that it made the gun go out of his hand and caused his head to bash in on the sharp corner of my glass table.

"Oh, no!" In a moment of panic, I reflexively covered my mouth with my hands. The sound of Gavin's head hitting the surface was distressingly loud, and I could tell it had been a hard impact, possibly deadly.

With my trembling hands still pressed against my quivering lips, I cautiously took small, silent steps toward Gavin's lifeless form, consumed by the dread of confirming my darkest apprehensions. Upon further inspection, from kicking him and yelling out his name multiple times, to the humungous gash in his forehead that oozed blood, it was evident that Gavin was dead.

"Shit! I didn't try to kill the nigga! I just wanted his ass to leave my house! Oh, fuck!" I screamed when a realization hit me. "I done killed this man's brother! Fuck! Fuck! Fuck! What the hell am I going to do?! Think, Dior!" I fretted as I paced back and forth in the living room.

Not only was I freaking out about having a dead body in my house, but also about what he dropped on me: Jace being his brother, Jace stalking me, and the biggest question I was curious to know was, who was their other brother?

25. Jenesis

As I stood in the kitchen, preparing the chicken spaghetti, Kelan approached me.

"Baby, I've never asked this before, and it's not something I plan to make a habit of, but would you mind watching Emmy for a few hours while I go over to Mama's place?"

"Of course not, babe, although Emmy *usually* goes to your mama's house with you." Despite my willingness, I couldn't help but feel curious about his unusual request.

"I know, but I need her to stay here with you this time. My mama invited me and Kane over for a meeting, if you could call it that, and she just wanted the two of us there, nobody extra, not even Emmy."

Concerned by his serious tone and the stress visible all over his face, I walked up to him and asked, "Is everything okay, babe?"

"To be honest, baby, nah, it isn't. This meeting is more so for Kane than it is for me."

"So, *you* know what it's about?"

"I do. Kane doesn't, though. Still, I don't know how it's going to turn out."

"Is it that bad?"

"Yeah, baby. I'm afraid it is. I'll explain it to you later. I gotta get ready to head over here, but... in case things go left, I need you to go to my crib and look in my nightstand. There will be a thick white folder in there. If something—"

"No, Kelan! Stop talking like that! You're talking like I won't see you again!" I sobbed, feeling overwhelmed.

Kelan held me close, and his embrace provided some solace. Gently lifting my head, Kelan wiped the tears from my cheeks.

"Baby, I'm sorry for dropping this on you at the last minute, but the notice of this meeting came suddenly to us as well. I don't mean to worry you. I just need you to be prepared if things go left. Can you do that for me?"

Fighting back tears, I nodded, my mind clouded with uncertainty about the situation and what I had just agreed to.

"Emmy!" Kelan called out to her as he prepared to leave.

She hurried into the kitchen.

"Slow down, baby, especially while Jenesis is cooking," Kelan gently reminded her.

"Yes, Daddy!" she responded cheerfully.

Kelan kneeled next to her, and said, "Daddy has to go handle something, and I need you to stay here with Jenesis until I get back. Are you cool with that?"

"Yes, Daddy! I love being with Jen!" She smiled brightly, which brought a temporary one to my face.

"That's my girl." Kelan gave her a tight hug and told her that he loved her.

After we exchanged our goodbyes, he left, leaving me feeling more than just worried. Despite my concerns, I made an effort to stay positive.

Alecia J.

"So, Emmy, it's just us girls. What would you like to do?"

"Hmm..." Emmy pondered, tapping her chin with her finger.

Mentally and physically, I prepared myself for whatever she had in mind.

"Emmy didn't wear you out today, did she?" Kelan chuckled as we Facetimed.

"Ha ha! But you know your daughter, so you know we had a *blast*," I exaggerated. "We painted each other's nails. I can't wait to show you mine." I chuckled. "We baked cookies. We watched one of her favorite movies. We went outside and did a few activities. And, of course, we had a tea party."

"Damn, I'm missing all the fun."

"Yeah, you are."

"She's just getting you prepared for stepmom and mommy mode for her siblings."

I shook my head, smiling. "Are y'all still waiting for Kane to arrive?"

I had texted Kelan earlier to check on him, and he told me that something was going on with the plane that Kane originally was supposed to arrive on, so they had to turn around and switch, which delayed his initial time of arrival. So, Kelan had been at his mom's house for seven hours, practically that entire day, waiting for Kane.

"Yeah, but I just talked to him. He said he'll be pulling up in ten minutes."

When Kelan said that, a reminder came to my mind.

"Oh, shit!"

"What's wrong, baby?"

One Drunk Night In Miami 2

"I was supposed to go by the house, get something for Dior, and take it to her. You know she's sick."

"Yeah. So, what's stopping you?"

"Emmy is asleep, and I don't want to wake her."

"Baby, Emmy is a hard sleeper. I can promise you if she wakes up when you get her out of her bed, she's going to go right back to sleep, especially if she's in a car. Go ahead and take her whatever she needs, and then y'all head back to the crib."

"Okay. Well, I love you. I'll talk to you later."

"Okay, baby. I love you, too. I'll call you when I'm on the way home."

If you make it home, I thought. The way Kelan was talking, there was a possibility that he wouldn't.

Once I managed to secure Emmy in the car, we set off for my house. As I turned into the driveway, a sense of unease washed over me. Firstly, I noticed the absence of my security guards, which was unusual. Secondly, the porch light was off, and I distinctly remembered leaving it on that morning, anticipating my return after dark. Trusting my instincts, I reached for my phone to call Kelan, only to realize I had left it behind in my rush to leave his house.

Shit!" I muttered, careful not to wake Emmy, who was still asleep.

Since I planned to run in and out of my house, and just drop off Dior's package on the way back to Kelan's house, I didn't dwell too much on my phone.

As I stepped out of the car, I looked around cautiously. Initially, I considered leaving Emmy in the car since she was asleep, and I would only be inside for a moment, but I quickly dismissed that idea. While I was trying to get Emmy out of her seat, I suddenly felt a hard object pressed against my back.

"Damn, that ass has gotten fat."

Alecia J.

When I heard the familiar voice, my heart sank. "Sin–Sincere?"

"Yeah, it's me, baby," he verified. "And don't even think about fuckin' yelling!" His voice was low and ominous.

"I won't! I promise!" I assured him, feeling the rapid thumping of my heart as I spoke those words.

"Good girl. Now, turn around so I can see that pretty face."

I reluctantly turned to face him with my heart pounding in my chest, and my trembling hands that I had held up as I obeyed his command.

As I stood face to face with him, I found myself gazing into the eyes of a man who I had once loved. However, on that day, all I felt toward him was pure, unadulterated disgust. Sincere was dressed entirely in black, like a true criminal. His clothes, his shoes, and even the black hat resting upon his head were all part of this dark ensemble.

He chuckled. "You can put your hands down, Jenesis. I'm not going to kill you, *unless* you give me a reason to."

I slowly put my hands by my side.

Sincere took a step forward and glided his hand over my face, which caused chills to run down my spine. "Still pretty. Actually, you're even more beautiful than you were the last time I saw you. Did you miss me, baby? 'Cause I surely did miss your fine ass."

This can't be the same nigga who gave me his ass to kiss five years ago, saying he missed me, I thought.

"Sin-Sincere, what are you doing here?"

"I'll explain all of that in a minute. So, you done went and had a baby by some nigga?"

"What?" I had a brief moment of confusion until I realized he was talking about Emmy. "Oh, she's... she's not my daughter."

"Then who in the fuck does she belong to?" he gritted,

looming over me with his body pressed against mine on the opened car door.

"She's... she's my boyfriend's daughter."

Sincere drew back a little and glanced at Emmy, who was thankfully still asleep, then he looked back at me.

"So, you call yourself got a boyfriend now, huh?"

I chose not to respond. For one, he clearly heard me say I did. Secondly, I wasn't sure if repeating that was the best choice.

"That's cool. You ain't got to answer. It's not like you'll be with the nigga for too much longer anyway."

"What?"

"Look, grab her, and let's go inside. We need to talk. We also got some making up to do." Sincere licked his lips as his eyes roamed lasciviously over my body while grabbing at his dick. Realizing that he was losing focus on his purpose for being there, Sincere's lustful desires quickly dissipated, and he harshly instructed, "But come on! Get the girl! I ain't got all fuckin' night!"

I hurriedly grabbed Emmy for her car seat, hoping and praying she wouldn't wake up to any of that chaos.

As I walked up to the door with Emmy draped across my shoulder, Sincere had the gun pressed into my back to ensure I didn't make a stupid move. Once I was on the doorstep, I went into my back pocket to retrieve my keys.

"What are you reaching for?" Sincere asked.

"I'm getting my keys."

"I'll get them. I don't trust you anymore." Sincere reached into my back pocket, but instead of just grabbing the keys, he began to caress that portion of my booty. "Damn, I can't wait to get back in that good shit," he whispered against my ear, causing tears to almost well up in my eyes.

Not only was he touching parts of my body that no longer

Alecia J.

belonged to him, but I wanted to get Emmy away from him as quickly as possible. I didn't think he'd *intentionally* harm her, but I took into account that I hadn't seen or heard from Sincere in five years, and people are known to definitely change within that amount of time. And since Kelan left her in my care, it was my duty to protect her at all costs.

"Here," he said, finally handing me the keys after getting his perverted feel on.

As I reached for the keyhole, my hand shook violently from a mix of nerves and adrenaline. With a deep breath, I steadied my hand and carefully inserted the keys. The door clicked open, allowing us to step inside.

"This shit is nice," Sincere said as he observed my home. "I can definitely get used to *us* living like this again. Go take her to the back so us grown people can talk."

"I'll be back," I said, turning to leave, but he quickly corrected me, "Nah, *we'll* be back up here together. "Jenesis, you should have enough sense to know that I'm not about to let you go to the back by yourself, although I'm sure you wouldn't be stupid enough to jeopardize putting that pretty lil' girl in harm's way. Now, move!" Sincere ordered and followed me to the back.

After laying Emmy down in one of the guest rooms, I kissed her forehead and whispered to her to sleep well. When I turned around, Sincere was standing at the door with a smirk resting on his face.

"I always knew you'd make a good mama. Let's go!"

"Sincere, where are my security guys?" I asked as we headed back up front.

"Oh, those niggas... they're dead!" he answered in an insensitive tone.

My eyes doubled in size as I turned to face him.

"Dead?!"

"Yeah, girl! Why are you looking at me like that? You're acting like I've never killed a nigga before. Then again, I did keep that kind of shit from you. I didn't want you to have nightmares about that shit, baby. So much for keeping secrets, huh?" He chuckled. "No worries; I cleaned up my mess... like I always do. However, you might want to advise your lil' boyfriend that he needs to up his game when it comes to security, especially *if* he hired them to protect you from niggas like *me*. Those niggas were not only not on their shit by not checking their surroundings, but they were weak as hell. None of them put up a fight with me! So, how the hell were they going to protect you? Three *easy* kills!" He laughed maniacally.

I just froze in place with my eyes fixed on him.

Who is this man standing before me? I questioned silently.

I wasn't sure what prison had done to him, but that wasn't the same Sincere I knew.

"Okay, so what do you want, Sincere?" I was feeling increasingly uncomfortable with his presence in my home. I was curious about how he managed to get released from prison with all the charges against him, but at that moment, I wasn't sure if I even wanted to know. If not knowing meant getting him out of my house and never having to see him again, I'd be perfectly fine with it.

"I told you that we needed to talk! Damn! Did you not hear me when I said that shit outside?" he bellowed, causing me to flinch.

I was a nurse, so I had extensive knowledge about drug addiction and its signs. Based on the way he constantly sniffed, flickered his nose, and fidgeted restlessly, it was evident to me that he was clearly under the influence of something. It didn't come as a complete surprise to me, as Sincere used to snort cocaine while we were together. To the best of my knowledge, he was unaware that I knew about his drug use. I had actually

Alecia J.

witnessed him in the act once—unbeknownst to him. During the nights when Sincere returned home in a heavily altered state, he would attempt to conceal it from me, but my nursing experience equipped me with the ability to recognize the telltale signs and symptoms of drug use, and they certainly did not go unnoticed by me.

"Sincere we can talk, but can you *please* keep your voice down?" I begged. "I don't want to wake his daughter and have her witness any of this."

"Damn, you must really love that nigga, huh? Well, let's see just how *much* you love him."

"What?" I questioned in confusion.

"I need a welcome home gift, and your pussy is the *perfect* gift." When I saw Sincere reach for his zipper, I started backing away.

"Sincere, no! I told you I have a boyfriend!"

Sincere laughed mockingly as he repeated my words, "Sincere, no! I told you that I have a boyfriend!" His evil laughter filled the room as he cornered me on the sofa, making me feel uncomfortable and trapped. "Jenesis, I'm well aware that you have a nigga! Hell, if I didn't know before coming to this bitch, you have made that shit *well* known by steadily bringing up the nigga!"

"Wait a minute! It was... it was you! It had to be you!"

"Had to be me what, baby? You gotta be a *little* more specific."

"Were you the one outside my house in an old Honda not too long ago?"

He chuckled. "Guilty as charged, baby. So, yeah, that's how I know about your lil' boyfriend. I just had to play it off earlier when I asked if you had one. But as you can see, or as you should know, no nigga puts fear in my heart, so fuck that nigga!

312

One Drunk Night In Miami 2

You might be his bitch, but I'ma about to have a lil' fun with his bitch!"

Sincere began to roughly tug at my pants.

"Sincere, please don't do this, especially while his daughter is in the back!" As much as I pleaded, hoping to soften his heart, he responded with cold indifference, saying, "I don't give a fuck. She ain't mine!" So those pleas fell on deaf ears.

As tears spilled from my eyes, I noticed that it didn't seem to have any impact on him whatsoever. Despite me fighting him back—and I put up a good ass fight—ultimately, Sincere's manly strength overpowered mine, and he managed to get my pants down.

"Oww!" escaped my lips as I felt the searing pain shoot through my pussy when Sincere forced himself inside me.

I knew I wasn't attracted to him anymore, and my pussy proved that when it didn't get wet for him. Unlike Kelan, whose dick was longer and perfect in every way, Sincere had a *thick* dick. Despite how long we were together, I never fully adjusted to his size. It was good but uncomfortable a lot of times, or maybe he chose to make it that way when we'd have sex. So when Sincere rammed himself inside me, his thickness alone brought on pain, and the fact that I wasn't prepared to have sex—to better put it, I was *dry* in that area—caused even more agony. However, the worst part of it all was that he went inside me raw. I didn't know what Sincere had endured while he was in prison, but I had to take into consideration that he could've possibly become gay or even contracted HIV or something.

All sorts of thoughts crossed my mind as Sincere gladly took advantage of me. I should've listened to Dior when she stressed to me to tell Kelan about the possibility of him being released early and had I, maybe I wouldn't have ended up in that situation. Maybe he could've relocated me or hired more security. So, I partially blamed myself for the predicament I was in.

Aside from Sincere being stronger than me, he also threatened to kill Emmy and me if I didn't cooperate, and for some reason, I believed he'd follow through on those words. So, instead of fighting him back, I lay there and fought back silent tears as I let him destroy me.

I could sense the fragile pieces of my inner self beginning to fracture irreparably. Sincere had committed a violation that went beyond physical harm, inflicting a deep wound on my soul and leaving me uncertain about the possibility of ever finding healing.

Kelan, I need you, baby.

26. Kelan

"**M**a..." I walked into her bedroom and found her on her knees, deep in prayer. As I was about to quietly step back and give her some privacy, she asked me to stay.

Concerned, I asked, "Are you good?"

"No, I'm not," she answered once she was on her feet. "For once in my life, I'm afraid of something. I'm afraid of the outcome of all of this." That confession came as a surprise, but given the circumstances we were facing, it was understandable.

During Emmy's party, my mom took Kane and me aside and mentioned that she needed to have a conversation with us in the upcoming week or weeks, but she didn't go into detail about the reason at that moment. Although I already had a feeling of what the meeting would be about once she mentioned it, later that night, I called her to confirm–she was ready to tell Kane the truth. Despite it being a long time coming, I was glad the time had finally come. At the same time, I was nervous as hell, too.

"I ain't gon' lie, Ma, part of me is scared too. Not so much about what Kane will do; I can handle him. I'm just scared of how this will affect our relationship. Kane isn't only my brother; he's my best friend, and I am his. So, do you know what this news could do to him? I mean, have you *really* thought this through?"

"I have, and I'm willing to accept whatever consequences come behind them. I just want to know one thing. This is something I've been questioning myself about over the last few weeks. Was I a good mom to you two?"

"Really, Ma? You're really questioning that? Hell yeah, you were and still are. You're an even better grandma to Emmy."

She smiled, more than likely thinking about Emmy. However, that smile went away just as fast as it came when I spoke the following words, "But that's not going to excuse what you did, especially not to a nigga like Kane. But regardless of how shit goes down today, I will always and forever look at that nigga as my biological brother. That half-brother shit don't even fly this way."

"What the fuck did you just say?" I heard Kane snarl from behind me.

Fuck! I cursed internally, then turned to face him and was met with the barrel of his gun.

"Kane, put the gun down, son!" Mama instructed.

"Son?" He scoffed. "Shid, from what I just heard from standing outside the door eavesdropping, you only got *one* son, and that's *this* nigga."

Kane's expression turned pained as he gestured toward me, his tone heavy with hurt.

"Kane, if you want to be mad at anybody, be mad at me! But please hear me out before you do something that you might regret!" Mama tried to plead with him.

"There's not a muthafucka whose life I have taken that I

have regretted taken 'til this day... not a single one. Ain't that right, *brother?*"

My heart shattered into countless pieces as I witnessed Kane, who was usually so strong and composed, shed a single tear before me. The tear that fell from his eye seemed to carry the weight of his unspoken pain. As I hung my head and shook it in disbelief, I couldn't contain my own emotions as a tear slid down my cheek.

Kane sniffled and wiped his face to rid himself of the tears. "But you know what? You might be right. It is you who I should have this muthafucka pointed at."

When Kane directed his gun at Mama, I pulled out mine and aimed it at him.

"Don't do this, bro. I know you're upset, hell, *pissed.* I get it, but like Ma said, hear her out first, *at the least.*"

"You gon' shoot me, Kelan? Yo' *brother?* At least that's what you *said* we'll still be once I found out this bullshit!"

With tears still rolling down my face, I responded, "You are my brother... for *life,* and for that reason, I *don't* want to shoot you, but I *will.*"

"And I don't want to *kill* her, but I'm *going* to!"

Phew! Phew! Phew!

To be continued...

Also by Alecia J.

One Drunk Night In Miami